T0038477

"Asimov is the reason I started reading science fiction. I cut my teeth (figuratively) on *The Caves of Steel* and followed it up with *The Naked Sun*. Some writers show us a different way of looking at the world, but Isaac Asimov opened up the door to the universe and invited us to come along for one hell of a fabulous ride."

—ESTHER FREISNER

"Isaac Asimov's ability to take the Big Ideas so crucial to the sense of wonder in science fiction and embody them in compellingly human stories and settings—particularly in his robot stories, Foundation works, and other speculative fiction both long and short—raised the bar high for all of us who have followed him in the tradition of idea-driven science fiction. Asimov was a law unto himself, yet he gave his fellow writers laws—of robotics, and psychohistory—that have shaped all of us who have tried to write of machine intelligence or of human civilizations vast in time and space. That is his great and vital legacy."

—HOWARD V. HENDRIX

"Asimov's Foundation trilogy was the pivotal touchstone in my life in creative fiction. His vision and scope spanned the galaxy across eons and at the same time he told deeply personal stories of living characters. The writer I am sprang from the boy that these books touched back then. They continue to move me still. Thank you, Isaac, for opening my mind and life to the possible."

—TRACY HICKMAN

"I grew up on the ABCs of science fiction—Asimov, Bradbury, Clarke. There's a reason Asimov's name comes first, and not just because of the alphabet."

—JANIS IAN

"Asimov's Foundation series stands the test of time. They were among the first science fiction books I ever read and I still enjoy them today as an adult. The genre owes much to his sprawling vision of galactic empire."

—KARIN LOWACHEE

"The idea of robots rising up against their human masters is at least as old as the word 'robot' itself. Asimov was unique in treating this as simply an engineering problem, which he solved with his famous Three Laws of Robotics. This by itself would have earned him a spot in history, but he went on (and on!) to explore the ramifications and unintended consequences of his solution. In so doing, he crafted one of the most vibrant, original, and enduring future histories the field of science fiction has ever seen, or probably ever will. Reader, you are in for a treat."

—WIL MCCARTHY

"If anything can be said to have been the launchpad for space age science fiction, it has to be the Foundation trilogy. It's a classic. And it's unforgettable."

—JACK MCDEVITT

"I'm sure there will be more Foundation stories, and more robot stories, and more science fictional mysteries, because those are Isaac's legacies to us. But reading them won't be quite the same. There was only one Isaac Asimov; there will never be another."

—MIKE RESNICK

"The Foundation series is one of the masterpieces of science fiction. If you've never read these novels, then you're in for a treat, and even if you've already read them, then you owe it to yourself to reread them, because they're still great."

—ALLEN M. STEELE

"Quite simply, Asimov got me started."

—LIZ WILLIAMS

"Isaac was still in his teens when I met him, a fan of mine before I was a fan of his. Writing for John W. Campbell back in the famous 'golden age of science fiction,' he became one of the founders of our field. With the robot stories and the Foundation stories, he helped to shape science fiction as we know it."

—JACK WILLIAMSON

BY ISAAC ASIMOV
AVAILABLE FROM DEL REY

The Foundation Series

Foundation
Foundation and Empire
Second Foundation
Foundation's Edge
Foundation and Earth
Prelude to Foundation
Forward the Foundation

The Galactic Empire Series

The Stars, Like Dust
The Currents of Space
Pebble in the Sky

The Robot Series

I, Robot
The Caves of Steel
The Naked Sun
The Robots of Dawn

The End of Eternity
Fantastic Voyage
The Gods Themselves
Nemesis
Nightfall and Other Stories

NIGHTFALL

AND OTHER STORIES

ISAAC
ASIMOV

NIGHTFALL
AND OTHER STORIES

DEL
REY

NEW YORK

2021 Del Rey Trade Paperback Edition

Published in the United States by Del Rey, an imprint of Random House, a division of Penguin Random House LLC, New York.

DEL REY is a registered trademark and the CIRCLE colophon is a trademark of Penguin Random House LLC.

Originally published in hardcover in the United States by Doubleday, an imprint of the Knopf Doubleday Publishing Group, a division of Penguin Random House LLC, in 1969. This edition published by arrangement with Doubleday, an imprint of the Knopf Doubleday Publishing Group, a division of Penguin Random House LLC.

ISBN 978-0-593-35746-0
Ebook ISBN 978-0-593-35795-8

Printed in the United States of America on acid-free paper

randomhousebooks.com

8th Printing

Book design by Alexis Capitini

*To John W. Campbell, Jr. for making "Nightfall" possible,
and for thirty years of friendship; and
To the memory of Anthony Boucher and Groff Conklin*

CONTENTS

NIGHTFALL

AND OTHER STORIES

PREFACE TO
NIGHTFALL

FIRST APPEARANCE—*ASTOUNDING SCIENCE FICTION,* September 1941. Copyright 1941, by Street & Smith Publications, Inc.; copyright renewed, 1968, by Isaac Asimov.

The writing of "Nightfall" was a watershed in my professional career. When I wrote it, I had just turned twenty-one. I had been writing professionally (in the sense that I was submitting my stories to magazines and occasionally selling them) for two and a half years, but had created no tidal wave. I had published about a dozen stories and had failed to sell a dozen others.

Then John W. Campbell, Jr., the editor of *Astounding Science Fiction,* showed me the Emerson quotation that starts "Nightfall." We discussed it; then I went home and, over the course of the next few weeks, wrote the story.

Now let's get something straight. I didn't write that story any differently from the way I had written my earlier stories—or, for that matter, from the way I wrote my later stories. As far as writing is concerned, I am a complete and utter primitive. I have no formal training at all and to this day I don't know How To Write.

I just write any old way it comes into my mind to write and just as fast as it comes into my mind.

And that's the way I wrote "Nightfall."

Mr. Campbell never sends letters of acceptance. He sends checks, instead, and very promptly, and that is an excellent way of handling the matter. I always found it thrilling. I received a check for "Nightfall" but my initial pang of delight was almost instantly snuffed out by the fact that Mr. Campbell had made a mistake.

Standard payment at that time was a munificent 1 ¢ a word. (No complaints, folks; I was glad to get it.) The story was 12,000 words long and therefore I expected $120.00, but the check was for $150.00.

I groaned. It would be so simple to cash the check and ask no questions, but the Ten Commandments, as preached to me by my stern and rockbound father, made it absolutely necessary to call Mr. Campbell at once and make arrangements for a new and smaller check.

It turned out there was no mistake. The story seemed so good to Mr. Campbell that he gave me a bonus of ¼ ¢ a word.

I had never, till then, received so huge a payment for any story, and that was just the beginning. When the story appeared, it was given the lead position *and* the cover.

What's more, I was suddenly taken seriously and the world of science fiction became aware that I existed. As the years passed, in fact, it became evident that I had written a "classic." It has appeared in ten anthologies that I know of—including one British, one Dutch, one German, one Italian, and one Russian.

I must say, though, that as time passed, I began to feel some irritation at being told, over and over again, that "Nightfall" was my best story. It seemed to me, after all, that although I know no more about Writing now than I knew then, sheer practice should have made me more proficient, technically, with each year.

The thing has preyed on my mind, in fact, until the idea of this book came to me.

I have never included "Nightfall" in any of my own collections of stories because it always seemed to me to have been so well anthologized that it must be familiar to all my readers. Yet perhaps that's not so. Most of my readers weren't even born when the story first appeared and perhaps many of them haven't seen the anthologies.

Besides, if it's my best story, then I want it in one of my own collec-

tions. I can also include other stories of mine that have proven successful in one way or another but have not appeared in any of my own
collections.

So, with Doubleday's kind permission, I have prepared *Nightfall and
Other Stories,* with all the tales in the order of publication. "Nightfall"
itself is the first and now you can see for yourself how my writing has
developed (or has failed to develop) with the years. Then you can decide for yourself why (or *if*) "Nightfall" is better than the others.

I don't know enough about Writing to be able to tell.

NIGHTFALL

"If the stars should appear one night in a thousand years. how would men believe and adore. and preserve for many generations the remembrance of the city of God?"

EMERSON

Aton 77, director of Saro University, thrust out a belligerent lower lip and glared at the young newspaperman in a hot fury.

Theremon 762 took that fury in his stride. In his earlier days, when his now widely syndicated column was only a mad idea in a cub reporter's mind, he had specialized in "impossible" interviews. It had cost him bruises, black eyes, and broken bones; but it had given him an ample supply of coolness and self-confidence.

So he lowered the outthrust hand that had been so pointedly ignored and calmly waited for the aged director to get over the worst. Astronomers were queer ducks, anyway, and if Aton's actions of the last two months meant anything, this same Aton was the queer-duckiest of the lot.

Aton 77 found his voice, and though it trembled with restrained emotion, the careful, somewhat pedantic phraseology, for which the famous astronomer was noted, did not abandon him.

"Sir," he said, "you display an infernal gall in coming to me with that impudent proposition of yours."

The husky telephotographer of the Observatory, Beenay 25, thrust a tongue's tip across dry lips and interposed nervously, "Now, sir, after all—"

The director turned to him and lifted a white eyebrow. "Do not interfere, Beenay. I will credit you with good intentions in bringing this man here; but I will tolerate no insubordination now."

Theremon decided it was time to take a part. "Director Aton, if you'll let me finish what I started saying, I think—"

"I don't believe, young man," retorted Aton, "that anything you could say now would count much as compared with your daily columns of these last two months. You have led a vast newspaper campaign against the efforts of myself and my colleagues to organize the world against the menace which it is now too late to avert. You have done your best with your highly personal attacks to make the staff of this Observatory objects of ridicule."

The director lifted a copy of the Saro City *Chronicle* from the table and shook it at Theremon furiously. "Even a person of your well-known impudence should have hesitated before coming to me with a request that he be allowed to cover today's events for his paper. Of all newsmen, you!"

Aton dashed the newspaper to the floor, strode to the window, and clasped his arms behind his back.

"You may leave," he snapped over his shoulder. He stared moodily out at the skyline where Gamma, the brightest of the planet's six suns, was setting. It had already faded and yellowed into the horizon mists, and Aton knew he would never see it again as a sane man.

He whirled. "No, wait, come here!" He gestured peremptorily. "I'll give you your story."

The newsman had made no motion to leave, and now he approached the old man slowly. Aton gestured outward. "Of the six suns, only Beta is left in the sky. Do you see it?"

The question was rather unnecessary. Beta was almost at zenith, its ruddy light flooding the landscape to an unusual orange as the brilliant rays of setting Gamma died. Beta was at aphelion. It was small; smaller than Theremon had ever seen it before, and for the moment it was undisputed ruler of Lagash's sky.

Lagash's own sun, Alpha, the one about which it revolved, was at the antipodes, as were the two distant companion pairs. The red dwarf Beta—Alpha's immediate companion—was alone, grimly alone.

Aton's upturned face flushed redly in the sunlight. "In just under four hours," he said, "civilization, as we know it, comes to an end. It will do so because, as you see, Beta is the only sun in the sky." He smiled grimly. "Print that! There'll be no one to read it."

"But if it turns out that four hours pass—and another four—and nothing happens?" asked Theremon softly.

"Don't let that worry you. Enough will happen."

"Granted! And *still*—if nothing happens?"

For a second time, Beenay 25 spoke. "Sir, I think you ought to listen to him."

Theremon said, "Put it to a vote, Director Aton."

There was a stir among the remaining five members of the Observatory staff, who till now had maintained an attitude of wary neutrality.

"That," stated Aton flatly, "is not necessary." He drew out his pocket watch. "Since your good friend, Beenay, insists so urgently, I will give you five minutes. Talk away."

"Good! Now, just what difference would it make if you allowed me to take down an eyewitness account of what's to come? If your prediction comes true, my presence won't hurt; for in that case my column would never be written. On the other hand, if nothing comes of it, you will just have to expect ridicule or worse. It would be wise to leave that ridicule to friendly hands."

Aton snorted. "Do you mean yours when you speak of friendly hands?"

"Certainly!" Theremon sat down and crossed his legs. "My columns may have been a little rough, but I gave you people the benefit of the doubt every time. After all, this is not the century to preach 'The end of the world is at hand' to Lagash. You have to understand that people don't believe the *Book of Revelations* anymore, and it annoys them to have scientists turn about-face and tell us the Cultists are right after all—"

"No such thing, young man," interrupted Aton. "While a great deal of our data has been supplied us by the Cult, our results contain none of the Cult's mysticism. Facts are facts, and the Cult's so-called mythology *has* certain facts behind it. We've exposed them and ripped away their mystery. I assure you that the Cult hates us now worse than you do."

"I don't hate you. I'm just trying to tell you that the public is in an ugly humor. They're angry."

Aton twisted his mouth in derision. "Let them be angry."

"Yes, but what about tomorrow?"

"There'll be no tomorrow!"

"But if there is. Say that there is—just to see what happens. That anger might take shape into something serious. After all, you know, business has taken a nosedive these last two months. Investors don't really believe the world is coming to an end, but just the same they're being cagy with their money until it's all over. Johnny Public doesn't believe you, either, but the new spring furniture might just as well wait a few months—just to make sure.

"You see the point. Just as soon as this is all over, the business interests will be after your hide. They'll say that if crackpots—begging your pardon—can upset the country's prosperity any time they want, simply by making some cockeyed prediction—it's up to the planet to prevent them. The sparks will fly, sir."

The director regarded the columnist sternly. "And just what were you proposing to do to help the situation?"

"Well"—Theremon grinned—"I was proposing to take charge of the publicity. I can handle things so that only the ridiculous side will show. It would be hard to stand, I admit, because I'd have to make you all out to be a bunch of gibbering idiots, but if I can get people laughing at you, they might forget to be angry. In return for that, all my publisher asks is an exclusive story."

Beenay nodded and burst out, "Sir, the rest of us think he's right. These last two months we've considered everything but the million-to-one chance that there is an error somewhere in our theory or in our calculations. We ought to take care of that, too."

There was a murmur of agreement from the men grouped about the table, and Aton's expression became that of one who found his mouth full of something bitter and couldn't get rid of it.

"You may stay if you wish, then. You will kindly refrain, however, from hampering us in our duties in any way. You will also remember that I am in charge of all activities here, and in spite of your opinions as expressed in your columns, I will expect full cooperation and full respect—"

His hands were behind his back, and his wrinkled face thrust forward determinedly as he spoke. He might have continued indefinitely but for the intrusion of a new voice.

"Hello, hello, hello!" It came in a high tenor, and the plump cheeks of the newcomer expanded in a pleased smile. "What's this morgue-like atmosphere about here? No one's losing his nerve, I hope."

Aton started in consternation and said peevishly, "Now what the devil are you doing here, Sheerin? I thought you were going to stay behind in the Hideout."

Sheerin laughed and dropped his stubby figure into a chair. "Hideout be blowed! The place bored me. I wanted to be here, where things are getting hot. Don't you suppose I have my share of curiosity? I want to see these Stars the Cultists are forever speaking about." He rubbed his hands and added in a soberer tone, "It's freezing outside. The wind's enough to hang icicles on your nose. Beta doesn't seem to give any heat at all, at the distance it is."

The white-haired director ground his teeth in sudden exasperation. "Why do you go out of your way to do crazy things, Sheerin? What kind of good are you around here?"

"What kind of good am I around there?" Sheerin spread his palms in comical resignation. "A psychologist isn't worth his salt in the Hideout. They need men of action and strong, healthy women that can breed children. Me? I'm a hundred pounds too heavy for a man of action, and I wouldn't be a success at breeding children. So why bother them with an extra mouth to feed? I feel better over here."

Theremon spoke briskly. "Just what is the Hideout, sir?"

Sheerin seemed to see the columnist for the first time. He frowned and blew his ample cheeks out. "And just who in Lagash are you, red-head?"

Aton compressed his lips and then muttered sullenly, "That's Theremon 762, the newspaper fellow. I suppose you've heard of him."

The columnist offered his hand. "And, of course, you're Sheerin 501 of Saro University. I've heard of you." Then he repeated, "What is this Hideout, sir?"

"Well," said Sheerin, "we have managed to convince a few people of the validity of our prophecy of—er—doom, to be spectacular about it, and those few have taken proper measures. They consist mainly of the immediate members of the families of the Observatory staff, certain of the faculty of Saro University, and a few outsiders. Altogether, they number about three hundred, but three quarters are women and children."

"I see! They're suppose to hide where the Darkness and the—er—Stars can't get at them, and then hold out when the rest of the world goes poof."

"If they can. It won't be easy. With all of mankind insane, with the great cities going up in flames—environment will not be conducive to survival. But they have food, water, shelter, and weapons—"

"They've got more," said Aton. "They've got all our records, except for what we will collect today. Those records will mean everything to the next cycle, and *that's* what must survive. The rest can go hang."

Theremon uttered a long, low whistle and sat brooding for several minutes. The men about the table had brought out a multi-chess board and started a six-member game. Moves were made rapidly and in silence. All eyes bent in furious concentration on the board. Theremon watched them intently and then rose and approached Aton, who sat apart in whispered conversation with Sheerin.

"Listen," he said, "let's go somewhere where we won't bother the rest of the fellows. I want to ask some questions."

The aged astronomer frowned sourly at him, but Sheerin chirped up, "Certainly. It will do me good to talk. It always does. Aton was telling me about your ideas concerning world reaction to a failure of the prediction—and I agree with you. I read your column pretty regularly, by the way, and as a general thing I like your views."

"Please, Sheerin," growled Aton.

"Eh? Oh, all right. We'll go into the next room. It has softer chairs, anyway."

There were softer chairs in the next room. There were also thick red curtains on the windows and a maroon carpet on the floor. With the bricky light of Beta pouring in, the general effect was one of dried blood.

Theremon shuddered. "Say, I'd give ten credits for a decent dose of white light for just a second. I wish Gamma or Delta were in the sky."

"What are your questions?" asked Aton. "Please remember that our time is limited. In a little over an hour and a quarter we're going upstairs, and after that there will be no time for talk."

"Well, here it is." Theremon leaned back and folded his hands on his chest. "You people seem so all-fired serious about this that I'm beginning to believe you. Would you mind explaining what it's all about?"

Aton exploded, "Do you mean to sit there and tell me that you've been bombarding us with ridicule without even finding out what we've been trying to say?"

The columnist grinned sheepishly. "It's not that bad, sir. I've got the general idea. You say there is going to be a world-wide Darkness in a few hours and that all mankind will go violently insane. What I want now is the science behind it."

"No, you don't. No, you don't," broke in Sheerin. "If you ask Aton for that—supposing him to be in the mood to answer at all—he'll trot out pages of figures and volumes of graphs. You won't make head or tail of it. Now if you were to ask me, I could give you the layman's standpoint."

"All right; I ask you."

"Then first I'd like a drink." He rubbed his hands and looked at Aton.

"Water?" grunted Aton.

"Don't be silly!"

"Don't you be silly. No alcohol today. It would be too easy to get my men drunk. I can't afford to tempt them."

The psychologist grumbled wordlessly. He turned to Theremon, impaled him with his sharp eyes, and began.

"You realize, of course, that the history of civilization on Lagash displays a cyclic character—but I mean, *cyclic*!"

"I know," replied Theremon cautiously, "that that is the current archaeological theory. Has it been accepted as a fact?"

"Just about. In this last century it's been generally agreed upon. This cyclic character is—or rather, was—one of the great mysteries. We've located series of civilizations, nine of them definitely, and indications of others as well, all of which have reached heights comparable to our own, and all of which, without exception, were destroyed by fire at the very height of their culture.

"And no one could tell why. All centers of culture were thoroughly gutted by fire, with nothing left behind to give a hint as to the cause."

Theremon was following closely. "Wasn't there a Stone Age, too?"

"Probably, but as yet practically nothing is known of it, except that men of that age were little more than rather intelligent apes. We can forget about that."

"I see. Go on!"

"There have been explanations of these recurrent catastrophes, all of a more or less fantastic nature. Some say that there are periodic rains of fire; some that Lagash passes through a sun every so often; some even wilder things. But there is one theory, quite different from all of these, that has been handed down over a period of centuries."

"I know. You mean this myth of the 'Stars' that the Cultists have in their *Book of Revelations*."

"Exactly," rejoined Sheerin with satisfaction. "The Cultists said that every two thousand and fifty years Lagash entered a huge cave, so that all the suns disappeared, and there came *total darkness all over the world!* And then, they say, things called Stars appeared, which robbed men of their souls and left them unreasoning brutes, so that they destroyed the civilization they themselves had built up. Of course they mix all this up with a lot of religio-mystic notions, but that's the central idea."

There was a short pause in which Sheerin drew a long breath. "And now we come to the Theory of Universal Gravitation." He pronounced the phrase so that the capital letters sounded—and at that point Aton turned from the window, snorted loudly, and stalked out of the room.

The two stared after him, and Theremon said, "What's wrong?"

"Nothing in particular," replied Sheerin. "Two of the men were due several hours ago and haven't shown up yet. He's terrifically shorthanded, of course, because all but the really essential men have gone to the Hideout."

"You don't think the two deserted, do you?"

"Who? Faro and Yimot? Of course not. Still, if they're not back within the hour, things would be a little sticky." He got to his feet suddenly, and his eyes twinkled. "Anyway, as long as Aton is gone—"

Tiptoeing to the nearest window, he squatted, and from the low window box beneath withdrew a bottle of red liquid that gurgled suggestively when he shook it.

"I *thought* Aton didn't know about this," he remarked as he trotted back to the table. "Here! We've only got one glass so, as the guest, you can have it. I'll keep the bottle." And he filled the tiny cup with judicious care.

Theremon rose to protest, but Sheerin eyed him sternly. "Respect your elders, young man."

The newsman seated himself with a look of anguish on his face. "Go ahead, then, you old villain."

The psychologist's Adam's apple wobbled as the bottle upended, and then, with a satisfied grunt and a smack of the lips, he began again. "But what do you know about gravitation?"

"Nothing, except that it is a very recent development, not too well established, and that the math is so hard that only twelve men in Lagash are supposed to understand it."

"*Tcha!* Nonsense! Baloney! I can give you all the essential math in a sentence. The Law of Universal Gravitation states that there exists a cohesive force among all bodies of the universe, such that the amount of this force between any two given bodies is proportional to the product of their masses divided by the square of the distance between them."

"Is that all?"

"That's enough! It took four hundred years to develop it."

"Why that long? It sounded simple enough, the way you said it."

"Because great laws are not divined by flashes of inspiration, whatever you may think. It usually takes the combined work of a world full of scientists over a period of centuries. After Genovi 41 discovered that Lagash rotated about the sun Alpha rather than vice versa—and that was four hundred years ago—astronomers have been working. The complex motions of the six suns were recorded and analyzed and unwoven. Theory after theory was advanced and checked and counterchecked and modified and abandoned and revived and converted to something else. It was a devil of a job."

Theremon nodded thoughtfully and held out his glass for more liquor. Sheerin grudgingly allowed a few ruby drops to leave the bottle.

"It was twenty years ago," he continued after remoistening his own throat, "that it was finally demonstrated that the Law of Universal Gravitation accounted exactly for the orbital motions of the six suns. It was a great triumph."

Sheerin stood up and walked to the window, still clutching his bottle. "And now we're getting to the point. In the last decade, the motions of Lagash about Alpha were computed according to gravity, and *it did not account for the orbit observed;* not even when all perturbations due to the other suns were included. Either the law was invalid, or there was another, as yet unknown, factor involved."

Theremon joined Sheerin at the window and gazed out past the wooded slopes to where the spires of Saro City gleamed bloodily on the horizon. The newsman felt the tension of uncertainty grow within him as he cast a short glance at Beta. It glowered redly at zenith, dwarfed and evil.

"Go ahead, sir," he said softly.

Sheerin replied, "Astronomers stumbled about for years, each proposed theory more untenable than the one before—until Aton had the inspiration of calling in the Cult. The head of the Cult, Sor 5, had access to certain data that simplified the problem considerably. Aton set to work on a new track.

"What if there were another nonluminous planetary body such as Lagash? If there were, you know, it would shine only by reflected light, and if it were composed of bluish rock, as Lagash itself largely is, then, in the redness of the sky, the eternal blaze of the suns would make it invisible—drown it out completely."

Theremon whistled. "What a screwy idea!"

"You think *that's* screwy? Listen to this: Suppose this body rotated about Lagash at such a distance and in such an orbit and had such a mass that its attraction would exactly account for the deviations of Lagash's orbit from theory—do you know what would happen?"

The columnist shook his head.

"Well, sometimes this body would get in the way of a sun." And Sheerin emptied what remained in the bottle at a draft.

"And it does, I suppose," said Theremon flatly.

"Yes! But only one sun lies in its plane of revolution." He jerked a thumb at the shrunken sun above. "Beta! And it has been shown that the eclipse will occur only when the arrangement of the suns is such that Beta is alone in its hemisphere and at maximum distance, at which time the moon is invariably at minimum distance. The eclipse that results, with the moon seven times the apparent diameter of Beta, covers all of Lagash and lasts well over half a day, so that no spot on the planet escapes the effects. *That eclipse comes once every two thousand and forty-nine years.*"

Theremon's face was drawn into an expressionless mask. "And that's my story?"

The psychologist nodded. "That's all of it. First the eclipse—which will start in three quarters of an hour—then universal Darkness and, maybe, these mysterious Stars—then madness, and end of the cycle."

He brooded. "We had two months' leeway—we at the Observatory— and that wasn't enough time to persuade Lagash of the danger. Two centuries might not have been enough. But our records are at the Hideout, and today we photograph the eclipse. The next cycle will *start off* with the truth, and when the *next* eclipse comes, mankind will at last be ready for it. Come to think of it, that's part of your story too."

A thin wind ruffled the curtains at the window as Theremon opened it and leaned out. It played coldly with his hair as he stared at the crimson sunlight on his hand. Then he turned in sudden rebellion.

"What is there in Darkness to drive *me* mad?"

Sheerin smiled to himself as he spun the empty liquor bottle with abstracted motions of his hand. "Have you ever experienced Darkness, young man?"

The newsman leaned against the wall and considered. "No. Can't say I have. But I know what it is. Just—uh—" He made vague motions with his fingers and then brightened. "Just no light. Like in caves."

"Have you ever been in a cave?"

"In a *cave!* Of course not!"

"I thought not. *I* tried last week—just to see—but I got out in a hurry. I went in until the mouth of the cave was just visible as a blur of light, with black everywhere else. I never thought a person my weight could run that fast."

Theremon's lip curled. "Well, if it comes to that, I guess I wouldn't have run if I had been there."

The psychologist studied the young man with an annoyed frown.

"My, don't you talk big! I dare you to draw the curtain."

Theremon looked his surprise and said, "What for? If we had four or five suns out there, we might want to cut the light down a bit for comfort, but now we haven't enough light as it is."

"That's the point. Just draw the curtain; then come here and sit down."

"All right." Theremon reached for the tasseled string and jerked. The red curtain slid across the wide window, the brass rings hissing their way along the crossbar, and a dusk-red shadow clamped down on the room.

Theremon's footsteps sounded hollowly in the silence as he made his way to the table, and then they stopped halfway. "I can't see you, sir," he whispered.

"Feel your way," ordered Sheerin in a strained voice.

"But I can't see you, sir." The newsman was breathing harshly. "I can't see anything."

"What did you expect?" came the grim reply. "Come here and sit down!"

The footsteps sounded again, waveringly, approaching slowly. There was the sound of someone fumbling with a chair. Theremon's voice came thinly, "Here I am. I feel . . . *ulp* . . . all right."

"You like it, do you?"

"N—no. It's pretty awful. The walls seem to be—" He paused. "They seem to be closing in on me. I keep wanting to push them away. But I'm not going *mad!* In fact, the feeling isn't as bad as it was."

"All right. Draw the curtain back again."

There were cautious footsteps through the dark, the rustle of Theremon's body against the curtain as he felt for the tassel, and then the triumphant *ro-o-osh* of the curtain slithering back. Red light flooded the room, and with a cry of joy Theremon looked up at the sun.

Sheerin wiped the moistness off his forehead with the back of a hand and said shakily, "And that was just a dark room."

"It can be stood," said Theremon lightly.

"Yes, a dark room can. But were you at the Jonglor Centennial Exposition two years ago?"

"No, it so happens I never got around to it. Six thousand miles was just a bit too much to travel, even for the exposition."

"Well, I was there. You remember hearing about the 'Tunnel of Mystery' that broke all records in the amusement area—for the first month or so, anyway?"

"Yes. Wasn't there some fuss about it?"

"Very little. It was hushed up. You see, that Tunnel of Mystery was just a mile-long tunnel—with no lights. You got into a little open car and jolted along through Darkness for fifteen minutes. It was very popular—while it lasted."

"Popular?"

"Certainly. There's a fascination in being frightened *when it's part of a game.* A baby is born with three instinctive fears: of loud noises, of falling, and of the absence of light. That's why it's considered so funny to jump at someone and shout 'Boo!' That's why it's such fun to ride a roller coaster. And that's why that Tunnel of Mystery started cleaning up. People came out of that Darkness shaking, breathless, half dead with fear, but they kept on paying to get in."

"Wait a while, I remember now. Some people came out dead, didn't they? There were rumors of that after it shut down."

The psychologist snorted. "Bah! Two or three died. That was nothing! They paid off the families of the dead ones and argued the Jonglor City Council into forgetting it. After all, they said, if people with weak hearts want to go through the tunnel, it was at their own risk—and besides, it wouldn't happen again. So they put a doctor in the front office and had every customer go through a physical examination before getting into the car. That actually *boosted* ticket sales."

"Well, then?"

"But you see, there was something else. People sometimes came out in perfect order, except that they refused to go into buildings—any buildings; including palaces, mansions, apartment houses, tenements, cottages, huts, shacks, lean-tos, and tents."

Theremon looked shocked. "You mean they refused to come in out of the open? Where'd they sleep?"

"In the open."

"They should have *forced* them inside."

"Oh, they did, they did. Whereupon these people went into violent hysterics and did their best to bat their brains out against the nearest wall. Once you got them inside, you couldn't keep them there without a strait jacket or a heavy dose of tranquilizer."

"They must have been crazy."

"Which is exactly what they were. One person out of every ten who went into that tunnel came out that way. They called in the psychologists, and we did the only thing possible. We closed down the exhibit." He spread his hands.

"What was the matter with these people?" asked Theremon finally.

"Essentially the same thing that was the matter with you when you thought the walls of the room were crushing in on you in the dark. There is a psychological term for mankind's instinctive fear of the absence of light. We call it 'claustrophobia,' because the lack of light is always tied up with enclosed places, so that fear of one is fear of the other. You see?"

"And those people of the tunnel?"

"Those people of the tunnel consisted of those unfortunates whose mentality did not quite possess the resiliency to overcome the claustrophobia that overtook them in the Darkness. Fifteen minutes without light is a long time; you only had two or three minutes, and I believe you were fairly upset.

"The people of the tunnel had what is called a 'claustrophobic fixation.' Their latent fear of Darkness and enclosed places had crystalized and become active, and, as far as we can tell, permanent. That's what fifteen minutes in the dark will do."

There was a long silence, and Theremon's forehead wrinkled slowly into a frown. "I don't believe it's that bad."

"You mean you don't want to believe," snapped Sheerin. "You're afraid to believe. Look out the window!"

Theremon did so, and the psychologist continued without pausing. "Imagine Darkness—everywhere. No light, as far as you can see. The houses, the trees, the fields, the earth, the sky—black! And Stars thrown in, for all I know—whatever *they* are. Can you conceive it?"

"Yes, I can," declared Theremon truculently.

And Sheerin slammed his fist down upon the table in sudden passion. "You lie! You can't conceive that. Your brain wasn't built for the conception any more than it was built for the conception of infinity or of eternity. You can only talk about it. A fraction of the reality upsets you, and when the real thing comes, your brain is going to be presented with the phenomenon outside its limits of comprehension. You will go mad, completely and permanently! There is no question of it!"

He added sadly, "And another couple of millennia of painful struggle comes to nothing. Tomorrow there won't be a city standing unharmed in all Lagash."

Theremon recovered part of his mental equilibrium. "That doesn't follow. I still don't see that I can go loony just because there isn't a sun in the sky—but even if I did, and everyone else did, how does that harm the cities? Are we going to blow them down?"

But Sheerin was angry, too. "If you were in Darkness, what would you want more than anything else; what would it be that every instinct would call for? Light, damn you, *light!*"

"Well?"

"And how would you get light?"

"I don't know," said Theremon flatly.

"What's the *only* way to get light, short of a sun?"

"How should I know?"

They were standing face to face and nose to nose.

Sheerin said, "You burn something, mister. Ever see a forest fire? Ever go camping and cook a stew over a wood fire? Heat isn't the only thing burning wood gives off, you know. It gives off light, and people know that. And when it's dark they want light, and they're going to *get* it."

"So they burn wood?"

"So they burn whatever they can get. They've got to have light. They've got to burn something, and wood isn't handy—so they'll burn whatever is nearest. They'll have their light—and every center of habitation goes up in flames!"

Eyes held each other as though the whole matter were a personal affair of respective will powers, and then Theremon broke away wordlessly. His breathing was harsh and ragged, and he scarcely noted the sudden hubbub that came from the adjoining room behind the closed door.

Sheerin spoke, and it was with an effort that he made it sound matter-of-fact. "I think I heard Yimot's voice. He and Faro are probably back. Let's go in and see what kept them."

"Might as well!" muttered Theremon. He drew a long breath and seemed to shake himself. The tension was broken.

THE ROOM WAS in an uproar, with members of the staff clustering about two young men who were removing outer garments even as they parried the miscellany of questions being thrown at them.

Aton bustled through the crowd and faced the newcomers angrily. "Do you realize that it's less than half an hour before deadline? Where have you two been?"

Faro 24 seated himself and rubbed his hands. His cheeks were red with the outdoor chill. "Yimot and I have just finished carrying through a little crazy experiment of our own. We've been trying to see if we couldn't construct an arrangement by which we could simulate the appearance of Darkness and Stars so as to get an advance notion as to how it looked."

There was a confused murmur from the listeners, and a sudden look of interest entered Aton's eyes. "There wasn't anything said of this before. How did you go about it?"

"Well," said Faro, "the idea came to Yimot and myself long ago, and we've been working it out in our spare time. Yimot knew of a low one-story house down in the city with a domed roof—it had once been used as a museum, I think. Anyway, we bought it—"

"Where did you get the money?" interrupted Aton peremptorily.

"Our bank accounts," grunted Yimot 70. "It cost two thousand credits." Then, defensively, "Well, what of it? Tomorrow, two thousand credits will be two thousand pieces of paper. That's all."

"Sure," agreed Faro. "We bought the place and rigged it up with black velvet from top to bottom so as to get as perfect a Darkness as possible. Then we punched tiny holes in the ceiling and through the roof and covered them with little metal caps, all of which could be shoved aside simultaneously at the close of a switch. At least we didn't do that part ourselves; we got a carpenter and an electrician and some others—money didn't count. The point was that we could get the light to shine through those holes in the roof, so that we could get a starlike effect."

Not a breath was drawn during the pause that followed. Aton said stiffly, "You had no right to make a private—"

Faro seemed abashed. "I know, sir—but frankly, Yimot and I thought the experiment was a little dangerous. If the effect really worked, we half expected to go mad—from what Sheerin says about all this, we thought that would be rather likely. We wanted to take the risk ourselves. Of course if we found we could retain sanity, it occurred to us that we might develop immunity to the real thing, and then expose the rest of you the same way. But things didn't work out at all—"

"Why, what happened?"

It was Yimot who answered. "We shut ourselves in and allowed our eyes to get accustomed to the dark. It's an extremely creepy feeling because the total Darkness makes you feel as if the walls and ceiling are crushing in on you. But we got over that and pulled the switch. The caps fell away and the roof glittered all over with little dots of light—"

"Well?"

"Well—nothing. That was the whacky part of it. Nothing happened. It was just a roof with holes in it, and that's just what it looked like. We tried it over and over again—that's what kept us so late—but there just isn't any effect at all."

There followed a shocked silence, and all eyes turned to Sheerin, who sat motionless, mouth open.

Theremon was the first to speak. "You know what this does to this whole theory you've built up, Sheerin, don't you?" He was grinning with relief.

But Sheerin raised his hand. "Now wait a while. Just let me think this through." And then he snapped his fingers, and when he lifted his head there was neither surprise nor uncertainty in his eyes. "Of course—"

He never finished. From somewhere up above there sounded a sharp clang, and Beenay, starting to his feet, dashed up the stairs with a "What the devil!"

The rest followed after.

Things happened quickly. Once up in the dome, Beenay cast one horrified glance at the shattered photographic plates and at the man bending over them; and then hurled himself fiercely at the intruder, getting a death grip on his throat. There was a wild threshing, and as others of the staff joined in, the stranger was swallowed up and smothered under the weight of half a dozen angry men.

Aton came up last, breathing heavily. "Let him up!"

There was a reluctant unscrambling and the stranger, panting harshly, with his clothes torn and his forehead bruised, was hauled to his feet. He had a short yellow beard curled elaborately in the style affected by the Cultists.

Beenay shifted his hold to a collar grip and shook the man savagely. "All right, rat, what's the idea? These plates—"

"I wasn't after *them,*" retorted the Cultist coldly. "That was an accident."

Beenay followed his glowering stare and snarled, "I see. You were after the cameras themselves. The accident with the plates was a stroke of luck for you, then. If you had touched Snapping Bertha or any of the others, you would have died by slow torture. As it is—" He drew his fist back.

Aton grabbed his sleeve. "Stop that! Let him go!"

The young technician wavered, and his arm dropped reluctantly. Aton pushed him aside and confronted the Cultist. "You're Latimer, aren't you?"

The Cultist bowed stiffly and indicated the symbol upon his hip. "I am Latimer 25, adjutant of the third class to his serenity, Sor 5."

"And"—Aton's white eyebrows lifted—"you were with his serenity when he visited me last week, weren't you?"

Latimer bowed a second time.

"Now, then, what do you want?"

"Nothing that you would give me of your own free will."

"Sor 5 sent you, I suppose—or is this your own idea?"

"I won't answer that question."

"Will there be any further visitors?"

"I won't answer that, either."

Aton glanced at his timepiece and scowled. "Now, man, what is it your master wants of me? I have fulfilled my end of the bargain."

Latimer smiled faintly, but said nothing.

"I asked him," continued Aton angrily, "for data only the Cult could supply, and it was given to me. For that, thank you. In return I promised to prove the essential truth of the creed of the Cult."

"There was no need to prove that," came the proud retort. "It stands proven by the *Book of Revelations*."

"For the handful that constitute the Cult, yes. Don't pretend to mistake my meaning. I offered to present scientific backing for your beliefs. And I did!"

The Cultist's eyes narrowed bitterly. "Yes, you did—with a fox's subtlety, for your pretended explanation backed our beliefs, and at the same time removed all necessity for them. You made of the Darkness and of the Stars a natural phenomenon and removed all its real significance. That was blasphemy."

"If so, the fault isn't mine. The facts exist. What can I do but state them?"

"Your 'facts' are a fraud and a delusion."

Aton stamped angrily. "How do you know?"

And the answer came with the certainty of absolute faith. "I know!"

The director purpled and Beenay whispered urgently. Aton waved him silent. "And what does Sor 5 want us to do? He still thinks, I suppose, that in trying to warn the world to take measures against the menace of madness, we are placing innumerable souls in jeopardy. We aren't succeeding, if that means anything to him."

"The attempt itself has done harm enough, and your vicious effort to gain information by means of your devilish instruments must be stopped. We obey the will of the Stars, and I only regret that my clumsiness prevented me from wrecking your infernal devices."

"It wouldn't have done you too much good," returned Aton. "All our data, except for the direct evidence we intend collecting right now, is already safely cached and well beyond possibility of harm." He smiled grimly. "But that does not affect your present status as an attempted burglar and criminal."

He turned to the men behind him. "Someone call the police at Saro City."

There was a cry of distaste from Sheerin. "Damn it, Aton, what's wrong with you? There's no time for that. Here"—he bustled his way forward—"let me handle this."

Aton stared down his nose at the psychologist. "This is not the time for your monkeyshines, Sheerin. Will you please let me handle this my own way? Right now you are a complete outsider here, and don't forget it."

Sheerin's mouth twisted eloquently. "Now why should we go to the impossible trouble of calling the police—with Beta's eclipse a matter of minutes from now—when this young man here is perfectly willing to pledge his word of honor to remain and cause no trouble whatsoever?"

The Cultist answered promptly, "I will do no such thing. You're free to do what you want, but it's only fair to warn you that just as soon as I get my chance I'm going to finish what I came out here to do. If it's my word of honor you're relying on, you'd better call the police."

Sheerin smiled in a friendly fashion. "You're a determined cuss, aren't you? Well, I'll explain something. Do you see that young man at the window? He's a strong, husky fellow, quite handy with his fists, and he's an outsider besides. Once the eclipse starts there will be nothing for him to do except keep an eye on you. Besides him, there will be myself—a little too stout for active fisticuffs, but still able to help."

"Well, what of it?" demanded Latimer frozenly.

"Listen and I'll tell you," was the reply. "Just as soon as the eclipse starts, we're going to take you, Theremon and I, and deposit you in a little closet with one door, to which is attached one giant lock and no windows. You will remain there for the duration."

"And afterward," breathed Latimer fiercely, "there'll be no one to let me out. I know as well as you do what the coming of the Stars means—I know it far better than you. With all your minds gone, you are not likely to free me. Suffocation or slow starvation, is it? About what I might have expected from a group of scientists. But I don't give my word. It's a matter of principle, and I won't discuss it further."

Aton seemed perturbed. His faded eyes were troubled. "Really, Sheerin, locking him—"

"Please!" Sheerin motioned him impatiently to silence. "I don't think for a moment things will go that far. Latimer has just tried a clever little bluff, but I'm not a psychologist just because I like the sound of the word." He grinned at the Cultist. "Come now, you don't really think I'm trying anything as crude as slow starvation. My dear Latimer, if I lock you in the closet, you are not going to see the Darkness, and you are not going to see the Stars. It does not take much knowledge of the fundamental creed of the Cult to realize that for you to be hidden from the Stars when they appear means the loss of your immortal soul. Now, I believe you to be an honorable man. I'll accept your word of honor to make no further effort to disrupt proceedings, if you'll offer it."

A vein throbbed in Latimer's temple, and he seemed to shrink within himself as he said thickly, "You have it!" And then he added with swift fury, "But it is my consolation that you will all be damned for your deeds of today." He turned on his heel and stalked to the high three-legged stool by the door.

Sheerin nodded to the columnist. "Take a seat next to him, Theremon—just as a formality. Hey, Theremon!"

But the newspaperman didn't move. He had gone pale to the lips. "Look at that!" The finger he pointed toward the sky shook, and his voice was dry and cracked.

There was one simultaneous gasp as every eye followed the pointing finger and, for one breathless moment, stared frozenly.

Beta was chipped on one side!

The tiny bit of encroaching blackness was perhaps the width of a fingernail, but to the staring watchers it magnified itself into the crack of doom.

Only for a moment they watched, and after that there was a shrieking confusion that was even shorter of duration and which gave way to an orderly scurry of activity—each man at his prescribed job. At the crucial moment there was no time for emotion. The men were merely scientists with work to do. Even Aton had melted away.

Sheerin said prosaically, "First contact must have been made fifteen minutes ago. A little early, but pretty good considering the uncertainties involved in the calculation." He looked about him and then tiptoed to Theremon, who still remained staring out the window, and dragged him away gently.

"Aton is furious," he whispered, "so stay away. He missed first contact on account of this fuss with Latimer, and if you get in his way he'll have you thrown out the window."

Theremon nodded shortly and sat down. Sheerin stared in surprise at him.

"The devil, man," he exclaimed, "you're shaking."

"Eh?" Theremon licked dry lips and then tried to smile. "I don't feel very well, and that's a fact."

The psychologist's eyes hardened. "You're not losing your nerve?"

"No!" cried Theremon in a flash of indignation. "Give me a chance, will you? I haven't really believed this rigmarole—not way down beneath, anyway—till just this minute. Give me a chance to get used to the idea. You've been preparing yourself for two months or more."

"You're right, at that," replied Sheerin thoughtfully. "Listen! Have you got a family—parents, wife, children?"

Theremon shook his head. "You mean the Hideout, I suppose. No, you don't have to worry about that. I have a sister, but she's two thousand miles away. I don't even know her exact address."

"Well, then, what about yourself? You've got time to get there, and they're one short anyway, since I left. After all, you're not needed here, and you'd make a darned fine addition—"

Theremon looked at the other wearily. "You think I'm scared stiff, don't you? Well, get this, mister, I'm a newspaperman and I've been assigned to cover a story. I intend covering it."

There was a faint smile on the psychologist's face. "I see. Professional honor, is that it?"

"You might call it that. But, man, I'd give my right arm for another bottle of that sockeroo juice even half the size of the one you hogged. If ever a fellow needed a drink, I do."

He broke off. Sheerin was nudging him violently. "Do you hear that? Listen!"

Theremon followed the motion of the other's chin and stared at the Cultist, who, oblivious to all about him, faced the window, a look of wild elation on his face, droning to himself the while in singsong fashion.

"What's he saying?" whispered the columnist.

"He's quoting *Book of Revelations*, fifth chapter," replied Sheerin. Then, urgently, "Keep quiet and listen, I tell you."

The Cultist's voice had risen in a sudden increase of fervor: " 'And it came to pass that in those days the Sun, Beta, held lone vigil in the sky for ever longer periods as the revolutions passed; until such time as for full half a revolution, it alone, shrunken and cold, shone down upon Lagash.

" 'And men did assemble in the public squares and in the highways, there to debate and to marvel at the sight, for a strange depression had seized them. Their minds were troubled and their speech confused, for the souls of men awaited the coming of the Stars.

" 'And in the city of Trigon, at high noon, Vendret 2 came forth and said unto the men of Trigon, "Lo, ye sinners! Though ye scorn the ways of righteousness, yet will the time of reckoning come. Even now the Cave approaches to swallow Lagash; yea, and all it contains.

" 'And even as he spoke the lip of the Cave of Darkness passed the edge of Beta so that to all Lagash it was hidden from sight. Loud were the cries of men as it vanished, and great the fear of soul that fell upon them.

" 'It came to pass that the Darkness of the Cave fell upon Lagash, and there was no light on all the surface of Lagash. Men were even as blinded, nor could one man see his neighbor, though he felt his breath upon his face.

" 'And in this blackness there appeared the Stars, in countless numbers, and to the strains of music of such beauty that the very leaves of the trees cried out in wonder.

" 'And in that moment the souls of men departed from them, and their abandoned bodies became even as beasts; yea, even as brutes of the wild; so that through the blackened streets of the cities of Lagash they prowled with wild cries.

" 'From the Stars there then reached down the Heavenly Flame, and where it touched, the cities of Lagash flamed to utter destruction, so that of man and of the works of man nought remained.

" 'Even then—' "

There was a subtle change in Latimer's tone. His eyes had not shifted, but somehow he had become aware of the absorbed attention of the other two. Easily, without pausing for breath, the timbre of his voice shifted and the syllables became more liquid.

Theremon, caught by surprise, stared. The words seemed on the border of familiarity. There was an elusive shift in the accent, a tiny change in the vowel stress; nothing more—yet Latimer had become thoroughly unintelligible.

Sheerin smiled slyly. "He shifted to some old-cycle tongue, probably their traditional second cycle. That was the language in which the *Book of Revelations* was originally written, you know."

"It doesn't matter; I've heard enough." Theremon shoved his chair back and brushed his hair back with hands that no longer shook. "I feel much better now."

"You do?" Sheerin seemed mildly surprised.

"I'll say I do. I had a bad case of jitters just a while back. Listening to you and your gravitation and seeing that eclipse start almost finished me. But this"—he jerked a contemptuous thumb at the yellow-bearded Cultist—"*this* is the sort of thing my nurse used to tell me. I've been laughing at that sort of thing all my life. I'm not going to let it scare me *now*."

He drew a deep breath and said with a hectic gaiety, "But if I expect to keep on the good side of myself, I'm going to turn my chair away from the window."

Sheerin said, "Yes, but you'd better talk lower. Aton just lifted his head out of that box he's got it stuck into and gave you a look that should have killed you."

Theremon made a mouth. "I forgot about the old fellow." With elaborate care he turned the chair from the window, cast one distasteful look over his shoulder, and said, "It has occurred to me that there must be considerable immunity against this Star madness."

The psychologist did not answer immediately. Beta was past its zenith now, and the square of bloody sunlight that outlined the window upon the floor had lifted into Sheerin's lap. He stared at its dusky color thoughtfully and then bent and squinted into the sun itself.

The chip in its side had grown to a black encroachment that covered a third of Beta. He shuddered, and when he straightened once more his florid cheeks did not contain quite as much color as they had had previously.

With a smile that was almost apologetic, he reversed his chair also. "There are probably two million people in Saro City that are all trying to join the Cult at once in one gigantic revival." Then, ironically, "The Cult is in for an hour of unexampled prosperity. I trust they'll make the most of it. Now, what was it you said?"

"Just this. How did the Cultists manage to keep the *Book of Revelations* going from cycle to cycle, and how on Lagash did it get written in the first place? There must have been some sort of immunity, for if everyone had gone mad, who would be left to write the book?"

Sheerin stared at his questioner ruefully. "Well, now, young man, there isn't any eyewitness answer to that, but we've got a few damned good notions as to what happened. You see, there are three kinds of people who might remain relatively unaffected. First, the very few who don't see the Stars at all: the seriously retarded or those who drink themselves into a stupor at the beginning of the eclipse and remain so to the end. We leave them out—because they aren't really witnesses.

"Then there are children below six, to whom the world as a whole is too new and strange for them to be too frightened at Stars and Darkness. They would be just another item in an already surprising world. You see that, don't you?"

The other nodded doubtfully. "I suppose so."

"Lastly, there are those whose minds are too coarsely grained to be entirely toppled. The very insensitive would be scarcely affected—oh, such people as some of our older, work-broken peasants. Well, the children would have fugitive memories, and that, combined with the confused, incoherent babblings of the half-mad morons, formed the basis for the *Book of Revelations*.

"Naturally, the book was based, in the first place, on the testimony of those least qualified to serve as historians; that is, children and morons; and was probably edited and re-edited through the cycles."

"Do you suppose," broke in Theremon, "that they carried the book through the cycles the way we're planning on handing on the secret of gravitation?"

Sheerin shrugged. "Perhaps, but their exact method is unimportant. They do it, somehow. The point I was getting at was that the book can't help but be a mass of distortion, even if it is based on fact. For instance, do you remember the experiment with the holes in the roof that Faro and Yimot tried—the one that didn't work?"

"Yes."

"You know why it didn't w—" He stopped and rose in alarm, for Aton was approaching, his face a twisted mask of consternation. "*What's happened?*"

Aton drew him aside and Sheerin could feel the fingers on his elbow twitching.

"Not so loud!" Aton's voice was low and tortured. "I've just gotten word from the Hideout on the private line."

Sheerin broke in anxiously. "They are in trouble?"

"Not *they.*" Aton stressed the pronoun significantly. "They sealed themselves off just a while ago, and they're going to stay buried till day after tomorrow. They're safe. But the *city,* Sheerin—it's a shambles. You have no idea—" He was having difficulty in speaking.

"Well?" snapped Sheerin impatiently. "What of it? It will get worse. What are you shaking about?" Then, suspiciously, "How do you feel?"

Aton's eyes sparked angrily at the insinuation, and then faded to anxiety once more. "You don't understand. The Cultists are active. They're rousing the people to storm the Observatory—promising them immediate entrance into grace, promising them salvation, promising them anything. What are we to do, Sheerin?"

Sheerin's head bent, and he stared in long abstraction at his toes. He tapped his chin with one knuckle, then looked up and said crisply, "Do? What is there to do? Nothing at all. Do the men know of this?"

"No, of course not!"

"Good! Keep it that way. How long till totality?"

"Not quite an hour."

"There's nothing to do but gamble. It will take time to organize any really formidable mob, and it will take more time to get them out here. We're a good five miles from the city—"

He glared out the window, down the slopes to where the farmed patches gave way to clumps of white houses in the suburbs; down to where the metropolis itself was a blur on the horizon—a mist in the waning blaze of Beta.

He repeated without turning, "It will take time. Keep on working and pray that totality comes first."

Beta was cut in half, the line of division pushing a slight concavity into the still-bright portion of the Sun. It was like a gigantic eyelid shutting slantwise over the light of a world.

The faint clatter of the room in which he stood faded into oblivion, and he sensed only the thick silence of the fields outside. The very insects seemed frightened mute. And things were dim.

He jumped at the voice in his ear. Theremon said, "Is something wrong?"

"Eh? Er—no. Get back to the chair. We're in the way." They slipped back to their corner, but the psychologist did not speak for a time. He lifted a finger and loosened his collar. He twisted his neck back and forth but found no relief. He looked up suddenly.

"Are you having any difficulty in breathing?"

The newspaperman opened his eyes wide and drew two or three long breaths. "No. Why?"

"I looked out the window too long, I suppose. The dimness got me.

Difficulty in breathing is one of the first symptoms of a claustrophobic attack."

Theremon drew another long breath. "Well, it hasn't got me yet. Say, here's another of the fellows."

Beenay had interposed his bulk between the light and the pair in the corner, and Sheerin squinted up at him anxiously. "Hello, Beenay."

The astronomer shifted his weight to the other foot and smiled feebly. "You won't mind if I sit down awhile and join in the talk? My cameras are set, and there's nothing to do till totality." He paused and eyed the Cultist, who fifteen minutes earlier had drawn a small, skinbound book from his sleeve and had been poring intently over it ever since. "That rat hasn't been making trouble, has he?"

Sheerin shook his head. His shoulders were thrown back and he frowned his concentration as he forced himself to breathe regularly. He said, "Have you had any trouble breathing, Beenay?"

Beenay sniffed the air in his turn. "It doesn't seem stuffy to me."

"A touch of claustrophobia," explained Sheerin apologetically.

"Ohhh! It worked itself differently with me. I get the impression that my eyes are going back on me. Things seem to blur and—well, nothing is clear. And it's cold, too."

"Oh, it's cold, all right. That's no illusion." Theremon grimaced. "My toes feel as if I've been shipping them cross-country in a refrigerating car."

"What we need," put in Sheerin, "is to keep our minds busy with extraneous affairs. I was telling you a while ago, Theremon, why Faro's experiments with the holes in the roof came to nothing."

"You were just beginning," replied Theremon. He encircled a knee with both arms and nuzzled his chin against it.

"Well, as I started to say, they were misled by taking the *Book of Revelations* literally. There probably wasn't any sense in attaching any physical significance to the Stars. It might be, you know, that in the presence of total Darkness, the mind finds it absolutely necessary to create light. This illusion of light might be all the Stars there really are."

"In other words," interposed Theremon, "you mean the Stars are the results of the madness and not one of the causes. Then, what good will Beenay's photographs be?"

"To prove that it is an illusion, maybe; or to prove the opposite; for all I know. Then again—"

But Beenay had drawn his chair closer, and there was an expression of sudden enthusiasm on his face. "Say, I'm glad you two got onto this subject." His eyes narrowed and he lifted one finger. "I've been thinking about these Stars and I've got a really cute notion. Of course it's strictly ocean foam, and I'm not trying to advance it seriously, but I think it's interesting. Do you want to hear it?"

He seemed half reluctant, but Sheerin leaned back and said, "Go ahead! I'm listening."

"Well, then, supposing there were other suns in the universe." He broke off a little bashfully. "I mean suns that are so far away that they're too dim to see. It sounds as if I've been reading some of that fantastic fiction, I suppose."

"Not necessarily. Still, isn't that possibility eliminated by the fact that, according to the Law of Gravitation, they would make themselves evident by their attractive forces?"

"Not if they were far enough off," rejoined Beenay, "really far off—maybe as much as four light years, or even more. We'd never be able to detect perturbations then, because they'd be too small. Say that there were a lot of suns that far off; a dozen or two, maybe."

Theremon whistled melodiously. "What an idea for a good Sunday supplement article. Two dozen suns in a universe eight light years across. Wow! That would shrink our world into insignificance. The readers would eat it up."

"Only an idea," said Beenay with a grin, "but you see the point. During an eclipse, these dozen suns would become visible because there'd be no *real* sunlight to drown them out. Since they're so far off, they'd appear small, like so many little marbles. Of course the Cultists talk of millions of Stars, but that's probably exaggeration. There just isn't any place in the universe you could put a million suns—unless they touch one another."

Sheerin had listened with gradually increasing interest. "You've hit something there, Beenay. And exaggeration is just exactly what would happen. Our minds, as you probably know, can't grasp directly any number higher than five; above that there is only the concept of 'many.' A dozen would become a million just like that. A damn good idea!"

"And I've got another cute little notion," Beenay said. "Have you ever thought what a simple problem gravitation would be if only you had a sufficiently simple system? Supposing you had a universe in which there was a planet with only one sun. The planet would travel in a perfect ellipse and the exact nature of the gravitational force would be so evident it could be accepted as an axiom. Astronomers on such a world would start off with gravity probably before they even invented the telescope. Naked-eye observation would be enough."

"But would such a system be dynamically stable?" questioned Sheerin doubtfully.

"Sure! They call it the 'one-and-one' case. It's been worked out mathematically, but it's the philosophical implications that interest me."

"It's nice to think about," admitted Sheerin, "as a pretty abstraction—like a perfect gas, or absolute zero."

"Of course," continued Beenay, "there's the catch that life would be impossible on such a planet. It wouldn't get enough heat and light, and if it rotated there would be total Darkness half of each day. You couldn't expect life—which is fundamentally dependent upon light—to develop under those conditions. Besides—"

Sheerin's chair went over backward as he sprang to his feet in a rude interruption. "Aton's brought out the lights."

Beenay said, "Huh," turned to stare, and then grinned halfway around his head in open relief.

There were half a dozen foot-long, inch-thick rods cradled in Aton's arms. He glared over them at the assembled staff members.

"Get back to work, all of you. Sheerin, come here and help me!"

Sheerin trotted to the older man's side and, one by one, in utter silence, the two adjusted the rods in makeshift metal holders suspended from the walls.

With the air of one carrying through the most sacred item of a religious ritual, Sheerin scraped a large, clumsy match into spluttering life and passed it to Aton, who carried the flame to the upper end of one of the rods.

It hesitated there awhile, playing futilely about the tip, until a sudden, crackling flare cast Aton's lined face into yellow highlights. He withdrew the match and a spontaneous cheer rattled the window.

The rod was topped by six inches of wavering flame! Methodically, the other rods were lighted, until six independent fires turned the rear of the room yellow.

The light was dim, dimmer even than the tenuous sunlight. The flames reeled crazily, giving birth to drunken, swaying shadows. The torches smoked devilishly and smelled like a bad day in the kitchen. But they emitted yellow light.

There was something about yellow light, after four hours of somber, dimming Beta. Even Latimer had lifted his eyes from his book and stared in wonder.

Sheerin warmed his hands at the nearest, regardless of the soot that gathered upon them in a fine, gray powder, and muttered ecstatically to himself. "Beautiful! Beautiful! I never realized before what a wonderful color yellow is."

But Theremon regarded the torches suspicously. He wrinkled his nose at the rancid odor and said, "What are those things?"

"Wood," said Sheerin shortly.

"Oh, no, they're not. They aren't burning. The top inch is charred and the flame just keeps shooting up out of nothing."

"That's the beauty of it. This is a really efficient artificial-light mechanism. We made a few hundred of them, but most went to the Hideout, of course. You see"—he turned and wiped his blackened hands upon his handkerchief—"you take the pithy core of coarse water reeds, dry them thoroughly, and soak them in animal grease. Then you set fire to it and the grease burns, little by little. These torches will burn for almost half an hour without stopping. Ingenious, isn't it? It was developed by one of our own young men at Saro University."

After the momentary sensation, the dome had quieted. Latimer had carried his chair directly beneath a torch and continued reading, lips moving in the monotonous recital of invocations to the Stars. Beenay had drifted away to his cameras once more, and Theremon seized the opportunity to add to his notes on the article he was going to write for the Saro City *Chronicle* the next day—a procedure he had been following for the last two hours in a perfectly methodical, perfectly conscientious and, as he was well aware, perfectly meaningless fashion.

But, as the gleam of amusement in Sheerin's eyes indicated, careful note-taking occupied his mind with something other than the fact that the sky was gradually turning a horrible deep purple-red, as if it were one gigantic, freshly peeled beet; and so it fulfilled its purpose.

The air grew, somehow, denser. Dusk, like a palpable entity, entered the room, and the dancing circle of yellow light about the torches etched itself into ever-sharper distinction against the gathering grayness beyond. There was the odor of smoke and the presence of little chuckling sounds that the torches made as they burned; the soft pad of one of the men circling the table at which he worked, on hesitant tip-toes; the occasional indrawn breath of someone trying to retain composure in a world that was retreating into the shadow.

It was Theremon who first heard the extraneous noise. It was a vague, unorganized *impression* of sound that would have gone unnoticed but for the dead silence that prevailed within the dome.

The newsman sat upright and replaced his notebook. He held his breath and listened; then, with considerable reluctance, threaded his way between the solarscope and one of Beenay's cameras and stood before the window.

The silence ripped to fragments at his startled shout: *"Sheerin!"*

Work stopped! The psychologist was at his side in a moment. Aton joined him. Even Yimot 70, high in his little lean-back seat at the eyepiece of the gigantic solarscope, paused and looked downward.

Outside, Beta was a mere smoldering splinter, taking one last desperate look at Lagash. The eastern horizon, in the direction of the city, was lost in Darkness, and the road from Saro to the Observatory was a dull-red line bordered on both sides by wooded tracts, the trees of which had somehow lost individuality and merged into a continuous shadowy mass.

But it was the highway itself that held attention, for along it there surged another, and infinitely menacing, shadowy mass.

Aton cried in a cracked voice, "The madmen from the city! They've come!"

"How long to totality?" demanded Sheerin.

"Fifteen minutes, but . . . but they'll be here in five."

"Never mind, keep the men working. We'll hold them off. This place is built like a fortress. Aton, keep an eye on our young Cultist just for luck. Theremon, come with me."

Sheerin was out the door, and Theremon was at his heels. The stairs stretched below them in tight, circular sweeps about the central shaft, fading into a dank and dreary grayness.

The first momentum of their rush had carried them fifty feet down, so that the dim, flickering yellow from the open door of the dome had disappeared and both above and below the same dusky shadow crushed in upon them.

Sheerin paused, and his pudgy hand clutched at his chest. His eyes bulged and his voice was a dry cough. "I can't . . . breathe. . . . Go down . . . yourself. Close all doors—"

Theremon took a few downward steps, then turned. "Wait! Can you hold out a minute?" He was panting himself. The air passed in and out his lungs like so much molasses, and there was a little germ of screeching panic in his mind at the thought of making his way into the mysterious Darkness below by himself.

Theremon, after all, was afraid of the dark!

"Stay here," he said. "I'll be back in a second." He dashed upward two steps at a time, heart pounding—not altogether from the exertion—tumbled into the dome and snatched a torch from its holder. It was foul-smelling, and the smoke smarted his eyes almost blind, but he clutched that torch as if he wanted to kiss it for joy, and its flame streamed backward as he hurtled down the stairs again.

Sheerin opened his eyes and moaned as Theremon bent over him. Theremon shook him roughly. "All right, get a hold on yourself. We've got light."

He held the torch at tiptoe height and, propping the tottering psychologist by an elbow, made his way downward in the middle of the protecting circle of illumination.

The offices on the ground floor still possessed what light there was, and Theremon felt the horror about him relax.

"Here," he said brusquely, and passed the torch to Sheerin. "You can hear *them* outside."

And they could. Little scraps of hoarse, wordless shouts.

But Sheerin was right; the Observatory was built like a fortress. Erected in the last century, when the neo-Gavottian style of architecture was at its ugly height, it had been designed for stability and durability rather than for beauty.

The windows were protected by the grillwork of inch-thick iron bars sunk deep into the concrete sills. The walls were solid masonry that an earthquake couldn't have touched, and the main door was a huge oaken slab reinforced with iron. Theremon shot the bolts and they slid shut with a dull clang.

At the other end of the corridor, Sheerin cursed weakly. He pointed to the lock of the back door which had been neatly jimmied into uselessness.

"That must be how Latimer got in," he said.

"Well, don't stand there," cried Theremon impatiently. "Help drag up the furniture—and keep that torch out of my eyes. The smoke's killing me."

He slammed the heavy table up against the door as he spoke, and in two minutes had built a barricade which made up for what it lacked in beauty and symmetry by the sheer inertia of its massiveness.

Somewhere, dimly, far off, they could hear the battering of naked fists upon the door; and the screams and yells from outside had a sort of half reality.

That mob had set off from Saro City with only two things in mind: the attainment of Cultist salvation by the destruction of the Observatory, and a maddening fear that all but paralyzed them. There was no time to think of ground cars, or of weapons, or of leadership, or even of organization. They made for the Observatory on foot and assaulted it with bare hands.

And now that they were there, the last flash of Beta, the last ruby-red drop of flame, flickered feebly over a humanity that had left only stark, universal fear!

Theremon groaned, "Let's get back to the dome!"

IN THE DOME, only Yimot, at the solarscope, had kept his place. The rest were clustered about the cameras, and Beenay was giving his instructions in a hoarse, strained voice.

"Get it straight, all of you. I'm snapping Beta just before totality and changing the plate. That will leave one of you to each camera. You all know about . . . about times of exposure—"

There was a breathless murmur of agreement.

Beenay passed a hand over his eyes. "Are the torches still burning? Never mind, I see them!" He was leaning hard against the back of a chair. "Now remember, don't . . . don't try to look for good shots. Don't waste time trying to get t-two stars at a time in the scope field. One is enough. And . . . and if you feel yourself going, *get away from the camera*."

At the door, Sheerin whispered to Theremon, "Take me to Aton. I don't see him."

The newsman did not answer immediately. The vague forms of the astronomers wavered and blurred, and the torches overhead had become only yellow splotches.

"It's dark," he whimpered.

Sheerin held out his hand. "Aton." He stumbled forward. "Aton!"

Theremon stepped after and seized his arm. "Wait, I'll take you." Somehow he made his way across the room. He closed his eyes against the Darkness and his mind against the chaos within it.

No one heard them or paid attention to them. Sheerin stumbled against the wall. "Aton!"

The psychologist felt shaking hands touching him, then withdrawing, a voice muttering, "Is that you, Sheerin?"

"Aton!" He strove to breathe normally. "Don't worry about the mob. The place will hold them off."

Latimer, the Cultist, rose to his feet, and his face twisted in desperation. His word was pledged, and to break it would mean placing his soul in mortal peril. Yet that word had been forced from him and had not been given freely. The Stars would come soon! He could not stand by and allow— And yet his word was pledged.

Beenay's face was dimly flushed as it looked upward at Beta's last ray, and Latimer, seeing him bend over his camera, made his decision. His nails cut the flesh of his palms as he tensed himself.

He staggered crazily as he started his rush. There was nothing before him but shadows; the very floor beneath his feet lacked substance. And then someone was upon him and he went down with clutching fingers at his throat.

He doubled his knee and drove it hard into his assailant. "Let me up or I'll kill you."

Theremon cried out sharply and muttered through a blinding haze of pain. "You double-crossing rat!"

The newsman seemed conscious of everything at once. He heard Beenay croak, "I've got it. At your cameras, men!" and then there was the strange awareness that the last thread of sunlight had thinned out and snapped.

Simultaneously he heard one last choking gasp from Beenay, and a queer little cry from Sheerin, a hysterical giggle that cut off in a rasp— and a sudden silence, a strange, deadly silence from outside.

And Latimer had gone limp in his loosening grasp. Theremon peered into the Cultist's eyes and saw the blankess of them, staring upward, mirroring the feeble yellow of the torches. He saw the bubble of froth upon Latimer's lips and heard the low animal whimper in Latimer's throat.

With the slow fascination of fear, he lifted himself on one arm and turned his eyes toward the blood-curdling blackness of the window.

Through it shone the Stars!

Not Earth's feeble thirty-six hundred Stars visible to the eye; Lagash was in the center of a giant cluster. Thirty thousand mighty suns shone down in a soul-searing splendor that was more frighteningly cold in its awful indifference than the bitter wind that shivered across the cold, horribly bleak world.

Theremon staggered to his feet, his throat constricting him to breathlessness, all the muscles of his body writhing in an intensity of terror and sheer fear beyond bearing. He was going mad and knew it, and somewhere deep inside a bit of sanity was screaming, struggling to fight off the hopeless flood of black terror. It was very horrible to go mad and know that you were going mad—to know that in a little minute you would be here physically and yet all the real essence would be dead and drowned in the black madness. For this was the Dark—the Dark and the Cold and the Doom. The bright walls of the universe were shattered and their awful black fragments were falling down to crush and squeeze and obliterate him.

He jostled someone crawling on hands and knees, but stumbled somehow over him. Hands groping at his tortured throat, he limped toward the flame of the torches that filled all his mad vision.

"Light!" he screamed.

Aton, somewhere, was crying, whimpering horribly like a terribly frightened child. "Stars—all the Stars—we didn't know at all. We didn't know anything. We thought six stars in a universe is something the Stars didn't notice is Darkness forever and ever and ever and the walls are breaking in and we didn't know we couldn't know and anything—"

Someone clawed at the torch, and it fell and snuffed out. In the instant, the awful splendor of the indifferent Stars leaped nearer to them.

On the horizon outside the window, in the direction of Saro City, a crimson glow began growing, strengthening in brightness, that was not the glow of a sun.

The long night had come again.

PREFACE TO
GREEN PATCHES

FIRST APPEARANCE—*GALAXY SCIENCE FICTION,* November 1950, under the title "Misbegotten Missionary." Copyright 1950, by World Editions, Inc.

In 1948, I woke up one morning to read in the *New York Times* that Street & Smith Publications had discontinued all its pulp magazines.

Since *Astounding Science Fiction* was one of the Street & Smith pulps, everything went black before my eyes. You see, during the six-year period from 1943 to 1948 inclusive, I had sold and published thirteen science fiction stories, every single one of them to *Astounding.* During that period I had labored constantly with the feeling that I was not a writer at all, but merely a person who happened to click it off with one particular market, and that if anything happened to *Astounding* or to Mr. Campbell, its editor, I was through.

With great difficulty I finished the article and found, near the end, the utterly casual statement (almost as an afterthought) that *Astounding* was the one exception. It was the only pulp magazine Street & Smith was going to retain.

I was retrieved, but I still felt in a most fragile situation. Something might still happen to either *Astounding* or to Mr. Campbell. (Nothing did! At least so far! At this moment of writing, more than twenty years after that article, *Astounding* still flourishes, although it has a different publisher and has changed its name to *Analog*. And the durable Mr. Campbell is *still* its editor.)

I sold four more stories to *Astounding* in 1949 and 1950 before breaking the string. Then, in 1950, a new science fiction magazine came into sudden, vigorous life under the energetic leadership of its editor, Horace L. Gold.

Mr. Gold searched strenuously for stories while the new magazine was being formed and he asked me if I would submit some. I hesitated, for I was not at all sure that Mr. Gold would like them and I was wondering whether I could bear rejections that would serve as "proof" that I was not a real writer but only a one-editor author.

Mr. Gold was, however, persuasive. I wrote two stories and he took them both. The first story, I felt, might have been a forced sale; he needed it for the maiden issue in a big hurry. The second story, which appeared in the second issue, did not have to be bought, it seemed to me. I accepted the sale as deserved and a more-than-seven-year agony of self-doubt was relieved. It is this second story which follows.

But one thing—editors have the frequent urge to change the titles of stories. Heaven knows why! Some editors have it worse than others and Mr. Gold had a rather acute case.

My own title for this story was "Green Patches" for reasons that will seem perfectly clear when you read the story. For some obscure reason, Mr. Gold didn't like it and when the story appeared, it bore the name "Misbegotten Missionary." Except for the alliteration, I could see no reason why this new title should appeal to any rational person.

So I am seizing the opportunity now to change the title back to what it had been. I don't think I'm being unduly hasty in doing so. I have been waiting eighteen years for a chance.

GREEN PATCHES

He had slipped aboard the ship! There had been dozens waiting outside the energy barrier when it had seemed that waiting would do no good. Then the barrier had faltered for a matter of two minutes (which showed the superiority of unified organisms over life fragments) and he was across.

None of the others had been able to move quickly enough to take advantage of the break, but that didn't matter. All alone, he was enough. No others were necessary.

And the thought faded out of satisfaction and into loneliness. It was a terribly unhappy and unnatural thing to be parted from all the rest of the unified organism, to be a life fragment oneself. How could these aliens stand being fragments?

It increased his sympathy for the aliens. Now that he experienced fragmentation himself, he could feel, as though from a distance, the terrible isolation that made them so afraid. It was fear born of that isolation that dictated their actions. What but the insane fear of their condition could have caused them to blast an area, one mile in diameter, into dull-red heat before landing their ship? Even the organized life ten feet deep in the soil had been destroyed in the blast.

He engaged reception, listening eagerly, letting the alien thought saturate him. He enjoyed the touch of life upon his consciousness. He would have to ration that enjoyment. He must not forget himself.

But it could do no harm to listen to thoughts. Some of the fragments of life on the ship thought quite clearly, considering that they were such primitive, incomplete creatures. Their thoughts were like tiny bells.

Roger Oldenn said, "I feel contaminated. You know what I mean? I keep washing my hands and it doesn't help."

Jerry Thorn hated dramatics and didn't look up. They were still maneuvering in the stratosphere of Saybrook's Planet and he preferred to watch the panel dials. He said, "No reason to feel contaminated. Nothing happened."

"I hope not," said Oldenn. "At least they had all the field men discard their spacesuits in the air lock for complete disinfection. They had a radiation bath for all men entering from outside. I *suppose* nothing happened."

"Why be nervous, then?"

"I don't know. I wish the barrier hadn't broken down."

"Who doesn't? It was an accident."

"I wonder." Oldenn was vehement. "I was here when it happened. My shift, you know. There was no reason to overload the power line. There was equipment plugged into it that had no damn business near it. None whatsoever."

"All right. People are stupid."

"Not that stupid. I hung around when the Old Man was checking into the matter. None of them had reasonable excuses. The armor-baking circuits, which were draining off two thousand watts, had been put into the barrier line. They'd been using the second subsidiaries for a week. Why not this time? They couldn't give any reason."

"Can you?"

Oldenn flushed. "No, I was just wondering if the men had been"—he searched for a word—"hypnotized into it. By those things outside."

Thorn's eyes lifted and met those of the other levelly. "I wouldn't repeat that to anyone else. The barrier was down only two minutes. If anything had happened, if even a spear of grass had drifted across it would have shown up in our bacteria cultures within half an hour, in the fruit-fly colonies in a matter of days. Before we got back it would show up in the hamsters, the rabbits, maybe the goats. Just get it through your head, Oldenn, that nothing happened. Nothing."

Oldenn turned on his heel and left. In leaving, his foot came within two feet of the object in the corner of the room. He did not see it.

HE DISENGAGED HIS reception centers and let the thoughts flow past him unperceived. These life fragments were not important, in any case, since they were not fitted for the continuation of life. Even as fragments, they were incomplete.

The other types of fragments now—they were different. He had to be careful of them. The temptation would be great, and he must give no indication, none at all, of his existence on board ship till they landed on their home planet.

He focused on the other parts of the ship, marveling at the diversity of life. Each item, no matter how small, was sufficient to itself. He forced himself to contemplate this, until the unpleasantness of the thought grated on him and he longed for the normality of home.

Most of the thoughts he received from the smaller fragments were vague and fleeting, as you would expect. There wasn't much to be had from them, but that meant their need for completeness was all the greater. It was that which touched him so keenly.

There was the life fragment which squatted on its haunches and fingered the wire netting that enclosed it. Its thoughts were clear, but limited. Chiefly, they concerned the yellow fruit a companion fragment was eating. It wanted the fruit very deeply. Only the wire netting that separated the fragments prevented its seizing the fruit by force.

He disengaged reception in a moment of complete revulsion. *These fragments competed for food!*

He tried to reach far outward for the peace and harmony of home, but it was already an immense distance away. He could reach only into the nothingness that separated him from sanity.

He longed at the moment even for the feel of the dead soil between the barrier and the ship. He had crawled over it last night. There had been no life upon it, but it had been the soil of home, and on the other side of the barrier there had still been the comforting feel of the rest of organized life.

He could remember the moment he had located himself on the surface of the ship, maintaining a desperate suction grip until the air lock opened. He had entered, moving cautiously between the outgoing feet. There had been an inner lock and that had been passed later. Now he lay here, a life fragment himself, inert and unnoticed.

Cautiously, he engaged reception again at the previous focus. The squatting fragment of life was tugging furiously at the wire netting. It still wanted the other's food, though it was the less hungry of the two.

LARSEN SAID, "DON'T feed the damn thing. She isn't hungry; she's just sore because Tillie had the nerve to eat before she herself was crammed full. The greedy ape! I wish we were back home and I never had to look another animal in the face again."

He scowled at the older female chimpanzee frowningly and the chimp mouthed and chattered back to him in full reciprocation.

Rizzo said, "Okay, okay. Why hang around here, then? Feeding time is over. Let's get out."

They went past the goat pens, the rabbit hutches, the hamster cages.

Larsen said bitterly, "You volunteer for an exploration voyage. You're a hero. They send you off with speeches—and make a zoo keeper out of you."

"They give you double pay."

"All right, so what? I didn't sign up just for the money. They said at the original briefing that it was even odds we wouldn't come back, that we'd end up like Saybrook. I signed up because I wanted to do something important."

"Just a bloomin' bloody hero," said Rizzo.

"I'm not an animal nurse."

Rizzo paused to lift a hamster out of the cage and stroke it. "Hey," he said, "did you ever think that maybe one of these hamsters has some cute little baby hamsters inside, just getting started?"

"Wise guy! They're tested every day."

"Sure, sure." He muzzled the little creature, which vibrated its nose at him. "But just suppose you came down one morning and found them there. New little hamsters looking up at you with soft, green patches of fur where the eyes ought to be."

"Shut up, for the love of Mike," yelled Larsen.

"Little soft, green patches of shining fur," said Rizzo, and put the hamster down with a sudden loathing sensation.

HE ENGAGED RECEPTION again and varied the focus. There wasn't a specialized life fragment at home that didn't have a rough counterpart on shipboard.

There were the moving runners in various shapes, the moving swimmers, and the moving fliers. Some of the fliers were quite large, with perceptible thoughts; others were small, gauzy-winged creatures. These last transmitted only patterns of sense perception, imperfect patterns at that, and added nothing intelligent of their own.

There were the non-movers, which, like the non-movers at home, were green and lived on the air, water, and soil. These were a mental blank. They knew only the dim, dim consciousness of light, moisture, and gravity.

And each fragment, moving and non-moving, had its mockery of life.

Not yet. Not yet. . . .

He clamped down hard upon his feelings. Once before, these life fragments had come, and the rest at home had tried to help them—too quickly. It had not worked. This time they must wait.

If only these fragments did not discover him.

They had not, so far. They had not noticed him lying in the corner of the pilot room. No one had bent down to pick up and discard him. Earlier, it had meant he could not move. Someone might have turned and stared at the stiff wormlike thing, not quite six inches long. First stare, then shout, and then it would all be over.

But now, perhaps, he had waited long enough. The takeoff was long past. The controls were locked; the pilot room was empty.

It did not take him long to find the chink in the armor leading to the recess where some of the wiring was. They were dead wires.

The front end of his body was a rasp that cut in two a wire of just the right diameter. Then, six inches away, he cut it in two again. He pushed the snipped-off section of the wire ahead of him packing it away neatly and invisibly into a corner of recess. Its outer covering was a brown elastic material and its core was gleaming, ruddy metal. He himself could not reproduce the core, of course, but that was not necessary. It was enough that the pellicle that covered him had been carefully bred to resemble a wire's surface.

He returned and grasped the cut sections of the wire before and behind. He tightened against them as his little suction disks came into play. Not even a seam showed.

They could not find him now. They could look right at him and see only a continuous stretch of wire.

Unless they looked very closely indeed and noted that, in a certain spot on this wire, there were two tiny patches of soft and shining green fur.

"IT IS REMARKABLE," said Dr. Weiss, "that little green hairs can do so much."

Captain Loring poured the brandy carefully. In a sense, this was a celebration. They would be ready for the jump through hyper-space in two hours, and after that, two days would see them back on Earth.

"You are convinced, then, the green fur is the sense organ?" he asked.

"It is," said Weiss. Brandy made him come out in splotches, but he was aware of the need of celebration—quite aware. "The experiments were conducted under difficulties, but they were quite significant."

The captain smiled stiffly. "'Under difficulties' is one way of phrasing it. I would never have taken the chances you did to run them."

"Nonsense. We're all heroes aboard this ship, all volunteers, all great men with trumpet, fife, and fanfarade. You took the chance of coming here."

"You were the first to go outside the barrier."

"No particular risk involved," Weiss said. "I burned the ground before me as I went, to say nothing of the portable barrier that surrounded me. Nonsense, Captain. Let's all take our medals when we come back; let's take them without attempt at gradation. Besides, I'm a male."

"But you're filled with bacteria to here." The captain's hand made a quick, cutting gesture three inches above his head. "Which makes you as vulnerable as a female would be."

They paused for drinking purposes.

"Refill?" asked the captain.

"No, thanks. I've exceeded my quota already."

"Then one last for the spaceroad." He lifted his glass in the general direction of Saybrook's Planet, no longer visible, its sun only a bright star in the visiplate. "To the little green hairs that gave Saybrook his first lead."

Weiss nodded. "A lucky thing. We'll quarantine the planet, of course."

The captain said, "That doesn't seem drastic enough. Someone might always land by accident someday and not have Saybrook's insight, or his guts. Suppose he did not blow up his ship, as Saybrook did. Suppose he got back to some inhabited place."

The captain was somber. "Do you suppose they might ever develop interstellar travel on their own?"

"I doubt it. No proof, of course. It's just that they have such a completely different orientation. Their entire organization of life has made tools unnecessary. As far as we know, even a stone ax doesn't exist on the planet."

"I hope you're right. Oh, and, Weiss, would you spend some time with Drake?"

"The Galactic Press fellow?"

"Yes. Once we get back, the story of Saybrook's Planet will be released for the public and I don't think it would be wise to oversensationalize it. I've asked Drake to let you consult with him on the story. You're a biologist and enough of an authority to carry weight with him. Would you oblige?"

"A pleasure."

The captain closed his eyes wearily and shook his head.

"Headache, Captain?"

"No. Just thinking of poor Saybrook."

HE WAS WEARY of the ship. Awhile back there had been a queer, momentary sensation, as though he had been turned inside out. It was alarming and he had searched the minds of the keen-thinkers for an explanation. Apparently the ship had leaped across vast stretches of empty space by cutting across something they knew as "hyper-space." The keen-thinkers were ingenious.

But—he was weary of the ship. It was such a futile phenomenon. These life fragments were skillful in their constructions, yet it was only a measure of their unhappiness, after all. They strove to find in the control of inanimate matter what they could not find in themselves. In their unconscious yearning for completeness, they built machines and scoured space, seeking, seeking . . .

These creatures, he knew, could never, in the very nature of things, find that for which they were seeking. At least not until such time as he gave it to them. He quivered a little at the thought.

Completeness!

These fragments had no concept of it, even. "Completeness" was a poor word.

In their ignorance they would even fight it. There had been the ship that had come before. The first ship had contained many of the keen-thinking fragments. There had been two varieties, life producers and the sterile ones. (How different this second ship was. The keen-thinkers were all sterile, while the other fragments, the fuzzy-thinkers and the no-thinkers, were all producers of life. It was strange.)

How gladly that first ship had been welcomed by all the planet! He could remember the first intense shock at the realization that the visitors were fragments and not complete. The shock had given way to pity, and the pity to action. It was not certain how they would fit into the community, but there had been no hesitation. All life was sacred and somehow room would have been made for them—for all of them, from the large keen-thinkers to the little multipliers in the darkness.

But there had been a miscalculation. They had not correctly analyzed the course of the fragments' ways of thinking. The keen-thinkers became aware of what had been done and resented it. They were frightened, of course; they did not understand.

They had developed the barrier first, and then, later, had destroyed themselves, exploding their ships to atoms.

Poor, foolish fragments.

This time, at least, it would be different. They would be saved, despite themselves.

JOHN DRAKE WOULD not have admitted it in so many words, but he was very proud of his skill on the photo-typer. He had a travel-kit model, which was a six-by-eight, featureless dark plastic slab, with cylindrical bulges on either end to hold the roll of thin paper. It fitted into a brown leather case, equipped with a beltlike contraption that held it closely about the waist and at one hip. The whole thing weighed less than a pound.

Drake could operate it with either hand. His fingers would flick quickly and easily, placing their light pressure at exact spots on the blank surface, and, soundlessly, words would be written.

He looked thoughtfully at the beginning of his story, then up at Dr. Weiss. "What do you think, Doc?"

"It starts well."

Drake nodded. "I thought I might as well start with Saybrook himself. They haven't released his story back home yet. I wish I could have seen Saybrook's original report. How did he ever get it through, by the way?"

"As near as I could tell, he spent one last night sending it through the sub-ether. When he was finished, he shorted the motors, and converted the entire ship into a thin cloud of vapor a millionth of a second later. The crew and himself along with it."

"What a man! You were in this from the beginning, Doc?"

"Not from the beginning," corrected Weiss gently. "Only since the receipt of Saybrook's report."

He could not help thinking back. He had read that report, realizing even then how wonderful the planet must have seemed when Saybrook's colonizing expedition first reached it. It was practically a duplicate of Earth, with an abounding plant life and a purely vegetarian animal life.

There had been only the little patches of green fur (how often had he used that phrase in his speaking and thinking!) which seemed strange. No living individual on the planet had eyes. Instead, there was this fur. Even the plants, each blade or leaf or blossom, possessed the two patches of richer green.

Then Saybrook had noticed, startled and bewildered, that there was no conflict for food on the planet. All plants grew pulpy appendages which were eaten by the animals. These were regrown in a matter of hours. No other parts of the plants were touched. It was as though the plants fed the animals as part of the order of nature. And the plants themselves did not grow in overpowering profusion. They might almost have been cultivated, they were spread across the available soil so discriminately.

How much time, Weiss wondered, had Saybrook had to observe the strange law and order on the planet?—the fact that insects kept their numbers reasonable, though no birds ate them; that the rodent-like things did not swarm, though no carnivores existed to keep them in check.

And then there had come the incident of the white rats.

That prodded Weiss. He said, "Oh, one correction, Drake. Hamsters were not the first animals involved. It was the white rats."

"White rats," said Drake, making the correction in his notes.

"Every colonizing ship," said Weiss, "takes a group of white rats for the purpose of testing any alien foods. Rats, of course, are very similar to human beings from a nutritional viewpoint. Naturally, only female white rats are taken."

Naturally. If only one sex was present, there was no danger of unchecked multiplication in case the planet proved favorable. Remember the rabbits in Australia.

"Incidentally, why not use males?" asked Drake.

"Females are hardier," said Weiss, "which is lucky, since that gave the situation away. It turned out suddenly that all the rats were bearing young."

"Right. Now that's where I'm up to, so here's my chance to get some things straight. For my own information, Doc, how did Saybrook find out they were in a family way?"

"Accidentally, of course. In the course of nutritional investigations, rats are dissected for evidence of internal damage. Their condition was bound to be discovered. A few more were dissected; same results. Eventually, all that lived gave birth to young—with *no* male rats aboard!"

"And the point is that all the young were born with little green patches of fur instead of eyes."

"That is correct. Saybrook said so and we corroborate him. After the rats, the pet cat of one of the children was obviously affected. When it finally kittened, the kittens were not born with closed eyes but with little patches of green fur. There was no tomcat aboard.

"Eventually Saybrook had the women tested. He didn't tell them what for. He didn't want to frighten them. Every single one of them was in the early stages of pregnancy, leaving out of consideration those few who had been pregnant at the time of embarkation. Saybrook never waited for any child to be born, of course. He knew they would have no eyes, only shining patches of green fur.

"He even prepared bacterial cultures (Saybrook was a thorough man) and found each bacillus to show microscopic green spots."

Drake was eager. "That goes way beyond our briefing—or, at least, the briefing I got. But granted that life on Saybrook's Planet is organized into a unified whole, how is it done?"

"How? How are your cells organized into a unified whole? Take an individual cell out of your body, even a brain cell, and what is it by itself? Nothing. A little blob of protoplasm with no more capacity for anything human than an amoeba. Less capacity, in fact, since it couldn't live by itself. But put the cells together and you have something that could invent a spaceship or write a symphony."

"I get the idea," said Drake.

Weiss went on, "*All* life on Saybrook's Planet is a *single* organism. In a sense, all life on Earth is too, but it's a fighting dependence, a dog-eat-dog dependence. The bacteria fix nitrogen; the plants fix carbon; animals eat plants and each other; bacterial decay hits everything. It comes full circle. Each grabs as much as it can, and is, in turn, grabbed.

"On Saybrook's Planet, each organism has its place, as each cell in our body does. Bacteria and plants produce food, on the excess of which animals feed, providing in turn carbon dioxide and nitrogenous wastes. Nothing is produced more or less than is needed. The scheme of life is intelligently altered to suit the local environment. No group of life forms multiplies more or less than is needed, just as the cells in our body stop multiplying when there are enough of them for a given purpose. When they don't stop multiplying, we call it cancer. And that's what life on Earth really is, the kind of organic organization we have, compared to that on Saybrook's Planet. One big cancer. Every species, every individual doing its best to thrive at the expense of every other species and individual."

"You sound as if you approve of Saybrook's Planet, Doc."

"I do, in a way. It makes sense out of the business of living. I can see their viewpoint toward us. Suppose one of the cells of your body could be conscious of the efficiency of the human body as compared with that of the cell itself, and could realize that this was only the result of the union of many cells into a higher whole. And then suppose it became conscious of the existence of free-living cells, with bare life and nothing more. It might feel a very strong desire to drag the poor thing into an organization. It might feel sorry for it, feel perhaps a sort of missionary spirit. The things on Saybrook's Planet—or the thing; one should use the singular—feels just that, perhaps."

"And went ahead by bringing about virgin births, eh, Doc? I've got to go easy on that angle of it. Post-office regulations, you know."

"There's nothing ribald about it, Drake. For centuries we've been able to make the eggs of sea urchins, bees, frogs, et cetera develop without the intervention of male fertilization. The touch of a needle was sometimes enough, or just immersion in the proper salt solution. The thing on Saybrook's Planet can cause fertilization by the controlled use of radiant energy. That's why an appropriate energy barrier stops it; interference, you see, or static.

"They can do more than stimulate the division and development of an unfertilized egg. They can impress their own characteristics upon its nucleoproteins, so that the young are born with the little patches of green fur, which serve as the planet's sense organ and means of communication. The young, in other words, are not individuals, but become part of the thing on Saybrook's Planet. The thing on the planet, not at all incidentally, can impregnate any species—plant, animal, or microscopic."

"Potent stuff," muttered Drake.

"Totipotent," Dr. Weiss said sharply. "Universally potent. Any fragment of it is totipotent. Given time, a single bacterium from Saybrook's Planet can convert *all of Earth* into a single organism! We've got the experimental proof of that."

Drake said unexpectedly, "You know, I think I'm a millionaire, Doc. Can you keep a secret?"

Weiss nodded, puzzled.

"I've got a souvenir from Saybrook's Planet," Drake told him, grinning. "It's only a pebble, but after the publicity the planet will get, combined with the fact that it's quarantined from here on in, the pebble will be all any human being will ever see of it. How much do you suppose I could sell the thing for?"

Weiss stared. "A pebble?" He snatched at the object shown him, a hard, gray ovoid. "You shouldn't have done that, Drake. It was strictly against regulations."

"I know. That's why I asked if you could keep a secret. If you could give me a signed note of authentication—*What's the matter, Doc?*"

Instead of answering, Weiss could only chatter and point. Drake ran over and stared down at the pebble. It was the same as before——

Except that the light was catching it at an angle, and it showed up two little green spots. Look very closely; they were patches of green hairs.

HE WAS DISTURBED. There was a definite air of danger within the ship. There was the suspicion of his presence aboard. How could that be? He had done nothing yet. Had another fragment of home come aboard and been less cautious? That would be impossible without his knowledge, and though he probed the ship intensely, he found nothing.

And then the suspicion diminished, but it was not quite dead. One of the keen-thinkers still wondered, and was treading close to the truth.

How long before the landing? Would an entire world of life fragments be deprived of completeness? He clung closer to the severed ends of the wire he had been specially bred to imitate, afraid of detection, fearful for his altruistic mission.

DR. WEISS HAD locked himself in his own room. They were already within the solar system, and in three hours they would be landing. He had to think. He had three hours in which to decide.

Drake's devilish "pebble" had been part of the organized life on Saybrook's Planet, of course, but it was dead. It was dead when he had first seen it, and if it hadn't been, it was certainly dead after they fed it into the hyper-atomic motor and converted it into a blast of pure heat. And the bacterial cultures still showed normal when Weiss anxiously checked.

That was not what bothered Weiss now.

Drake had picked up the "pebble" during the last hours of the stay on Saybrook's Planet—*after* the barrier breakdown. What if the breakdown had been the result of a slow, relentless mental pressure on the part of the thing on the planet? What if parts of its being waited to invade as the barrier dropped? If the "pebble" had not been fast enough and had moved only after the barrier was reestablished, it would have been killed. It would have lain there for Drake to see and pick up.

It was a "pebble," not a natural life form. But did that mean it was not *some* kind of life form? It might have been a deliberate production of the planet's single organism—a creature deliberately designed to look like a pebble, harmless-seeming, unsuspicious. Camouflage, in other words—a shrewd and frighteningly successful camouflage.

Had any other camouflaged creature succeeded in crossing the barrier *before* it was re-established—with a suitable shape filched from the minds of the humans aboard ship by the mind-reading organism of the planet? Would it have the casual appearance of a paperweight? Of an ornamental brass-head nail in the captain's old-fashioned chair? And how would they locate it? Could they search every part of the ship for the telltale green patches—even down to individual microbes?

And why camouflage? Did it intend to remain undetected for a time? Why? So that it might wait for the landing on Earth?

An infection *after landing* could not be cured by blowing up a ship. The bacteria of Earth, the molds, yeasts, and protozoa, would go first. Within a year the non-human young would be arriving by the uncountable billions.

Weiss closed his eyes and told himself it might not be such a bad thing. There would be no more disease, since no bacterium would multiply at the expense of its host, but instead would be satisfied with its fair share of what was available. There would be no more overpopulation; the hordes of mankind would decline to adjust themselves to the food supply. There would be no more wars, no crime, no greed.

But there would be no more individuality, either.

Humanity would find security by becoming a cog in a biological machine. A man would be brother to a germ, or to a liver cell.

He stood up. He would have a talk with Captain Loring. They would send their report and blow up the ship, just as Saybrook had done.

He sat down again. Saybrook had had proof, while he had only the conjectures of a terrorized mind, rattled by the sight of two green spots on a pebble. Could he kill the two hundred men on board ship because of a feeble suspicion?

He had to *think!*

HE WAS STRAINING. Why did he have to wait? If he could only welcome those who were aboard now. *Now!*

Yet a cooler, more reasoning part of himself told him that he could not. The little multipliers in the darkness would betray their new status in fifteen minutes, and the keen-thinkers had them under continual observation. Even one mile from the surface of their planet would be too soon, since they might still destroy themselves and their ship out in space.

Better to wait for the main air locks to open, for the planetary air to swirl in with millions of the little multipliers. Better to greet each one of them into the brotherhood of unified life and let them swirl out again to spread the message.

Then it would be done! Another world organized, complete!

He waited. There was the dull throbbing of the engines working mightily to control the slow dropping of the ship; the shudder of contact with planetary surface, then——

He let the jubilation of the keen-thinkers sweep into reception, and his own jubilant thoughts answered them. Soon they would be able to receive as well as himself. Perhaps not these particular fragments, but the fragments that would grow out of those which were fitted for the continuation of life.

The main air locks were about to be opened——

And all thought ceased.

JERRY THORN THOUGHT, Damn it, something's wrong *now*.

He said to Captain Loring, "Sorry. There seems to be a power breakdown. The locks won't open."

"Are you sure, Thorn? The lights are on."

"Yes, sir. We're investigating it now."

He tore away and joined Roger Oldenn at the air-lock wiring box. "What's wrong?"

"Give me a chance, will you?" Oldenn's hands were busy. Then he said, "For the love of Pete, there's a six-inch break in the twenty-amp lead."

"What? That can't be!"

Oldenn held up the broken wires with their clean, sharp, sawn-through ends.

Dr. Weiss joined them. He looked haggard and there was the smell of brandy on his breath.

He said shakily, "What's the matter?"

They told him. At the bottom of the compartment, in one corner, was the missing section.

Weiss bent over. There was a black fragment on the floor of the compartment. He touched it with his finger and it smeared, leaving a sooty smudge on his finger tip. He rubbed it off absently.

There might have been something taking the place of the missing section of wire. Something that had been alive and only looked like wire, yet something that would heat, die, and carbonize in a tiny fraction of a second once the electrical circuit which controlled the air lock had been closed.

He said, "How are the bacteria?"

A crew member went to check, returned and said, "All normal, Doc."

The wires had meanwhile been spliced, the locks opened, and Dr. Weiss stepped out into the anarchic world of life that was Earth.

"Anarchy," he said, laughing a little wildly. "And it will stay that way."

PREFACE TO
HOSTESS

First appearance—*Galaxy Science Fiction,* May 1951. Copyright 1951, by World Editions, Inc.

By late 1950, my wife and I had come to the sad and reluctant conclusion that we were not going to have any children. There was nothing particularly wrong that anyone could find, but neither was anything happening.

My wife therefore decided we might as well adjust our way of life to childlessness and prepared to take a greater role in my continuing-to-expand writing career. It seemed to us that efficiency might be increased if we worked as a team. I would dictate my stories and she would type them.

I was a little dubious. It sounded great in theory, but I had never dictated a story. I was used to typing my stories and watching the sentences appear steadily, word by word. So I did not buy a dictating machine outright. I talked the salesman into letting me have it on thirty-day approval.

In the course of the next month, I dictated three stories into the machine, of which "Hostess" was one. It was a frightening experience that taught me a few things. For instance, I discovered that I participated in a story to a greater extent than I realized, when my wife came to me with a little plastic record and said "I can't type this."

I listened to the passage she objected to, one in which two of my characters were quarreling with greater and greater vehemence. I found that as they grew more emotional, so did I, and when their quarrel reached its peak, I was making nothing more than incoherent sounds of rage. I had to dictate that part over again. Heavens, it never happens when I type.

But it worked out well. When the stories were typed up, they sounded just like me; just as though I had typed them from the start. (At least so it seemed to me. You can read "Hostess" and judge for yourself.)

Naturally, I was delighted. I looked up the salesman and told him I would buy the machine. I made out a check for the entire payment in a lump sum.

Within a week, however, according to later calculation, we managed to get a child started. When the fact became unmistakable, we had a conversation in which my contribution consisted entirely of a frequently interjected "You're kidding!"

Anyway, the dictating machine was never used again, though we still own it. Four months after "Hostess" appeared, my son, David, was born.

HOSTESS

Rose Smollett was happy about it; almost triumphant. She peeled off her gloves, put her hat away, and turned her brightening eyes upon her husband.

She said, "Drake, we're going to have him here."

Drake looked at her with annoyance. "You've missed supper. I thought you were going to be back by seven."

"Oh, that doesn't matter. I ate something on the way home. But, Drake, we're going to have him here!"

"*Who* here? What are you talking about?"

"The doctor from Hawkin's Planet! Didn't you realize that was what today's conference was about? We spent all day talking about it. It's the most exciting thing that could possibly have happened!"

Drake Smollett removed the pipe from the vicinity of his face. He stared first at it and then at his wife. "Let me get this straight. When you say the doctor from Hawkin's Planet, do you mean the Hawkinsite you've got at the Institute?"

"Well, of course. Who else could I possibly mean?"

"And may I ask what the devil you mean by saying we'll have him here?"

"Drake, don't you understand?"

"What is there to understand? Your Institute may be interested in the thing, but I'm not. What have we to do with it personally? It's Institute business, isn't it?"

"But, darling," Rose said, patiently, "the Hawkinsite would like to stay at a private house somewhere, where he won't be bothered with official ceremony, and where he'll be able to proceed more according to his own likes and dislikes. I find it quite understandable."

"Why at *our* house?"

"Because our place is convenient for the purpose, I suppose. They asked if I would allow it, and frankly," she added with some stiffness, "I consider it a privilege."

"Look!" Drake put his fingers through his brown hair and succeeded in rumpling it. "We've got a convenient little place here— granted! It's not the most elegant place in the world, but it does well enough for us. However, I don't see where we've got room for extra-terrestrial visitors."

ROSE BEGAN TO look worried. She removed her glasses and put them away in their case. "He can stay in the spare room. He'll take care of it himself. I've spoken to him and he's very pleasant. Honestly, all we have to do is show a certain amount of adaptability."

Drake said, "Sure, just a little adaptability! The Hawkinsites breathe cyanide. We'll just adapt ourselves to that, I suppose!"

"He carries cyanide in a little cylinder. You won't even notice it."

"And what else about them that I won't notice?"

"*Nothing* else. They're perfectly harmless. Goodness, they're even vegetarians."

"And what does that mean? Do we feed him a bale of hay for dinner?"

Rose's lower lip trembled. "Drake, you're being deliberately hateful. There are many vegetarians on Earth; they don't eat hay."

"And what about us? Do we eat meat ourselves or will that make us look like cannibals to him? I won't live on salads to suit him; I warn you."

"You're being quite ridiculous."

Rose felt helpless. She had married late in life, comparatively. Her career had been chosen; she herself had seemed well settled in it. She was a fellow in biology at the Jenkins Institute for the Natural Sciences, with over twenty publications to her credit. In a word, the line was hewed, the path cleared; she had been set for a career and spinsterhood. And now, at 35, she was still a little amazed to find herself a bride of less than a year.

Occasionally, it embarrassed her, too, since she sometimes found that she had not the slightest idea of how to handle her husband. What *did* one do when the man of the family became mulish? That was not included in any of her courses. As a woman of independent mind and career, she couldn't bring herself to cajolery.

So she looked at him steadily and said simply, "It means very much to me."

"Why?"

"Because, Drake, if he stays here for any length of time, I can study him really closely. Very little work has been done on the biology and psychology of the individual Hawkinsite or of any of the extraterrestrial intelligences. We have some of their sociology and history, of course, but that's all. Surely, you must see the opportunity. He stays here; we watch him, speak to him, observe his habits—"

"Not interested."

"Oh, Drake, I don't understand you."

"You're going to say I'm not usually like this, I suppose."

"Well, you're not."

DRAKE WAS SILENT for a while. He seemed withdrawn and his high cheekbones and large chin were twisted and frozen into a brooding position.

He said finally, "Look, I've heard a bit about the Hawkinsites in the way of my own business. You say there have been investigations of their sociology, but not of their biology. Sure. It's because the Hawkinsites don't like to be studied as specimens any more than we would. I've spoken to men who were in charge of security groups watching various Hawkinsite missions on Earth. The missions stay in the rooms assigned to them and don't leave for anything but the most important official business. They have nothing to do with Earthmen. It's quite obvious that they are as revolted by us as I personally am by them.

"In fact, I just don't understand why this Hawkinsite at the Institute should be any different. It seems to me to be against all the rules to have him come here by himself, anyway—and to have him want to stay in an Earthman's home just puts the maraschino cherry on top."

Rose said, wearily, "This is different. I'm surprised you can't understand it, Drake. He's a doctor. He's coming here in the way of medical research, and I'll grant you that he probably doesn't enjoy staying with human beings and will find us perfectly horrible. But he must stay just the same! Do you suppose human doctors enjoy going into the tropics, or that they are particularly fond of letting themselves be bitten by infected mosquitoes?"

Drake said sharply, "What's this about mosquitoes? What have they to do with it?"

"Why, nothing," Rose answered, surprised. "It just came to my mind, that's all. I was thinking of Reed and his yellow-fever experiments."

Drake shrugged. "Well, have it your own way."

For a moment, Rose hesitated. "You're not angry about this, are you?" To her own ears she sounded unpleasantly girlish.

"No."

And that, Rose knew, meant that he was.

ROSE SURVEYED HERSELF doubtfully in the full-length mirror. She had never been beautiful and was quite reconciled to the fact; so much so that it no longer mattered. Certainly, it would not matter to a being from Hawkin's Planet. What *did* bother her was this matter of being a hostess under the very queer circumstances of having to be tactful to an extraterrestrial creature and, at the same time, to her husband as well. She wondered which would prove the more difficult.

Drake was coming home late that day; he was not due for half an hour. Rose found herself inclined to believe that he had arranged that purposely in a sullen desire to leave her alone with her problem. She found herself in a state of mild resentment.

He had called her just before noon at the Institute and had asked abruptly, "When are you taking him home?"

She answered, curtly, "In about three hours."

"All right. What's his name? His Hawkinsite name?"

"Why do you want to know?" She could not keep the chill from her words.

"Let's call it a small investigation of my own. After all, the thing will be in my house."

"Oh, for heaven's sake, Drake, don't bring your job home with you!"

Drake's voice sounded tinny and nasty in her ears. "Why not, Rose? Isn't that exactly what you're doing?"

It was, of course, so she gave him the information he wanted.

This was the first time in their married life that they had had even the semblance of a quarrel, and, as she sat there before the full-length mirror, she began to wonder if perhaps she ought not make an attempt to see his side of it. In essence, she had married a policeman. Of course he was more than simply a policeman; he was a member of the World Security Board.

It had been a surprise to her friends. The fact of the marriage itself had been the biggest surprise, but if she had decided on marriage, the attitude was, why not with another biologist? Or, if she had wanted to go afield, an anthropologist, perhaps; even a chemist; but why, of all people, a policeman? Nobody had exactly said those things, naturally, but it had been in the very atmosphere at the time of her marriage.

She had resented it then, and ever since. A man could marry whom he chose, but if a doctor of philosophy, female variety, chose to marry a man who never went past the bachelor's degree, there was shock. Why should there be? What business was it of theirs? He was handsome, in a way, intelligent, in another way, and she was perfectly satisfied with her choice.

Yet how much of this same snobbishness did she bring home with her? Didn't she always have the attitude that her own work, her biological investigations, were important, while his job was merely something to be kept within the four walls of his little office in the old U.N. buildings on the East River?

She jumped up from her seat in agitation and, with a deep breath, decided to leave such thoughts behind her. She desperately did not want to quarrel with him. And she just wasn't going to interfere with him. She was committed to accepting the Hawkinsite as guest, but otherwise she would let Drake have his own way. He was making enough of a concession as it was.

———

HARG THOLAN WAS standing quietly in the middle of the living room when she came down the stairs. He was not sitting, since he was not anatomically constructed to sit. He stood on two sets of limbs placed close together, while a third pair entirely different in construction were suspended from a region that would have been the upper chest in a human being. The skin of his body was hard, glistening and ridged, while his face bore a distant resemblance to something alienly bovine. Yet he was not completely repulsive, and he wore clothes of a sort over the lower portion of his body in order to avoid offending the sensibilities of his human hosts.

He said, "Mrs. Smollett, I appreciate your hospitality beyond my ability to express it in your language," and he drooped so that his forelimbs touched the ground for a moment.

Rose knew this to be a gesture signifying gratitude among the beings of Hawkin's Planet. She was grateful that he spoke English as well as he did. The construction of his mouth, combined with an absence of incisors, gave a whistling sound to the sibilants. Aside from that, he might have been born on Earth for all the accent his speech showed.

She said, "My husband will be home soon, and then we will eat."

"Your husband?" For a moment, he said nothing more, and then added, "Yes, of course."

She let it go. If there was one source of infinite confusion among the five intelligent races of the known Galaxy, it lay in the differences among them with regard to their sex life and the social institutions that grew around it. The concept of husband and wife, for instance, existed only on Earth. The other races could achieve a sort of intellectual understanding of what it meant, but never an emotional one.

She said, "I have consulted the Institute in preparing your menu. I trust you will find nothing in it that will upset you."

The Hawkinsite blinked its eyes rapidly. Rose recalled this to be a gesture of amusement.

He said, "Proteins are proteins, my dear Mrs. Smollett. For those trace factors which I need but are not supplied in your food, I have brought concentrates that will be most adequate."

And proteins *were* proteins. Rose knew this to be true. Her concern for the creature's diet had been largely one of formal politeness. In the discovery of life on the planets of the outer stars, one of the most interesting generalizations that had developed was the fact that, although life could be formed on the basis of substances other than proteins—even on elements other than carbon—it remained true that the only known intelligences were proteinaceous in nature. This meant that each of the five forms of intelligent life could maintain themselves over prolonged periods on the food of any of the other four.

SHE HEARD DRAKE'S key in the door and went stiff with apprehension.

She had to admit he did well. He strode in, and, without hesitation, thrust his hand out at the Hawkinsite, saying firmly, "Good evening, Dr. Tholan."

The Hawkinsite put out his large and rather clumsy forelimb and the two, so to speak, shook hands. Rose had already gone through that procedure and knew the queer feeling of a Hawkinsite hand in her own. It had felt rough and hot and dry. She imagined that, to the Hawkinsite, her own and Drake's felt cold and slimy.

At the time of the formal greeting, she had taken the opportunity to observe the alien hand. It was an excellent case of converging evolution. Its morphological development was entirely different from that of the human hand, yet it had brought itself into a fairly approximate similarity. There were four fingers but no thumb. Each finger had five independent ball-and-socket joints. In this way, the flexibility lost with the absence of the thumb was made up for by the almost tentacular properties of the fingers. What was even more interesting to her biologist's eyes was the fact that each Hawkinsite finger ended in a vestigial hoof, very small and, to the layman, unidentifiable as such, but clearly adapted at one time to running, just as man's had been to climbing.

Drake said, in friendly enough fashion, "Are you quite comfortable, sir?"

The Hawkinsite answered, "Quite. Your wife has been most thoughtful in all her arrangements."

"Would you care for a drink?"

The Hawkinsite did not answer but looked at Rose with a slight facial contortion that indicated some emotion which, unfortunately, Rose could not interpret. She said, nervously, "On Earth there is the custom of drinking liquids which have been fortified with ethyl alcohol. We find it stimulating."

"Oh, yes. I am afraid, then, that I must decline. Ethyl alcohol would interfere most unpleasantly with my metabolism."

"Why, so it does to Earthmen, too, but I understand, Dr. Tholan," Drake replied. "Would you object to *my* drinking?"

"Of course not."

Drake passed close to Rose on his way to the sideboard and she caught only one word. He said, "God!" in a tightly controlled whisper, yet he managed to put seventeen exclamation points after it.

THE HAWKINSITE *STOOD* at the table. His fingers were models of dexterity as they wove their way around the cutlery. Rose tried not to look at him as he ate. His wide lipless mouth split his face alarmingly as he ingested food, and, in chewing, his large jaws moved disconcertingly from side to side. It was another evidence of his ungulate ancestry. Rose found herself wondering if, in the quiet of his own room, he would later chew his cud, and was then panic-stricken lest Drake get the same idea and leave the table in disgust. But Drake was taking everything quite calmly.

He said, "I imagine, Dr. Tholan, that the cylinder at your side holds cyanide?"

Rose started. She had actually not noticed it. It was a curved metal object, something like a water canteen, that fitted flatly against the creature's skin, half-hidden behind its clothing. But, then, Drake had a policeman's eyes.

The Hawkinsite was not in the least disconcerted. "Quite so," he said, and his hoofed fingers held out a thin, flexible hose that ran up his body, its tint blending into that of his yellowish skin, and entered the corner of his wide mouth. Rose felt slightly embarrassed, as though at the display of intimate articles of clothing.

Drake said, "And does it contain pure cyanide?"

The Hawkinsite humorously blinked his eyes. "I hope you are not considering possible danger to Earthites. I know the gas is highly poisonous to you and I do not need a great deal. The gas contained in the cylinder is five percent hydrogen cyanide, the remainder oxygen. None of it emerges except when I actually suck at the tube, and that need not be done frequently."

"I see. And you really must have the gas to live?"

Rose was slightly appalled. One simply did not ask such questions without careful preparation. It was impossible to foresee where the sensitive points of an alien psychology might be. And Drake *must* be doing this deliberately, since he could not help realizing that he could get answers to such questions as easily from herself. Or was it that he preferred not to ask her?

The Hawkinsite remained apparently unperturbed. "Are you not a biologist, Mr. Smollett?"

"No, Dr. Tholan."

"But you are in close association with Mrs. *Dr.* Smollett."

Drake smile a bit. "Yes, I am married to a Mrs. doctor, but just the same I am not a biologist; merely a minor government official. My wife's friends," he added, "call me a policeman."

ROSE BIT THE inside of her cheek. In this case it was the Hawkinsite who had impinged upon the sensitive point of an alien psychology. On Hawkin's Planet, there was a tight caste system and intercaste associations were limited. But Drake wouldn't realize that.

The Hawkinsite turned to her. "May I have your permission, Mrs. Smollett, to explain a little of our biochemistry to your husband? It will be dull for you, since I am sure you must understand it quite well already."

She said, "By all means do, Dr. Tholan."

He said, "You see, Mr. Smollett, the respiratory system in your body and in the bodies of all air-breathing creatures on Earth is controlled by certain metal-containing enzymes, I am taught. The metal is usually iron, though sometimes it is copper. In either case, small traces of cyanide would combine with these metals and immobilize the respiratory system of the terrestrial living cell. They would be prevented from using oxygen and killed in a few minutes.

"The life on my own planet is not quite so constituted. The key respiratory compounds contain neither iron nor copper; no metal at all, in fact. It is for this reason that my blood is colorless. Our compounds contain certain organic groupings which are essential to life, and these groupings can only be maintained intact in the presence of a small concentration of cyanide. Undoubtedly, this type of protein has developed through millions of years of evolution on a world which has a few tenths of a percent of hydrogen cyanide occurring naturally in the atmosphere. Its presence is maintained by a biological cycle. Various of our native micro-organisms liberate the free gas."

"You make it extremely clear, Dr. Tholan, and very interesting," Drake said. "What happens if you don't breathe it? Do you just go, like that?" He snapped his fingers.

"Not quite. It isn't equivalent to the presence of cyanide for you. In my case, the absence of cyanide would be equivalent to slow strangulation. It happens sometimes, in ill-ventilated rooms on my world, that the cyanide is gradually consumed and falls below the minimum necessary concentration. The results are very painful and difficult to treat."

Rose had to give Drake credit; he really sounded interested. And the alien, thank heaven, did not mind the catechism.

The rest of the dinner passed without incident. It was almost pleasant.

Throughout the evening, Drake remained that way; interested. Even more than that—absorbed. He drowned her out, and she was glad of it. *He* was the one who was really colorful and it was only her job, her specialized training, that stole the color from him. She looked at him gloomily and thought, *Why did he marry me?*

Drake sat, one leg crossed over the other, hands clasped and tapping his chin gently, watching the Hawkinsite intently. The Hawkinsite faced him, standing in his quadruped fashion.

Drake said, "I find it difficult to keep thinking of you as a doctor."

The Hawkinsite laughingly blinked his eyes. "I understand what you mean," he said. "I find it difficult to think of you as a policeman. On my world, policemen are very specialized and distinctive people."

"Are they?" said Drake, somewhat drily, and then changed the subject. "I gather that you are not here on a pleasure trip."

"No, I am here very much on business. I intend to study this queer planet you call Earth, as it has never been studied before by any of my people."

"Queer?" asked Drake. "In what way?"

The Hawkinsite looked at Rose. "Does he know of the Inhibition Death?"

Rose felt embarrassed. "His work is important," she said. "I am afraid that my husband has little time to listen to the details of my work." She knew that this was not really adequate and she felt herself to be the recipient, yet again, of one of the Hawkinsite's unreadable emotions.

The extraterrestrial creature turned back to Drake. "It is always amazing to me to find how little you Earthmen understand your own unusual characteristics. Look, there are five intelligent races in the Galaxy. These have all developed independently, yet have managed to converge in remarkable fashion. It is as though, in the long run, intelligence requires a certain physical makeup to flourish. I leave that question for philosophers. But I need not belabor the point, since it must be a familiar one to you.

"Now when the differences among the intelligences are closely investigated, it is found over and over again that it is you Earthmen, more than any of the others, who are unique. For instance, it is only on Earth that life depends upon metal enzymes for respiration. Your people are the only ones which find hydrogen cyanide poisonous. Yours is the only form of intelligent life which is carnivorous. Yours is the only form of life which has not developed from a grazing animal. And, most interesting of all, yours is the only form of intelligent life known which stops growing upon reaching maturity."

Drake grinned at him. Rose felt her heart suddenly race. It was the nicest thing about him, that grin, and he was using it perfectly naturally. It wasn't forced or false. He was adjusting to the presence of this alien creature. He was being pleasant—and he must be doing it for her. She loved that thought and repeated it to herself. He was doing it for her; he was being nice to the Hawkinsite for her sake.

DRAKE WAS SAYING with his grin, "You don't look very large, Dr. Tholan. I should say that you are an inch taller than I am, which would make you six feet two inches tall. Is it that you are young, or is it that the others on your world are generally small?"

"Neither," said the Hawkinsite. "We grow at a diminishing rate with the years, so that at my age it would take fifteen years to grow an additional inch, but—and this is the important point—we never *entirely* stop. And, of course, as a consequence, we never entirely die."

Drake gasped and even Rose felt herself sitting stiffly upright. This was something new. This was something which, to her knowledge, the few expeditions to Hawkin's Planet had never brought back. She was torn with excitement but held an exclamation back and let Drake speak for her.

He said, "They don't entirely die? You're not trying to say, sir, that the people on Hawkin's Planet are immortal?"

"No people are truly immortal. If there were no other way to die, there would always be accident, and if that fails, there is boredom. Few of us live more than several centuries of your time. Still, it is unpleasant to think that death may come involuntarily. It is something which, to us, is extremely horrible. It bothers me even as I think of it now, this thought that *against my will and despite all care*, death may come."

"We," said Drake, grimly, "are quite used to it."

"You Earthmen live with the thought; we do not. And this is why we are disturbed to find that the incidence of Inhibition Death has been increasing in recent years."

"You have not yet explained," said Drake, "just what the Inhibition Death is, but let me guess. Is the Inhibition Death a pathological cessation of growth?"

"Exactly."

"And how long after growth's cessation does death follow?"

"Within the year. It is a wasting disease, a tragic one, and absolutely incurable."

"What causes it?"

The Hawkinsite paused a long time before answering, and even then there was something strained and uneasy about the way he spoke. "Mr. Smollett, we know nothing about the cause of the disease."

Drake nodded thoughtfully. Rose was following the conversation as though she were a spectator at a tennis match.

Drake said, "And why do you come to Earth to study this disease?"

"Because again Earthmen are unique. They are the only intelligent beings who are immune. The Inhibition Death affects *all* the other races. Do your biologists know that, Mrs. Smollett?"

He had addressed her suddenly, so that she jumped slightly. She said, "No, they don't."

"I am not surprised. That piece of information is the result of very recent research. The Inhibition Death is easily diagnosed incorrectly and the incidence is much lower on the other planets. In fact, it is a strange thing, something to philosophize over, that the incidence of the Death is highest on my world, which is closest to Earth, and lower on each more distant planet—so that it is lowest on the world of the star Tempora, which is farthest from Earth, while Earth itself is immune. Somewhere in the biochemistry of the Earthite, there is the secret of that immunity. How interesting it would be to find it."

Drake said, "But look here, you can't say Earth is immune. From where I sit, it looks as if the incidence is a hundred percent. All Earthmen stop growing and all Earthmen die. We've *all* got the Inhibition Death."

"Not at all. Earthmen live up to seventy years after the cessation of growth. That is not the Death as *we* know it. *Your* equivalent disease is rather one of unrestrained growth. Cancer, you call it.—But come, I bore you."

Rose protested instantly. Drake did likewise with even more vehemence, but the Hawkinsite determinedly changed the subject. It was then that Rose had her first pang of suspicion, for Drake circled Harg Tholan warily with his words, worrying him, jabbing at him, attempting always to get the information back to the point where the Hawkinsite had left off. Not badly, not unskillfully, but Rose knew him, and could tell what he was after. And what could he be after but that which was demanded by his profession? And, as though in response to her thoughts, the Hawkinsite took up the phrase which had begun careening in her mind like a broken record on a perpetual turntable.

He asked, "Did you not say you were a policeman?"

Drake said, curtly, "Yes."

"Then there is something I would like to request you to do for me. I have been wanting to all this evening, since I discovered your profession, and yet I hesitate. I do not wish to be troublesome to my host and hostess."

"We'll do what we can."

"I have a profound curiosity as to how Earthmen live; a curiosity which is not perhaps shared by the generality of my countrymen. So I wonder, could you show me through one of the police departments on your planet?"

"I do not belong to a police department in exactly the way you imagine," said Drake, cautiously. "However, I am known to the New York police department. I can manage it without trouble. Tomorrow?"

"That would be most convenient for me. Would I be able to visit the Missing Persons Bureau?"

"The what?"

The Hawkinsite drew his four standing legs closer together, as if he were becoming more intense. "It is a hobby of mine, a little queer corner of interest I have always had. I understand you have a group of police officers whose sole duty it is to search for men who are missing."

"And women and children," added Drake. "But why should that interest you so particularly?"

"Because there again you are unique. There is no such thing as a missing person on our planet. I can't explain the mechanism to you, of course, but among the people of other worlds, there is always an awareness of one another's presence, especially if there is a strong, affectionate tie. We are always aware of each other's exact location, no matter where on the planet we might be."

Rose grew excited again. The scientific expeditions to Hawkin's Planet had always had the greatest difficulty in penetrating the internal emotional mechanisms of the natives, and here was one who talked freely, who would explain! She forgot to worry about Drake and intruded into the conversations. "Can you feel such awareness even now? On Earth?"

The Hawkinsite said, "You mean across space? No, I'm afraid not. But you see the importance of the matter. All the uniqueness of Earth should be linked. If the lack of this sense can be explained, perhaps the immunity to Inhibition Death can be, also. Besides, it strikes me as very curious that any form of intelligent community life can be built among people who lack this community awareness. How can an Earthman tell, for instance, when he has formed a congenial sub-group, a family? How can you two, for instance, know that there is a true tie between you?"

Rose found herself nodding. How strongly she missed such a sense!

But Drake only smiled. "We have our ways. It is as difficult to explain what we call 'love' to you as it is for you to explain your sense to us."

"I suppose so. Yet tell me truthfully, Mr. Smollett—if Mrs. Smollett were to leave this room and enter another without your having seen her do so, would you really not be aware of her location?"

"I really would not."

The Hawkinsite said, "Amazing." He hesitated, then added, "Please do not be offended at the fact that I find it revolting as well."

AFTER THE LIGHT in the bedroom had been put out, Rose went to the door three times, opening it a crack and peering out. She could feel Drake watching her. There was a hard kind of amusement in his voice as he asked, finally, "What's the matter?"

She said, "I want to talk to you."

"Are you afraid our friend can hear?"

Rose was whispering. She got into bed and put her head on his pillow so that she could whisper better. She said, "Why were you talking about the Inhibition Death to Dr. Tholan?"

"I am taking an interest in your work, Rose. You've always wanted me to take an interest."

"I'd rather you weren't sarcastic." She was almost violent, as nearly violent as she could be in a whisper. "I know that there's something of your own interest in this—of *police* interest, probably. What is it?"

He said, "I'll talk to you tomorrow."

"No, right now."

He put his hand under her head, lifting it. For a wild moment she thought he was going to kiss her—just kiss her on impulse the way husbands sometimes did, or as she imagined they sometimes did. Drake never did, and he didn't now.

He merely held her close and whispered, "Why are you so interested?"

His hand was almost brutally hard upon the nape of her neck, so that she stiffened and tried to draw back. Her voice was more than a whisper now. "Stop it, Drake."

He said, "I want no questions from you and no interference. You do your job, and I'll do mine."

"The nature of my job is open and known."

"The nature of my job," he retorted, "isn't, by definition. But I'll tell you this. Our six-legged friend is here in this house for some definite reason. You weren't picked as biologist in charge for any random reason. Do you know that two days ago, he'd been inquiring about me at the Commission?"

"You're joking."

"Don't believe that for a minute. There are depths to this that you know nothing about. But that's my job and I won't discuss it with you any further. Do you understand?"

"No, but I won't question you if you don't want me to."

"Then go to sleep."

She lay stiffly on her back and the minutes passed, and then the quarter-hours. She was trying to fit the pieces together. Even with what Drake had told her, the curves and colors refused to blend. She wondered what Drake would say if he knew she had a recording of that night's conversation!

One picture remained clear in her mind at that moment. It hovered over her mockingly. The Hawkinsite, at the end of the long evening, had turned to her and said gravely, "Good night, Mrs. Smollett. You are a most charming hostess."

She had desperately wanted to giggle at the time. How could he call her a charming hostess? To him, she could only be a horror, a monstrosity with too few limbs and a too-narrow face.

And then, as the Hawkinsite delivered himself of this completely meaningless piece of politeness, Drake had turned white! For one instant, his eyes had burned with something that looked like terror.

She had never before known Drake to show fear of anything, and the picture of that instant of pure panic remained with her until all her thoughts finally sagged into the oblivion of sleep.

IT WAS NOON before Rose was at her desk the next day. She had deliberately waited until Drake and the Hawkinsite had left, since only then was she able to remove the small recorder that had been behind Drake's armchair the previous evening. She had had no original intention of keeping its presence secret from him. It was just that he had come home so late, and she couldn't say anything about it with the Hawkinsite present. Later on, of course, things had changed—

The placing of the recorder had been only a routine maneuver. The Hawkinsite's statements and intonations needed to be preserved for future intensive studies by various specialists at the Institute. It had been hidden in order to avoid the distortions of self-consciousness that the visibility of such a device would bring, and now it couldn't be shown to the members of the Institute at all. It would have to serve a different function altogether. A rather nasty function.

She was going to spy on Drake.

She touched the little box with her fingers and wondered, irrelevantly, how Drake was going to manage, that day. Social intercourse between inhabited worlds was, even now, not so commonplace that the sight of a Hawkinsite on the city streets would not succeed in drawing crowds. But Drake would manage, she knew. Drake always managed.

She listened once again to the sounds of last evening, repeating the interesting moments. She was dissatisfied with what Drake had told her. Why should the Hawkinsite have been interested in the two of them particularly? Yet Drake wouldn't lie. She would have liked to check at the Security Commission, but she knew she could not do that. Besides, the thought made her feel disloyal; Drake would definitely not lie.

But, then again, why should Harg Tholan not have investigated them? He might have inquired similarly about the families of all the biologists at the Institute. It would be no more than natural to attempt to choose the home he would find most pleasant by his own standards, whatever they were.

And if he had—even if he had investigated only the Smolletts— why should that create the great change in Drake from intense hostility to intense interest? Drake undoubtedly had knowledge he was keeping to himself. Only heaven knew how much.

Her thoughts churned slowly through the possibilities of interstellar intrigue. So far, to be sure, there were no signs of hostility or ill-feeling among any of the five intelligent races known to inhabit the Galaxy. As yet they were spaced at intervals too wide for enmity. Even the barest contact among them was all but impossible. Economic and political interests just had no point at which to conflict.

BUT THAT WAS only her idea and she was not a member of the Security Commission. If there *were* conflict, if there *were* danger, if there *were* any reason to suspect that the mission of a Hawkinsite might be other than peaceful—Drake would know.

Yet was Drake sufficiently high in the councils of the Security Commission to know, off-hand, the dangers involved in the visit of a Hawkinsite physician? She had never thought of his position as more than that of a very minor functionary in the Commission; he had never presented himself as more. And yet—

Might he be more?

She shrugged at the thought. It was reminiscent of Twentieth Century spy novels and of costume dramas of the days when there existed such things as atom bomb secrets.

The thought of costume dramas decided her. Unlike Drake, she wasn't a real policeman, and she didn't know how a real policeman would go about it. But she knew how such things were done in the old dramas.

She drew a piece of paper toward her and, with a quick motion, slashed a vertical pencil mark down its center. She headed one column "Harg Tholan," the other "Drake." Under "Harg Tholan" she wrote "bonafide" and thoughtfully put three question marks after it. After all, was he a doctor at all, or was he what could only be described as an interstellar agent? What proof had even the Institute of his profession except his own statements? Was that why Drake had quizzed him so relentlessly concerning the Inhibition Death? Had he boned up in advance and tried to catch the Hawkinsite in an error?

For a moment, she was irresolute; then, springing to her feet, she folded the paper, put it in the pocket of her short jacket, and swept out of her office. She said nothing to any of those she passed as she left the Institute. She left no word at the reception desk as to where she was going, or when she would be back.

Once outside, she hurried into the third-level tube and waited for an empty compartment to pass. The two minutes that elapsed seemed unbearably long. It was all she could do to say, "New York Academy of Medicine," into the mouthpiece just above the seat.

The door of the little cubicle closed, and the sound of the air flowing past the compartment hissed upward in pitch.

THE NEW YORK Academy of Medicine had been enlarged both vertically and horizontally in the past two decades. The library alone occupied one entire wing of the third floor. Undoubtedly, if all the books, pamphlets and periodicals it contained were in their original printed form, rather than in microfilm, the entire building, huge though it was, would not have been sufficiently vast to hold them. As it was, Rose knew there was already talk of limiting printed works to the last five years, rather than to the last ten, as was now the case.

Rose, as a member of the Academy, had free entry to the library. She hurried toward the alcoves devoted to extraterrestrial medicine and was relieved to find them unoccupied.

It might have been wiser to have enlisted the aid of a librarian, but she chose not to. The thinner and smaller the trail she left, the less likely it was that Drake might pick it up.

And so, without guidance, she was satisfied to travel along the shelves, following the titles anxiously with her fingers. The books were almost all in English, though some were in German or Russian. None, ironically enough, were in extraterrestrial symbolisms. There was a room somewhere for such originals, but they were available only to official translators.

Her traveling eye and finger stopped. She had found what she was looking for.

She dragged half a dozen volumes from the shelf and spread them out upon the small dark table. She fumbled for the light switch and opened the first of the volumes. It was entitled *Studies on Inhibition*. She leafed through it and then turned to the author index. The name of Harg Tholan was there.

One by one, she looked up the references indicated, then returned to the shelves for translations of such original papers as she could find.

She spent more than two hours in the Academy. When she was finished, she knew this much—there was a Hawkinsite doctor named Harg Tholan, who was an expert on the Inhibition Death. He was connected with the Hawkinsite research organization with which the Institute had been in correspondence. Of course, the Harg Tholan she knew might simply be impersonating an actual doctor to make the role more realistic, but why should that be necessary?

SHE TOOK THE paper out of her pocket and, where she had written "bonafide" with three question marks, she now wrote a YES in capitals. She went back to the Institute and at 4 P.M. was once again at her desk. She called the switchboard to say that she would not answer any phone calls and then she locked her door.

Underneath the column headed "Harg Tholan" she now wrote two questions: "Why did Harg Tholan come to Earth alone?" She left considerable space. Then, "What is his interest in the Missing Persons Bureau?"

Certainly, the Inhibition Death was all the Hawkinsite said it was. From her reading at the Academy, it was obvious that it occupied the major share of medical effort on Hawkin's Planet. It was more feared there than cancer was on Earth. If they had thought the answer to it lay on Earth, the Hawkinsites would have sent a full-scale expedition. Was it distrust and suspicion on their part that made them send only one investigator?

What was it Harg Tholan had said the night before? The incidence of the Death was highest upon his own world, which was closest to Earth, lowest upon the world farthest from Earth. Add to that the fact implied by the Hawkinsite, and verified by her own readings at the Academy, that the incidence had expanded enormously since interstellar contact had been made with Earth. . . .

Slowly and reluctantly she came to one conclusion. The inhabitants of Hawkin's Planet might have decided that somehow Earth had discovered the cause of the Inhibition Death, and was deliberately fostering it among the alien peoples of the Galaxy, with the intention, perhaps, of becoming supreme among the stars.

She rejected this conclusion with what was almost panic. It could not be; it was impossible. In the first place, Earth *wouldn't* do such a horrible thing. Secondly, it *couldn't*.

As far as scientific advance was concerned, the beings of Hawkin's Planet were certainly the equals of Earthmen. The Death had occurred there for thousands of years and their medical record was one of total failure. Surely, Earth, in its long-distance investigations into alien biochemistry, could not have succeeded so quickly. In fact, as far as she knew, there were no investigations to speak of into Hawkinsite pathology on the part of Earth biologists and physicians.

Yet all the evidence indicated that Harg Tholan had come in suspicion and had been received in suspicion. Carefully, she wrote down under the question, "Why did Harg Tholan come to Earth alone?" the answer, "Hawkin's Planet *believes* Earth is causing the Inhibition Death."

But, then, what was this business about the Bureau of Missing Persons? As a scientist, she was rigorous about the theories she developed. *All* the facts had to fit in, not merely some of them.

Missing Persons Bureau! If it was a false trail, deliberately intended to deceive Drake, it had been done clumsily, since it came only after an hour of discussion of the Inhibition Death.

Was it intended as an opportunity to study Drake? If so, why? Was this perhaps the *major* point? The Hawkinsite had investigated Drake before coming to them. Had he come because Drake was a policeman with entry to Bureaus of Missing Persons?

But why? Why?

———

SHE GAVE IT up and turned to the column headed "Drake."

And there a question wrote itself, not in pen and ink upon the paper, but in the much more visible letters of thought on mind. *Why did he marry me?* thought Rose, and she covered her eyes with her hands so that the unfriendly light was excluded.

They had met quite by accident somewhat more than a year before, when he had moved into the apartment house in which she then lived. Polite greetings had somehow become friendly conversation and this, in turn, had led to occasional dinners in a neighborhood restaurant. It had been very friendly and normal and an exciting new experience, and she had fallen in love.

When he asked her to marry him, she was pleased—and overwhelmed. At the time, she had many explanations for it. He appreciated her intelligence and friendliness. She was a nice girl. She would make a good wife, a splendid companion.

She had tried all those explanations and had half-believed every one of them. But half-belief was not enough.

It was not that she had any definite fault to find in Drake as a husband. He was always thoughtful, kind and a gentleman. Their married life was not one of passion, and yet it suited the paler emotional surges of the late thirties. She wasn't nineteen. What did she expect?

That was it; she wasn't nineteen. She wasn't beautiful, or charming, or glamorous. What did she expect? Could she have expected Drake— handsome and rugged, whose interest in intellectual pursuits was quite minor, who neither asked about her work in all the months of their marriage, nor offered to discuss his own with her? Why, then, did he marry her?

But there was no answer to that question, and it had nothing to do with what Rose was trying to do now. It was extraneous, she told herself fiercely; it was a childish distraction from the task she had set herself. She was acting like a girl of nineteen, after all, with no chronological excuse for it.

She found that the point of her pencil had somehow broken, and took a new one. In the column headed "Drake" she wrote, "Why is he suspicious of Harg Tholan?" and under it she put an arrow pointing to the other column.

What she had already written there was sufficient explanation. If Earth was spreading the Inhibition Death, or if Earth knew it was suspected of such a deed, then, obviously, it would be preparing for eventual retaliation on the part of the aliens. In fact, the setting would actually be one of preliminary maneuvering for the first interstellar war of history. It was an adequate but horrible explanation.

Now there was left the second question, the one she could not answer. She wrote it slowly, "Why Drake's reaction to Tholan's words, 'You are a most charming hostess'?"

SHE TRIED TO bring back the exact setting. The Hawkinsite had said it innocuously, matter-of-factly, politely, and Drake had frozen at the sound of it. Over and over, she had listened to that particular passage in the recording. An Earthman might have said it in just such an inconsequential tone on leaving a routine cocktail party. The recording did not carry the sight of Drake's face; she had only her memory for that. Drake's eyes had become alive with fear and hate, and Drake was one who feared practically nothing. What was there to fear in the phrase, "You are a most charming hostess," that could upset him so? Jealousy? Absurd. The feeling that Tholan had been sarcastic? Maybe, though unlikely. She was sure Tholan was sincere.

She gave it up and put a large question mark under that second question. There were two of them now, one under "Harg Tholan" and one under "Drake." Could there be a connection between Tholan's interest in missing persons and Drake's reaction to a polite party phrase? She could think of none.

She put her head down upon her arms. It was getting dark in the office and she was very tired. For a while, she must have hovered in that queer land between waking and sleeping, when thoughts and phrases lose the control of the conscious and disport themselves erratically and surrealistically through one's head. But, no matter where they danced and leaped, they always returned to that one phrase, "You are a most charming hostess." Sometimes she heard it in Harg Tholan's cultured, lifeless voice, and sometimes in Drake's vibrant one. When Drake said it, it was full of love, full of a love she never heard from him. She liked to hear him say it.

She startled herself to wakefulness. It was quite dark in the office now, and she put on the desk light. She blinked, then frowned a little. Another thought must have come to her in that fitful half-sleep. There had been another phrase which had upset Drake. What was it? Her forehead furrowed with mental effort. It had not been last evening. It was not anything in the recorded conversation, so it must have been before that. Nothing came and she grew restless.

Looking at her watch, she gasped. It was almost eight. They would be at home waiting for her.

But she did not want to go home. She did not want to face them. Slowly, she took up the paper upon which she had scrawled her thoughts of the afternoon, tore it into little pieces and let them flutter into the little atomic-flash ashtray upon her desk. They were gone in a little flare and nothing was left of them.

If only nothing were left of the thoughts they represented as well.

It was no use. She would have to go home.

THEY WERE NOT there waiting for her, after all. She came upon them getting out of a gyrocab just as she emerged from the tubes onto street level. The gyrocabbie, wide-eyed, gazed after his fares for a moment, then hovered upward and away. By unspoken mutual consent, the three waited until they had entered the apartment before speaking.

Rose said disinterestedly, "I hope you have had a pleasant day, Dr. Tholan."

"Quite. And a fascinating and profitable one as well, I think."

"Have you had a chance to eat?" Though Rose had not herself eaten, she was anything but hungry.

"Yes, indeed."

Drake interrupted, "We had lunch and supper sent up to us. Sandwiches." He sounded tired.

Rose said, "Hello, Drake." It was the first time she had addressed him.

Drake scarcely looked at her. "Hello."

The Hawkinsite said, "Your tomatoes are remarkable vegetables. We have nothing to compare with them in taste on our own planet. I believe I ate two dozen, as well as an entire bottle of tomato derivative."

"Ketchup," explained Drake, briefly.

Rose said, "And your visit at the Missing Persons Bureau, Dr. Tholan? You say you found it profitable?"

"I should say so. Yes."

Rose kept her back to him. She plumped up sofa cushions as she said, "In what way?"

"I find it most interesting that the large majority of missing persons are males. Wives frequently report missing husbands, while the reverse is practically never the case."

Rose said, "Oh, that's not mysterious, Dr. Tholan. You simply don't realize the economic setup we have on Earth. On this planet, you see, it is the male who is usually the member of the family that maintains it as an economic unit. He is the one whose labor is repaid in units of currency. The wife's function is generally that of taking care of home and children."

"Surely this is not universal!"

Drake put in, "More or less. If you are thinking of my wife, she is an example of the minority of women who are capable of making their own way in the world."

Rose looked at him swiftly. Was he being sarcastic?

THE HAWKINSITE SAID, "Your implication, Mrs. Smollett, is that women, being economically dependent upon their male companions, find it less feasible to disappear?"

"That's a gentle way of putting it," said Rose, "but that's about it."

"And would you call the Missing Persons Bureau of New York a fair sampling of such cases in the planet at large?"

"Why, I should think so."

The Hawkinsite said, abruptly, "And is there, then, an economic explanation for the fact that since interstellar travel has been developed, the percentage of young males among the missing is more pronounced than ever?"

It was Drake who answered, with a verbal snap. "Good lord, that's even less of a mystery than the other. Nowadays, the runaway has all space to disappear into. Anyone who wants to get away from trouble need only hop the nearest space freighter. They're always looking for crewmen, no questions asked, and it would be almost impossible to locate the runaway after that, if he really wanted to stay out of circulation."

"And almost always young men in their first year of marriage."

Rose laughed suddenly. She said, "Why, that's just the time a man's troubles seem the greatest. If he survives the first year, there is usually no need to disappear at all."

Drake was obviously not amused. Rose thought again that he looked tired and unhappy. *Why* did he insist on bearing the load alone? And then she thought that perhaps he had to.

The Hawkinsite said, suddenly, "Would it offend you if I disconnected for a period of time?"

Rose said, "Not at all. I hope you haven't had too exhausting a day. Since you come from a planet whose gravity is greater than that of Earth's, I'm afraid we too easily presume that you would show greater endurance than we do."

"Oh, I am not tired in a physical sense." He looked for a moment at her legs and blinked very rapidly, indicating amusement. "You know, I keep expecting Earthmen to fall either forward or backward in view of their meager equipment of standing limbs. You must pardon me if my comment is overfamiliar, but your mention of the lesser gravity of Earth brought it to my mind. On my planet, two legs would simply not be enough. But this is all beside the point at the moment. It is just that I have been absorbing so many new and unusual concepts that I feel the desire for a little disconnection."

Rose shrugged inwardly. Well, that was as close as one race could get to another, anyway. As nearly as the expeditions to Hawkin's Planet could make out, Hawkinsites had the faculty for disconnecting their conscious mind from all its bodily functions and allowing it to sink into an undisturbed meditative process for periods of time lasting up to terrestrial days. Hawkinsites found the process pleasant, even necessary sometimes, though no Earthman could truly say what function it served.

Conversely, it had never been entirely possible for Earthmen to explain the concept of "sleep" to a Hawkinsite, or to any extraterrestrial. What an Earthman would call sleep or a dream, a Hawkinsite would view as an alarming sign of mental disintegration.

Rose thought uneasily, *Here is another way Earthmen are unique.*

The Hawkinsite was backing away, drooping so that his forelimbs swept the floor in polite farewell. Drake nodded curtly at him as he disappeared behind the bend in the corridor. They heard his door open, close, then silence.

After minutes in which the silence was thick between them, Drake's chair creaked as he shifted restlessly. With a mild horror, Rose noticed blood upon his lips. She thought to herself, *He's in some kind of trouble, I've got to talk to him. I can't let it go on like this.*

She said, "Drake!"

Drake seemed to look at her from a far, far distance. Slowly, his eyes focused closer at hand and he said, "What is it? Are you through for the day, too?"

"No, I'm ready to begin. It's the tomorrow you spoke of. Aren't you going to speak to me?"

"Pardon me?"

"Last night, you said you would speak to me tomorrow. I am ready now."

DRAKE FROWNED. HIS eyes withdrew beneath a lowered brow and Rose felt some of her resolution begin to leave her. He said, "I thought it was agreed that you would not question me about my business in this matter."

"I think it's too late for that. I know too much about your business by now."

"What do you mean?" he shouted, jumping to his feet. Recollecting himself, he approached, laid his hands upon her shoulders and repeated in a lower voice, "What do you mean?"

Rose kept her eyes upon her hands, which rested limply in her lap. She bore the painfully gripping fingers patiently, and said slowly, "Dr. Tholan thinks that Earth is spreading the Inhibition Death purposely. That's it, isn't it?"

She waited. Slowly, the grip relaxed and he was standing there, hands at his side, face baffled and unhappy. He said, "Where did you get that notion?"

"It's true, isn't it?"

He said breathlessly, unnaturally, "I want to know exactly why you say that. Don't play foolish games with me, Rose. This is for keeps."

"If I tell you, will you answer one question?"

"What question?"

"Is Earth spreading the disease deliberately, Drake?"

Drake flung his hands upward. "Oh, for Heaven's sake!"

He knelt before her. He took her hands in his and she could feel their trembling. He was forcing his voice into soothing, loving syllables.

He was saying, "Rose dear, look, you've got something red-hot by the tail and you think you can use it to tease me in a little husband-wife repartee. No, I'm not asking much. Just tell me exactly what causes you to say what—what you have just said." He was terribly earnest about it.

"I was at the New York Academy of Medicine this afternoon. I did some reading there."

"But why? What made you do it?"

"You seemed so interested in the Inhibition Death, for one thing. And Dr. Tholan made those statements about the incidence increasing since interstellar travel, and being the highest on the planet nearest Earth." She paused.

"And your reading?" he prompted. "What about your reading, Rose?"

SHE SAID, "IT backs him up. All I could do was to skim hastily into the direction of their research in recent decades. It seems obvious to me, though, that at least some of the Hawkinsites are considering the possibility the Inhibition Death originates on Earth."

"Do they say so outright?"

"No. Or, if they have, I haven't seen it." She gazed at him in surprise. In a matter like this, certainly the government would have investigated Hawkinsite research on the matter. She said, gently, "Don't you know about Hawkinsite research in the matter, Drake? The government—"

"Never mind about that." Drake had moved away from her and now he turned again. His eyes were bright. He said, as though making a wonderful discovery, "Why, you're an expert in this!"

Was she? Did he find that out only now that he needed her? Her nostrils flared and she said flatly, "I am a biologist."

He said, "Yes, I know that, but I mean your particular specialty is growth. Didn't you once tell me you had done work on growth?"

"You might call it that. I've had twenty papers published on the relationship of nucleic acid fine structure and embryonic development on my Cancer Society grant."

"Good. I should have thought of that." He was choked with a new excitement. "Tell me, Rose—Look, I'm sorry if I lost my temper with you a moment ago. You'd be as competent as anyone to understand the direction of their researches if you read about it, wouldn't you?"

"Fairly competent, yes."

"Then tell me how they think the disease is spread. The details, I mean."

"Oh, now look, that's asking a little too much. I spent a few hours in the Academy, that's all. I'd need much more time than that to be able to answer your question."

"An intelligent guess, at least. You can't imagine how important it is."

She said, doubtfully, "Of course, 'Studies on Inhibition' is a major treatise in the field. It would summarize all of the available research data."

"Yes? And how recent is it?"

"It's one of those periodic things. The last volume is about a year old."

"Does it have any account of *his* work in it?" His finger jabbed in the direction of Harg Tholan's bedroom.

"More than anyone else's. He's an outstanding worker in the field. I looked over his papers especially."

"And what are his theories about the origin of the disease? Try to remember, Rose."

She shook her head at him. "I could swear he blames Earth, but he admits they know nothing about how the disease is spread. I could swear to that, too."

He stood stiffly before her. His strong hands were clenched into fists at his side and his words were scarcely more than a mutter. "It could be a matter of complete overestimation. Who knows—"

He whirled away. "I'll find out about this right now, Rose. Thank you for your help."

She ran after him. "What are you going to do?"

"Ask him a few questions." He was rummaging through the drawers of his desk and now his right hand withdrew. It held a needle-gun.

She cried, "No, Drake!"

He shook her off roughly, and turned down the corridor toward the Hawkinsite's bedroom.

DRAKE THREW THE door open and entered. Rose was at his heels, still trying to grasp his arm, but now he stopped and looked at Harg Tholan.

The Hawkinsite was standing there motionless, eyes unfocused, his four standing limbs sprawled out in four directions as far as they would go. Rose felt ashamed of intruding, as though she were violating an intimate rite. But Drake, apparently unconcerned, walked to within four feet of the creature and stood there. They were face to face, Drake holding the needle-gun easily at a level of about the center of the Hawkinsite's torso.

Drake said, "Now keep quiet. He'll gradually become aware of me."

"How do you know?"

The answer was flat. "I *know*. Now get out of here."

But she did not move and Drake was too absorbed to pay her further attention.

Portions of the skin on the Hawkinsite's face were beginning to quiver slightly. It was rather repulsive and Rose found herself preferring not to watch.

Drake suddenly, "That's about all, Dr. Tholan. Don't throw in connection with any of the limbs. Your sense organs and voice box will be quiet enough."

The Hawkinsite's voice was dim. "Why do you invade my disconnection chamber?" Then, more strongly, "And why are you armed?"

His head wobbled sightly atop a still frozen torso. He had, apparently, followed Drake's suggestion against limb connection. Rose wondered how Drake knew such partial reconnection to be possible. She herself had not known of it.

The Hawkinsite spoke again. "What do you want?"

And this time Drake answered. He said, "The answer to certain questions."

"With a gun in your hand? I would not humor your discourtesy so far."

"You would not merely be humoring me. You might be saving your own life."

"That would be a matter of considerable indifference to me, under the circumstances. I am sorry, Mr. Smollett, that the duties toward a guest are so badly understood on Earth."

"You are no guest of mine, Dr. Tholan," said Drake. "You entered my house on false pretenses. You had some reason for it, some way you had planned of using me to further your own purposes. I have no compunction in reversing the process."

"You had better shoot. It will save time."

"You are convinced that you will answer no questions? That, in itself, is suspicious. It seems that you consider certain answers to be more important than your life."

"I consider the principles of courtesy to be very important. You, as an Earthman, may not understand."

"Perhaps not. But I, as an Earthman, understand one thing." Drake had jumped forward, faster than Rose could cry out, faster than the Hawkinsite could connect his limbs. When he sprang backward, the flexible hose of Harg Tholan's cyanide cylinder was in his hand. At the corner of the Hawkinsite's wide mouth, where the hose had once been affixed, a droplet of colorless liquid oozed sluggishly from a break in the rough skin, and slowly solidified into a brown jellylike globule, as it oxidized.

DRAKE YANKED AT the hose and the cylinder jerked free. He plunged home the knob that controlled the needle valve at the head of the cylinder and the small hissing ceased.

"I doubt," said Drake, "that enough will have escaped to endanger us. I hope, however, that you realize what will happen to you *now*, if you do not answer the questions I am going to ask you—and answer them in such a way that I am convinced you are being truthful."

"Give me back my cylinder," said the Hawkinsite, slowly. "If not, it will be necessary for me to attack you and then it will be necessary for you to kill me."

Drake stepped back. "Not at all. Attack me and I shoot your legs from under you. You will lose them; all four, if necessary, but you will still live, in a horrible way. You will live to die of cyanide lack. It would be a most uncomfortable death. I am only an Earthman and I can't appreciate its true horrors, but you can, can't you?"

The Hawkinsite's mouth was open and something within quivered yellow-green. Rose wanted to throw up. She wanted to scream. *Give him back the cylinder, Drake!* But nothing would come. She couldn't even turn her head.

Drake said, "You have about an hour, I think, before the effects are irreversible. Talk quickly, Dr. Tholan, and you will have your cylinder back."

"And after that—" said the Hawkinsite.

"After that, what does it matter to you? Even if I kill you then, it will be a clean death; not cyanide lack."

Something seemed to pass out of the Hawkinsite. His voice grew guttural and his words blurred as though he no longer had the energy to keep his English perfect. He said, "What are your questions?" and as he spoke, his eyes followed the cylinder in Drake's hand.

Drake swung it deliberately, tantalizingly, and the creature's eyes followed—followed—

Drake said, "What are your theories concerning the Inhibition Death? Why did you really come to Earth? What is your interest in the Missing Persons Bureau?"

Rose found herself waiting in breathless anxiety. These were the questions she would like to have asked, too. Not in this manner, perhaps, but in Drake's job, kindness and humanity had to take second place to necessity.

She repeated that to herself several times in an effort to counteract the fact that she found herself loathing Drake for what he was doing to Dr. Tholan.

THE HAWKINSITE SAID, "The proper answer would take more than the hour I have left me. You have bitterly shamed me by forcing me to talk under duress. On my own planet, you could not have done so under any circumstances. It is only here, on this revolting planet, that I can be deprived of cyanide."

"You are wasting your hour, Dr. Tholan."

"I would have told you this eventually, Mr. Smollett. I needed your help. It is why I came here."

"You are still not answering my questions."

"I will answer them now. For years, in addition to my regular scientific work, I have been privately investigating the cells of my patients suffering from Inhibition Death. I have been forced to use the utmost secrecy and to work without assistance, since the methods I used to investigate the bodies of my patients were frowned upon by my people.

Your society would have similar feelings against human vivisection, for instance. For this reason, I could not present the results I obtained to my fellow physicians until I had verified my theories here on earth."

"What were your theories?" demanded Drake. The feverishness had returned to his eyes.

"It became more and more obvious to me as I proceeded with my studies that the entire direction of research into the Inhibition Death was wrong. Physically, there was no solution to its mystery. The Inhibition Death is entirely a disease of the mind."

Rose interrupted, "Surely, Dr. Tholan, it isn't psychosomatic."

A thin, gray translucent film had passed over the Hawkinsite's eyes. He no longer looked at them. He said, "No, Mrs. Smollett, it is not psychosomatic. It is a true disease of the mind; a mental infection. My patients had double minds. Beyond and beneath the one that obviously belonged to them, there was evidence of *another* one—an *alien* mind. I worked with Inhibition Death patients of other races than my own, and the same could be found. In short, there are not five intelligences in the Galaxy, but six. And the sixth is parasitic."

Rose said, "This is wild—impossible! You *must* be mistaken, Dr. Tholan."

"I am not mistaken. Until I came to Earth, I thought I might be. But my stay at the Institute and my researches at the Missing Persons Bureau convinced me that is not so. What is so impossible about the concept of a parasitic intelligence? Intelligences like these would not leave fossil remains, nor even leave artifacts—if their only function is to derive nourishment somehow from the mental activities of other creatures. One can imagine such a parasite, through the course of millions of years, perhaps, losing all portions of its physical being but that which remains necessary, just as a tapeworm, among your Earthly physical parasites, eventually lost all its functions but the single one of reproduction. In the case of the parasitic intelligence, all physical attributes would eventually be lost. It would become nothing but pure mind, living in some mental fashion we cannot conceive of on the minds of others. Particularly on the minds of Earthmen."

Rose said, "Why particularly Earthmen?"

Drake simply stood apart, intent, asking no further questions. He was content, apparently, to let the Hawkinsite speak.

"Have you not surmised that the sixth intelligence is a native of

Earth? Mankind from the beginning has lived with it, has adapted to it, is unconscious of it. It is why the higher species of terrestrial animals, including man, do not grow after maturity and, eventually, die what is called natural death. It is the result of this universal parasitic infestation. It is why you sleep and dream, since it is then that the parasitic mind must feed and then that you are a little more conscious of it, perhaps. It is why the terrestrial mind alone of the intelligences is so subject to instability. Where else in the Galaxy are found split personalities and other such manifestations? After all, even now there must be occasional human minds which are visibly harmed by the presence of the parasite.

"Somehow, these parasitic minds could traverse space. They had no physical limitations. They could drift between the stars in what would correspond to a state of hibernation. Why the first ones did it, I don't know; probably no one will ever know. But once those first discovered the presence of intelligence on other planets in the Galaxy, there was a small, steady stream of parasitic intelligences making their way through space. We of the outer worlds must have been a gourmet's dish for them or they would have never struggled so hard to get to us. I imagine many must have failed to make the trip, but it must have been worth the effort to those who succeeded.

"But you see, we of the other worlds had not lived with these parasites for millions of years, as man and his ancestors had. We had not adapted ourselves to it. Our weak strains had not been killed off gradually through hundreds of generations until only the resistants were left. So, where Earthmen could survive the infection for decades with little harm, we others die a quick death within a year."

"And is that why the incidence has increased since interstellar travel between Earth and the other planets has begun?"

"Yes." For a moment there was silence, and then the Hawkinsite said with a sudden access of energy, "Give me back my cylinder. You have your answer."

Drake said, coolly, "What about the Missing Persons Bureau?" He was swinging the cylinder again; but now the Hawkinsite did not follow its movements. The gray translucent film on his eyes had deepened and Rose wondered whether that was simply an expression of weariness or an example of the changes induced by cyanide lack.

The Hawkinsite said, "As we are not well adapted to the intelligence that infests man, neither is it well adapted to us. It can live on us—it even prefers to, apparently—but it cannot reproduce with ourselves alone as the source of its life. The Inhibition Death is therefore not directly contagious among our people."

Rose looked at him with growing horror. "What are you implying, Dr. Tholan?"

"The Earthman remains the prime host for the parasite. An Earthman may infect one of us if he remains among us. But the parasite, once it is located in an intelligence of the outer worlds, must somehow return to an Earthman, if it expects to reproduce. Before interstellar travel, this was possible only by a re-passage of space and therefore the incidence of infection remained infinitesimal. Now we are infected and reinfected as the parasites return to Earth and come back to us via the mind of Earthmen who travel through space."

Rose said faintly, "And the missing persons—"

"Are the intermediate hosts. The exact process by which it is done, I, of course, do not know. The masculine terrestrial mind seems better suited for their purposes. You'll remember that at the Institute I was told that the life expectancy of the average human male is three years less than that of the average female. Once reproduction has been taken care of, the infested male leaves, by spaceship, for the outer worlds. He disappears."

"But this is impossible," insisted Rose. "What you say implies that the parasite mind can control the actions of its host! This cannot be, or we of Earth would have noticed their presence."

"The control, Mrs. Smollett, may be very subtle, and may, moreover, be exerted only during the period of active reproduction. I simply point to your Missing Persons Bureau. Why do the young men disappear? You have economic and psychological explanations, but they are not sufficient.—But I am quite ill now and cannot speak much longer. I have only this to say. In the mental parasite, your people and mine have a common enemy. Earthmen, too, need not die involuntarily, except for its presence. I thought that if I found myself unable to return to my own world with my information because of the unorthodox methods I used to obtain it, I might bring it to the authorities on Earth, and ask their help in stamping out this menace. Imagine my pleasure when I found that the husband of one of the biologists at the Institute was a member of one of Earth's most important investigating bodies. Naturally, I did what I could to be made a guest at his home in order that I might deal with him privately; convince him of the terrible truth; utilize his position to help in the attack on the parasites.

"This is, of course, now impossible. I cannot blame you too far. As Earthmen, you cannot be expected to understand the psychology of my people. Nevertheless, you must understand this. I can have no further dealing with either of you. I could not even bear to remain any longer on Earth."

Drake said, "Then you alone, of all your people, have any knowledge of this theory of yours."

"I alone."

Drake held out the cylinder. "Your cyanide, Dr. Tholan."

The Hawkinsite groped for it eagerly. His supple fingers manipulated the hose and the needle valve with the utmost delicacy. In the space of ten seconds, he had it in place and was inhaling the gas in huge breaths. His eyes were growing clear and transparent.

Drake waited until the Hawkinsite breathings had subsided to normal, and then, without expression, he raised his needlegun and fired. Rose screamed. The Hawkinsite remained standing. His four lower limbs were incapable of buckling, but his head lolled and from his suddenly flaccid mouth, the cyanide hose fell, disregarded. Once again, Drake closed the needle valve and now he tossed the cylinder aside and stood there somberly, looking at the dead creature. There was no external mark to show that he had been killed. The needlegun's pellet, thinner than the needle which gave the gun its name, entered the body noiselessly and easily, and exploded with devastating effect only within the abdominal cavity.

Rose ran from the room, still screaming. Drake pursued her, seized her arm. She heard the hard, flat sounds of his palm against her face without feeling them and subsided into little bubbling sobs.

Drake said, "I told you to have nothing to do with this. Now what do you think you'll do?"

She said, "Let me go. I want to leave. I want to go away."

"Because of something it was my job to do? You heard what the creature was saying. Do you suppose I could allow him to return to his world and spread those lies? They would believe him. And what do you think would happen then? Can you imagine what an interstellar war might be like? They would imagine they would have to kill us all to stop the disease."

With an effort that seemed to turn her inside out, Rose steadied. She looked firmly into Drake's eyes and said, "What Dr. Tholan said were no lies and no mistakes, Drake."

"Oh, come now, you're hysterical. You need sleep."

"I know what he said is so because the Security Commission knows all about that same theory, and knows it to be true."

"Why do you say such a preposterous thing?"

"Because you yourself let that slip twice."

Drake said, "Sit down." She did so, and he stood there, looking curiously at her. "So I have given myself away twice, have I? You've had a busy day of detection, my dear. You have facets you keep well hidden." He sat down and crossed his legs.

Rose thought, yes, she had had a busy day. She could see the electric clock on the kitchen wall from where she sat; it was more than two hours past midnight. Harg Tholan had entered their house thirty-five hours before and now he lay murdered in the spare bedroom.

Drake said, "Well, aren't you going to tell me where I pulled my two boners?"

"You turned white when Harg Tholan referred to me as a charming hostess. Hostess has a double meaning, you know, Drake. A host is one who harbors a parasite."

"Number one," said Drake. "What's number two?"

"That's something you did before Harg Tholan entered the house. I've been trying to remember it for hours. Do *you* remember, Drake? You spoke about how unpleasant it was for Hawkinsites to associate with Earthmen, and I said Harg Tholan was a doctor and had to. I asked you if you thought that human doctors particularly enjoyed going to the tropics, or letting infected mosquitoes bite them. Do you remember how upset you became?"

Drake laughed. "I had no idea I was so transparent. Mosquitoes are hosts for the malaria and yellow fever parasites." He sighed. "I've done my best to keep you out of this. I tried to keep the Hawkinsite away. I tried threatening you. Now there's nothing left but to tell you the truth. I must, because only the truth—or death—will keep you quiet. And I don't want to kill you."

She shrank back in her chair, eyes wide.

Drake said, "The Commission knows the truth. It does us no good. We can only do all in our power to prevent the other worlds from finding out."

"But the truth can't be held down forever! Harg Tholan found out. You've killed him, but another extraterrestrial will repeat the same discovery—over and over again. You can't kill them all."

"We know that, too," agreed Drake. "We have no choice."

"Why?" cried Rose. "Harg Tholan gave you the solution. He made no suggestions or threats of war between worlds. He suggested that we combine with the other intelligences and help to wipe out the parasite. And we can! If we, in common with all the others, put every scrap of effort into it—"

"You mean we can trust him? Does he speak for his government or for the other races?"

"Can we dare to refuse the risk?"

Drake said, "You don't understand." He reached toward her and took one of her cold, unresisting hands between both of his. He went on, "I may seem silly trying to teach you anything about your specialty, but I want you to hear me out. Harg Tholan was right. Man and his prehistoric ancestors have been living with this parasitic intelligence for uncounted ages; certainly for a much longer period than we have been truly *Homo sapiens*. In that interval, we have not only become adapted to it, we have become dependent upon it. It is no longer a case of parasitism. It is a case of mutual cooperation. You biologists have a name for it."

She tore her hand away. "What are you talking about? Symbiosis?"

"Exactly. We have a disease of our own, remember. It is a reverse disease; one of unrestrained growth. We've mentioned it already as a contrast to the Inhibition Death. Well, what is the cause of cancer? How long have biologists, physiologists, biochemists and all the others been working on it? How much success have they had with it? Why? Can't you answer that for yourself now?"

She said, slowly, "No, I can't. What are you talking about?"

"It's all very well to say that if we could remove the parasite, we would have eternal growth and life if we wanted it; or at least until we got tired of being too big or of living too long, and did away with ourselves neatly. But how many millions of years has it been since the human body has had occasion to grow in such an unrestrained fashion? Can it do so any longer? Is the chemistry of the body adjusted to that? Has it got the proper whatchamacallits?"

"Enzymes," Rose supplied in a whisper.

"Yes, enzymes. It's impossible for us. If for any reason the parasitic intelligence, as Harg Tholan calls it, does leave the human body, or if its relationship to the human mind is in any way impaired, growth does take place, but not in any orderly fashion. We call the growth cancer. And there you have it. There's no way of getting rid of the parasite. We're together for all eternity. To get rid of their Inhibition Death, extraterrestrials must first wipe out all vertebrate life on Earth. There is no other solution for them, and so we must keep knowledge of it from them. Do you understand?"

Her mouth was dry and it was difficult to talk. "I understand, Drake." She noticed that his forehead was damp and that there was a line of perspiration down each cheek. "And now you'll have to get it out of the apartment."

"It's late at night and I'll be able to get the body out of the building. From there on—" He turned to her. "I don't know when I'll be back."

"I understand, Drake," she said again.

Harg Tholan was heavy. Drake had to drag him through the apartment. Rose turned away, retching. She hid her eyes until she heard the front door close. She whispered to herself, "I understand, Drake."

IT WAS 3 A.M. Nearly an hour had passed since she had heard the front door click gently into place behind Drake and his burden. She didn't know where he was going, what he intended doing—

She sat there numbly. There was no desire to sleep; no desire to move. She kept her mind traveling in tight circles, away from the thing she knew and which she wanted not to know.

Parasitic minds! Was it only a coincidence or was it some queer racial memory, some tenuous long-sustained wisp of tradition or insight, stretching back through incredible millennia, that kept current the odd myth of human beginnings? She thought to herself, there were two intelligences on Earth to begin with. There were humans in the Garden of Eden and also the serpent, which "was more subtil than any beast of the field." The serpent infected man and, as a result, it lost its limbs. Its physical attributes were no longer necessary. And because of the infection, man was driven out of the Garden of eternal life. Death entered the world.

Yet, despite her efforts, the circle of her thoughts expanded and returned to Drake. She shoved and it returned; she counted to herself, she recited the names of the objects in her field of vision, she cried, "No, no, no," and it returned. It kept returning.

Drake had lied to her. It had been a plausible story. It would have held good under most circumstances; but Drake was not a biologist. Cancer could not be, as Drake had said, a disease that was an expression of a lost ability for normal growth. Cancer attacked children while they were still growing; it could even attack embryonic tissue. It attacked fish, which, like extraterrestrials, never stopped growing while they lived, and died only by disease or accident. It attacked plants which had no minds and could not be parasitized. Cancer had nothing to do with the presence or absence of normal growth; it was the general disease of life, to which *no* tissue of *no* multicellular organism was completely immune.

He should not have bothered lying. He should not have allowed some obscure sentimental weakness to persuade him to avoid the necessity of killing her in that manner. She would tell them at the Institute. The parasite *could* be beaten. Its absence would *not* cause cancer. But who would believe her?

She put her hands over her eyes. The young men who disappeared were usually in the first year of their marriage. Whatever the process of reproduction of the parasite intelligences, it must involve close association with another parasite—the type of close and continuous association that might only be possible if their respective hosts were in equally close relationship. As in the case of newly married couples.

She could feel her thoughts slowly disconnect. They would be coming to her. They would be saying, "Where is Harg Tholan?" And she would answer, "With my husband." Only they would say, "Where is your husband?" because he would be gone, too. He needed her no longer. He would never return. They would never find him, because he would be out in space. She would report them both, Drake Smollett and Harg Tholan, to the Missing Persons Bureau.

She wanted to weep, but couldn't; she was dry-eyed and it was painful.

And then she began to giggle and couldn't stop. It was very funny. She had looked for the answers to so many questions and had found them all. She had even found the answer to the question she thought had no bearing on the subject.

She had finally learned why Drake had married her.

PREFACE TO
BREEDS THERE
A MAN . . . ?

FIRST APPEARANCE—*ASTOUNDING SCIENCE FICTION,* June 1951. Copyright 1951, by Street & Smith Publications, Inc.

The dropping of the atomic bomb in 1945 made science fiction respectable. Once the horror at Hiroshima took place, anyone could see that science fiction writers were not merely dreamers and crackpots after all, and that many of the motifs of that class of literature were now permanently part of the newspaper headlines.

I suppose that science fiction writers and readers were, on the whole, pleased—if not at the effect of the atom bomb itself, then at least at the crystallization into fact of something that had been so science fictional.

I myself was ambivalent. Quite apart from the frightening aspects of nuclear explosions and the mildly irrational feeling that such things as atom bombs belonged to *us* and not to the real world, I also felt that reality might have a stultifying effect on the field.

And I think it did to a certain extent. There was a tendency for the new reality to nail the science fiction writer to the ground. Prior to 1945, science fiction had been wild and free. All its motifs and plot varieties remained in the realm of fantasy and we could do as we pleased. After 1945, there came the increasing need to talk about the AEC and to mold all the infinite scope of our thoughts to the small bit of them that had become real.

In fact, there was the birth of something I called "tomorrow fiction"; the science fiction story that was no more new than tomorrow's headlines.

Believe me, there can be nothing duller than tomorrow's headlines in science fiction. As an example, consider Nevil Shute's *On the Beach*. Surely to the science fiction fan—as opposed to the general public— this must seem very milk-and-watery. So there's a nuclear war to start the story with—and what else is new?

I resisted the temptation to base a story slavishly on the present until I could think of a way to do so without making myself a minion of the headlines and of topicality. I wanted to write a story that would deal with the things of tomorrow without becoming outdated the day after tomorrow.

The result was "Breeds There a Man . . . ?" which, despite all its topicality, is as much science fiction now as it was in 1951 when it was written.

BREEDS THERE
A MAN . . . ?

Police Sergeant Mankiewicz was on the telephone and he wasn't enjoying it. His conversation was sounding like a one-sided view of a firecracker.

He was saying, "That's right! He came in here and said, 'Put me in jail, because I want to kill myself.'

". . . I can't help that. Those were his exact words. It sounds crazy to me, too.

". . . Look, mister, the guy answers the description. You asked me for information and I'm giving it to you.

". . . He has exactly that scar on his right cheek and he said his name was John Smith. He didn't say it was Doctor anything-at-all.

". . . Well, sure it's a phony. Nobody is named John Smith. Not in a police station, anyway.

". . . He's in jail now.

". . . Yes, I mean it.

". . . Resisting an officer; assault and battery; malicious mischief. That's three counts.

". . . I don't care who he is.

". . . All right. I'll hold on."

He looked up at Officer Brown and put his hand over the mouthpiece of the phone. It was a ham of a hand that nearly swallowed up the phone altogether. His blunt-featured face was ruddy and steaming under a thatch of pale-yellow hair.

He said, "Trouble! Nothing but trouble at a precinct station. I'd rather be pounding a beat any day."

"Who's on the phone?" asked Brown. He had just come in and didn't really care. He thought Mankiewicz would look better on a suburban beat, too.

"Oak Ridge. Long Distance. A guy called Grant. Head of somethingological division, and now he's getting somebody else at seventy-five cents a min . . . Hello!"

Mankiewicz got a new grip on the phone and held himself down.

"Look," he said, "let me go through this from the beginning. I want you to get it straight and then if you don't like it, you can send someone down here. The guy doesn't want a lawyer. He claims he just wants to stay in jail and, brother, that's all right with me.

"Well, will you listen? He came in yesterday, walked right up to me, and said, 'Officer, I want you to put me in jail because I want to kill myself.' So I said, 'Mister, I'm sorry you want to kill yourself. Don't do it, because if you do, you'll regret it the rest of your life.'

". . . I *am* serious. I'm just telling you what I said. I'm not saying it was a funny joke, but I've got my own troubles here, if you know what I mean. Do you think all I've got to do here is to listen to cranks who walk in and——

". . . Give me a chance, will you? I said, 'I can't put you in jail for wanting to kill yourself. That's no crime.' And he said, 'But I don't want to die.' So I said, 'Look, bud, get out of here.' I mean if a guy wants to commit suicide, all right, and if he doesn't want to, all right, but I don't want him weeping on my shoulder.

". . . I'm *getting* on with it. So he said to me. 'If I commit a crime, will you put me in jail?' I said, 'If you're caught and if someone files a charge and you can't put up bail, we will. Now beat it.' So he picked up the inkwell on my desk and, before I could stop him, he turned it upside down on the open police blotter.

". . . That's right! Why do you think we have 'malicious mischief' tabbed on him? The ink ran down all over my pants."

". . . Yes, assault and battery, too! I came hopping down to shake a little sense into him, and he kicked me in the shins and handed me one in the eye.

". . . I'm not making this up. You want to come down here and look at my face?

". . . He'll be up in court one of these days. About Thursday, maybe.

". . . Ninety days is the least he'll get, unless the psychos say otherwise. I think he belongs in the loony-bin myself.

". . . Officially, he's John Smith. That's the only name he'll give.

". . . No, sir, he doesn't get released without the proper legal steps.

". . . O.K., you do that, if you want to, bud! I just do my job here."

He banged the phone into its cradle, glowered at it, then picked it up and began dialing. He said "Gianetti?," got the proper answer and began talking.

"What's the A.E.C.? I've been talking to some Joe on the phone and he says——

". . . No, I'm not kidding, lunk-head. If I were kidding, I'd put up a sign. What's the alphabet soup?"

He listened, said "Thanks" in a small voice and hung up again.

He had lost some of his color. "That second guy was the head of the Atomic Energy Commission," he said to Brown. "They must have switched me from Oak Ridge to Washington."

Brown lounged to his feet, "Maybe the F.B.I. is after this John Smith guy. Maybe he's one of these here scientists." He felt moved to philosophy. "They ought to keep atomic secrets away from those guys. Things were O.K. as long as General Groves was the only fella who knew about the atom bomb. Once they cut in these here scientists on it, though——"

"Ah, shut up," snarled Mankiewicz.

DR. OSWALD GRANT kept his eyes fixed on the white line that marked the highway and handled the car as though it were an enemy of his. He always did. He was tall and knobby with a withdrawn expression stamped on his face. His knees crowded the wheel, and his knuckles whitened whenever he made a turn.

Inspector Darrity sat beside him with his legs crossed so that the sole of his left shoe came up hard against the door. It would leave a sandy mark when he took it away. He tossed a nut-brown penknife from hand to hand. Earlier, he had unsheathed its wicked, gleaming blade and scraped casually at his nails as they drove, but a sudden swerve had nearly cost him a finger and he desisted.

He said, "What do you know about this Ralson?"

Dr. Grant took his eyes from the road momentarily, then returned them. He said, uneasily, "I've known him since he took his doctorate at Princeton. He's a very brilliant man."

"Yes? Brilliant, huh? Why is it that all you scientific men describe one another as 'brilliant'? Aren't there any mediocre ones?"

"Many. I'm one of them. But Ralson isn't. You ask anyone. Ask Oppenheimer. Ask Bush. He was the youngest observer at Alamogordo."

"O.K. He was brilliant. What about his private life?"

Grant waited. "I wouldn't know."

"You know him since Princeton. How many years is that?"

They had been scouring north along the highway from Washington for two hours with scarcely a word between them. Now Grant felt the atmosphere change and the grip of the law on his coat collar.

"He got his degree in '43."

"You've known him eight years then."

"That's right."

"And you don't know about his private life?"

"A man's life is his own, Inspector. He wasn't very sociable. A great many of the men are like that. They work under pressure and when they're off the job, they're not interested in continuing the lab acquaintanceships."

"Did he belong to any organizations that you know of?"

"No."

The inspector said, "Did he ever say anything to you that might indicate he was disloyal?"

Grant shouted "No!" and there was silence for a while.

Then Darrity said, "How important is Ralson in atomic research?"

Grant hunched over the wheel and said, "As important as any one man can be. I grant you that no one is indispensable, but Ralson has always seemed to be rather unique. He has the engineering mentality."

"What does that mean?"

"He isn't much of a mathematician himself, but he can work out the gadgets that put someone else's math into life. There's no one like him when it comes to that. Time and again, Inspector, we've had a problem to lick and no time to lick it in. There were nothing but blank minds all around until he put some thought into it and said, 'Why don't you try so-and-so?' Then he'd go away. He wouldn't even be interested enough to see if it worked. But it always did. Always! Maybe we would have got it ourselves eventually, but it might have taken months of additional time. I don't know how he does it. It's no use asking him either. He just looks at you and says 'It was obvious,' and walks away. Of course, once he's shown us how to do it, it *is* obvious."

The inspector let him have his say out. When no more came, he said, "Would you say he was queer, mentally? Erratic, you know."

"When a person is a genius, you wouldn't expect him to be normal, would you?"

"Maybe not. But just how abnormal was this particular genius?"

"He never talked, particularly. Sometimes, he wouldn't work."

"Stayed at home and went fishing instead?"

"No. He came to the labs all right; but he would just sit at his desk. Sometimes that would go on for weeks. Wouldn't answer you, or even look at you, when you spoke to him."

"Did he ever actually leave work altogether?"

"Before now, you mean? Never!"

"Did he ever claim he wanted to commit suicide? Ever say he wouldn't feel safe except in jail?"

"No."

"You're sure this John Smith is Ralson?"

"I'm almost positive. He has a chemical burn on his right cheek that can't be mistaken."

"O.K. That's that, then I'll speak to him and see what he sounds like."

The silence fell for good this time. Dr. Grant followed the snaking line as Inspector Darrity tossed the penknife in low arcs from hand to hand.

The warden listened to the call-box and looked up at his visitors. "We can have him brought up here, Inspector, regardless."

"No," Dr. Grant shook his head. "Let's go to him."

Darrity said, "Is that normal for Ralson, Dr. Grant? Would you expect him to attack a guard trying to take him out of a prison cell?"

Grant said, "I can't say."

The warden spread a calloused palm. His thick nose twitched a little. "We haven't tried to do anything about him so far because of the telegram from Washington, but, frankly, he doesn't belong here. I'll be glad to have him taken off my hands."

"We'll see him in his cell," said Darrity.

They went down the hard, barlined corridor. Empty, in-curious eyes watched their passing.

Dr. Grant felt his flesh crawl. "Has he been kept *here* all the time?"

Darrity did not answer.

The guard, pacing before them, stopped. "This is the cell."

Darrity said, "Is that Dr. Ralson?"

Dr. Grant looked silently at the figure upon the cot. The man had been lying down when they first reached the cell, but now he had risen to one elbow and seemed to be trying to shrink into the wall. His hair was sandy and thin, his figure slight, his eyes blank and china-blue. On his right cheek there was a raised pink patch that tailed off like a tadpole.

Dr. Grant said, "That's Ralson."

The guard opened the door and stepped inside, but Inspector Darrity sent him out again with a gesture. Ralson watched them mutely. He had drawn both feet up to the cot and was pushing backwards. His Adam's apple bobbled as he swallowed.

Darrity said quietly, "Dr. Elwood Ralson?"

"What do you want?" The voice was a surprising baritone.

"Would you come with us, please? We have some questions we would like to ask you."

"No! Leave me alone!"

"Dr. Ralson," said Grant, "I've been sent here to ask you to come back to work."

Ralson looked at the scientist and there was a momentary glint of something other than fear in his eyes. He said, "Hello, Grant." He got off his cot. "Listen, I've been trying to have them put me into a padded cell. Can't you make them do that for me? You know me, Grant, I wouldn't ask for something I didn't feel was necessary. Help me. I can't stand the hard walls. It makes me want to . . . bash—" He brought the flat of his palm thudding down against the hard, dull-gray concrete behind his cot.

Darrity looked thoughtful. He brought out his penknife and unbent the gleaming blade. Carefully, he scraped at his thumbnail, and said, "Would you like to see a doctor?"

But Ralson didn't answer that. He followed the gleam of metal and his lips parted and grew wet. His breath became ragged and harsh.

He said, "Put that away!"

Darrity paused. "Put what away?"

"The knife. Don't hold it in front of me. I can't stand looking at it."

Darrity said, "Why not?" He held it out. "Anything wrong with it? It's a good knife."

Ralson lunged. Darrity stepped back and his left hand came down on the other's wrist. He lifted the knife high in the air. "What's the matter, Ralson? What are you after?"

Grant cried a protest but Darrity waved him away.

Darrity said, "What do you want, Ralson?"

Ralson tried to reach upward, and bent under the other's appalling grip. He gasped, "Give me the knife."

"Why, Ralson? What do you want to do with it?"

"Please. I've got to——" He was pleading. "I've got to stop living."

"You want to die?"

"No. But I must."

Darrity shoved. Ralson flailed backward and tumbled into his cot, so that it squeaked noisily. Slowly, Darrity bent the blade of his penknife into its sheath and put it away. Ralson covered his face. His shoulders were shaking but otherwise he did not move.

There was the sound of shouting from the corridor, as the other prisoners reacted to the noise issuing from Ralson's cell. The guard came hurrying down, yelling "Quiet!" as he went.

Darrity looked up. "It's all right, guard."

He was wiping his hands upon a large white handkerchief. "I think we'll get a doctor for him."

DR. GOTTFRIED BLAUSTEIN was small and dark and spoke with a trace of an Austrian accent. He needed only a small goatee to be the layman's caricature of a psychiatrist. But he was clean-shaven, and very carefully dressed. He watched Grant closely, assessing him, blocking in certain observations and deductions. He did this automatically, now, with everyone he met.

He said, "You give me a sort of picture. You describe a man of great

talent, perhaps even genius. You tell me he has always been uncomfortable with people; that he has never fitted in with his laboratory environment, even though it was there that he met the greatest of success.
Is there another environment to which he has fitted himself?"

"I don't understand."

"It is not given to all of us to be so fortunate as to find a congenial
type of company at the place or in the field where we find it necessary
to make a living. Often, one compensates by playing an instrument, or
going hiking, or joining some club. In other words, one creates a new
type of society, when not working, in which one can feel more at
home. It need not have the slightest connection with what one's ordinary occupation is. It is an escape, and not necessarily an unhealthy
one." He smiled and added, "Myself, I collect stamps. I am an active
member of the American Society of Philatelists."

Grant shook his head. "I don't know what he did outside working
hours. I doubt that he did anything like what you've mentioned."

"Um-m-m. Well, that would be sad. Relaxation and enjoyment are
wherever you find them; but you must find them somewhere, no?"

"Have you spoken to Dr. Ralson, yet?"

"About his problems? No."

"Aren't you going to?"

"Oh, yes. But he has been here only a week. One must give him a
chance to recover. He was in a highly excited state when he first came
here. It was almost a delirium. Let him rest and become accustomed to
the new environment. I will question him, then."

"Will you be able to get him back to work?"

Blaustein smiled. "How should I know? I don't even know what his
sickness is."

"Couldn't you at least get rid of the worst of it; this suicidal obses-
sion of his, and take care of the rest of the cure while he's at work?"

"Perhaps. I couldn't even venture an opinion so far without several
interviews."

"How long do you suppose it will all take?"

"In these matters, Dr. Grant, nobody can say."

Grant brought his hands together in a sharp slap. "Do what seems
best then. But this is more important than you know."

"Perhaps. But you may be able to help me, Dr. Grant."

"How?"

"Can you get me certain information which may be classified as top secret?"

"What kind of information?"

"I would like to know the suicide rate, since 1945, among nuclear scientists. Also, how many have left their jobs to go into other types of scientific work, or to leave science altogether."

"Is this in connection with Ralson?"

"Don't you think it might be an occupational disease, this terrible unhappiness of his?"

"Well—a good many have left their jobs, naturally."

"Why naturally, Dr. Grant?"

"You must know how it is, Dr. Blaustein. The atmosphere in modern atomic research is one of great pressure and red tape. You work with the government; you work with military men. You can't talk about your work; you have to be careful what you say. Naturally, if you get a chance at a job in a university, where you can fix your own hours, do your own work, write papers that don't have to be submitted to the A.E.C., attend conventions that aren't held behind locked doors, you take it."

"And abandon your field of specialty forever."

"There are always non-military applications. Of course, there was one man who did leave for another reason. He told me once he couldn't sleep nights. He said he'd hear one hundred thousand screams coming from Hiroshima, when he put the lights out. The last I heard of him he was a clerk in a haberdashery."

"And do you ever hear a few screams yourself?"

Grant nodded. "It isn't a nice feeling to know that even a little of the responsibility of atomic destruction might be your own."

"How did Ralson feel?"

"He never spoke of anything like that."

"In other words, if he felt it, he never even had the safety-valve effect of letting off steam to the rest of you."

"I guess he hadn't."

"Yet nuclear research must be done, no?"

"I'll say."

"What would you do, Dr. Grant, if you felt you *had* to do something that you *couldn't* do."

Grant shrugged. "I don't know."

"Some people kill themselves."

"You mean that's what has Ralson down."

"I don't know. I do not know. I will speak to Dr. Ralson this evening. I can promise nothing, of course, but I will let you know whatever I can."

Grant rose. "Thanks, Doctor. I'll try to get the information you want."

ELWOOD RALSON'S APPEARANCE had improved in the week he had been at Dr. Blaustein's sanatorium. His face had filled out and some of the restlessness had gone out of him. He was tieless and beltless. His shoes were without laces.

Blaustein said, "How do you feel, Dr. Ralson?"

"Rested."

"You have been treated well?"

"No complaints, Doctor."

Blaustein's hand fumbled for the letter-opener with which it was his habit to play during moments of abstraction, but his fingers met nothing. It had been put away, of course, with anything else possessing a sharp edge. There was nothing on his desk, now, but papers.

He said, "Sit down, Dr. Ralson. How do your symptoms progress?"

"You mean, do I have what you would call a suicidal impulse? Yes. It gets worse or better, depending on my thoughts, I think. But it's always with me. There is nothing you can do to help."

"Perhaps you are right. There are often things I cannot help. But I would like to know as much as I can about you. You are an important man——"

Ralson snorted.

"You do not consider that to be so?" asked Blaustein.

"No, I don't. There are no important men, any more than there are important individual bacteria."

"I don't understand."

"I don't expect you to."

"And yet it seems to me that behind your statement there must have been much thought. It would certainly be of the greatest interest to have you tell me some of this thought."

For the first time, Ralson smiled. It was not a pleasant smile. His nostrils were white. He said, "It is amusing to watch you, Doctor. You go about your business so conscientiously. You must listen to me, mustn't you, with just that air of phony interest and unctuous sympathy. I can tell you the most ridiculous things and still be sure of an audience, can't I?"

"Don't you think my interest can be real, even granted that it is professional, too?"

"No, I don't."

"Why not?"

"I'm not interested in discussing it."

"Would you rather return to your room?"

"If you don't mind. No!" His voice had suddenly suffused with fury as he stood up, then almost immediately sat down again. "Why shouldn't I use you? I don't like to talk to people. They're stupid. They don't see things. They stare at the obvious for hours and it means nothing to them. If I spoke to them, they wouldn't understand; they'd lose patience; they'd laugh. Whereas you must listen. It's your job. You can't interrupt to tell me I'm mad, even though you may think so."

"I'd be glad to listen to whatever you would like to tell me."

Ralson drew a deep breath. "I've known something for a year now, that very few people know. Maybe it's something no *live* person knows. Do you know that human cultural advances come in spurts? Over a space of two generations in a city containing thirty thousand free men, enough literary and artistic genius of the first rank arose to supply a nation of millions for a century under ordinary circumstances. I'm referring to the Athens of Pericles.

"There are other examples. There is the Florence of the Medicis, the England of Elizabeth, the Spain of the Cordovan Emirs. There was the spasm of social reformers among the Israelites of the Eighth and Seventh centuries before Christ. Do you know what I mean?"

Blaustein nodded. "I see that history is a subject that interests you."

"Why not? I suppose there's nothing that says I must restrict myself to nuclear cross-sections and wave mechanics."

"Nothing at all. Please proceed."

"At first, I thought I could learn more of the true inwardness of historical cycles by consulting a specialist. I had some conferences with a professional historian. A waste of time!"

"What was his name; this professional historian?"

"Does it matter?"

"Perhaps not, if you would rather consider it confidential. What did he tell you?"

"He said I was wrong; that history only appeared to go in spasms. He said that after closer studies the great civilizations of Egypt and Sumeria did not arise suddenly or out of nothing, but upon the basis of a long-developing sub-civilization that was already sophisticated in its arts. He said that Periclean Athens built upon a pre-Periclean Athens of lower accomplishments, without which the age of Pericles could not have been.

"I asked why was there not a post-Periclean Athens of higher accomplishments still, and he told me that Athens was ruined by a plague and by a long war with Sparta. I asked about other cultural spurts and each time it was a war that ended it, or, in some cases, even accompanied it. He was like all the rest. The truth was there; he had only to bend and pick it up; but he didn't."

Ralson stared at the floor, and said in a tired voice, "They come to me in the laboratory sometimes, Doctor. They say, 'How the devil are we going to get rid of the such-and-such effect that is ruining all our measurements, Ralson?' They show me the instruments and the wiring diagrams and I say, 'It's staring at you. Why don't you do so-and-so? A child could tell you that.' Then I walk away because I can't endure the slow puzzling of their stupid faces. Later, they come to me and say, 'It worked, Ralson. How did you figure it out?' I can't explain to them, Doctor; it would be like explaining that water is wet. And I couldn't explain to the historian. And I can't explain to you. It's a waste of time."

"Would you like to go back to your room?"

"Yes."

Blaustein sat and wondered for many minutes after Ralson had been escorted out of his office. His fingers found their way automatically into the upper right drawer of his desk and lifted out the letter-opener. He twiddled it in his fingers.

Finally, he lifted the telephone and dialed the unlisted number he had been given.

He said, "This is Blaustein. There is a professional historian who was consulted by Dr. Ralson some time in the past, probably a bit over a year ago. I don't know his name. I don't even know if he was connected with a university. If you could find him, I would like to see him."

THADDEUS MILTON, PH.D., blinked thoughtfully at Blaustein and brushed his hand through his iron-gray hair. He said, "They came to me and I said that I had indeed met this man. However, I have had very little connection with him. None, in fact, beyond a few conversations of a professional nature."

"How did he come to you?"

"He wrote me a letter; why me, rather than someone else, I do not know. A series of articles written by myself had appeared in one of the semi-learned journals of semi-popular appeal about that time. It may have attracted his attention."

"I see. With what general topic were the articles concerned?"

"They were a consideration of the validity of the cyclic approach to history. That is, whether one can really say that a particular civilization must follow laws of growth and decline in any matter analogous to those involving individuals."

"I have read Toynbee, Dr. Milton."

"Well, then, you know what I mean."

Blaustein said, "And when Dr. Ralson consulted you, was it with reference to this cyclic approach to history?"

"U-m-m-m. In a way, I suppose. Of course, the man is not an historian and some of his notions about cultural trends are rather dramatic and . . . what shall I say . . . tabloidish. Pardon me, Doctor, if I ask a question which may be improper. Is Dr. Ralson one of your patients?"

"Dr. Ralson is not well and is in my care. This, and all else we say here, is confidential, of course."

"Quite. I understand that. However, your answer explains something to me. Some of his ideas almost verged on the irrational. He was always worried, it seemed to me, about the connection between what he called 'cultural spurts' and calamities of one sort or another. Now such connections have been noted frequently. The time of a nation's greatest vitality may come at a time of great national insecurity. The Netherlands is a good case in point. Her great artists, statesmen, and explorers belong to the early Seventeenth Century at the time when she was locked in a death struggle with the greatest European power of the time, Spain. When at the point of destruction at home, she was building an empire in the Far East and had secured footholds on the northern coast of South America, the southern tip of Africa, and the Hudson Valley of North America. Her fleets fought England to a standstill. And then, once her political safety was assured, she declined.

"Well, as I say, that is not unusual. Groups, like individuals, will rise to strange heights in answer to a challenge, and vegetate in the absence of a challenge. Where Dr. Ralson left the paths of sanity, however, was in insisting that such a view amounted to confusing cause and effect. He declared that it was not times of war and danger that stimulated 'cultural spurts,' but rather vice versa. He claimed that each time a group of men showed too much vitality and ability, a war became necessary to destroy the possibility of their further development."

"I see," said Blaustein.

"I rather laughed at him, I am afraid. It may be that that was why he did not keep the last appointment we made. Just toward the end of that last conference he asked me, in the most intense fashion imaginable, whether I did not think it queer that such an improbable species as man was dominant on earth, when all he had in his favor was intelligence. There I laughed aloud. Perhaps I should not have, poor fellow."

"It was a natural reaction," said Blaustein, "but I must take no more of your time. You have been most helpful."

They shook hands, and Thaddeus Milton took his leave.

"WELL," SAID DARRITY, "there are your figures on the recent suicides among scientific personnel. Get any deductions out of it?"

"I should be asking you that," said Blaustein, gently. "The F.B.I. must have investigated thoroughly."

"You can bet the national debt on that. They *are* suicides. There's no mistake about it. There have been people checking on it in another department. The rate is about four times above normal, taking age, social status, economic class into consideration."

"What about British scientists?"

"Just about the same."

"And the Soviet Union?"

"Who can tell?" The investigator leaned forward. "Doc, you don't think the Soviets have some sort of ray that can make people want to commit suicide, do you? It's sort of suspicious that men in atomic research are the only ones affected."

"Is it? Perhaps not. Nuclear physicists may have peculiar strains imposed upon them. It is difficult to tell without thorough study."

"You mean complexes might be coming through?" asked Darrity, warily.

Blaustein made a face. "Psychiatry is becoming too popular. Everybody talks of complexes and neuroses and psychoses and compulsions and what-not. One man's guilt complex is another man's good night's sleep. If I could talk to each one of the men who committed suicide, maybe I could know something."

"You're talking to Ralson."

"Yes, I'm talking to Ralson."

"Has *he* got a guilt complex?"

"Not particularly. He has a background out of which it would not surprise me if he obtained a morbid concern with death. When he was twelve he saw his mother die under the wheels of an automobile. His father died slowly of cancer. Yet the effect of those experiences on his present troubles is not clear."

Darrity picked up his hat. "Well, I wish you'd get a move on, Doc. There's something big on, bigger than the H-Bomb. I don't know how anything *can* be bigger than that, but it is."

RALSON INSISTED ON standing. "I had a bad night last night, Doctor."

"I hope," said Blaustein, "these conferences are not disturbing you."

"Well, maybe they are. They have me thinking on the subject again. It makes things bad, when I do that. How do you imagine it feels being part of a bacterial culture, Doctor?"

"I had never thought of that. To a bacterium, it probably feels quite normal."

Ralson did not hear. He said, slowly, "A culture in which intelligence is being studied. We study all sorts of things as far as their genetic relationships are concerned. We take fruit flies and cross red eyes and white eyes to see what happens. We don't care anything about red eyes and white eyes, but we try to gather from them certain basic genetic principles. You see what I mean?"

"Certainly."

"Even in humans, we can follow various physical characteristics. There are the Hapsburg lips, and the hæmophilia that started with Queen Victoria and cropped up in her descendants among the Spanish and Russian royal families. We can even follow feeble-mindedness in the Jukeses and Kallikakas. You learn about it in high-school biology. But you can't breed human beings the way you do fruit flies. Humans live too long. It would take centuries to draw conclusions. It's a pity we don't have a special race of men that reproduce at weekly intervals, eh?"

He waited for an answer, but Blaustein only smiled.

Ralson said, "Only that's exactly what we would be for another group of beings whose life span might be thousands of years. To them, we would reproduce rapidly enough. We would be short-lived creatures and they could study the genetics of such things as musical aptitude, scientific intelligence, and so on. Not that those things would interest them as such, any more than the white eyes of the fruit fly interest us as white eyes."

"This is a very interesting notion," said Blaustein.

"It is not simply a notion. It is true. To me, it is obvious, and I don't care how it seems to you. Look around you. Look at the planet, Earth. What kind of a ridiculous animal are we to be lords of the world after the dinosaurs had failed? Sure, we're intelligent, but what's intelligence? We think it is important because we have it. If the Tyrannosaurus could have picked out the one quality that he thought would ensure species domination, it would be size and strength. And he would make a better case for it. He lasted longer than we're likely to.

"Intelligence in itself isn't much as far as survival values are concerned. The elephant makes out very poorly indeed when compared to the sparrow even though he is much more intelligent. The dog does well, under man's protection, but not as well as the house-fly against whom every human hand is raised. Or take the primates as a group. The small ones cower before their enemies; the large ones have always been remarkably unsuccessful in doing more than barely holding their own. The baboons do the best and that is because of their canines, not their brains."

A light film of perspiration covered Ralson's forehead. "And one can see that man has been tailored, made to careful specifications for those things that study us. Generally, the primate is short-lived. Naturally, the larger ones live longer, which is a fairly general rule in animal life. Yet the human being has a life span twice as long as any of the other great apes; considerably longer even than the gorilla that outweighs him. We mature later. It's as though we've been carefully bred to live a little longer so that our life cycle might be of a more convenient length."

He jumped to his feet, shaking his fists above his head. "A thousand years are but as yesterday——"

Blaustein punched a button hastily.

For a moment, Ralson struggled against the white-coated orderly who entered, and then he allowed himself to be led away.

Blaustein looked after him, shook his head, and picked up the telephone.

He got Darrity. "Inspector, you may as well know that this may take a long time."

He listened and shook his head. "I know. I don't minimize the urgency."

The voice in the receiver was tinny and harsh. "Doctor, you *are* minimizing it. I'll send Dr. Grant to you. He'll explain the situation to you."

DR. GRANT ASKED how Ralson was, then asked somewhat wistfully if he could see him. Blaustein shook his head gently.

Grant said, "I've been directed to explain the current situation in atomic research to you."

"So that I will understand, no?"

"I hope so. It's a measure of desperation. I'll have to remind you——"

"Not to breathe a word of it. Yes, I know. This insecurity on the part of you people is a very bad symptom. You must know these things cannot be hidden."

"You live with secrecy. It's contagious."

"Exactly. What is the current secret?"

"There is . . . or, at least, there might be a defense against the atomic bomb."

"And that is a secret? It would be better if it were shouted to all the people of the world instantly."

"For heaven's sake, no. Listen to me, Dr. Blaustein. It's only on paper so far. It's at the E equals mc squared stage, almost. It may not be practical. It would be bad to raise hopes we would have to disappoint. On the other hand, if it were known that we *almost* had a defense, there *might* be a desire to start and win a war before the defense were completely developed."

"That I don't believe. But, nevertheless, I distract you. What is the nature of this defense, or have you told me as much as you dare?"

"No, I can go as far as I like; as far as is necessary to convince you we have to have Ralson—and fast!"

"Well, then tell me, and I too, will know secrets. I'll feel like a member of the Cabinet."

"You'll know more than most. Look, Dr. Blaustein, let me explain it in lay language. So far, military advances have been made fairly equally in both offensive and defensive weapons. Once before there seemed to be a definite and permanent tipping of all warfare in the direction of the offense, and that was with the invention of gunpowder. But the defense caught up. The medieval man-in-armor-on-horse became the modern man-in-tank-on-treads, and the stone castle became the concrete pillbox. The same thing, you see, except that everything has been boosted several orders of magnitude."

"Very good. You make it clear. But with the atomic bomb comes more orders of magnitude, no? You must go past concrete and steel for protection."

"Right. Only we can't just make thicker and thicker walls. We've run out of materials that are strong enough. So we must abandon materials altogether. If the atom attacks, we must let the atom defend. We will use energy itself; a force field."

"And what," asked Blaustein, gently, "is a force field?"

"I wish I could tell you. Right now, it's an equation on paper. Energy can be so channeled as to create a wall of matterless inertia, theoretically. In practice, we don't know how to do it."

"It would be a wall you could not go through, is that it? Even for atoms?"

"Even for atom bombs. The only limit on its strength would be the amount of energy we could pour into it. It could even theoretically be made to be impermeable to radiation. The gamma rays would bounce off it. What we're dreaming of is a screen that would be in permanent place about cities; at minimum strength, using practically no energy. It could then be triggered to maximum intensity in a fraction of a millisecond at the impingement of short-wave radiation; say the amount radiating from the mass of plutonium large enough to be an atomic war head. All this is theoretically possible."

"And why must you have Ralson?"

"Because he is the only one who can reduce it to practice, if it can be made practical at all, quickly enough. Every minute counts these days. You know what the international situation is. Atomic defense *must* arrive before atomic war."

"You are so sure of Ralson?"

"I am as sure of him as I can be of anything. The man is amazing, Dr. Blaustein. He is always right. Nobody in the field knows how he does it."

"A sort of intuition, no?" the psychiatrist looked disturbed. "A kind of reasoning that goes beyond ordinary human capacities. Is that it?"

"I make no pretense of knowing what it is."

"Let me speak to him once more then. I will let you know."

"Good." Grant rose to leave; then, as if in afterthought, he said, "I might say, Doctor, that if you don't do something, the Commission plans to take Dr. Ralson out of your hands."

"And try another psychiatrist? If they wish to do that, of course, I will not stand in their way. It is my opinion, however, that no reputable practitioner will pretend there is a rapid cure."

"We may not intend further mental treatment. He may simply be returned to work."

"That, Dr. Grant, I will fight. You will get nothing out of him. It will be his death."

"We get nothing out of him anyway."

"This way there is at least a chance, no?"

"I hope so. And by the way, please don't mention the fact that I said anything about taking Ralson away."

"I will not, and I thank you for the warning. Good-bye, Dr. Grant."

"I MADE A fool of myself last time, didn't I, Doctor?" said Ralson. He was frowning.

"You mean you don't believe what you said then?"

"*I do!*" Ralson's slight form trembled with the intensity of his affirmation.

He rushed to the window, and Blaustein swiveled in his chair to keep him in view. There were bars in the window. He couldn't jump. The glass was unbreakable.

Twilight was ending, and the stars were beginning to come out.

Ralson stared at them in fascination, then he turned to Blaustein and flung a finger outward. "Every single one of them is an incubator. They maintain temperatures at the desired point. Different experiments; different temperatures. And the planets that circle them are just huge cultures, containing different nutrient mixtures and different life forms. The experimenters are economical, too—whatever and whoever they are. They've cultured many types of life forms in this particular test-tube. Dinosaurs in a moist, tropical age and ourselves among the glaciers. They turn the sun up and down and we try to work out the physics of it. Physics!" He drew his lips back in a snarl.

"Surely," said Dr. Blaustein, "it is not possible that the sun can be turned up and down at will."

"Why not? It's just like a heating element in an oven. You think bacteria know what it is that works the heat that reaches them? Who knows? Maybe they evolve theories, too. Maybe they have their cosmogonies about cosmic catastrophes, in which clashing light-bulbs create strings of Petri dishes. Maybe they think there must be some beneficent creator that supplies them with food and warmth and says to them, 'Be fruitful and multiply!'

"We breed like them, not knowing why. We obey the so-called laws of nature which are only our interpretation of the not-understood forces imposed upon us.

"And now they've got the biggest experiment of any yet on their hands. It's been going on for two hundred years. They decided to develop a strain for mechanical aptitude in England in the seventeen hundreds, I imagine. We call it the Industrial Revolution. It began with steam, went on to electricity, then atoms. It was an interesting experiment, but they took their chances on letting it spread. Which is why they'll have to be very drastic indeed in ending it."

Blaustein said, "And how would they plan to end it? Do you have an idea about that?"

"You ask *me* how they plan to end it. You can look about the world today and still ask what is likely to bring our technological age to an end. All the earth fears an atomic war and would do anything to avoid it; yet all the earth fears that an atomic war is inevitable."

"In other words, the experimenters will arrange an atom war whether we want it or not, to kill off the technological era we are in, and to start fresh. That is it, no?"

"Yes. It's logical. When we sterilize an instrument, do the germs know where the killing heat comes from? Or what has brought it about? There is some way the experimenters can raise the heat of our emotions; some way they can handle us that passes our understanding."

"Tell me," said Blaustein, "is that why you want to die? Because you think the destruction of civilization is coming and can't be stopped?"

Ralson said, "I *don't* want to die. It's just that I must." His eyes were tortured. "Doctor, if you had a culture of germs that were highly dangerous and that you had to keep under absolute control, might you not have an agar medium impregnated with, say, penicillin, in a circle at a certain distance from the center of inoculation? Any germs spreading out too far from the center would die. You would have nothing against the particular germs who were killed; you might not even know that any germs had spread that far in the first place. It would be purely automatic.

"Doctor, there is a penicillin ring about our intellects. When we stray too far; when we penetrate the true meaning of our own existence, we have reached into the penicillin and we must die. It works slowly—but it's hard to stay alive."

He smiled briefly and sadly. Then he said, "May I go back to my room now, Doctor?"

DR. BLAUSTEIN WENT to Ralson's room about noon the next day. It was a small room and featureless. The walls were gray with padding. Two small windows were high up and could not be reached. The mattress lay directly on the padded floor. There was nothing of metal in the room; nothing that could be utilized in tearing life from body. Even Ralson's nails were clipped short.

Ralson sat up. "Hello!"

"Hello, Dr. Ralson. May I speak to you?"

"Here? There isn't any seat I can offer you."

"It is all right. I'll stand. I have a sitting job and it is good for my sitting-down place that I should stand sometimes. Dr. Ralson, I have thought all night of what you told me yesterday and in the days before."

"And now you are going to apply treatment to rid me of what you think are delusions."

"No. It is just that I wish to ask questions and perhaps to point out some consequences of your theories which . . . you will forgive me? . . . you may not have thought of."

"Oh?"

"You see, Dr. Ralson, since you have explained your theories, I, too, know what you know. Yet I have no feeling about suicide."

"Belief is more than something intellectual, Doctor. You'd have to believe this with all your insides, which you don't."

"Do you not think perhaps it is rather a phenomenon of adaptation?"

"How do you mean?"

"You are not really a biologist, Dr. Ralson. And although you are very brilliant indeed in physics, you do not think of everything with respect to these bacterial cultures you use as analogies. You know that it is possible to breed bacterial strains that are resistant to penicillin or to almost any bacterial posion."

"Well?"

"The experimenters who breed us have been working with humanity for many generations, no? And this particular strain which they have been culturing for two centuries shows no sign of dying out spontaneously. Rather, it is a vigorous strain and a very infective one. Older high-culture strains were confined to single cities or to small areas and lasted only a generation or two. This one is spreading throughout the world. It is a *very* infective strain. Do you not think it may have developed penicillin immunity? In other words, the methods the experimenters use to wipe out the culture may not work too well anymore, no?"

Ralson shook his head. "It's working on me."

"You are perhaps non-resistant. Or you have stumbled into a very high concentration of penicillin indeed. Consider all the people who have been trying to outlaw atomic warfare and to establish some form of world government and lasting peace. The effort has risen in recent years, without too awful results."

"It isn't stopping the atomic war that's coming."

"No, but maybe only a little more effort is all that is required. The peace-advocates do not kill themselves. More and more humans are immune to the experimenters. Do you know what they are doing in the laboratory?"

"I don't want to know."

"You *must* know. They are trying to invent a force field that will stop the atom bomb. Dr. Ralson, if I am culturing a virulent and pathological bacterium; then, even with all precautions, it may sometimes happen that I will start a plague. We may be bacteria to them, but we are dangerous to them, also, or they wouldn't wipe us out so carefully after each experiment.

"They are not quick, no? To them a thousand years is as a day, no? By the time they realize we are out of the culture, past the penicillin, it will be too late for them to stop us. They have brought us to the atom, and if we can only prevent ourselves from using it upon one another, we may turn out to be too much even for the experimenters."

Ralson rose to his feet. Small though he was, he was an inch and a half taller than Blaustein. "They are really working on a force field?"

"They are trying to. But they need you."

"No. I can't."

"They must have you in order that you might see what is so obvious to you. It is not obvious to them. Remember, it is your help, or else— defeat of man by the experimenters."

Ralson took a few rapid steps away, staring into the blank, padded wall. He muttered, "But there must be that defeat. If they build a force field, it will mean death for all of them before it can be completed."

"Some or all of them may be immune, no? And in any case, it will be death for them anyhow. They are trying."

Ralson said, "I'll try to help them."

"Do you still want to kill yourself?"

"Yes."

"But you'll try not to, no?"

"I'll *try* not to, Doctor." His lip quivered. "I'll have to be watched."

Blaustein climbed the stairs and presented his pass to the guard in the lobby. He had already been inspected at the outer gate, but he, his pass, and its signature were now scrutinized once again. After a moment, the guard retired to his little booth and made a phone call. The answer satisfied him. Blaustein took a seat and, in half a minute, was up again, shaking hands with Dr. Grant.

"The President of the United States would have trouble getting in here, no?" said Blaustein.

The lanky physicist smiled. "You're right, if he came without warning."

They took an elevator which traveled twelve floors. The office to which Grant led the way had windows in three directions. It was sound-proofed and air-conditioned. Its walnut furniture was in a state of high polish.

Blaustein said, "My goodness. It is like the office of the chairman of a board of directors. Science is becoming big business."

Grant looked embarrassed. "Yes, I know, but government money flows easily and it is difficult to persuade a congressman that your work is important unless he can see, smell, and touch the surface shine."

Blaustein sat down and felt the upholstered seat give way slowly. He said, "Dr. Elwood Ralson has agreed to return to work."

"Wonderful. I was hoping you would say that. I was hoping that was why you wanted to see me." As though inspired by the news, Grant offered the psychiatrist a cigar, which was refused.

"However," said Blaustein, "he remains a very sick man. He will have to be treated carefully and with insight."

"Of course. Naturally."

"It's not quite as simple as you may think. I want to tell you something of Ralson's problems, so that you will really understand how delicate the situation is."

He went on talking and Grant listened first in concern, and then in astonishment. "But then the man is out of his head, Dr. Blaustein. He'll be of no use to us. He's crazy."

Blaustein shrugged. "It depends on how you define 'crazy.' It's a bad word; don't use it. He had delusions, certainly. Whether they will affect his peculiar talents one cannot know."

"But surely no sane man could possibly——"

"Please. Please. Let us not launch into long discussions on psychiatric definitions of sanity and so on. The man has delusions and, ordinarily, I would dismiss them from all consideration. It is just that I have been given to understand that the man's particular ability lies in his manner of proceeding to the solution of a problem by what seems to be outside ordinary reason. That is so, no?"

"Yes. That *must* be admitted."

"How can you and I judge then as to the worth of one of his conclusions. Let me ask you, do *you* have suicidal impulses lately?"

"I don't think so."

"And other scientists here?"

"No, of course not."

"I would suggest, however, that while research on the force field proceeds, the scientists concerned be watched here and at home. It might even be a good enough idea that they should not go home. Offices like these could be arranged to be a small dormitory——"

"Sleep at work. You would never get them to agree."

"Oh, yes. If you do not tell them the real reason but say it is for security purposes, they will agree. 'Security purposes' is a wonderful phrase these days, no? Ralson must be watched more than anyone."

"Of course."

"But all this is minor. It is something to be done to satisfy my conscience in case Ralson's theories are correct. Actually, I don't believe them. They *are* delusions, but once that is granted, it is necessary to ask what the causes of those delusions are. What is it in Ralson's mind, in his background, in his life that makes it so necessary for him to have these particular delusions? One cannot answer that simply. It may well take years of constant psychoanalysis to discover the answer. And until the answer is discovered, he will not be cured.

"But, meanwhile, we can perhaps make intelligent guesses. He has had an unhappy childhood, which, in one way or another, has brought him face to face with death in very unpleasant fashion. In addition, he has never been able to form associations with other children, or, as he grew older, with other men. He was always impatient with their slower forms of reasoning. Whatever difference there is between his mind and that of others, it has built a wall between him and society as strong as the force field you are trying to design. For similar reasons, he has been unable to enjoy a normal sex life. He has never married; he has had no sweethearts.

"It is easy to see that he could easily compensate to himself for this failure to be accepted by his social milieu by taking refuge in the thought that other human beings are inferior to himself. Which is, of course, true, as far as mentality is concerned. There are, of course, many, many facets to the human personality and in not all of them is he superior. No one is. Others, then, who are more prone to see merely what is inferior, just as he himself is, would not accept his affected preeminence of position. They would think him queer, even laughable, which would make it even more important to Ralson to prove how miserable and inferior the human species was. How could he better do that than to show that mankind was simply a form of bacteria to other superior creatures which experiment upon them. And then his impulses to suicide would be a wild desire to break away completely from being a man at all; to stop this identification with the miserable species he has created in his mind. You see?"

Grant nodded. "Poor guy."

"Yes, it is a pity. Had he been properly taken care of in childhood—— Well, it is best for Dr. Ralson that he have no contact with any of the other men here. He is too sick to be trusted with them. You, yourself, must arrange to be the only man who will see him or speak to him. Dr. Ralson has agreed to that. He apparently thinks you are not as stupid as some of the others."

Grant smiled faintly. "That is agreeable to me."

"You will, of course, be careful. I would not discuss anything with him but his work. If he should volunteer information about his theories, which I doubt, confine yourself to something non-committal, and leave. And at all times, keep away anything that is sharp and pointed. Do not let him reach a window. Try to have his hands kept in view. You understand. I leave my patient in your care, Dr. Grant."

"I will do my best, Dr. Blaustein."

FOR TWO MONTHS, Ralson lived in a corner of Grant's office, and Grant lived with him. Gridwork had been built up before the windows, wooden furniture was removed and upholstered sofas brought in. Ralson did his thinking on the couch and his calculating on a desk pad atop a hassock.

The "Do Not Enter" was a permanent fixture outside the office. Meals were left outside. The adjoining men's room was marked off for private use and the door between it and the office removed. Grant switched to an electric razor. He made certain that Ralson took sleeping pills each night and waited till the other slept before sleeping himself.

And always reports were brought to Ralson. He read them while Grant watched and tried to seem not to watch.

Then Ralson would let them drop and stare at the ceiling, with one hand shading his eyes.

"Anything?" asked Grant.

Ralson shook his head from side to side.

Grand said, "Look, I'll clear the building during the swing shift. It's important that you see some of the experimental jigs we've been setting up."

They did so, wandering through the lighted, empty buildings like drifting ghosts, hand in hand. Always hand in hand. Grant's grip was tight. But after each trip, Ralson would still shake his head from side to side.

Half a dozen times he would begin writing; each time there would be a few scrawls and then he would kick the hassock over on its side.

Until, finally, he began writing once again and covered half a page rapidly. Automatically, Grant approached. Ralson looked up, covering the sheet of paper with a trembling hand.

He said, "Call Blaustein."

"What?"

"I said, 'Call Blaustein.' Get him here. Now!"

Grant moved to the telephone.

Ralson was writing rapidly now, stopping only to brush wildly at his forehead with the back of a hand. It came away wet.

He looked up and his voice was cracked, "Is he coming?"

Grant looked worried. "He isn't at his office."

"Get him at his home. Get him wherever he is. *Use* that telephone. Don't play with it."

Grant used it; and Ralson pulled another sheet toward himself.

Five minutes later, Grant said, "He's coming. What's wrong? You're looking sick."

Ralson could speak only thickly, "No time—— Can't talk——"

He was writing, scribbling, scrawling, shakily diagraming. It was as though he were driving his hands, fighting it.

"Dictate!" urged Grant. "I'll write."

Ralson shook him off. His words were unintelligible. He held his wrist with his other hand, shoving it as though it were a piece of wood, and then he collapsed over the papers.

Grant edged them out from under and laid Ralson down on the couch. He hovered over him restlessly and hopelessly until Blaustein arrived.

Blaustein took one look. "What happened?"

Grant said, "I think he's alive," but by that time Blaustein had verified that for himself, and Grant told him what had happened.

Blaustein used a hypodermic and they waited. Ralson's eyes were blank when they opened. He moaned.

Blaustein leaned close. "Ralson."

Ralson's hands reached out blindly and clutched at the psychiatrist. "Doc. Take me back."

"I will. Now. It is that you have the force field worked out, no?"

"It's on the papers. Grant, it's on the papers."

Grant had them and was leafing through them dubiously. Ralson said, weakly, "It's not *all* there. It's all I can write. You'll *have* to make it out of that. Take me back, Doc!"

"Wait," said Grant. He whispered urgently to Blaustein. "Can't you leave him here till we test this thing? I can't make out what most of this is. The writing is illegible. Ask him what makes him think this will work."

"Ask *him?*" said Blaustein, gently. "Isn't he the one who always knows?"

"Ask me, anyway," said Ralson, overhearing from where he lay on the couch. His eyes were suddenly wide and blazing.

They turned to him.

He said, "*They* don't want a force field. *They!* The experimenters! As long as I had no true grasp, things remained as they were. But I hadn't followed up that thought—*that* thought which is there in the papers—I hadn't followed it up for thirty seconds before I felt . . . I felt—— Doctor——"

Blaustein said, "What is it?"

Ralson was whispering again, "I'm deeper in the penicillin. I could feel myself plunging in and in, the further I went with that. I've never been in . . . so deep. That's how I knew I was right. Take me away."

Blaustein straightened. "I'll have to take him away, Grant. There's no alternative. If you can make out what he's written, that's it. If you can't make it out, I can't help you. That man can do no more work in his field without dying, do you understand?"

"But," said Grant, "he's dying of something imaginary."

"All right. Say that he is. But he will be really dead just the same, no?"

Ralson was unconscious again and heard nothing of this. Grant looked at him somberly, then said, "Well, take him away, then."

TEN OF THE top men at the Institute watched glumly as slide after slide filled the illuminated screen. Grant faced them, expression hard and frowning.

He said, "I think the idea is simple enough. You're mathematicians and you're engineers. The scrawl may seem illegible, but it was done with meaning behind it. That meaning must somehow remain in the writing, distorted though it is. The first page is clear enough. It should be a good lead. Each one of you will look at every page over and over again. You're going to put down every possible version of each page as it seems it might be. You will work independently. I want no consultations."

One of them said, "How do you know it means *anything*, Grant?"

"Because those are Ralson's notes."

"*Ralson!* I thought he was——"

"You thought he was sick," said Grant. He had to shout over the rising hum of conversation. "I know. He is. That's the writing of a man who was nearly dead. It's all we'll ever get from Ralson, anymore. Somewhere in that scrawl is the answer to the force field problem. If we can't find it, we may have to spend ten years looking for it elsewhere."

They bent to their work. The night passed. Two nights passed. Three nights——

Grant looked at the results. He shook his head. "I'll take your word for it that it is all self-consistent. I can't say I understand it."

Lowe, who, in the absence of Ralson, would readily have been rated the best nuclear engineer at the Institute, shrugged. "It's not exactly clear to me. If it works, he hasn't explained why."

"He had no time to explain. Can you build the generator as he describes it?"

"I could try."

"Would you look at all the other versions of the pages?"

"The others are definitely not self-consistent."

"Would you double-check?"

"Sure."

"And could you start construction anyway?"

"I'll get the shop started. But I tell you frankly that I'm pessimistic."

"I know. So am I."

THE THING GREW. Hal Ross, Senior Mechanic, was put in charge of the actual construction, and he stopped sleeping. At any hour of the day or night, he could be found at it, scratching his bald head.

He asked questions only once, "What is it, Dr. Lowe? Never saw anything like it? What's it supposed to do?"

Lowe said, "You know where you are, Ross. You know we don't ask questions here. Don't ask again."

Ross did not ask again. He was known to dislike the structure that was being built. He called it ugly and unnatural. But he stayed at it.

BLAUSTEIN CALLED ONE day.

Grant said, "How's Ralson?"

"Not good. He wants to attend the testing of the Field Projector he designed."

Grant hesitated, "I suppose we should. It's his after all."

"I would have to come with him."

Grant looked unhappier. "It might be dangerous, you know. Even in a pilot test, we'd be playing with tremendous energies."

Blaustein said, "No more dangerous for us than for you."

"Very well. The list of observers will have to be cleared through the Commission and the F.B.I., but I'll put you in."

BLAUSTEIN LOOKED ABOUT him. The field projector squatted in the very center of the huge testing laboratory, but all else had been cleared. There was no visible connection with the plutonium pile which served as energy-source, but from what the psychiatrist heard in scraps about him—he knew better than to ask Ralson—the connection was from beneath.

At first, the observers had circled the machine, talking in incomprehensibles, but they were drifting away now. The gallery was filling up. There were at least three men in generals' uniforms on the other side, and a real coterie of lower-scale military. Blaustein chose an unoccupied portion of the railing; for Ralson's sake, most of all.

He said, "Do you still think you would like to stay?"

It was warm enough within the laboratory, but Ralson was in his coat, with his collar turned up. It made little difference, Blaustein felt. He doubted that any of Ralson's former acquaintances would now recognize him.

Ralson said, "I'll stay."

Blaustein was pleased. He wanted to see the test. He turned again at a new voice.

"Hello, Dr. Blaustein."

For a minute, Blaustein did not place him, then he said, "Ah, Inspector Darrity. What are you doing here?"

"Just what you would suppose." He indicated the watchers. "There isn't any way you can weed them out so that you can be sure there won't be any mistakes. I once stood as near to Klaus Fuchs as I am standing to you." He tossed his pocketknife into the air and retrieved it with a dexterous motion.

"Ah, yes. Where shall one find perfect security? What man can trust even his own unconscious? And you will now stand near to me, no?"

"Might as well." Darrity smiled. "You were very anxious to get in here, weren't you?"

"Not for myself, Inspector. And would you put away the knife, please."

Darrity turned in surprise in the direction of Blaustein's gentle head-gesture. He put his knife away and looked at Blaustein's companion for the second time. He whistled softly.

He said, "Hello, Dr. Ralson."

Ralson croaked, "Hello."

Blaustein was not surprised at Darrity's reaction. Ralson had lost twenty pounds since returning to the sanatorium. His face was yellow and wrinkled; the face of a man who had suddenly become sixty.

Blaustein said, "Will the test be starting soon?"

Darrity said, "It looks as if they're starting now."

He turned and leaned on the rail. Blaustein took Ralson's elbow and began leading him away, but Darrity said, softly, "Stay here, Doc. I don't want you wandering about."

Blaustein looked across the laboratory. Men were standing about with the uncomfortable air of having turned half to stone. He could recognize Grant, tall and gaunt, moving his hand slowly to light a cigarette, then changing his mind and putting lighter and cigarette in his pocket. The young men at the control panels waited tensely.

Then there was a low humming and the faint smell of ozone filled the air.

Ralson said harshly, "Look!"

Blaustein and Darrity looked along the pointing finger. The projec-

tor seemed to flicker. It was as though there were heated air rising between it and them. An iron ball came swinging down pendulum fashion
and passed through the flickering area.

"It slowed up, no?" said Blaustein, excitedly.

Ralson nodded. "They're measuring the height of rise on the other
side to calculate the loss of momentum. Fools! I *said* it would work."
He was speaking with obvious difficulty.

Blaustein said, "Just watch, Dr. Ralson. I would not allow myself to
grow needlessly excited."

The pendulum was stopped in its swinging, drawn up. The flickering about the projector became a little more intense and the iron sphere
arced down once again.

Over and over again, and each time the sphere's motion was slowed
with more of a jerk. It made a clearly audible sound as it struck the flicker.
And eventually, it *bounced*. First, soggily, as though it hit putty, and then
ringingly, as though it hit steel, so that the noise filled the place.

They drew back the pendulum bob and used it no longer. The projector could hardly be seen behind the haze that surrounded it.

Grant gave an order and the odor of ozone was suddenly sharp and
pungent. There was a cry from the assembled observers; each one ex-
claiming to his neighbor. A dozen fingers were pointing.

Blaustein leaned over the railing, as excited as the rest. Where the
projector had been, there was now only a huge semi-globular mirror. It
was perfectly and beautifully clear. He could see himself in it, a small
man standing on a small balcony that curved up on each side. He could
see the fluorescent lights reflected in spots of glowing illumination. It
was wonderfully sharp.

He was shouting, "Look, Ralson. It is reflecting energy. It is reflecting light waves like a mirror. Ralson—"

He turned, "Ralson! Inspector, where is Ralson?"

"What?" Darrity whirled. "I haven't seen him."

He looked about, wildly. "Well, he won't get away. No way of getting out of here now. You take the other side." And then he clapped
hand to thigh, fumbled for a moment in his pocket, and said, "My knife
is gone."

Blaustein found him. He was inside the small office belonging to
Hal Ross. It led off the balcony, but under the circumstances, of course,
it had been deserted. Ross himself was not even an observer. A senior

mechanic need not observe. But his office would do very well for the final end of the long fight against suicide.

Blaustein stood in the doorway for a sick moment, then turned. He caught Darrity's eye as the latter emerged from a similar office a hundred feet down the balcony. He beckoned, and Darrity came at a run.

DR. GRANT WAS trembling with excitement. He had taken two puffs at each of two cigarettes and trodden each underfoot thereafter. He was fumbling with the third now.

He was saying, "This is better than any of us could possibly have hoped. We'll have the gunfire test tomorrow. I'm sure of the result now, but we've planned it; we'll go through with it. We'll skip the small arms and start with the bazooka levels. Or maybe not. It might be necessary to construct a special testing structure to take care of the ricochet problem."

He discarded his third cigarette.

A general said, "We'd have to try a literal atom-bombing, of course."

"Naturally. Arrangements have already been made to build a mock-city at Eniwetok. We could build a generator on the spot and drop the bomb. There'd be animals inside."

"And you really think if we set up a field in full power it would hold the bomb?"

"It's not just that, general. There'd be no noticeable field at all until the bomb is dropped. The radiation of the plutonium would have to energize the field before explosion. As we did here in the last step. That's the essence of it all."

"You know," said a Princeton professor, "I see disadvantages, too. When the field is on full, anything it protects is in total darkness, as far as the sun is concerned. Besides that, it strikes me that the enemy can adopt the practice of dropping harmless radioactive missiles to set off the field at frequent intervals. It would have nuisance value and be a considerable drain on our pile as well."

"Nuisances," said Grant, "can be survived. These difficulties will be met eventually, I'm sure, now that the main problem has been solved."

The British observer had worked his way toward Grant and was shaking hands. He said, "I feel better about London already. I cannot help but wish your government would allow me to see the complete plans. What I have seen strikes me as completely ingenious. It seems obvious now, of course, but how did anyone ever come to think of it?"

Grant smiled. "That question has been asked before with reference to Dr. Ralson's devices——"

He turned at the touch of a hand upon his shoulder. "Dr. Blaustein! I had nearly forgotten. Here, I want to talk to you."

He dragged the small psychiatrist to one side and hissed in his ear, "Listen, can you persuade Ralson to be introduced to these people? This is his triumph."

Blaustein said, "Ralson is dead."

"What!"

"Can you leave these people for a time?"

"Yes . . . yes—— Gentlemen, you will excuse me for a few minutes?"

He hurried off with Blaustein.

The Federal men had already taken over. Unobtrusively, they barred the doorway to Ross's office. Outside there were the milling crowd discussing the answer to Alamogordo that they had just witnessed. Inside, unknown to them, was the death of the answerer. The G-man barrier divided to allow Grant and Blaustein to enter. It closed behind them again.

For a moment, Grant raised the sheet. He said, "He looks peaceful."

"I would say—happy," said Blaustein.

Darrity said, colorlessly, "The suicide weapon was my own knife. It was my negligence; it will be reported as such."

"No, no," said Blaustein, "that would be useless. He was my patient and I am responsible. In any case, he would not have lived another week. Since he invented the projector, he was a dying man."

Grant said, "How much of this has to be placed in the Federal files? Can't we forget all about his madness?"

"I'm afraid not, Dr. Grant," said Darrity.

"I have told him the whole story," said Blaustein, sadly.

Grant looked from one to the other. "I'll speak to the Director. I'll go to the President, if necessary. I don't see that there need be any mention of suicide or of madness. He'll get full publicity as inventor of the field projector. It's the least we can do for him." His teeth were gritting.

Blaustein said, "He left a note."

"A note?"

Darrity handed him a sheet of paper and said, "Suicides almost always do. This is one reason the doctor told me about what really killed Ralson."

The note was addressed to Blaustein and it went:

"The projector works; I knew it would. The bargain is done. You've got it and you don't need me anymore. So I'll go. You needn't worry about the human race, Doc. You were right. They've bred us too long; they've taken too many chances. We're out of the culture now and they won't be able to stop us. I know. That's all I can say. I know."

He had signed his name quickly and then underneath there was one scrawled line, and it said:

"Provided enough men are penicillin-resistant."

Grant made a motion to crumple the paper, but Darrity held out a quick hand.

"For the record, Doctor," he said.

Grant gave it to him and said, "Poor Ralson! He died believing all that trash."

Blaustein nodded. "So he did. Ralson will be given a great funeral, I suppose, and the fact of his invention will be publicized without the madness and the suicide. But the government men will remain interested in his mad theories. They may not be so mad, no, Mr. Darrity?"

"That's ridiculous, Doctor," said Grant. "There isn't a scientist on the job who has shown the least uneasiness about it at all."

"Tell him, Mr. Darrity," said Blaustein.

Darrity said, "There has been another suicide. No, no, none of the scientists. No one with a degree. It happened this morning, and we investigated because we thought it might have some connection with today's test. There didn't seem any, and we were going to keep it quiet till the test was over. Only now there seems to be a connection.

"The man who died was just a guy with a wife and three kids. No reason to die. No history of mental illness. He threw himself under a car. We have witnesses, and it's certain he did it on purpose. He didn't die right away and they got a doctor to him. He was horribly mangled, but his last words were 'I feel much better now' and he died."

"But who was he?" cried Grant.

"Hal Ross. The guy who actually built the projector. The guy whose office this is."

Blaustein walked to the window. The evening sky was darkening into starriness.

He said, "The man knew nothing about Ralson's views. He had never spoken to Ralson, Mr. Darrity tells me. Scientists are probably resistant as a whole. They must be or they are quickly driven out of the profession. Ralson was an exception, a penicillin-sensitive who insisted on remaining. You see what happened to him. But what about the others; those who have remained in walks of life where there is no constant weeding out of the sensitive ones. How much of humanity *is* penicillin-resistant?"

"You *believe* Ralson?" asked Grant in horror.

"I don't really know."

Blaustein looked at the stars.

Incubators?

PREFACE TO
C-CHUTE

FIRST APPEARANCE—*GALAXY SCIENCE FICTION,* October 1951. Copyright 1951, by Galaxy Publishing Corporation.

In 1950, the Korean War broke out and that was a depressing time indeed, almost as depressing as the present. I will not conceal from you that I am not enthusiastic over what Othello called the "quality, pride, pomp, and circumstance of glorious war."

World War II had been something unique. That was one war there could be few idealistic qualms over. We were fighting an absolute evil that seemed quite beyond the usual defame-the-enemy routine; and there seemed a reasonable hope that once the war was over there would be some way of setting up a form of world organization to prevent future wars.

The euphoria of the days of the immediate end of the war and of the setting up of the United Nations didn't last long and the Korean War spelled final ruin to the first great hopes.

You might think that we science fiction writers were luckier than most. We had so nice a way of "escaping." Off we could go into space, leaving the Earth-bound problems of the day behind us. Well, escape isn't that easy. It is harder than you think to divorce yourself from reality, and when, in the days of Korea, I blasted off in my spaceship for the empty distances between the stars, what did I find? An interstellar war, a battle for a spaceship.

I wasn't escaping at all!

But one more thing. Before the days of television there was something called radio, and in the late 1940s and early 1950s, we had science fiction on it. Radio didn't have the problem of the complicated and expensive sets that television requires in order to give a semblance of reality to science fiction. It can do everything with sound effects, and the proper sounds can be made into the most bizarre visual effects in the mind.

The programs involved—"Two Thousand Plus" and "Dimension X"—were, unfortunately, not heavily sponsored when they were sponsored at all and they did not last long, but while they were on, they were intensely satisfying to me. What's more, they ran no less than three of my stories. One of them was "Nightfall" (of course), and a second was "C-Chute."

In the radio version of "C-Chute," Mullen was played by an actor with a distinctive voice—dry, restrained, unemotional, and gentle. It was exactly Mullen's voice. Once television came in, I found that voice, and matched the face to it, and that *looked* like Mullen.

It is so pleasant, every time I see him, to be able to say (despite the fact that he is a fairly tall man), "There's Mullen." Mullen is the only one of all my characters I have seen in the flesh, and I have carefully refrained from ever finding out the actor's real name. I want him to remain Mullen.

C-CHUTE

Even from the cabin into which he and the other passengers had been herded, Colonel Anthony Windham could still catch the essence of the battle's progress. For a while, there was silence, no jolting, which meant the spaceships were fighting at astronomical distance in a duel of energy blasts and powerful force-field defenses.

He knew that could have only one end. Their Earth ship was only an armed merchantman and his glimpse of the Kloro enemy just before he had been cleared off deck by the crew was sufficient to show it to be a light cruiser.

And in less than half an hour, there came those hard little shocks he was waiting for. The passengers swayed back and forth as the ship pitched and veered, as though it were an ocean liner in a storm. But space was calm and silent as ever. It was their pilot sending desperate bursts of steam through the steam-tubes, so that by reaction the ship would be sent rolling and tumbling. It could only mean that the inevitable had occurred. The Earth ship's screens had been drained and it no longer dared withstand a direct hit.

Colonel Windham tried to steady himself with his aluminum cane.

He was thinking that he was an old man; that he had spent his life in the militia and had never seen a battle; that now, with a battle going on around him, he was old and fat and lame and had no men under his command.

They would be boarding soon, those Kloro monsters. It was their way of fighting. They would be handicapped by spacesuits and their casualties would be high, but they wanted the Earth ship. Windham considered the passengers. For a moment, he thought, *if they were armed and I could lead them—*

He abandoned the thought. Porter was in an obvious state of funk and the young boy, Leblanc, was hardly better. The Polyorketes brothers—dash it, he *couldn't* tell them apart—huddled in a corner speaking only to one another. Mullen was a different matter. He sat perfectly erect, with no signs of fear or any other emotion in his face. But the man was just about five feet tall and had undoubtedly never held a gun of any sort in his hands in all his life. He could do nothing.

And there was Stuart, with his frozen half-smile and the high-pitched sarcasm which saturated all he said. Windham looked sidelong at Stuart now as Stuart sat there, pushing his dead-white hands through his sandy hair. With those artificial hands he was useless, anyway.

Windham felt the shuddering vibration of ship-to-ship contact; and in five minutes, there was the noise of the fight through the corridors. One of the Polyorketes brothers screamed and dashed for the door. The other called, "Aristides! Wait!" and hurried after.

It happened so quickly. Aristides was out the door and into the corridor, running in brainless panic. A carbonizer glowed briefly and there was never even a scream. Windham, from the doorway, turned in horror at the blackened stump of what was left. Strange—a lifetime in uniform and he had never before seen a man killed in violence.

It took the combined force of the rest to carry the other brother back struggling into the room.

The noise of battle subsided.

Stuart said, "That's it. They'll put a prize crew of two aboard and take us to one of their home planets. We're prisoners of war, naturally."

"Only two of the Kloros will stay aboard?" asked Windham, astonished.

Stuart said, "It is their custom. Why do you ask, Colonel? Thinking of leading a gallant raid to retake the ship?"

Windham flushed. "Simply a point of information, dash it." But the dignity and tone of authority he tried to assume failed him, he knew. He was simply an old man with a limp.

And Stuart was probably right. He had lived among the Kloros and knew their ways.

JOHN STUART HAD claimed from the beginning that the Kloros were gentlemen. Twenty-four hours of imprisonment had passed, and now he repeated the statement as he flexed the fingers of his hands and watched the crinkles come and go in the soft artiplasm.

He enjoyed the unpleasant reaction it aroused in the others. People were made to be punctured; windy bladders, all of them. And they had hands of the same stuff as their bodies.

There was Anthony Windham, in particular. Colonel Windham, he called himself, and Stuart was willing to believe it. A retired colonel who had probably drilled a home guard militia on a village green, forty years ago, with such lack of distinction that he was not called back to service in any capacity, even during the emergency of Earth's first interstellar war.

"Dashed unpleasant thing to be saying about the enemy, Stuart. Don't know that I like your attitude." Windham seemed to push the words through his clipped mustache. His head had been shaven, too, in imitation of the current military style, but now a gray stubble was beginning to show about a centered bald patch. His flabby cheeks dragged downward. That and the fine red lines on his thick nose gave him a somewhat undone appearance, as though he had been wakened too suddenly and too early in the morning.

Stuart said, "Nonsense. Just reverse the present situation. Suppose an Earth warship had taken a Kloro liner. What do you think would have happened to any Kloro civilians aboard?"

"I'm sure the Earth fleet would observe all the interstellar rules of war," Windham said stiffly.

"Except that there aren't any. If we landed a prize crew on one of their ships, do you think we'd take the trouble to maintain a chlorine atmosphere for the benefit of the survivors; allow them to keep their non-contraband possessions; give them the use of the most comfortable stateroom, etcetera, etcetera, etcetera?"

Ben Porter said, "Oh, shut up, for God's sake. If I hear your etcetera, etcetera once again, I'll go nuts."

Stuart said, "Sorry!" He wasn't.

Porter was scarcely responsible. His thin face and beaky nose glistened with perspiration, and he kept biting the inside of his cheek until he suddenly winced. He put his tongue against the sore spot, which made him look even more clownish.

Stuart was growing weary of baiting them. Windham was too flabby a target and Porter could do nothing but writhe. The rest were silent. Demetrios Polyorketes was off in a world of silent internal grief for the moment. He had not slept the night before, most probably. At least, whenever Stuart woke to change his position—he himself had been rather restless—there had been Polyorketes' thick mumble from the next cot. It said many things, but the moan to which it returned over and over again was, "Oh, my brother!"

He sat dumbly on his cot now, his red eyes rolling at the other prisoners out of his broad swarthy, unshaven face. As Stuart watched, his face sank into calloused palms so that only his mop of crisp and curly black hair could be seen. He rocked gently, but now that they were all awake, he made no sound.

Claude Leblanc was trying very unsuccessfully, to read a letter. He was the youngest of the six, scarcely out of college, returning to Earth to get married. Stuart had found him that morning weeping quietly, his pink and white face flushed and blotched as though it were a heartbroken child's. He was very fair, with almost a girl's beauty about his large blue eyes and full lips. Stuart wondered what kind of girl it was who had promised to be his wife. He had seen her picture. Who on the ship had not? She had the characterless prettiness that makes all pictures of fiancees indistinguishable. It seemed to Stuart that if he were a girl, however, he would want someone a little more pronouncedly masculine.

That left only Randolph Mullen. Stuart frankly did not have the least idea what to make of him. He was the only one of the six that had been on the Arcturian worlds for any length of time. Stuart, himself, for instance, had been there only long enough to give a series of lectures on astronautical engineering at the provincial engineering institute. Colonel Windham had been on a Cook's tour; Porter was trying to buy concentrated alien vegetables for his canneries on Earth; and the Polyorketes brothers had attempted to establish themselves in Arcturus as truck farmers and, after two growing seasons, gave it up, had somehow unloaded at a profit, and were returning to Earth.

Randolph Mullen, however, had been in the Arcturian system for seventeen years. How did voyagers discover so much about one another so quickly? As far as Stuart knew, the little man had scarcely spoken aboard ship. He was unfailingly polite, always stepped to one side to allow another to pass, but his entire vocabulary appeared to consist only of "Thank you" and "Pardon me." Yet the word had gone around that this was his first trip to Earth in seventeen years.

He was a little man, very precise, almost irritatingly so. Upon awaking that morning, he had made his cot neatly, shaved, bathed and dressed. The habit of years seemed not in the least disturbed by the fact that he was a prisoner of the Kloros now. He was unobtrusive about it, it had to be admitted, and gave no impression of disapproving of the sloppiness of the others. He simply sat there, almost apologetic, trussed in his overconservative clothing, and hands loosely clasped in his lap. The thin line of hair on his upper lip, far from adding character to his face, absurdly increased its primness.

He looked like someone's idea of a caricature of a bookkeeper. And the queer thing about it all, Stuart thought, was that that was exactly what he was. He had noticed it on the registry—Randolph Fluellen Mullen; occupation, bookkeeper; employers, Prime Paper Box Co.; 27 Tobias Avenue, New Warsaw, Arcturus II.

"MR. STUART?"

Stuart looked up. It was Leblanc, his lower lip trembling slightly. Stuart tried to remember how one went about being gentle. He said, "What is it, Leblanc?"

"Tell me, when will they let us go?"

"How should I know?"

"Everyone says you lived on a Kloro planet, and just now you said they were gentlemen."

"Well, yes. But even gentlemen fight wars in order to win. Probably, we'll be interned for the duration."

"But that could be *years!* Margaret is waiting. She'll think I'm *dead!*"

"I suppose they'll allow messages to be sent through once we're on their planet."

Porter's hoarse voice sounded in agitation. "Look here, if you know so much about these devils, what will they do to us while we're interned? What will they feed us? Where will they get oxygen for us? They'll kill us, I tell you." And as an afterthought, "I've got a wife waiting for me, too," he added.

But Stuart had heard him speaking of his wife in the days before the attack. He wasn't impressed. Porter's nail-bitten fingers were pulling and plucking at Stuart's sleeve. Stuart drew away in sharp revulsion. He couldn't stand those ugly hands. It angered him to desperation that such monstrosities should be real while his own white and perfectly shaped hands were only mocking imitations grown out of an alien latex.

He said, "They won't kill us. If they were going to, they would have done it before now. Look, we capture Kloros too, you know, and it's just a matter of common sense to treat your prisoners decently if you want the other side to be decent to your men. They'll do their best. The food may not be very good, but they're better chemists than we are. It's what they're best at. They'll know exactly what food factors we'll need and how many calories. We'll live. They'll see to that."

Windham rumbled, "You sound more and more like a blasted greenie sympathizer, Stuart. It turns my stomach to hear an Earthman speak well of the green fellas the way you've been doing. Burn it, man, where's your loyalty?"

"My loyalty's where it belongs. With honesty and decency, regardless of the shape of the being it appears in." Stuart held up his hands. "See these? Kloros made them. I lived on one of their planets for six months. My hands were mangled in the conditioning machinery of my own quarters. I thought the oxygen supply they gave me was a little poor—it wasn't, by the way—and I tried making the adjustments on my own. It was my fault. You should never trust yourself with the machines of another culture. By the time someone among the Kloros could put on an atmosphere suit and get to me, it was too late to save my hands.

"They grew these artiplasm things for me and operated. You know what that meant? It meant designing equipment and nutrient solutions that would work in oxygen atmosphere. It meant that their surgeons had to perform a delicate operation while dressed in atmosphere suits. And now I've got hands again." He laughed harshly, and clenched them into weak fists. "Hands—"

Windham said, "And you'd sell your loyalty to Earth for that?"

"Sell my loyalty? You're mad. For years, I hated the Kloros for this. I was a master pilot on the Trans-Galactic Spacelines before it happened. Now? Desk job. Or an occasional lecture. It took me a long time to pin the fault on myself and to realize that the only role played by the Kloros was a decent one. They have their code of ethics, and it's as good as ours. If it weren't for the stupidity of some of their people—and, by God, of some of ours—we wouldn't be at war. And after it's over—"

Polyorketes was on his feet. His thick fingers curved inward before him and his dark eyes glittered. "I don't like what you say, mister."

"Why don't you?"

"Because you talk too nice about these damned green bastards. The Kloros were good to you, eh? Well, they weren't good to my brother. They killed him. I think maybe I kill you, you damned greenie spy."

And he charged.

Stuart barely had time to raise his arms to meet the infuriated farmer. He gasped out, "What the hell—" as he caught one wrist and heaved a shoulder to block the other which groped toward his throat.

His artiplasm hand gave way. Polyorketes wrenched free with scarcely an effort.

Windham was bellowing incoherently, and Leblanc was calling out in his reedy voice, "Stop it! Stop it!" But it was little Mullen who threw his arms about the farmer's neck from behind and pulled with all his might. He was not very effective; Polyorketes seemed scarcely aware of the little man's weight upon his back. Mullen's feet left the floor so that he tossed helplessly to right and left. But he held his grip and it hampered Polyorketes sufficiently to allow Stuart to break free long enough to grasp Windham's aluminum cane.

He said, "Stay away, Polyorketes."

He was gasping for breath and fearful of another rush. The hollow aluminum cylinder was scarcely heavy enough to accomplish much, but it was better than having only his weak hands to defend himself with.

Mullen had loosed his hold and was now circling cautiously, his breathing roughened and his jacket in disarray.

Polyorketes, for a moment, did not move. He stood there, his shaggy head bent low. Then he said, "It is no use. I must kill Kloros. Just watch your tongue, Stuart. If it keeps on rattling too much, you're liable to get hurt. Really hurt, I mean."

Stuart passed a forearm over his forehead and thrust the cane back at Windham, who seized it with his left hand, while mopping his bald pate vigorously with a handkerchief in his right.

Windham said, "Gentlemen, we must avoid this. It lowers our prestige. We must remember the common enemy. We are Earthmen and we must act what we are—the ruling race of the Galaxy. We dare not demean ourselves before the lesser breeds."

"Yes, Colonel," said Stuart, wearily. "Give us the rest of the speech tomorrow."

He turned to Mullen, "I want to say thanks."

He was uncomfortable about it, but he had to. The little accountant had surprised him completely.

But Mullen said, in a dry voice that scarcely raised above a whisper, "Don't thank me, Mr. Stuart. It was the logical thing to do. If we are to be interned, we would need you as an interpreter, perhaps, one who would understand the Kloros."

Stuart stiffened. It was, he thought, too much of the bookkeeper type of reasoning, too logical, too dry of juice. Present risk and ultimate advantage. The assets and debits balanced neatly. He would have liked Mullen to leap to his defense out of—well, out of what? Out of pure, unselfish decency?

Stuart laughed silently at himself. He was beginning to expect idealism of human beings, rather than good, straightforward, self-centered motivation.

POLYORKETES WAS NUMB. His sorrow and rage were like acid inside him, but they had no words to get out. If he were Stuart, big-mouth, white-hands Stuart, he could talk and talk and maybe feel better. Instead, he had to sit there with half of him dead; with no brother, no Aristides—

It had happened so quickly. If he could only go back and have one second more warning, so that he might snatch Aristides, hold him, save him.

But mostly he hated the Kloros. Two months ago, he had hardly ever heard of them, and now he hated them so hard, he would be glad to die if he could kill a few.

He said, without looking up, "What happened to start this war, eh?"

He was afraid Stuart's voice would answer. He hated Stuart's voice. But it was Windham, the bald one.

Windham said, "The immediate cause, sir, was a dispute over mining concessions in the Wyandotte system. The Kloros had poached on Earth property."

"Room for both, Colonel!"

Polyorketes looked up at that, snarling. Stuart could not be kept quiet for long. He was speaking again; the cripple-hand, wiseguy, Kloros-lover.

Stuart was saying, "Is that anything to fight over, Colonel? We can't use one another's worlds. Their chlorine planets are useless to us and our oxygen ones are useless to them. Chlorine is deadly to us and oxygen is deadly to them. There's no way we could maintain permanent hostility. Our races just don't coincide. Is there reason to fight then because both races want to dig iron out of the same airless planetoids when there are millions like them in the Galaxy?"

Windham said, "There is the question of planetary honor—"

"Planetary fertilizer. How can it excuse a ridiculous war like this one? It can only be fought on outposts. It has to come down to a series of holding actions and eventually be settled by negotiations that might just as easily have been worked out in the first place. Neither we nor the Kloros will gain a thing."

Grudgingly, Polyorketes found that he agreed with Stuart. What did he and Aristides care where Earth or the Kloros got their iron?

Was that something for Aristides to die over?

The little warning buzzer sounded.

Polyorketes' head shot up and he rose slowly, his lips drawing back. Only one thing could be at the door. He waited, arms tense, fists balled. Stuart was edging toward him. Polyorketes saw that and laughed to himself. Let the Kloro come in, and Stuart, along with all the rest, could not stop him.

Wait, Aristides, wait just a moment, and a fraction of revenge will be paid back.

The door opened and a figure entered, completely swathed in a shapeless, billowing travesty of a spacesuit.

An odd, unnatural, but not entirely unpleasant voice began, "It is with some misgivings, Earthmen, that my companion and myself—"

It ended abruptly as Polyorketes, with a roar, charged once again. There was no science in the lunge. It was sheer bull-momentum. Dark head low, burly arms spread out with the hair-tufted fingers in choking position, he clumped on. Stuart was whirled to one side before he had a chance to intervene, and was spun tumbling across a cot.

The Kloro might have, without undue exertion, straight-armed Polyorketes to a halt, or stepped aside, allowing the whirlwind to pass. He did neither. With a rapid movement, a hand-weapon was up and a gentle pinkish line of radiance connected it with the plunging Earthman. Polyorketes stumbled and crashed down, his body maintaining its last curved position, one foot raised, as though a lightning paralysis had taken place. It toppled to one side and he lay there, eyes all alive and wild with rage.

The Kloro said, "He is not permanently hurt." He seemed not to resent the offered violence. Then he began again, "It is with some misgiving, Earthmen, that my companion and myself were made aware of a certain commotion in this room. Are you in any need which we can satisfy?"

Stuart was angrily nursing his knee which he had scraped in colliding with the cot. He said, "No, thank you, Kloro."

"Now, look here," puffed Windham, "this is a dashed outrage. We demand that our release be arranged."

The Kloro's tiny, insectlike head turned in the fat old man's direction. He was not a pleasant sight to anyone unused to him. He was about the height of an Earthman, but the top of him consisted of a thin stalk of a neck with a head that was the merest swelling. It consisted of a blunt triangular proboscis in front and two bulging eyes on either side. That was all. There was no brain pan and no brain. What corresponded to the brain in a Kloro was located in what would be an Earthly abdomen, leaving the head as a mere sensory organ. The Kloro's spacesuit followed the outlines of the head more or less faithfully, the two eyes being exposed by two clear semicircles of glass, which looked faintly green because of the chlorine atmosphere inside.

One of the eyes was now cocked squarely at Windham, who quivered uncomfortably under the glance, but insisted, "You have no right to hold us prisoner. We are noncombatants."

The Kloro's voice, sounding thoroughly artificial, came from a small attachment of chromium mesh on what served as its chest. The voice box was manipulated by compressed air under the control of one or two of the many delicate, forked tendrils that radiated from two circles about its upper body and were, mercifully enough, hidden by the suit.

The voice said, "Are you serious, Earthman? Surely you have heard of war and rules of war and prisoners of war."

It looked about, shifting eyes with quick jerks of its head, staring at a particular object first with one, then with another. It was Stuart's understanding that each eye transferred a separate message to the abdominal brain, which had to coordinate the two to obtain full information.

Windham had nothing to say. No one had. The Kloro, its four main limbs, roughly arms and legs in pairs, had a vaguely human appearance under the masking of the suit, if you looked no higher than its chest, but there was no way of telling what it felt.

They watched it turn and leave.

PORTER COUGHED AND said in a strangled voice, "God, smell that chlorine. If they don't do something, we'll all die of rotted lungs."

Stuart said, "Shut up. There isn't enough chlorine in the air to make a mosquito sneeze, and what there is will be swept out in two minutes. Besides, a little chlorine is good for you. It may kill your cold virus."

Windham coughed and said, "Stuart, I feel that you might have said something to your Kloro friend about releasing us. You are scarcely as bold in their presence, dash it, as you are once they are gone."

"You heard what the creature said, Colonel. We're prisoners of war, and prisoner exchanges are negotiated by diplomats. We'll just have to wait."

Leblanc, who had turned pasty white at the entrance of the Kloro, rose and hurried into the privy. There was the sound of retching.

An uncomfortable silence fell while Stuart tried to think of something to say to cover the unpleasant sound. Mullen filled in. He had rummaged through a little box he had taken from under his pillow.

He said, "Perhaps Mr. Leblanc had better take a sedative before retiring. I have a few. I'd be glad to give him one." He explained his generosity immediately, "Otherwise he may keep the rest of us awake, you see."

"Very logical," said Stuart, dryly. "You'd better save one for Sir Launcelot here; save half a dozen." He walked to where Polyorketes still sprawled and knelt at his side. "Comfortable, baby?"

Windham said, "Deuced poor taste speaking like that, Stuart."

"Well, if you're so concerned about him, why don't you and Porter hoist him onto his cot?"

He helped them do so. Polyorketes' arms were trembling erratically now. From what Stuart knew of the Kloro's nerve weapons, the man should be in an agony of pins and needles about now.

Stuart said, "And don't be too gentle with him, either. The damned fool might have gotten us all killed. And for what?"

He pushed Polyorketes' stiff carcass to one side and sat at the edge of the cot. He said, "Can you hear me, Polyorketes?"

Polyorketes' eyes gleamed. An arm lifted abortively and fell back.

"Okay then, listen. Don't try anything like that again. The next time it may be the finish for all of us. If you had been a Kloro and he had been an Earthman, we'd be dead now. So just get one thing through your skull. We're sorry about your brother and it's a rotten shame, but it was his own fault."

Polyorketes tried to heave and Stuart pushed him back.

"No, you keep on listening," he said. "Maybe this is the only time I'll get to talk to you when you *have* to listen. Your brother had no right leaving passengers' quarters. There was no place for him to go. He just got in the way of our own men. We don't even know for certain that it was a Kloro gun that killed him. It might have been one of our own."

"Oh, I say, Stuart," objected Windham.

Stuart whirled at him. "Do you have proof it wasn't? Did you see the shot? Could you tell from what was left of the body whether it was Kloro energy or Earth energy?"

Polyorketes found his voice, driving his unwilling tongue into a fuzzy verbal snarl. "Damned stinking greenie bastard."

"Me?" said Stuart. "I know what's going on in your mind, Polyorketes. You think that when the paralysis wears off, you'll ease your feelings by slamming me around. Well, if you do, it will probably be curtains for all of us."

He rose, put his back against the wall. For the moment, he was fighting all of them. "None of you know the Kloros the way I do. The physical differences you see are not important. The differences in their temperament are. They don't understand our views on sex, for instance. To them, it's just a biological reflex like breathing. They attach no importance to it. But they *do* attach importance to social groupings. Remember, their evolutionary ancestors had lots in common with our insects. They always assume that any group of Earthmen they find together makes up a social unit.

"That means just about everything to them. I don't understand exactly *what* it means. No Earthman can. But the result is that they never break up a group, just as we don't separate a mother and her children if we can help it. One of the reasons they may be treating us with kid gloves right now is that they imagine we're all broken up over the fact that they killed one of us, and they feel guilt about it.

"But this is what you'll have to remember. We're going to be interned together and *kept* together for duration. I don't like the thought. I wouldn't have picked any of you for co-internees and I'm pretty sure none of you would have picked me. But there it is. The Kloros could never understand that our being together on the ship is only accidental.

"That means we've got to get along somehow. That's not just goodie-goodie talk about birds in their little nest agreeing. What do you think would have happened if the Kloros had come in earlier and found Polyorketes and myself trying to kill each other? You don't know? Well, what do you suppose *you* would think of a mother you caught trying to kill her children?

"That's it, then. They would have killed every one of us as a bunch of Kloro-type perverts and monsters. Got that? How about you, Polyorketes? Have *you* got it? So let's call names if we have to, but let's keep our hands to ourselves. And now, if none of you mind, I'll massage my hands back into shape—these synthetic hands that I got from the Kloros and that one of my own kind tried to mangle again."

FOR CLAUDE LEBLANC, the worst was over. He had been sick enough; sick with many things; but sick most of all over having ever left Earth. It had been a great thing to go to college off Earth. It had been an adventure and had taken him away from his mother. Somehow, he had been sneakingly glad to make that escape after the first month of frightened adjustment.

And then on the summer holidays, he had been no longer Claude, the shy-spoken scholar, but Leblanc, space traveler. He had swaggered the fact for all it was worth. It made him feel such a man to talk of stars and Jumps and the customs and environments of other worlds; it had given him courage with Margaret. She had loved him for the dangers he had undergone—

Except that this had been the first one, really, and he had not done so well. He knew it and was ashamed and wished he were like Stuart.

He used the excuse of mealtime to approach. He said, "Mr. Stuart."

Stuart looked up and said shortly, "How do you feel?"

Leblanc felt himself blush. He blushed easily and the effort not to blush only made it worse. He said, "Much better, thank you. We are eating. I thought I'd bring you your ration."

Stuart took the offered can. It was standard space ration; thoroughly synthetic, concentrated, nourishing and, somehow, unsatisfying. It heated automatically when the can was opened, but could be eaten cold, if necessary. Though a combined fork-spoon utensil was enclosed, the ration was of a consistency that made the use of fingers practical and not particularly messy.

Stuart said, "Did you hear my little speech?"

"Yes, sir. I want you to know you can count on me."

"Well, good. Now go and eat."

"May I eat here?"

"Suit yourself."

For a moment, they ate in silence, and then Leblanc burst out, "You are so sure of yourself, Mr. Stuart! It must be very wonderful to be like that!"

"Sure of myself? Thanks, but there's your self-assured one."

Leblanc followed the direction of the nod in surprise. "Mr. Mullen? That little man? Oh, no!"

"You don't think he's self-assured?"

Leblanc shook his head. He looked at Stuart intently to see if he could detect humor in his expression. "That one is just cold. He has no emotion in him. He's like a little machine. I find him repulsive. You're different, Mr. Stuart. You have it all inside, but you control it. I would like to be like that."

And as though attracted by the magnetism of the mention, even though unheard, of his name, Mullen joined them. His can of ration was barely touched. It was still steaming gently as he squatted opposite them.

His voice had its usual quality of furtively rustling underbrush. "How long, Mr. Stuart, do you think the trip will take?"

"Can't say, Mullen. They'll undoubtedly be avoiding the usual trade routes and they'll be making more Jumps through hyper-space than usual to throw off possible pursuit. I wouldn't be surprised if it took as long as a week. Why do you ask? I presume you have a very practical and logical reason?"

"Why, yes. Certainly." He seemed quite shellbacked to sarcasm. He said, "It occurred to me that it might be wise to ration the rations, so to speak."

"We've got enough food and water for a month. I checked on that first thing."

"I see. In that case, I will finish the can." He did, using the all-purpose utensil daintily and patting a handkerchief against his unstained lips from time to time.

POLYORKETES STRUGGLED TO his feet some two hours later. He swayed a bit, looking like the Spirit of Hangover. He did not try to come closer to Stuart, but spoke from where he stood.

He said, "You stinking greenie spy, you watch yourself."

"You heard what I said before, Polyorketes."

"I heard. But I also heard what you said about Aristides. I won't bother with you, because you're a bag of nothing but noisy air. But wait, someday you'll blow your air in one face too many and it will be let out of you."

"I'll wait," said Stuart.

Windham hobbled over, leaning heavily on his cane. "Now, now," he called with a wheezing joviality that overlaid his sweating anxiety so thinly as to emphasize it. "We're all Earthmen, dash it. Got to remember that; keep it as a glowing light of inspiration. Never let down before the blasted Kloros. We've got to forget private feuds and remember only that we are Earthmen united against alien blighters."

Stuart's comment was unprintable.

Porter was right behind Windham. He had been in a close conference with the shaven-headed colonel for an hour, and now he said with indignation, "It doesn't help to be a wiseguy, Stuart. You listen to the colonel. We've been doing some hard thinking about the situation."

He had washed some of the grease off his face, wet his hair and slicked it back. It did not remove the little tic on his right cheek just at the point where his lips ended, or make his hangnail hands more attractive in appearance.

"All right, Colonel," said Stuart. "What's on your mind?"

Windham said, "I'd prefer to have all the men together."

"Okay, call them."

Leblanc hurried over; Mullen approached with greater deliberation. Stuart said, "You want that fellow?" He jerked his head at Polyorketes.

"Why, yes. Mr. Polyorketes, may we have you, old fella?"

"Ah, leave me alone."

"Go ahead," said Stuart, "leave him alone. I don't want him."

"No, no," said Windham. "This is a matter for all Earthmen. Mr. Polyorketes, we must have you."

Polyorketes rolled off one side of his cot. "I'm close enough, I can hear you."

Windham said to Stuart, "Would they—the Kloros, I mean—have this room wired?"

"No," said Stuart. "Why should they?"

"Are you sure?"

"Of course I'm sure. They didn't know what happened when Polyorketes jumped me. They just heard the thumping when it started rattling the ship."

"Maybe they were trying to give us the impression the room wasn't wired."

"Listen, Colonel, I've never known a Kloro to tell a deliberate lie—"

Polyorketes interrupted calmly, "That lump of noise just *loves* the Kloros."

Windham said hastily, "Let's not begin that. Look, Stuart, Porter and I have been discussing matters and we have decided that you know the Kloros well enough to think of some way of getting us back to Earth."

"It happens that you're wrong. I can't think of any way."

"Maybe there is some way we can take the ship back from the blasted green fellas," suggested Windham. "Some weakness they may have. Dash it, you know what I mean."

"Tell me, Colonel, what are you after? Your own skin or Earth's welfare?"

"I resent that question. I'll have you know that while I'm as careful of my own life as anyone has a right to be, I'm thinking of Earth primarily. And I think that's true of all of us."

"Damn right," said Porter, instantly. Leblanc looked anxious, Polyorketes resentful; and Mullen had no expression at all.

"Good," said Stuart. "Of course, I don't think we can take the ship. They're armed and we aren't. But there's this. You know why the Kloros took this ship intact. It's because they need ships. They may be better chemists than Earthmen are, but Earthmen are better astronautical engineers. We have bigger, better and more ships. In fact, if our crew had had a proper respect for military axioms in the first place, they would have blown the ship up as soon as it looked as though the Kloros were going to board."

Leblanc looked horrified. "And kill the passengers?"

"Why not? You heard what the good colonel said. Every one of us puts his own lousy little life after Earth's interests. What good are we to Earth alive right now? None at all. What harm will this ship do in Kloro hands? A hell of a lot, probably."

"Just why," asked Mullen, "did our men refuse to blow up the ship? They must have had a reason."

"They did. It's the firmest tradition of Earth's military men that there must never be an unfavorable ratio of casualties. If we had blown ourselves up, twenty fighting men and seven civilians of Earth would be dead as compared with an enemy casualty total of zero. So what happens? We let them board, kill twenty-eight—I'm sure we killed at least that many—and let them have the ship."

"Talk, talk, talk," jeered Polyorketes.

"There's a moral to this," said Stuart. "We can't take the ship away from the Kloros. We *might* be able to rush them, though, and keep them busy long enough to allow one of us enough time to short the engines."

"What?" yelled Porter, and Windham shushed him in fright.

"Short the engines," Stuart repeated. "That would destroy the ship, of course, which is what we want to do, isn't it?"

Leblanc's lips were white. "I don't think that would work."

"We can't be sure till we try. But what have we to lose by trying?"

"Our lives, damn it!" cried Porter. "You insane maniac, you're crazy!"

"If I'm a maniac," said Stuart, "and insane to boot, then naturally I'm crazy. But just remember that if we lose our lives, which is over-whelmingly probable, we lose nothing of value to Earth; whereas if we destroy the ship, as we just barely might, we do Earth a lot of good. What patriot would hesitate? Who here would put himself ahead of his world?" He looked about in the silence. "Surely not you, Colonel Windham."

Windham coughed tremendously. "My dear man, that is not the question. There must be a way to save the ship for Earth *without* losing our lives, eh?"

"All right. You name it."

"Let's all think about it. Now there are only two of the Kloros aboard ship. If one of us could sneak up on them and—"

"How? The rest of the ship's all filled with chlorine. We'd have to wear a spacesuit. Gravity in their part of the ship is hopped up to Kloro level, so whoever is patsy in the deal would be clumping around, metal on metal, slow and heavy. Oh, he could sneak up on them, sure—like a skunk trying to sneak downwind."

"Then we'll drop it all," Porter's voice shook. "Listen, Windham, there's not going to be any destroying the ship. My life means plenty to me and if any of you try anything like that, I'll call the Kloros. I mean it."

"Well," said Stuart, "there's hero number one."

Leblanc said, "I want to go back to Earth, but I—"

Mullen interrupted, "I don't think our chances of destroying the ship are good enough unless—"

"Heroes number two and three. What about you, Polyorketes? You would have the chance of killing two Kloros."

"I want to kill them with my bare hands," growled the farmer, his heavy fists writhing. "On their planet, I will kill dozens."

"That's a nice safe promise for now. What about you, Colonel? Don't you want to march to death and glory with me?"

"Your attitude is very cynical and unbecoming, Stuart. It's obvious that if the rest are unwilling, then your plan will fall through."

"Unless I do it myself, huh?"

"You won't, do you hear?" said Porter, instantly.

"Damn right I won't," agreed Stuart. "I don't claim to be a hero. I'm just an average patriot, perfectly willing to head for any planet they take me to and sit out the war."

MULLEN SAID, THOUGHTFULLY, "Of course, there *is* a way we could surprise the Kloros."

The statement would have dropped flat except for Polyorketes. He pointed a black-nailed, stubby forefinger and laughed harshly. "Mr. Bookkeeper!" he said. "Mr. Bookkeeper is a big shot talker like this damned greenie spy, Stuart. All right, Mr. Bookkeeper, go ahead. You make big speeches also. Let the words roll like an empty barrel."

He turned to Stuart and repeated venomously, "Empty barrel! Cripple-hand empty barrel! No good for anything but talk."

Mullen's soft voice could make no headway until Polyorketes was through, but then he said, speaking directly to Stuart, "We might be able to reach them from outside. This room has a C-chute I'm sure."

"What's a C-chute?" asked Leblanc.

"Well—" began Mullen, and then stopped, at a loss.

Stuart said, mockingly, "It's a euphemism, my boy. Its full name is 'casualty chute.' It doesn't get talked about, but the main rooms on any ship would have them. They're just little airlocks down which you slide a corpse. Burial at space. Always lots of sentiment and bowed heads, with the captain making a rolling speech of the type Polyorketes here wouldn't like."

Leblanc's face twisted. "Use *that* to leave the ship?"

"Why not? Superstitious?—Go on, Mullen."

The little man had waited patiently. He said, "Once outside, one could re-enter the ship by the steam-tubes. It can be done—with luck. And then you would be an unexpected visitor in the control room."

Stuart stared at him curiously. "How do you figure this out? What do *you* know about steam-tubes?"

Mullen coughed. "You mean because I'm in the paper-box business? Well—" He grew pink, waited a moment, then made a new start in a colorless, unemotional voice. "My company, which manufactures fancy paper boxes and novelty containers, made a line of spaceship candy boxes for the juvenile trade some years ago. It was designed so that if a string were pulled, small pressure containers were punctured and jets of compressed air shot out through the mock steam-tubes, sailing the box across the room and scattering candy as it went. The sales theory was that the youngsters would find it exciting to play with the ship and fun to scramble for the candy.

"Actually, it was a complete failure. The ship would break dishes and sometimes hit another child in the eye. Worse still, the children would not only scramble for the candy but would fight over it. It was almost our worst failure. We lost thousands.

"Still, while the boxes were being designed, the entire office was extremely interested. It was like a game, very bad for efficiency and office morale. For a while, we all became steam-tube experts. I read quite a few books on ship construction. On my own time, however, not the company's."

Stuart was intrigued. He said, "You know it's a video sort of idea, but it might work if we had a hero to spare. Have we?"

"What about you?" demanded Porter, indignantly. "You go around

sneering at us with your cheap wisecracks. I don't notice you volun-
teering for anything."

"That's because I'm no hero, Porter. I admit it. My object is to stay
alive, and shinnying down steam-tubes is no way to go about staying
alive. But the rest of you are noble patriots. The colonel says so. What
about you, Colonel? You're the senior hero here."

Windham said, "If I were younger, blast it, and if you had your
hands, I would take pleasure, sir, in trouncing you soundly."

"I've no doubt of it, but that's no answer."

"You know very well that at my time of life and with my leg—" he
brought the flat of his hand down upon his stiff knee—"I am in no
position to do anything of the sort, however much I should wish to."

"Ah, yes," said Stuart, "and I, myself, am crippled in the hands, as
Polyorketes tells me. That saves us. And what unfortunate deformities
do the rest of us have?"

"Listen," cried Porter, "I want to know what this is all about. How
can anyone go down the steam-tubes? What if the Kloros use them
while one of us is inside?"

"Why, Porter, that's part of the sporting chance. It's where the excitement comes in."

"But he'd be boiled in the shell like a lobster."

"A pretty image, but inaccurate. The steam wouldn't be on for more
than a very short time, maybe a second or two, and the suit insulation
would hold that long. Besides, the jet comes scooting out at several
hundred miles a minute, so that you would be blown clear of the ship
before the steam could even warm you. In fact, you'd be blown quite a
few miles out into space, and after that you would be quite safe from
the Kloros. Of course, you couldn't get back to the ship."

Porter was sweating freely. "You don't scare me for one minute,
Stuart."

"I don't? Then you're offering to go? Are you sure you've thought
out what being stranded in space means? You're all alone, you know;
really all alone. The steam-jet will probably leave you turning or tumbling pretty rapidly. You won't feel that. You'll seem to be motionless.
But all the stars will be going around and around so that they're just
streaks in the sky. They won't ever stop. They won't even slow up.
Then your heater will go off, your oxygen will give out, and you will
die very slowly. You'll have lots of time to think. Or, if you are in a

hurry, you could open your suit. That wouldn't be pleasant, either. I've seen faces of men who had a torn suit happen to them accidentally, and it's pretty awful. But it would be quicker. Then—"

Porter turned and walked unsteadily away.

Stuart said, lightly, "Another failure. One act of heroism still ready to be knocked down to the highest bidder with nothing offered yet."

Polyorketes spoke up and his harsh voice roughed the words. "You keep on talking, Mr. Big Mouth. You just keep banging that empty barrel. Pretty soon, we'll kick your teeth in. There's one boy I think would be willing to do it now, eh, Mr. Porter?"

Porter's look at Stuart confirmed the truth of Polyorketes' remarks, but he said nothing.

Stuart said, "Then what about you, Polyorketes? You're the bare-hand man with guts. Want me to help you into a suit?"

"I'll ask you when I want help."

"What about you, Leblanc?"

The young man shrank away.

"Not even to get back to Margaret?"

But Leblanc could only shake his head.

"Mullen?"

"Well—I'll try."

"You'll what?"

"I said, yes, I'll try. After all, it's my idea."

Stuart looked stunned. "You're serious? How come?"

Mullen's prim mouth pursed. "Because no one else will."

"But that's no reason. Especially for you."

Mullen shrugged.

There was a thump of a cane behind Stuart. Windham brushed past. He said, "Do you really intend to go, Mullen?"

"Yes, Colonel."

"In that case, dash it, let me shake your hand. I like you. You're an—an Earthman, by heaven. Do this, and win or die, I'll bear witness for you."

Mullen withdrew his hand awkwardly from the deep and vibrating grasp of the other.

And Stuart just stood there. He was in a very unusual position. He was, in fact, in the particular position of all positions in which he most rarely found himself.

He had nothing to say.

THE QUALITY OF tension had changed. The gloom and frustration had lifted a bit, and the excitement of conspiracy had replaced it. Even Polyorketes was fingering the spacesuits and commenting briefly and hoarsely on which he considered preferable.

Mullen was having a certain amount of trouble. The suit hung rather limply upon him even though the adjustable joints had been tightened nearly to minimum. He stood there now with only the helmet to be screwed on. He wiggled his neck.

Stuart was holding the helmet with an effort. It was heavy, and his artiplasmic hands did not grip it well. He said, "Better scratch your nose if it itches. It's your last chance for a while." He didn't add, "Maybe forever," but he thought it.

Mullen said, tonelessly, "I think perhaps I had better have a spare oxygen cylinder."

"Good enough."

"With a reducing valve."

Stuart nodded. "I see what you're thinking of. If you do get blown clear of the ship, you could try to blow yourself back by using the cylinder as an action-reaction motor."

They clamped on the headpiece and buckled the spare cylinder to Mullen's waist. Polyorketes and Leblanc lifted him up to the yawning opening of the C-tube. It was ominously dark inside, the metal lining of the interior having been painted a mournful black. Stuart thought he could detect a musty odor about it, but that, he knew, was only imagination.

He stopped the proceedings when Mullen was half within the tube. He tapped upon the little man's faceplate.

"Can you hear me?"

Within, there was a nod.

"Air coming through all right? No last-minute troubles?"

Mullen lifted his armored arm in a gesture of reassurance.

"Then remember, don't use the suit-radio out there. The Kloros might pick up the signals."

Reluctantly, he stepped away. Polyorketes' brawny hands lowered Mullen until they could hear the thumping sound made by the steel-shod feet against the outer valve. The inner valve then swung shut with a dreadful finality, its beveled silicone gasket making a slight soughing noise as it crushed hard. They clamped it into place.

Stuart stood at the toggle-switch that controlled the outer valve. He threw it and the gauge that marked the air pressure within the tube fell to zero. A little pinpoint of red light warned that the outer valve was open. Then the light disappeared, the valve closed, and the gauge climbed slowly to fifteen pounds again.

They opened the inner valve again and found the tube empty.

Polyorketes spoke first. He said, "The little son-of-a-gun. He went!" He looked wonderingly at the others. "A little fellow with guts like that."

Stuart said, "Look, we'd better get ready in here. There's just a chance that the Kloros may have detected the valves opening and closing. If so, they'll be here to investigate and we'll have to cover up."

"How?" asked Windham.

"They won't see Mullen anywhere around. We'll say he's in the head. The Kloros know that it's one of the peculiar characteristics of Earthmen that they resent intrusion on their privacy in lavatories, and they'll make no effort to check. If we can hold them off—"

"What if they wait, or if they check the spacesuits?" asked Porter.

Stuart shrugged. "Let's hope they don't. And listen, Polyorketes, don't make any fuss when they come in."

Polyorketes grunted, "With that little guy out there? What do you think I am?" He stared at Stuart without animosity, then scratched his curly hair vigorously. "You know, I laughed at him. I thought he was an old woman. It makes me ashamed."

Stuart cleared his throat. He said, "Look, I've been saying some things that maybe weren't too funny after all, now that I come to think of it. I'd like to say I'm sorry if I have."

He turned away morosely and walked toward his cot. He heard the steps behind him, felt the touch on his sleeve. He turned; it was Leblanc.

The youngster said softly, "I keep thinking that Mr. Mullen is an old man."

"Well, he's not a kid. He's about forty-five or fifty, I think."

Leblanc said, "Do you think, Mr. Stuart, that *I* should have gone, instead? I'm the youngest here. I don't like the thought of having let an old man go in my place. It makes me feel like the devil."

"I know. If he dies, it will be too bad."

"But he volunteered. We didn't make him, did we?"

"Don't try to dodge responsibility, Leblanc. It won't make you feel better. There isn't one of us without a stronger motive to run the risk than he had." And Stuart sat there silently, thinking.

MULLEN FELT THE obstruction beneath his feet yield and the walls about him slip away quickly, too quickly. He knew it was the puff of air escaping, carrying him with it, and he dug arms and legs frantically against the wall to brake himself. Corpses were supposed to be flung well clear of the ship, but he was no corpse—for the moment.

His feet swung free and threshed. He heard the *clunk* of one magnetic boot against the hull just as the rest of his body puffed out like a tight cork under air pressure. He teetered dangerously at the lip of the hole in the ship—he had changed orientation suddenly and was looking down on it—then took a step backward as its lid came down of itself and fitted smoothly against the hull.

A feeling of unreality overwhelmed him. Surely, it wasn't he standing on the outer surface of a ship. Not Randolph F. Mullen. So few human beings could ever say they had, even those who traveled in space constantly.

He was only gradually aware that he was in pain. Popping out of that hole with one foot clamped to the hull had nearly bent him in two. He tried moving, cautiously, and found his motions to be erratic and almost impossible to control. He *thought* nothing was broken, though the muscles of his left side were badly wrenched.

And then he came to himself and noticed that the wristlights of his suit were on. It was by their light that he had stared into the blackness of the C-chute. He stirred with the nervous thought that from within, the Kloros might see the twin spots of moving light just outside the hull. He flicked the switch upon the suit's midsection.

Mullen had never imagined that, standing on a ship, he would fail to see its hull. But it was dark, as dark below as above. There were the stars, hard and bright little non-dimensional dots. Nothing more. Nothing more anywhere. Under his feet, not even the stars—*not even his feet*.

He bent back to look at the stars. His head swam. They were moving slowly. Or, rather, they were standing still and the ship was rotating, but he could not tell his eyes that. *They* moved. His eyes followed—down and behind the ship. New stars up and above from the other side. A black horizon. The ship existed only as a region where there were no stars.

No stars? Why, there was one almost at his feet. He nearly reached for it; then he realized that it was only a glittering reflection in the mirroring metal.

They were moving thousands of miles an hour. The stars were. The ship was. He was. But it meant nothing. To his senses, there was only silence and darkness and that slow wheeling of the stars. His eyes followed the wheeling—

And his head in its helmet hit the ship's hull with a soft bell-like ring.

He felt about in panic with his thick, insensitive, spun-silicate gloves. His feet were still firmly magnetized to the hull, that was true, but the rest of his body bent backward at the knees in a right angle. There was no gravity outside the ship. If he bent back, there was nothing to pull the upper part of his body down and tell his joints they were bending. His body stayed as he put it.

He pressed wildly against the hull and his torso shot upward and refused to stop when upright. He fell forward.

He tried more slowly, balancing with both hands against the hull, until he squatted evenly. Then upward. Very slowly. Straight up. Arms out to balance.

He was straight now, aware of his nausea and lightheadedness.

He looked about. My God, where were the steam-tubes? He couldn't see them. They were black on black, nothing on nothing.

Quickly, he turned on the wrist-lights. In space, there were no beams, only elliptical, sharply defined spots of blue steel, winking light back at him. Where they struck a rivet, a shadow was cast, knife-sharp and as black as space, the lighted region illuminated abruptly and without diffusion.

He moved his arms, his body swaying gently in the opposite direction; action and reaction. The vision of a steam-tube with its smooth cylindrical sides sprang at him.

He tried to move toward it. His foot held firmly to the hull. He pulled and it slogged upward, straining against quicksand that eased quickly. Three inches up and it had almost sucked free; six inches up and he thought it would fly away.

He advanced it and let it down, felt it enter the quicksand. When the sole was within two inches of the hull, it snapped down; out of control, hitting the hull ringingly. His spacesuit carried the vibrations, amplifying them in his ears.

He stopped in absolute terror. The dehydrators that dried the atmosphere within his suit could not handle the sudden gush of perspiration that drenched his forehead and armpits.

He waited, then tried lifting his foot again—a bare inch, holding it there by main force and moving it horizontally. Horizontal motion involved no effort at all; it was motion perpendicular to the lines of magnetic force. But he had to keep the foot from snapping down as he did so, and then lower it slowly.

He puffed with the effort. Each step was agony. The tendons of his knees were cracking, and there were knives in his side.

Mullen stopped to let the perspiration dry. It wouldn't do to steam up the inside of his faceplate. He flashed his wrist-lights, and the steam-cylinder was right ahead.

The ship had four of them, at ninety degree intervals, thrusting out at an angle from the midgirdle. They were the "fine adjustment" of the ship's course. The coarse adjustment was the powerful thrusters back and front which fixed final velocity by their accelerative and the decelerative force, and the hyperatomics that took care of the space-swallowing Jumps.

But occasionally the direction of flight had to be adjusted slightly and then the steam-cylinders took over. Singly, they could drive the ship up, down, right, left. By twos, in appropriate ratios of thrust, the ship could be turned in any desired direction.

The device had been unimproved in centuries, being too simple to improve. The atomic pile heated the water content of a closed container into steam, driving it, in less than a second, up to temperatures where it would have broken down into a mixture of hydrogen and oxygen, and then into a mixture of electrons and ions. Perhaps the breakdown actually took place. No one ever bothered testing; it worked, so there was no need to.

At the critical point, a needle valve gave way and the steam thrust madly out in a short but incredible blast. And the ship, inevitably and majestically, moved in the opposite direction, veering about its own center of gravity. When the degrees of turn were sufficient, an equal and opposite blast would take place and the turning would be canceled. The ship would be moving at its original velocity, but in a new direction.

Mullen had dragged himself out to the lip of the steam-cylinder. He had a picture of himself—a small speck teetering at the extreme end of a structure thrusting out of an ovoid that was tearing through space at ten thousand miles an hour.

But there was no air-stream to whip him off the hull, and his magnetic soles held him more firmly than he liked.

With lights on, he bent down to peer into the tube and the ship dropped down precipitously as his orientation changed. He reached out to steady himself, but he was not falling. There was no up or down in space except for what his confused mind chose to consider up or down.

The cylinder was just large enough to hold a man, so that it might be entered for repair purposes. His light caught the rungs almost directly opposite his position at the lip. He puffed a sigh of relief with what breath he could muster. Some ships didn't have ladders.

He made his way to it, the ship appearing to slip and twist beneath him as he moved. He lifted an arm over the lip of the tube, feeling for the rung, loosened each foot, and drew himself within.

The knot in his stomach that had been there from the first was a convulsed agony now. If they should choose to manipulate the ship, if the steam should whistle out now—

He would never hear it; never know it. One instant he would be holding a rung, feeling slowly for the next with a groping arm. The next moment he would be alone in space, the ship a dark, dark nothingness lost forever among the stars. There would be, perhaps, a brief glory of swirling ice crystals drifting with him, shining in his wrist-lights and slowly approaching and rotating about him, attracted by his mass like infinitesimal planets to an absurdly tiny Sun.

He was trickling sweat again, and now he was also conscious of thirst. He put it out of his mind. There would be no drinking until he was out of his suit—if ever.

Up a rung; up another; and another. How many were there? His hand slipped and he stared in disbelief at the glitter that showed under his light.

Ice?

Why not? The steam, incredibly hot as it was, would strike metal that was at nearly absolute zero. In the few split-seconds of thrust, there would not be time for the metal to warm above the freezing point of water. A sheet of ice would condense that would sublime slowly into the vacuum. It was the speed of all that happened that prevented the fusion of the tubes and of the original water-container itself.

His groping hand reached the end. Again the wrist-lights. He stared with crawling horror at the steam nozzle, half an inch in diameter. It looked dead, harmless. But it always would, right up to the micro-second before—

Around it was the outer steam lock. It pivoted on a central hub that was springed on the portion toward space, screwed on the part toward the ship. The springs allowed it to give under the first wild thrust of steam pressure before the ship's mighty inertia could be overcome. The steam was bled into the inner chamber, breaking the force of the thrust, leaving the total energy unchanged, but spreading it over time so that the hull itself was in that much less danger of being staved in.

Mullen braced himself firmly against a rung and pressed against the outer lock so that it gave a little. It was stiff, but it didn't have to give much, just enough to catch on the screw. He felt it catch.

He strained against it and turned it, feeling his body twist in the opposite direction. It held tight, the screw taking up the strain as he carefully adjusted the small control switch that allowed the springs to fall free. How well he remembered the books he had read!

He was in the interlock space now, which was large enough to hold a man comfortably, again for convenience in repairs. He could no longer be blown away from the ship. If the steam blast were turned on now, it would merely drive him against the inner lock—hard enough to crush him to a pulp. A quick death he would never feel, at least.

Slowly, he unhooked his spare oxygen cylinder. There was only an inner lock between himself and the control room now. This lock opened outward into space so that the steam blast could only close it tighter, rather than blow it open. And it fitted tightly and smoothly. There was absolutely no way to open it from without.

He lifted himself above the lock, forcing his bent back against the inner surface of the interlock area. It made breathing difficult. The spare oxygen cylinder dangled at a queer angle. He held its metal-mesh hose and straightened it, forcing it against the inner lock so that vibration thudded. Again—again—

It would *have* to attract the attention of the Kloros. They would *have* to investigate.

He would have no way of telling when they were about to do so. Ordinarily, they would first let air into the interlock to force the outer lock shut. But now the outer lock was on the central screw, well away from its rim. Air would suck about it ineffectually, dragging out into space.

Mullen kept on thumping. Would the Kloros look at the air-gauge, note that it scarcely lifted from zero, or would they take its proper working for granted?

PORTER SAID, "HE'S been gone an hour and a half."

"I know," said Stuart.

They were all restless, jumpy, but the tension among themselves had disappeared. It was as though all the threads of emotion extended to the hull of the ship.

Porter was bothered. His philosophy of life had always been simple—take care of yourself because no one will take care of you for you. It upset him to see it shaken.

He said, "Do you suppose they've caught him?"

"If they had, we'd hear about it," replied Stuart, briefly.

Porter felt, with a miserable twinge, that there was little interest on the part of the others in speaking to him. He could understand it; he had not exactly earned their respect. For the moment, a torrent of self-excuse poured through his mind. The others had been frightened, too. A man had a right to be afraid. No one likes to die. At least, he hadn't broken like Aristides Polyorketes. He hadn't wept like Leblanc. He—

But there was Mullen, out there on the hull.

"Listen," he cried, "why did he do it?" They turned to look at him, not understanding, but Porter didn't care. It bothered him to the point where it had to come out. "I want to know why Mullen is risking his life."

"The man," said Windham, "is a patriot—"

"No, none of that!" Porter was almost hysterical. "That little fellow has no emotions at all. He just has reasons and I want to know what those reasons are, because—"

He didn't finish the sentence. Could he say that if those reasons applied to a little middle-aged bookkeeper, they might apply even more forcibly to himself?

Polyorketes said, "He's one brave damn little fellow."

Porter got to his feet. "Listen," he said, "he may be stuck out there. Whatever he's doing, he may not be able to finish it alone. I—I volunteer to go out after him."

He was shaking as he said it and he waited in fear for the sarcastic lash of Stuart's tongue. Stuart was staring at him, probably with surprise, but Porter dared not meet his eyes to make certain.

Stuart said, mildly, "Let's give him another half-hour."

Porter looked up, startled. There was no sneer on Stuart's face. It was even friendly. They *all* looked friendly.

He said, "And then—"

"And then all those who do volunteer will draw straws or something equally democratic. Who volunteers, besides Porter?"

They all raised their hands; Stuart did, too.

But Porter was happy. He had volunteered first. He was anxious for the half-hour to pass.

It caught Mullen by surprise. The outer lock flew open and the long, thin, snakelike, almost headless neck of a Kloro sucked out, unable to fight the blast of escaping air.

Mullen's cylinder flew away, almost tore free. After one wild moment of frozen panic, he fought for it, dragging it above the airstream, waiting as long as he dared to let the first fury die down as the air of the control room thinned out, then bringing it down with force.

It caught the sinewy neck squarely, crushing it. Mullen, curled above the lock, almost entirely protected from the stream, raised the cylinder again and plunging it down again striking the head, mashing the staring eyes to liquid ruin. In the near-vacuum, green blood was pumping out of what was left of the neck.

Mullen dared not vomit, but he wanted to.

With eyes averted, he backed away, caught the outer lock with one hand and imparted a whirl. For several seconds, it maintained that whirl. At the end of the screw, the springs engaged automatically and pulled it shut. What was left of the atmosphere tightened it and the laboring pumps could now begin to fill the control room once again.

Mullen crawled over the mangled Kloro and into the room. It was empty.

He had barely time to notice that when he found himself on his knees. He rose with difficulty. The transition from non-gravity to gravity had taken him entirely by surprise. It was Klorian gravity, too, which meant that with this suit, he carried a fifty percent overload for his small frame. At least, though, his heavy metal clogs no longer clung so exasperatingly to the metal underneath. Within the ship, floors and wall were of cork-covered aluminum alloy.

He circled slowly. The neckless Kloro had collapsed and lay with only an occasional twitch to show it had once been a living organism. He stepped over it, distastefully, and drew the steam-tube lock shut.

The room had a depressing bilious cast and the lights shone yellow-green. It was the Kloro atmosphere, of course.

Mullen felt a twinge of surprise and reluctant admiration. The Kloros obviously had some way of treating materials so that they were impervious to the oxidizing effect of chlorine. Even the map of Earth on the wall, printed on glossy plastic-backed paper, seemed fresh and untouched. He approached, drawn by the familiar outlines of the continents—

There was a flash of motion caught in the corner of his eyes. As quickly as he could in his heavy suit, he turned, then screamed. The Kloro he had thought dead was rising to its feet.

Its neck hung limp, an oozing mass of tissue mash, but its arms reached out blindly, and the tentacles about its chest vibrated rapidly like innumerable snakes' tongues.

It was blind, of course. The destruction of its neck-stalk had deprived it of all sensory equipment, and partial asphyxiation had disorganized it. But the brain remained whole and safe in the abdomen. It still lived.

Mullen backed away. He circled, trying clumsily and unsuccessfully to tiptoe, though he knew that what was left of the Kloro was also deaf. It blundered on its way, struck a wall, felt to the base and began sidling along it.

Mullen cast about desperately for a weapon, found nothing. There was the Kloro's holster, but he dared not reach for it. Why hadn't he snatched it at the very first? Fool!

The door to the control room opened. It made almost no noise. Mullen turned, quivering.

The other Kloro entered, unharmed, entire. It stood in the doorway for a moment, chest-tendrils stiff and unmoving; its neck-stalk stretched forward; its horrible eyes flickering first at him and then at its nearly dead comrade.

And then its hand moved quickly to its side.

Mullen, without awareness, moved as quickly in pure reflex. He stretched out the hose of the spare oxygen-cylinder, which, since entering the control room, he had replaced in its suit-clamp, and cracked the valve. He didn't bother reducing the pressure. He let it gush out unchecked so that he nearly staggered under the backward push.

He could *see* the oxygen stream. It was a pale puff, billowing out amid the chlorine-green. It caught the Kloro with one hand on the weapon's holster.

The Kloro threw its hands up. The little beak on its head-nodule opened alarmingly but noiselessly. It staggered and fell, writhed for a moment, then lay still. Mullen approached and played the oxygen-stream upon its body as though he were extinguishing a fire. And then he raised his heavy foot and brought it down upon the center of the neck-stalk and crushed it on the floor.

He turned to the first. It was sprawled, rigid.

The whole room was pale with oxygen, enough to kill whole legions of Kloros, and his cylinder was empty.

Mullen stepped over the dead Kloro, out of the control room and along the main corridor toward the prisoners' room.

Reaction had set in. He was whimpering in blind, incoherent fright.

STUART WAS TIRED. False hands and all, he was at the controls of a ship once again. Two light cruisers of Earth were on the way. For better than twenty-four hours he had handled the controls virtually alone. He had discarded the chlorinating equipment, rerigged the old atmospherics, located the ship's position in space, tried to plot a course, and sent out carefully guarded signals—which had worked.

So when the door of the control room opened, he was a little annoyed. He was too tired to play conversational handball. Then he turned, and it was Mullen stepping inside.

Stuart said, "For God's sake, get back into bed, Mullen!"

Mullen said, "I'm tired of sleeping, even though I never thought I would be a while ago."

"How do you feel?"

"I'm stiff all over. Especially my side." He grimaced and stared involuntarily around.

"Don't look for the Kloros," Stuart said. "We dumped the poor devils." He shook his head. "I was sorry for them. To themselves, *they're* the human beings, you know, and *we're* the aliens. Not that I'd rather they'd killed you, you understand."

"I understand."

Stuart turned a sidelong glance upon the little man who sat looking at the map of Earth and went on, "I owe you a particular and personal apology, Mullen. I didn't think much of you."

"It was your privilege," said Mullen in his dry voice. There was no feeling in it.

"No, it wasn't. It is no one's privilege to despise another. It is only a hard-won right after long experience."

"Have you been thinking about this?"

"Yes, all day. Maybe I can't explain. It's these hands." He held them up before him, spread out. "It was hard knowing that other people had hands of their own. I had to hate them for it. I always had to do my best to investigate and belittle their motives, point up their deficiencies, expose their stupidities. I had to do anything that would prove to myself that they weren't worth envying."

Mullen moved restlessly. "This explanation is not necessary."

"It is. It is!" Stuart felt his thoughts intently, strained to put them into words. "For years I've abandoned hope of finding any decency in human beings. Then you climbed into the C-chute."

"You had better understand," said Mullen, "that I was motivated by practical and selfish considerations. I will not have you present me to myself as a hero."

"I wasn't intending to. I know that you would do nothing without a reason. It was what your action did to the rest of us. It turned a collection of phonies and fools into decent people. And not by magic either. They were decent all along. It was just that they needed something to live up to and you supplied it. And—I'm one of them. I'll have to live up to you, too. For the rest of my life, probably."

Mullen turned away uncomfortably. His hand straightened his sleeves, which were not in the least twisted. His finger rested on the map.

He said, "I was born in Richmond, Virginia, you know. Here it is. I'll be going there first. Where were you born?"

"Toronto," said Stuart.

"That's right here. Not very far apart on the map, is it?"

Stuart said, "Would you tell me something?"

"If I can."

"Just why *did* you go out there?"

Mullen's precise mouth pursed. He said, dryly, "Wouldn't my rather prosaic reason ruin the inspirational effect?"

"Call it intellectual curiosity. Each of the rest of us had such obvious motives. Porter was scared to death of being interned; Leblanc wanted to get back to his sweetheart; Polyorketes wanted to kill Kloros; and Windham was a patriot according to his lights. As for me, I thought of myself as a noble idealist, I'm afraid. Yet in none of us was the motivation strong enough to get us into a spacesuit and out the C-chute. Then what made *you* do it, *you,* of all people?"

"Why the phrase, 'of all people'?"

"Don't be offended, but you seem devoid of all emotion."

"Do I?" Mullen's voice did not change. It remained precise and soft, yet somehow a tightness had entered it. "That's only training, Mr. Stuart, and self-discipline; not nature. A small man can have no respectable emotions. Is there anything more ridiculous than a man like myself in a state of rage? I'm five feet and one-half inch tall, and one hundred and two pounds in weight, if you care for exact figures. I insist on the half inch and the two pounds.

"Can I be dignified? Proud? Draw myself to my full height without inducing laughter? Where can I meet a woman who will not dismiss me instantly with a giggle? Naturally, I've had to learn to dispense with external display of emotion.

"*You* talk about deformities. No one would notice your hands or know they were different, if you weren't so eager to tell people all about it the instant you meet them. Do you think that the eight inches of height I do not have can be hidden? That it is not the first and, in most cases, the only thing about me that a person will notice?"

Stuart was ashamed. He had invaded a privacy he ought not have. He said, "I'm sorry."

"Why?"

"I should not have forced you to speak of this. I should have seen for myself that you—that you—"

"That I what? Tried to prove myself? Tried to show that while I might be small in body, I held within it a giant's heart?"

"I would not have put it mockingly."

"Why not? It's a foolish idea, and nothing like it is the reason I did what I did. What would I have accomplished if that's what was in my mind? Will they take me to Earth now and put me up before the television cameras—pitching them low, of course, to catch my face, or standing me on a chair—and pin medals on me?"

"They are quite likely to do exactly that."

"And what good would it do me? They would say, 'Gee, and he's such a little guy.' And afterward, what? Shall I tell each man I meet, 'You know, I'm the fellow they decorated for incredible valor last month?' How many medals, Mr. Stuart, do you suppose it would take to put eight inches and sixty pounds on me?"

Stuart said, "Put that way, I see your point."

Mullen was speaking a trifle more quickly now; a controlled heat had entered his words, warming them to just a tepid room temperature. "There *were* days when I thought I would show them, the mysterious 'them' that includes all the world. I was going to leave Earth and carve out worlds for myself. I would be a new and even smaller Napoleon. So I left Earth and went to Arcturus. And what could I do on Arcturus that I could not have done on Earth? Nothing. I balance books. So I am past the vanity, Mr. Stuart, of trying to stand on tiptoe."

"Then why *did* you do it?"

"I left Earth when I was twenty-eight and came to the Arcturian System. I've been there ever since. This trip was to be my first vacation, my first visit back to Earth in all that time. I was going to stay on Earth for six months. The Kloros instead captured us and would have kept us interned indefinitely. But I couldn't—I *couldn't* let them stop me from traveling to Earth. No matter what the risk, I had to prevent their interference. It wasn't love of woman, or fear, or hate, or idealism of any sort. It was stronger than any of those."

He stopped, and stretched out a hand as though to caress the map on the wall.

"Mr. Stuart," Mullen asked quietly, "haven't you ever been homesick?"

PREFACE TO
IN A GOOD CAUSE—

FIRST APPEARANCE—*NEW TALES OF Space and Time,* 1951. Copyright 1951, by Henry Holt and Company, Inc.

There is a perennial question among readers as to whether the views contained in a story reflect the views of the author. The answer is, "Not necessarily—" And yet one ought to add another short phrase "—but usually."

When I write a story in which opposing characters have opposing viewpoints, I do my best, insofar as it lies within my capabilities, to let each character express his own viewpoint honestly.

There are few people who, like Richard III in Shakespeare's play, are willing to say: "since I cannot prove a lover to entertain these fair and well-spoken days, I am determined to prove a villain."

No matter how villainous Tom may appear to Dick, Tom undoubtedly has arguments, quite sincerely felt, to prove to himself that he is not villainous at all. It is therefore quite ridiculous to have a villain act ostentatiously like a villain (unless you have the genius of a Shakespeare and can carry off anything—and I'm afraid I haven't).

Still, no matter how I try to be fair, and how I try to present each person's views honestly, I cannot make myself be as convincing in presenting views that don't appeal to me, as in presenting those that do. Besides, the general working out of my story usually proceeds as I want it to; the victory, in one way or another, tends to lie with those characters whom I particularly like. Even if the ending is tragic, the point of the story (I hate to use the word "moral") is usually one that satisfies me.

In short, if you ignore the fine details of any of my stories and consider it as a whole, I think you will find that the feeling it leaves with you is the feeling that I myself feel. It isn't a matter of conscious propaganda; it's just that I am a human being who feels something and who cannot help having that feeling show in the story.

But there are exceptions—

In 1951, Mr. Raymond J. Healy, an anthologist of note, was planning a collection of original science fiction stories, and asked me to write one. He made only one specification. He wanted an upbeat story—something which, in my own more unsophisticated way, I called a "happy ending" story.

So I wrote a happy ending, but since I always try to beat the rules out of sheer bravado, I tried to write an unexpected happy ending, one in which the reader doesn't find out till the very end what the happy ending really is.

It was only after I had successfully (I think) managed this particular *tour de force* and had had the story published, that I realized that my interest in technique had for once blinded me to content. Somehow this particular story, "In a Good Cause—," doesn't quite reflect my own feelings.

Groff Conklin, the late perceptive science fiction critic, once said that he liked this story, even though he disagreed with its philosophy, and to my embarrassment, I find that that is exactly how I myself feel.

IN A GOOD CAUSE—

In the Great Court, which stands as a patch of untouched peace among the fifty busy square miles devoted to the towering buildings that are the pulse beat of the United Worlds of the Galaxy, stands a statue.

It stands where it can look at the stars at night. There are other statues ringing the court, but this one stands in the center and alone.

It is not a very good statue. The face is too noble and lacks the lines of living. The brow is a shade too high, the nose a shade too symmetrical, the clothing a shade too carefully disposed. The whole bearing is by far too saintly to be true. One can suppose that the man in real life might have frowned at times, or hiccuped, but the statue seemed to insist that such imperfections were impossible.

All this, of course, is understandable overcompensation. The man had no statues raised to him while alive, and succeeding generations, with the advantage of hindsight, felt guilty.

The name on the pedestal reads "Richard Sayama Altmayer." Underneath it is a short phrase and, vertically arranged, three dates. The phrase is: *"In a good cause, there are no failures."* The three dates are June 17, 2755; September 5, 2788; December 32, 2800;—the years being counted in the usual manner of the period, that is, from the date of the first atomic explosion in 1945 of the ancient era.

None of those dates represents either his birth or death. They mark neither a date of marriage or of the accomplishment of some great deed or, indeed, of anything that the inhabitants of the United Worlds can remember with pleasure and pride. Rather, they are the final expression of the feeling of guilt.

Quite simply and plainly, they are the three dates upon which Richard Sayama Altmayer was sent to prison for his opinions.

1—JUNE 17, 2755

At the age of twenty-two, certainly, Dick Altmayer was fully capable of feeling fury. His hair was as yet dark brown and he had not grown the mustache which, in later years, would be so characteristic of him. His nose was, of course, thin and high-bridged, but the contours of his face were youthful. It would only be later that the growing gauntness of his cheeks would convert that nose into the prominent landmark that it now is in the minds of trillions of school children.

Geoffrey Stock was standing in the doorway, viewing the results of his friend's fury. His round face and cold, steady eyes were there, but he had yet to put on the first of the military uniforms in which he was to spend the rest of his life.

He said, "Great Galaxy!"

Altmayer looked up. "Hello, Jeff."

"What's been happening, Dick? I thought your principles, pal, forbid destruction of any kind. Here's a book-viewer that looks somewhat destroyed." He picked up the pieces.

Altmayer said, "I was holding the viewer when my wave-receiver came through with an official message. You know which one, too."

"I know. It happened to me, too. Where is it?"

"On the floor. I tore it off the spool as soon as it belched out at me. Wait, let's dump it down the atom chute."

"Hey, hold on. You can't—"

"Why not?"

"Because you won't accomplish anything. You'll have to report."

"And just why?"

"Don't be an ass, Dick."

"This is a matter of principle, by Space."

"Oh, nuts! You can't fight the whole planet."

"I don't intend to fight the whole planet; just the few who get us into wars."

Stock shrugged. "That means the whole planet. That guff of yours of leaders tricking poor innocent people into fighting is just so much space-dust. Do you think that if a vote were taken the people wouldn't be overwhelmingly in favor of fighting this fight?"

"That means nothing, Jeff. The government has control of—"

"The organs of propaganda. Yes, I know. I've listened to you often enough. Buy why not report, anyway?"

Altmayer turned away.

Stock said, "In the first place, you might not pass the physical examination."

"I'd pass. I've been in Space."

"That doesn't mean anything. If the doctors let you hop a liner, that only means you don't have a heart murmur or an aneurysm. For military duty aboard ship in Space you need much more than just that. How do you know you qualify?"

"That's a side issue, Jeff, and an insulting one. It's not that I'm afraid to fight."

"Do you think you can stop the war this way?"

"I wish I could," Altmayer's voice almost shook as he spoke. "It's this idea I have that all mankind should be a single unit. There shouldn't be wars or space-fleets armed only for destruction. The Galaxy stands ready to be opened to the united efforts of the human race. Instead, we have been factioned for nearly two thousand years, and we throw away all the Galaxy."

Stock laughed, "We're doing all right. There are more than eighty independent planetary systems."

"And are we the only intelligences in the Galaxy?"

"Oh, the Diaboli, your particular devils," and Stock put his fists to his temples and extended the two forefingers, waggling them.

"And yours, too, and everybody's. They have a single government extending over more planets than all those occupied by our precious eighty independents."

"Sure, and their nearest planet is only fifteen hundred light years away from Earth and they can't live on oxygen planets anyway."

Stock got out of his friendly mood. He said, curtly, "Look, I dropped by here to say that I was reporting for examination next week. Are you coming with me?"

"No."

"You're really determined."

"I'm really determined."

"You know you'll accomplish nothing. There'll be no great flame ignited on Earth. It will be no case of millions of young men being excited by your example into a no-war strike. You will simply be put in jail."

"Well, then, jail it is."

And jail it was. On June 17, 2755, of the atomic era, after a short trial in which Richard Sayama Altmayer refused to present any defense, he was sentenced to jail for the term of three years or for the duration of the war, whichever should be longer. He served a little over four years and two months, at which time the war ended in a definite though not shattering Santannian defeat. Earth gained complete control of certain disputed asteroids, various commercial advantages, and a limitation of the Santannian navy.

The combined human losses of the war were something over two thousand ships with, of course, most of their crews, and in addition, several millions of lives due to the bombardment of planetary surfaces from space. The fleets of the two contending powers had been sufficiently strong to restrict this bombardment to the outposts of their respective systems, so that the planets of Earth and Santanni, themselves, were little affected.

The war conclusively established Earth as the strongest single human military power.

Geoffrey Stock fought throughout the war, seeing action more than once and remaining whole in life and limb despite that. At the end of the war he had the rank of major. He took part in the first diplomatic mission sent out by Earth to the worlds of the Diaboli, and that was the first step in his expanding role in Earth's military and political life.

2—SEPTEMBER 5, 2788

They were the first Diaboli ever to have appeared on the surface of Earth itself. The projection posters and the newscasts of the Federalist party made that abundantly clear to any who were unaware of that. Over and over, they repeated the chronology of events.

It was toward the beginning of the century that human explorers first came across the Diaboli. They were intelligent and had discovered interstellar travel independently somewhat earlier than had the humans. Already the galactic volume of their dominions was greater than that which was human-occupied.

Regular diplomatic relationships between the Diaboli and the major human powers had begun twenty years earlier, immediately after the war between Santanni and Earth. At that time, outposts of Diaboli power were already within twenty light years of the outermost human centers. Their missions went everywhere, drawing trade treaties, obtaining concessions on unoccupied asteroids.

And now they were on Earth itself. They were treated as equals and perhaps as more than equals by the rulers of the greatest center of human population in the Galaxy. The most damning statistic of all was the most loudly proclaimed by the Federalists. It was this: Although the number of living Diaboli was somewhat less than the total number of living humans, humanity had opened up not more than five new worlds to colonization in fifty years, while the Diaboli had begun the occupation of nearly five hundred.

"A hundred to one against us," cried the Federalists, "because they are one political organization and we are a hundred." But relatively few on Earth, and fewer in the Galaxy as a whole, paid attention to the Federalists and their demands for Galactic Union.

The crowds that lined the streets along which nearly daily the five Diaboli of the mission traveled from their specially conditioned suite in the best hotel of the city to the Secretariat of Defense were, by and large, not hostile. Most were merely curious, and more than a little revolted.

The Diaboli were not pleasant creatures to look at. They were larger and considerably more massive than Earthmen. They had four stubby legs set close together below and two flexibly-fingered arms above. Their skin was wrinkled and naked and they wore no clothing. Their broad, scaly faces wore no expressions capable of being read by Earthmen, and from flattened regions just above each large-pupiled eye there sprang short horns. It was these last that gave the creatures their names. At first they had been called devils, and later the politer Latin equivalent.

Each wore a pair of cylinders on its back from which flexible tubes extended to the nostrils; there they clamped on tightly. These were packed with soda-lime which absorbed the, to them, poisonous carbon dioxide from the air they breathed. Their own metabolism revolved about the reduction of sulfur and sometimes those foremost among the humans in the crowd caught a foul whiff of the hydrogen sulfide exhaled by the Diaboli.

The leader of the Federalists was in the crowd. He stood far back where he attracted no attention from the police who had roped off the avenues and who now maintained a watchful order on the little hoppers that could be maneuvered quickly through the thickest crowd. The Federalist leader was gaunt-faced, with a thin and prominently bridged nose and straight, graying hair.

He turned away, "I cannot bear to look at them."

His companion was more philosophic. He said, "No uglier in spirit, at least, than some of our handsome officials. These creatures are at least true to their own."

"You are sadly right. Are we entirely ready?"

"Entirely. There won't be one of them alive to return to his world."

"Good! I will remain here to give the signal."

THE DIABOLI WERE talking as well. This fact could not be evident to any human, no matter how close. To be sure, they could communicate by making ordinary sounds to one another but that was not their method of choice. The skin between their horns could, by the actions of muscles which differed in their construction from any known to humans, vibrate rapidly. The tiny waves which were transmitted in this manner to the air were too rapid to be heard by the human ear and too delicate to be detected by any but the most sensitive of human instrumentation. At that time, in fact, humans remained unaware of this form of communication.

A vibration said, "Did you know that this is the planet of origin of the Two-legs?"

"No." There was a chorus of such no's, and then one particular vibration said, "Do you get that from the Two-leg communications you have been studying, queer one?"

"Because I study the communications? More of our people should do so instead of insisting so firmly on the complete worthlessness of Two-leg culture. For one thing, we are in a much better position to deal with the Two-legs if we know something about them. Their history is interesting in a horrible way. I am glad I brought myself to view their spools."

"And yet," came another vibration, "from our previous contacts with Two-legs, one would be certain that they did not know their planet of origin. Certainly there is no veneration of this planet, Earth, or any memorial rites connected with it. Are you sure the information is correct?"

"Entirely so. The lack of ritual, and the fact that this planet is by no means a shrine, is perfectly understandable in the light of Two-leg history. The Two-legs on the other worlds would scarcely concede the honor. It would somehow lower the independent dignity of their own worlds."

"I don't quite understand."

"Neither do I, exactly, but after several days of reading I think I catch a glimmer. It would seem that, originally, when interstellar travel was first discovered by the Two-legs, they lived under a single political unit."

"Naturally."

"Not for these Two-legs. This was an unusual stage in their history and did not last. After the colonies on the various worlds grew and came to reasonable maturity, their first interest was to break away from the mother world. The first in the series of interstellar wars among these Two-legs began then."

"Horrible. Like cannibals."

"Yes, isn't it? My digestion has been upset for days. My cud is sour. In any case, the various colonies gained independence, so that now we have the situation of which we are well aware. All of the Two-leg kingdoms, republics, aristocracies, etc., are simply tiny clots of worlds, each consisting of a dominant world and a few subsidiaries which, in turn, are forever seeking their independence or being shifted from one dominant to another. This Earth is the strongest among them and yet less than a dozen worlds owe it allegiance."

"Incredible that these creatures should be so blind to their own interests. Do they not have a tradition of the single government that existed when they consisted of but one world?"

"As I said that was unusual for them. The single government had existed only a few decades. Prior to that, this very planet itself was split into a number of subplanetary political units."

"Never heard anything like it." For a while, the supersonics of the various creatures interfered with one another.

"It's a fact. It is simply the nature of the beast."

And with that, they were at the Secretariat of Defense.

The five Diaboli stood side by side along the table. They stood because their anatomy did not admit of anything that could correspond to "sitting." On the other side of the table, five Earthmen stood as well. It would have been more convenient for the humans to sit but, understandably, there was no desire to make the handicap of smaller size any more pronounced than it already was. The table was a rather wide one; the widest, in fact, that could be conveniently obtained. This was out of respect for the human nose, for from the Diaboli, slightly so as they breathed, much more so when they spoke, there came the gentle and continuous drift of hydrogen sulfide. This was a difficulty rather unprecedented in diplomatic negotiations.

Ordinarily the meetings did not last for more than half an hour, and at the end of this interval the Diaboli ended their conversations without ceremony and turned to leave. This time, however, the leave-taking was interrupted. A man entered, and the five human negotiators made way for him. He was tall, taller than any of the other Earthmen, and he wore a uniform with the ease of long usage. His face was round and his eyes cold and steady. His black hair was rather thin but as yet untouched by gray. There was an irregular blotch of scar tissue running from the point of his jaw downward past the line of his high, leather-brown collar. It might have been the result of a hand energy-ray, wielded by some forgotten human enemy in one of the five wars in which the man had been an active participant.

"Sirs," said the Earthman who had been chief negotiator hitherto, "may I introduce the Secretary of Defense?"

The Diaboli were somewhat shocked and, although their expressions were in repose and inscrutable, the sound plates on their foreheads vibrated actively. Their strict sense of hierarchy was disturbed. The Secretary was only a Two-leg, but by Two-leg standards, he outranked them. They could not properly conduct official business with him.

The Secretary was aware of their feelings but had no choice in the matter. For at least ten minutes, their leaving must be delayed and no ordinary interruption could serve to hold back the Diaboli.

"Sirs," he said, "I must ask your indulgence to remain longer this time."

The central Diabolus replied in the nearest approach to English any Diabolus could manage. Actually, a Diabolus might be said to have two mouths. One was hinged at the outermost extremity of the jawbone and was used in eating. In this capacity, the motion of the mouth was rarely seen by human beings, since the Diaboli much preferred to eat in the company of their own kind, exclusively. A narrower mouth opening, however, perhaps two inches in width, could be used in speaking. It pursed itself open, revealing the gummy gap where a Diabolus' missing incisors ought to have been. It remained open during speech, the necessary consonantal blockings being performed by the palate and back of the tongue. The result was hoarse and fuzzy, but understandable.

The Diabolus said, "You will pardon us, already we suffer." And by his forehead, he twittered unheard, "They mean to suffocate us in their vile atmosphere. We must ask for larger poison-absorbing cylinders."

The Secretary of Defense said, "I am in sympathy with your feelings, and yet this may be my only opportunity to speak with you. Perhaps you would do us the honor to eat with us."

The Earthman next to the Secretary could not forbear a quick and passing frown. He scribbled rapidly on a piece of paper and passed it to the Secretary, who glanced momentarily at it.

It read, "No. They eat sulfuretted hay. Stinks unbearably." The Secretary crumbled the note and let it drop.

The Diabolus said, "The honor is ours. Were we physically able to endure your strange atmosphere for so long a time, we would accept most gratefully."

And via forehead, he said with agitation, "They cannot expect us to eat with them and watch them consume the corpses of dead animals. My cud would never be sweet again."

"We respect your reasons," said the Secretary. "Let us then transact our business now. In the negotiations that have so far proceeded, we have been unable to obtain from your government, in the persons of you, their representatives, any clear indication as to what the boundaries of your sphere of influence are in your own minds. We have presented several proposals in this matter."

"As far as the territories of Earth are concerned, Mr. Secretary, a definition has been given."

"But surely you must see that this is unsatisfactory. The boundaries of Earth and your lands are nowhere in contact. So far, you have done nothing but state this fact. While true, the mere statement is not satisfying."

"We do not completely understand. Would you have us discuss the boundaries between ourselves and such independent human kingdoms as that of Vega?"

"Why, yes."

"That cannot be done, sir. Surely, you realize that any relations between ourselves and the sovereign realm of Vega cannot be possibly any concern of Earth. They can be discussed only with Vega."

"Then you will negotiate a hundred times with the hundred human world systems?"

"It is necessary. I would point out, however, that the necessity is imposed not by us but by the nature of your human organization."

"Then that limits our field of discussion drastically." The Secretary seemed abstracted. He was listening, not exactly to the Diaboli opposite, but, rather, it would seem, to something at a distance.

And now there was a faint commotion, barely heard from outside the Secretariat. The babble of distant voices, the brisk crackle of energy-guns muted by distance to nearly nothingness, and the hurried click-clacking of police hoppers.

The Diaboli showed no indication of hearing, nor was this simply another affectation of politeness. If their capacity for receiving supersonic sound waves was far more delicate and acute than almost anything human ingenuity had ever invented, their reception for ordinary sound waves was rather dull.

The Diabolus was saying, "We beg leave to state our surprise. We were of the opinion that all this was known to you."

A man in police uniform appeared in the doorway. The Secretary turned to him and, with the briefest of nods, the policeman departed.

The Secretary said suddenly and briskly, "Quite. I merely wished to ascertain once again that this was the case. I trust you will be ready to resume negotiations tomorrow?"

"Certainly, sir."

One by one, slowly, with a dignity befitting the heirs of the universe, the Diaboli left.

An Earthman said, "I'm glad they refused to eat with us."

"I knew they couldn't accept," said the Secretary, thoughtfully. "They're vegetarian. They sicken thoroughly at the very thought of eating meat. I've seen them eat, you know. Not many humans have. They resemble our cattle in the business of eating. They bolt their food and then stand solemnly about in circles, chewing their cuds in a great community of thought. Perhaps they intercommunicate by a method we are unaware of. The huge lower jaw rotates horizontally in a slow, grinding process—"

The policeman had once more appeared in the doorway.

The Secretary broke off, and called, "You have them all?"

"Yes, sir."

"Do you have Altmayer?"

"Yes, sir."

"Good."

THE CROWD HAD gathered again when the five Diaboli emerged from the Secretariat. The schedule was strict. At 3:00 P.M. each day they left their suite and spent five minutes walking to the Secretariat. At 3:35, they emerged therefrom once again and returned to their suite, the way being kept clear by the police. They marched stolidly, almost mechanically, along the broad avenue.

Halfway in their trek there came the sounds of shouting men. To most of the crowd, the words were not clear but there was the crackle of an energy-gun and the pale blue fluorescence split the air overhead. Police wheeled, their own energy-guns drawn, hoppers springing seven feet into the air, landing delicately in the midst of groups of people, touching none of them, jumping again almost instantly. People scattered and their voices were joined to the general uproar.

Through it all, the Diaboli, either through defective hearing or excessive dignity, continued marching as mechanically as ever.

At the other end of the gathering, almost diametrically opposing the region of excitement, Richard Sayama Altmayer stroked his nose in a moment of satisfaction. The strict chronology of the Diaboli had made a split-second plan possible. The first diversionary disturbance was only to attract the attention of the police. It was now—

And he fired a harmless sound pellet into the air.

Instantly, from four directions, concussion pellets split the air. From the roofs of buildings lining the way, snipers fired.

Each of the Diaboli, torn by the shells, shuddered and exploded as the pellets detonated within them. One by one, they toppled.

And from nowhere, the police were at Altmayer's side. He stared at them with some surprise.

Gently, for in twenty years he had lost his fury and learned to be gentle, he said, "You come quickly, but even so you come too late." He gestured in the direction of the shattered Diaboli.

The crowd was in simple panic now. Additional squadrons of police, arriving in record time, could do nothing more than herd them off into harmless directions.

The policeman, who now held Altmayer in a firm grip, taking the sound gun from him and inspecting him quickly for further weapons, was a captain by rank. He said, stiffly, "I think you've made a mistake, Mr. Altmayer. You'll notice you've drawn no blood." And he, too, waved toward where the Diaboli lay motionless.

Altmayer turned, startled. The creatures lay there on their sides, some in pieces, tattered skin shredding away, frames distorted and bent, but the police captain was correct. There was no blood, no flesh. Altmayer's lips, pale and stiff, moved soundlessly.

The police captain interpreted the motion accurately enough. He said, "You are correct, sir, they are robots."

And from the great doors of the Secretariat of Defense the true Diaboli emerged. Clubbing policemen cleared the way, but another way, so that they need not pass the sprawled travesties of plastic and aluminum which for three minutes had played the role of living creatures.

The police captain said, "I'll ask you to come without trouble, Mr. Altmayer. The Secretary of Defense would like to see you."

"I am coming, sir." A stunned frustration was only now beginning to overwhelm him.

GEOFFREY STOCK AND Richard Altmayer faced one another for the first time in almost a quarter of a century, there in the Defense Secretary's private office. It was a rather straitlaced office: a desk, an armchair, and two additional chairs. All were a dull brown in color, the chairs being topped by brown foamite which yielded to the body enough for comfort, not enough for luxury. There was a micro-viewer on the desk and a little cabinet big enough to hold several dozen opto-spools. On the wall opposite the desk was a trimensional view of the old *Dauntless*, the Secretary's first command.

Stock said, "It is a little ridiculous meeting like this after so many years. I find I am sorry."

"Sorry about what, Jeff?" Altmayer tried to force a smile, "I am sorry about nothing but that you tricked me with those robots."

"You were not difficult to trick," said Stock, "and it was an excellent opportunity to break your party. I'm sure it will be quite discredited after this. The pacifist tries to force war; the apostle of gentleness tries assassination."

"War against the true enemy," said Altmayer sadly. "But you are right. It is a sign of desperation that this was forced on me."—Then, "How did you know my plans?"

"You still overestimate humanity, Dick. In any conspiracy the weakest points are the people that compose it. You had twenty-five co-conspirators. Didn't it occur to you that at least one of them might be an informer, or even an employee of mine?"

A dull red burned slowly on Altmayer's high cheekbones. "Which one?" he said.

"Sorry. We may have to use him again."

Altmayer sat back in his chair wearily. "What have you gained?"

"What have *you* gained? You are as impractical now as on that last day I saw you; the day you decided to go to jail rather than report for induction. You haven't changed."

Altmayer shook his head, "The truth doesn't change."

Stock said impatiently, "If it is truth, why does it always fail? Your stay in jail accomplished nothing. The war went on. Not one life was saved. Since then, you've started a political party; and every cause it has backed has failed. Your conspiracy has failed. You're nearly fifty, Dick, and what have you accomplished? Nothing."

Altmayer said, "And you went to war, rose to command a ship, then to a place in the Cabinet. They say you will be the next Coordinator. You've accomplished a great deal. Yet success and failure do not exist in themselves. Success in what? Success in working the ruin of humanity. Failure in what? In saving it? I wouldn't change places with you. Jeff, remember this. In a good cause, there are no failures; there are only delayed successes."

"Even if you are executed for this day's work?"

"Even if I am executed. There will be someone else to carry on, and his success will be my success."

"How do you envisage this success? Can you really see a union of worlds, a Galactic Federation? Do you want Santanni running our affairs? Do you want a Vegan telling you what to do? Do you want Earth to decide its own destiny or to be at the mercy of any random combination of powers?"

"We would be at their mercy no more than they would be at ours."

"Except that we are the richest. We would be plundered for the sake of the depressed worlds of the Sirius Sector."

"And pay the plunder out of what we would save in the wars that would no longer occur."

"Do you have answers for all questions, Dick?"

"In twenty years we have been asked all questions, Jeff."

"Then answer this one. How would you force this union of yours on unwilling humanity?"

"That is why I wanted to kill the Diaboli." For the first time, Altmayer showed agitation. "It would mean war with them, but all humanity would unite against the common enemy. Our own political and ideological differences would fade in the face of that."

"You really believe that? Even when the Diaboli have never harmed us? They cannot live on our worlds. They must remain on their own worlds of sulfide atmosphere and oceans which are sodium sulfate solutions."

"Humanity knows better, Jeff. They are spreading from world to world like an atomic explosion. They block space-travel into regions where there are unoccupied oxygen worlds, the kind *we* could use. They are planning for the future; making room for uncounted future generations of Diaboli, while we are being restricted to one corner of the Galaxy, and fighting ourselves to death. In a thousand years we will be their slaves; in ten thousand we will be extinct. Oh, yes, they are the common enemy. Mankind knows that. You will find that out sooner than you think, perhaps."

The Secretary said, "Your party members speak a great deal of ancient Greece of the preatomic age. They tell us that the Greeks were a marvelous people, the most culturally advanced of their time, perhaps of all times. They set mankind on the road it has never yet left entirely. They had only one flaw. They could not unite. They were conquered and eventually died out. And we follow in their footsteps now, eh?"

"You have learned your lesson well, Jeff."

"But have you, Dick?"

"What do you mean?"

"Did the Greeks have no common enemy against whom they could unite?"

Altmayer was silent.

Stock said, "The Greeks fought Persia, their great common enemy. Was it not a fact that a good proportion of the Greek states fought on the Persian side?"

Altmayer said finally, "Yes. Because they thought Persian victory was inevitable and they wanted to be on the winning side."

"Human beings haven't changed, Dick. Why do you suppose the Diaboli are here? What is it we are discussing?"

"I am not a member of the government."

"No," said Stock, savagely, "but I am. The Vegan League has allied itself with the Diaboli."

"I don't believe you. It can't be."

"It can be and is. The Diaboli have agreed to supply them with five hundred ships at any time they happen to be at war with Earth. In return, Vega abandons all claims to the Nigellian star cluster. So if you had really assassinated the Diaboli, it would have been war, but with half of humanity probably fighting on the side of your so-called common enemy. We are trying to prevent that."

Altmayer said slowly, "I am ready for trial. Or am I to be executed without one?"

Stock said, "You are still foolish. If we shoot you, Dick, we make a martyr. If we keep you alive and shoot only your subordinates, you will be suspected of having turned state's evidence. As a presumed traitor, you will be quite harmless in the future."

And so, on September 5th, 2788, Richard Sayama Altmayer, after the briefest of secret trials, was sentenced to five years in prison. He served his full term. The year he emerged from prison, Geoffrey Stock was elected Coordinator of Earth.

3—DECEMBER 21, 2800

Simon Devoire was not at ease. He was a little man, with sandy hair and a freckled, ruddy face. He said, "I'm sorry I agreed to see you, Altmayer. It won't do you any good. It might do me harm."

Altmayer said, "I am an old man. I won't hurt you." And he was indeed a very old man somehow. The turn of the century found his years at two-thirds of a century, but he was older than that, older inside and older outside. His clothes were too big for him, as if he were shrinking away inside them. Only his nose had not aged; it was still the thin, aristocratic, high-beaked Altmayer nose.

Devoire said, "It's not you I'm afraid of."

"Why not? Perhaps you think I betrayed the men of '88."

"No, of course not. No man of sense believes that you did. But the days of the Federalists are over, Altmayer."

Altmayer tried to smile. He felt a little hungry; he hadn't eaten that day—no time for food. Was the day of the Federalists over? It might seem so to others. The movement had died on a wave of ridicule. A conspiracy that fails, a "lost cause," is often romantic. It is remembered and draws adherents for generations, *if* the loss is at least a dignified one. But to shoot at living creatures and find the mark to be robots; to be outmaneuvered and outfoxed; to be made ridiculous—that is deadly. It is deadlier than treason, wrong, and sin. Not many had believed Altmayer had bargained for his life by betraying his associates, but the universal laughter killed Federalism as effectively as though they had.

But Altmayer had remained stolidly stubborn under it all. He said, "The day of the Federalists will never be over, while the human race lives."

"Words," said Devoire impatiently. "They meant more to me when I was younger. I am a little tired now."

"Simon, I need access to the subetheric system."

Devoire's face hardened. He said, "And you thought of me. I'm sorry, Altmayer, but I can't let you use my broadcasts for your own purposes."

"You were a Federalist once."

"Don't rely on that," said Devoire. "That's in the past. Now I am—nothing. I am a Devoirist, I suppose. I want to live."

"Even if it is under the feet of the Diaboli? Do you want to live when they are willing; die when they are ready?"

"Words!"

"Do you approve of the all-Galactic conference?"

Devoire reddened past his usual pink level. He gave the sudden impression of a man with too much blood for his body. He said smolderingly, "Well, why not? What does it matter how we go about establishing the Federation of Man? If you're still a Federalist, what have you to object to in a united humanity?"

"United under the Diaboli?"

"What's the difference? Humanity can't unite by itself. Let us be driven to it, as long as the fact is accomplished. I am sick of it all, Altmayer, sick of all our stupid history. I'm tired of trying to be an idealist with nothing to be idealistic over. Human beings are human beings and that's the nasty part of it. Maybe we've *got* to be whipped into line. If so, I'm perfectly willing to let the Diaboli do the whipping."

Altmayer said gently, "You're very foolish, Devoire. It won't be a real union, you know that. The Diaboli called this conference so that they might act as umpires on all current interhuman disputes to their own advantage, and remain the supreme court of judgment over us hereafter. You know they have no intention of establishing a real central human government. It will only be a sort of interlocking directorate; each human government will conduct its own affairs as before and pull in various directions as before. It is simply that we will grow accustomed to running to the Diaboli with our little problems."

"How do you know that will be the result?"

"Do you seriously think any other result is possible?"

Devoire chewed at his lower lip, "Maybe not!"

"Then see through a pane of glass, Simon. Any true independence we now have will be lost."

"A lot of good this independence has ever done us.—Besides, what's the use? We can't stop this thing. Coordinator Stock is probably no keener on the conference than you are, but that doesn't help him. If Earth doesn't attend, the union will be formed without us, and then we will face war with the rest of humanity and the Diaboli. And that goes for any other government that wants to back out."

"What if *all* the governments back out? Wouldn't the conference break up completely?"

"Have you ever known all the human governments to do *anything* together? You never learn, Altmayer."

"There are new facts involved."

"Such as? I know I am foolish for asking, but go ahead."

Altmayer said, "For twenty years most of the Galaxy has been shut to human ships. You know that. None of us has the slightest notion of what goes on within the Diaboli sphere of influence. And yet some human colonies exist within that sphere."

"So?"

"So occasionally, human beings escape into the small portion of the Galaxy that remains human and free. The government of Earth receives reports; reports which they don't dare make public. But not *all* officials of the government can stand the cowardice involved in such actions forever. One of them has been to see me. I can't tell you which one, of course— So I have documents, Devoire; official, reliable, and true."

Devoire shrugged, "About what?" He turned the desk chronometer rather ostentatiously so that Altmayer could see its gleaming metal face on which the red, glowing figures stood out sharply. They read 22:31, and even as it was turned, the 1 faded and the new glow of a 2 appeared.

Altmayer said, "There is a planet called by its colonists Chu Hsi. It did not have a large population; two million, perhaps. Fifteen years ago the Diaboli occupied worlds on various sides of it; and in all those fifteen years, no human ship ever landed on the planet. Last year the Diaboli themselves landed. They brought with them huge freight ships filled with sodium sulfate and bacterial cultures that are native to their own worlds."

"What?—You can't make me believe it."

"Try," said Altmayer, ironically. "It is not difficult. Sodium sulfate will dissolve in the oceans of any world. In a sulfate ocean, their bacteria will grow, multiply, and produce hydrogen sulfide in tremendous quantities which will fill the oceans and the atmosphere. They can then introduce their plants and animals and eventually themselves. Another planet will be suitable for Diaboli life—and unsuitable for any human. It would take time, surely, but the Diaboli have time. They are a united people and . . ."

"Now, look," Devoire waved his hand in disgust, "that just doesn't hold water. The Diaboli have more worlds than they know what to do with."

"For their present purposes, yes, but the Diaboli are creatures that look toward the future. Their birth rate is high and eventually they will fill the Galaxy. And how much better off they would be if they were the only intelligence in the universe."

"But it's impossible on purely physical grounds. Do you know how many millions of tons of sodium sulfate it would take to fill up the oceans to their requirements?"

"Obviously a planetary supply."

"Well, then, do you suppose they would strip one of their own worlds to create a new one? Where is the gain?"

"Simon, Simon, there are millions of planets in the Galaxy which through atmospheric conditions, temperature, or gravity are forever uninhabitable either to humans or to Diaboli. Many of these are quite adequately rich in sulfur."

Devoire considered, "What about the human beings on the planet?"

"On Chu Hsi? Euthanasia—except for the few who escaped in time. Painless I suppose. The Diaboli are not needlessly cruel, merely efficient."

Altmayer waited. Devoire's fist clenched and unclenched.

Altmayer said, "Publish this news. Spread it out on the interstellar subetheric web. Broadcast the documents to the reception centers on the various worlds. You can do it, and when you do, the all-Galactic conference will fall apart."

Devoire's chair tilted forward. He stood up. "Where's your proof?"

"Will you do it?"

"I want to see your proof."

Altmayer smiled, "Come with me."

THEY WERE WAITING for him when he came back to the furnished room he was living in. He didn't notice them at first. He was completely unaware of the small vehicle that followed him at a slow pace and a prudent distance. He walked with his head bent, calculating the length of time it would take for Devoire to put the information through the reaches of space; how long it would take for the receiving stations on Vega and Santanni and Centaurus to blast out the news; how long it would take to spread it over the entire Galaxy. And in this way he passed, unheeding, between the two plainclothes men who flanked the entrance of the rooming house.

It was only when he opened the door to his own room that he stopped and turned to leave but the plainclothes men were behind him now. He made no attempt at violent escape. He entered the room instead and sat down, feeling so old. He thought feverishly, I need only hold them off an hour and ten minutes.

The man who occupied the darkness reached up and flicked the switch that allowed the wall lights to operate. In the soft wall glow, the man's round face and balding gray-fringed head were startlingly clear.

Altmayer said gently, "I am honored with a visit by the Coordinator himself."

And Stock said, "We are old friends, you and I, Dick. We meet every once in a while."

Altmayer did not answer.

Stock said, "You have certain government papers in your possession, Dick."

Altmayer said, "If you think so, Jeff, you'll have to find them."

Stock rose wearily to his feet. "No heroics, Dick. Let me tell you what those papers contained. They were circumstantial reports of the sulfation of the planet Chu Hsi. Isn't that true?"

Altmayer looked at the clock.

Stock said, "If you are planning to delay us, to angle us as though we were fish, you will be disappointed. We know where you've been, we know Devoire has the papers, we know exactly what he's planning to do with them."

Altmayer stiffened. The thin parchment of his cheeks trembled. He said, "How long have you known?"

"As long as you have, Dick. You are a very predictable man. It is the very reason we decided to use you. Do you suppose the Recorder would really come to see you as he did, without our knowledge?"

"I don't understand."

Stock said, "The Government of Earth, Dick, is not anxious that the all-Galactic conference be continued. However, we are not Federalists; we know humanity for what it is. What do you suppose would happen if the rest of the Galaxy discovered that the Diaboli were in the process of changing a salt-oxygen world into a sulfate-sulfide one?

"No, don't answer. You are Dick Altmayer and I'm sure you'd tell me that with one fiery burst of indignation, they'd abandon the conference, join together in a loving and brotherly union, throw themselves at the Diaboli, and overwhelm them."

Stock paused such a long time that for a moment it might have seemed he would say no more. Then he continued in half a whisper, "Nonsense. The other worlds would say that the Government of Earth for purposes of its own had initiated a fraud, had forged documents in a deliberate attempt to disrupt the conference. The Diaboli would deny everything, and most of the human worlds would find it to their interests to believe the denial. They would concentrate on the iniquities of Earth and forget about the iniquities of the Diaboli. So you see, we could sponsor no such exposé."

Altmayer felt drained, futile. "Then you will stop Devoire. It is always that you are so sure of failure beforehand; that you believe the worst of your fellow man—"

"Wait! I said nothing of stopping Devoire. I said only that the government could not sponsor such an exposé and we will not. But the exposé will take place just the same, except that afterward we will arrest Devoire and yourself and denounce the whole thing as vehemently as will the Diaboli. The whole affair would then be changed. The Government of Earth will have dissociated itself from the claims. It will then seem to the rest of the human government that for our own selfish purposes we are trying to hide the actions of the Diaboli, that we have, perhaps, a special understanding with them. They will fear that special understanding and unite against us. But *then* to be against us will mean that they are also against the Diaboli. They will insist on believing the exposé to be the truth, the documents to be real—and the conference will break up."

"It will mean war again," said Altmayer hopelessly, "and not against the real enemy. It will mean fighting among the humans and a victory all the greater for the Diaboli when it is all over."

"No war," said Stock. "No government will attack Earth with the Diaboli on our side. The other governments will merely draw away from us and grind a permanent anti-Diaboli bias into their propaganda. Later, if there should be war between ourselves and the Diaboli, the other governments will at least remain neutral."

He looks very old, thought Altmayer. We are all old, dying men. Aloud, he said, "Why would you expect the Diaboli to back Earth? You may fool the rest of mankind by pretending to attempt suppression of the facts concerning the planet Chu Hsi, but you won't fool the Diaboli. They won't for a moment believe Earth to be sincere in its claim that it believes the documents to be forgeries."

"Ah, but they will." Geoffrey Stock stood up, "You see, the documents *are* forgeries. The Diaboli may be planning sulfation of planets in the future, but to our knowledge, they have not tried it yet."

———

On December 21, 2800, Richard Sayama Altmayer entered prison for the third and last time. There was no trial, no definite sentence, and scarcely a real imprisonment in the literal sense of the word. His movements were confined and only a few officials were allowed to communicate with him, but otherwise his comforts were looked to assiduously. He had no access to news, of course, so that he was not aware that in the second year of this third imprisonment of his, the war between Earth and the Diaboli opened with the surprise attack near Sirius by an Earth squadron upon certain ships of the Diaboli navy.

In 2802, Geoffrey Stock came to visit Altmayer in his confinement. Altmayer rose in surprise to greet him.

"You're looking well, Dick," Stock said.

He himself was not. His complexion had grayed. He still wore his naval captain's uniform, but his body stooped slightly within it. He was to die within the year, a fact of which he was not completely unaware. It did not bother him much. He thought repeatedly, I have lived the years I've had to live.

Altmayer, who looked the older of the two, had yet more than nine years to live. He said, "An unexpected pleasure, Jeff, but this time you can't have come to imprison me. I'm in prison already."

"I've come to set you free, if you would like."

"For what purpose, Jeff? Surely you have a purpose? A clever way of using me?"

Stock's smile was merely a momentary twitch. He said, "A way of using you, truly, but this time you will approve. . . . We are at war."

"With whom?" Altmayer was startled.

"With the Diaboli. We have been at war for six months."

Altmayer brought his hands together, thin fingers interlacing nervously, "I've heard nothing of this."

"I know." The Coordinator clasped his hands behind his back and was distantly surprised to find that they were trembling. He said, "It's been a long journey for the two of us, Dick. We've had the same goal, you and I— No, let me speak. I've often wanted to explain my point of view to you, but you would never have understood. You weren't the kind of man to understand, until I had the results for you.—I was twenty-five when I first visited a Diaboli world, Dick. I knew then it was either they or we."

"I said so," whispered Altmayer, "from the first."

"Merely saying so was not enough. You wanted to force the human governments to unite against them and that notion was politically unrealistic and completely impossible. It wasn't even desirable. Humans are not Diaboli. Among the Diaboli individual consciousness is low, almost nonexistent. Ours is almost overpowering. They have no such thing as politics; we have nothing else. They can never disagree, can have nothing but a single government. We can never agree; if we had a single island to live on, we would split it in three.

"*But our very disagreements are our strength!* Your Federalist party used to speak of ancient Greece a great deal once. Do you remember? But your people always missed the point. To be sure, Greece could never unite and was therefore ultimately conquered. But even in her state of disunion, she defeated the gigantic Persian Empire. Why?

"I would like to point out that the Greek city-states over centuries had fought with one another. They were forced to specialize in things military to an extent far beyond the Persians. Even the Persians themselves realized that, and in the last century of their imperial existence, Greek mercenaries formed the most valued parts of their armies.

"The same might be said of the small nation-states of preatomic Europe, which in centuries of fighting had advanced their military arts to the point where they could overcome and hold for two hundred years the comparatively gigantic empires of Asia.

"So it is with us. The Diaboli, with vast extents of galactic space, have never fought a war. Their military machine is massive, but untried. In fifty years, only such advances have been made by them as they have been able to copy from the various human navies. Humanity, on the other hand, has competed ferociously in warfare. Each government has raced to keep ahead of its neighbors in military science. They've had to! It was our own disunion that made the terrible race for survival necessary, so that in the end almost any one of us was a match for all the Diaboli, provided only that none of us would fight on their side in a general war.

"It was toward the prevention of such a development that all of Earth's diplomacy has been aimed. Until it was certain that in a war between Earth and the Diaboli, the rest of humanity would be at least neutral, there could be no war, and no union of human governments could be allowed, since the race for military perfection must continue. Once we were sure of neutrality, through the hoax that broke up the conference two years ago, we sought the war, and now we have it."

Altmayer, through all this, might have been frozen. It was a long time before he could say anything.

Finally, "What if the Diaboli are victorious after all?"

Stock said, "They aren't. Two weeks ago, the main fleets joined action and theirs was annihilated with practically no loss to ourselves, although we were greatly outnumbered. We might have been fighting unarmed ships. We had stronger weapons of greater range and more accurate sighting. We had three times their effective speed since we had antiacceleration devices which they lacked. Since the battle a dozen of the other human governments have decided to join the winning side and have declared war on the Diaboli. Yesterday the Diaboli requested that negotiations for an armistice be opened. The war is practically over; and henceforward the Diaboli will be confined to their original planets with only such future expansions as we permit."

Altmayer murmured incoherently.

Stock said, "And now union becomes necessary. After the defeat of Persia by the Greek city-states, they were ruined because of their continued wars among themselves, so that first Macedon and then Rome conquered them. After Europe colonized the Americas, cut up Africa, and conquered Asia, a series of continued European wars led to European ruin.

"Disunion until conquest; union thereafter! But now union is easy. Let one subdivision succeed by itself and the rest will clamor to become part of that success. The ancient writer, Toynbee, first pointed out this difference between what he called a 'dominant minority' and a 'creative minority.'

"We are a creative minority now. In an almost spontaneous gesture, various human governments have suggested the formation of a United Worlds organization. Over seventy governments are willing to attend the first sessions in order to draw up a Charter of Federation. The others will join later, I am sure. We would like you to be one of the delegates from Earth, Dick."

Altmayer found his eyes flooding, "I—I don't understand your purpose. Is this all true?"

"It is all exactly as I say. You were a voice in the wilderness, Dick, crying for union. Your words will carry much weight. What did you once say: 'In a good cause, there are no failures.' "

"No!" said Altmayer, with sudden energy. "It seems your cause was the good one."

Stock's face was hard and devoid of emotion, "You were always a misunderstander of human nature, Dick. When the United Worlds is a reality and when generations of men and women look back to these days of war through their centuries of unbroken peace, they will have forgotten the purpose of my methods. To them they will represent war and death. *Your* calls for union, *your* idealism, will be remembered forever."

HE TURNED AWAY and Altmayer barely caught his last words: "And when they build their statues, they will build none for me."

In the Great Court, which stands as a patch of untouched peace among the fifty busy square miles devoted to the towering buildings that are the pulse beat of the United Worlds of the Galaxy, stands a statue . . .

PREFACE TO
WHAT IF—

First appearance—*FANTASTIC*, Summer 1952. Copyright 1952, by Ziff-Davis Publishing Company.

Easily the most frequently asked question put to any writer of science fiction stories is: "Where do you get your ideas?"

I imagine the person who asks the question is sure that there is some mysterious kind of inspiration that can only be produced by odd and possibly illicit means, or that the writer goes through an eldritch ritual that may even involve calling up the devil.

But the answer is only, "You can get an idea from anything if you are willing to think hard enough and long enough."

That long-and-hard bit seems to disillusion people. Their admiration for you drops precipitously and you get the feeling you have exposed yourself as an impostor. After all, if long-and-hard is all it takes, *anyone* can do it.

Strange, then, that so few do.

Anyway, my wife once broke down and asked me that question even though she knows I dislike having it asked. We had moved to the

Boston area in 1949, when I took my position with Boston University School of Medicine, and periodically we made a train trip back to New York to visit our respective families.

Once, on one of those train trips, perhaps out of boredom, she asked The Question. I said, "From anything. I can probably get one out of this train trip, if I try."

"Go ahead," she said, naturally enough.

So I thought hard and told her the story of a train trip which, when I got back home, I typed up in permanent form and called "What If—."

The story is unusual for me in another respect, too. I am not strong on romance in my stories. Why that should be, I will leave to the parlor psychoanalyst. I merely state the fact.

Sometimes, I do have women in my stories. On rare occasions, as in "Hostess," the woman is even the protagonist. But even then romance is a minor factor, if it appears at all.

In "What If—," however, the story is all romance. Each time I think of that, the fact startles me. I believe it is the only one of my many stories that is all serious (as opposed to ribald) romance. Heavens!

WHAT IF—

Norman and Livvy were late, naturally, since catching a train is always a matter of last-minute delays, so they had to take the only available seat in the coach. It was the one toward the front; the one with nothing before it but the seat that faced wrong way, with its back hard against the front partition. While Norman heaved the suitcase onto the rack, Livvy found herself chafing a little.

If a couple took the wrong-way seat before them, they would be staring self-consciously into each others' faces all the hours it would take to reach New York; or else, which was scarcely better, they would have to erect synthetic barriers of newspaper. Still, there was no use in taking a chance on there being another unoccupied double seat elsewhere in the train.

Norman didn't seem to mind, and that was a little disappointing to Livvy. Usually they held their moods in common. That, Norman claimed, was why he remained sure that he had married the right girl.

He would say, "We fit each other, Livvy, and that's the key fact. When you're doing a jigsaw puzzle and one piece fits another, that's it. There are no other possibilities, and of course there are no other girls."

And she would laugh and say, "If you hadn't been on the streetcar that day, you would probably never have met me. What would you have done then?"

"Stayed a bachelor. Naturally. Besides, I would have met you through Georgette another day."

"It wouldn't have been the same."

"Sure it would."

"No, it wouldn't. Besides, Georgette would never have introduced me. She was interested in you herself, and she's the type who knows better than to create a possible rival."

"What nonsense."

Livvy asked her favorite question: "Norman, what if you had been one minute later at the streetcar corner and had taken the next car? What *do* you suppose would have happened?"

"And what if fish had wings and all of them flew to the top of the mountains? What would we have to eat on Fridays then?"

But they *had* caught the streetcar, and fish *didn't* have wings, so that now they had been married five years and ate fish on Fridays. And because they had been married five years, they were going to celebrate by spending a week in New York.

Then she remembered the present problem. "I wish we could have found some other seat."

Norman said, "Sure. So do I. But no one has taken it yet, so we'll have relative privacy as far as Providence, anyway."

Livvy was unconsoled, and felt herself justified when a plump little man walked down the central aisle of the coach. Now, where had he come from? The train was halfway between Boston and Providence, and if he had had a seat, why hadn't he kept it? She took out her vanity and considered her reflection. She had a theory that if she ignored the little man, he would pass by. So she concentrated on her light-brown hair which, in the rush of catching the train, had become disarranged just a little; at her blue eyes, and at her little mouth with the plump lips which Norman said looked like a permanent kiss.

Not bad, she thought.

Then she looked up, and the little man was in the seat opposite. He caught her eye and grinned widely. A series of lines curled about the edges of his smile. He lifted his hat hastily and put it down beside him on top of the little black box he had been carrying. A circle of white hair instantly sprang up stiffly about the large bald spot that made the center of his skull a desert.

She could not help smiling back a little, but then she caught sight of the black box again and the smile faded. She yanked at Norman's elbow.

Norman looked up from his newspaper. He had startlingly dark eyebrows that almost met above the bridge of his nose, giving him a formidable first appearance. But they and the dark eyes beneath bent upon her now with only the usual look of pleased and somewhat amused affection.

He said, "What's up?" He did not look at the plump little man opposite.

Livvy did her best to indicate what she saw by a little unobtrusive gesture of her hand and head. But the little man was watching and she felt a fool, since Norman simply stared at her blankly.

Finally she pulled him closer and whispered, "Don't you see what's printed on his box?"

She looked again as she said it, and there was no mistake. It was not very prominent, but the light caught it slantingly and it was a slightly more glistening area on a black background. In flowing script it said, "What If."

The little man was smiling again. He nodded his head rapidly and pointed to the words and then to himself several times over.

Norman said in an aside, "Must be his name."

Livvy replied, "Oh, how could that be anybody's name?"

Norman put his paper aside. "I'll show you." He leaned over and said, "Mr. If?"

The little man looked at him eagerly.

"Do you have the time, Mr. If?"

The little man took out a large watch from his vest pocket and displayed the dial.

"Thank you, Mr. If," said Norman. And again in a whisper, "See, Livvy."

He would have returned to his paper, but the little man was opening his box and raising a finger periodically as he did so, to enforce their attention. It was just a slab of frosted glass that he removed—about six by nine inches in length and width and perhaps an inch thick. It had beveled edges, rounded corners, and was completely featureless. Then he took out a little wire stand on which the glass slab fitted comfortably. He rested the combination on his knees and looked proudly at them.

Livvy said, with sudden excitement, "Heavens, Norman, it's a picture of some sort."

Norman bent close. Then he looked at the little man. "What's this? A new kind of television?"

The little man shook his head, and Livvy said, "No, Norman, it's *us*."

"What?"

"Don't you see? That's the streetcar we met on. There you are in the back seat wearing that old fedora I threw away three years ago. And that's Georgette and myself getting on. The fat lady's in the way. Now! Can't you see us?"

He muttered, "It's some sort of illusion."

"But you see it too, don't you? That's why he calls this 'What If.' It will *show* us what if. What if the streetcar hadn't swerved . . ."

She was sure of it. She was very excited and very sure of it. As she looked at the picture in the glass slab, the late afternoon sunshine grew dimmer and the inchoate chatter of the passengers around and behind them began fading.

How she remembered that day. Norman knew Georgette and had been about to surrender his seat to her when the car swerved and threw Livvy into his lap. It was such a ridiculously corny situation, but it had worked. She had been so embarrassed that he was forced first into gallantry and then into conversation. An introduction from Georgette was not even necessary. By the time they got off the streetcar, he knew where she worked.

She could still remember Georgette glowering at her, sulkily forcing a smile when they themselves separated. Georgette said, "Norman seems to like you."

Livvy replied, "Oh, don't be silly! He was just being polite. But he is nice-looking, isn't he?"

It was only six months after that that they married.

And now here was that same streetcar again, with Norman and herself and Georgette. As she thought that, the smooth train noises, the rapid clack-clack of the wheels, vanished completely. Instead, she was in the swaying confines of the streetcar. She had just boarded it with Georgette at the previous stop.

Livvy shifted weight with the swaying of the streetcar, as did forty others, sitting and standing, all to the same monotonous and rather ridiculous rhythm. She said, "Somebody's motioning at you, Georgette. Do you know him?"

"At me?" Georgette directed a deliberately casual glance over her shoulder. Her artificially long eyelashes flickered. She said, "I know him a little. What do you suppose he wants?"

"Let's find out," said Livvy. She felt pleased and a little wicked.

Georgette had a well-known habit of hoarding her male acquaintances, and it was rather fun to annoy her this way. And besides, this one seemed quite . . . interesting.

She snaked past the line of standees, and Georgette followed without enthusiasm. It was just as Livvy arrived opposite the young man's seat that the streetcar lurched heavily as it rounded a curve. Livvy snatched desperately in the direction of the straps. Her fingertips caught and she held on. It was a long moment before she could breathe. For some reason, it had seemed that there were no straps close enough to be reached. Somehow, she felt that by all the laws of nature she should have fallen.

The young man did not look at her. He was smiling at Georgette and rising from his seat. He had astonishing eyebrows that gave him a rather competent and self-confident appearance. Livvy decided that she definitely liked him.

Georgette was saying, "Oh no, don't bother. We're getting off in about two stops."

They did. Livvy said, "I thought we were going to Sach's."

"We are. There's just something I remember having to attend to here. It won't take but a minute."

"Next stop, Providence!" the loud-speakers were blaring. The train was slowing and the world of the past had shrunk itself into the glass slab once more. The little man was still smiling at them.

Livvy turned to Norman. She felt a little frightened. "Were you through all that, too?"

He said, "What happened to the time? We *can't* be reaching Providence yet?" He looked at his watch. "I guess we are." Then, to Livvy, "You didn't fall that time."

"Then you *did* see it?" She frowned. "Now, that's like Georgette. I'm sure there was no reason to get off the streetcar except to prevent my meeting you. How long had you known Georgette before then, Norman?"

"Not very long. Just enough to be able to recognize her at sight and to feel that I ought to offer her my seat."

Livvy curled her lip.

Norman grinned, "You can't be jealous of a might-have-been, kid. Besides, what difference would it have made? I'd have been sufficiently interested in you to work out a way of meeting you."

"You didn't even look at me."

"I hardly had the chance."

"Then how would you have met me?"

"Some way. I don't know how. But you'll admit this is a rather foolish argument we're having."

They were leaving Providence. Livvy felt a trouble in her mind. The little man had been following their whispered conversation, with only the loss of his smile to show that he understood. She said to him, "Can you show us more?"

Norman interrupted, "Wait now, Livvy. What are you going to try to do?"

She said, "I want to see our wedding day. What it would have been if I had caught the strap."

Norman was visibly annoyed. "Now, that's not fair. We might not have been married on the same day, you know."

But she said, "Can you show it to me, Mr. If?" and the little man nodded.

The slab of glass was coming alive again, glowing a little. Then the light collected and condensed into figures. A tiny sound of organ music was in Livvy's ears without there actually being sound.

Norman said with relief, "Well, there I am. That's our wedding. Are you satisfied?"

The train sounds were disappearing again, and the last thing Livvy heard was her own voice saying, "Yes, there *you* are. But where am *I*?"

LIVVY WAS WELL back in the pews. For a while she had not expected to attend at all. In the past months she had drifted further and further away from Georgette, without quite knowing why. She had heard of her engagement only through a mutual friend, and, of course, it was to

Norman. She remembered very clearly that day, six months before, when she had first seen him on the streetcar. It was the time Georgette had so quickly snatched her out of sight. She had met him since on several occasions, but each time Georgette was with him, standing between.

Well, she had no cause for resentment; the man was certainly none of hers. Georgette, she thought, looked more beautiful than she really was. And *he* was very handsome indeed.

She felt sad and rather empty, as though something had gone wrong—something that she could not quite outline in her mind. Georgette had moved up the aisle without seeming to see her, but earlier she had caught *his* eyes and smiled at him. Livvy thought he had smiled in return.

She heard the words distantly as they drifted back to her, "I now pronounce you—"

THE NOISE OF the train was back. A woman swayed down the aisle, herding a little boy back to their seats. There were intermittent bursts of girlish laughter from a set of four teenage girls halfway down the coach. A conductor hurried past on some mysterious errand.

Livvy was frozenly aware of it all.

She sat there, staring straight ahead, while the trees outside blended into a fuzzy, furious green and the telephone poles galloped past.

She said, "It was *she* you married."

He stared at her for a moment and then one side of his mouth quirked a little. He said lightly, "I didn't really, Olivia. You're still my wife, you know. Just think about it for a few minutes."

She turned to him. "Yes, you married me—because I fell in your lap. If I hadn't, you would have married Georgette. If she hadn't wanted you, you would have married someone else. You would have married *anybody*. So much for your jigsaw-puzzle pieces."

Norman said very slowly, "Well—I'll—be—darned!" He put both hands to his head and smoothed down the straight hair over his ears where it had a tendency to tuft up. For the moment it gave him the appearance of trying to hold his head together. He said, "Now, look here, Livvy, you're making a silly fuss over a stupid magician's trick. You can't blame me for something I haven't done."

"You would have done it."

"How do you know?"

"You've seen it."

"I've seen a ridiculous piece of—of hypnotism, I suppose." His voice suddenly raised itself into anger. He turned to the little man opposite. "Off with you, Mr. If, or whatever your name is. Get out of here. We don't want you. Get out before I throw your little trick out the window and you after it."

Livvy yanked at his elbow. "Stop it. *Stop it!* You're in a crowded train."

The little man shrank back into the corner of the seat as far as he could go and held his little black bag behind him. Norman looked at him, then at Livvy, then at the elderly lady across the way who was regarding him with patent disapproval.

He turned pink and bit back a pungent remark. They rode in frozen silence to and through New London.

Fifteen minutes past New London, Norman said, "Livvy!"

She said nothing. She was looking out the window but saw nothing but the glass.

He said again, "Livvy! Livvy! Answer me!"

She said dully, "What do you want?"

He said, "Look, this is all nonsense. I don't know how the fellow does it, but even granting it's legitimate, you're not being fair. Why stop where you did? Suppose I *had* married Georgette, do you suppose *you* would have stayed single? For all I know, you were already married at the time of my supposed wedding. Maybe that's why I married Georgette."

"I wasn't married."

"How do you know?"

"I would have been able to tell. I knew what my own thoughts were."

"Then you would have been married within the next year."

Livvy grew angrier. The fact that a sane remnant within her clamored at the unreason of her anger did not soothe her. It irritated her further, instead. She said, "And if I did, it would be no business of yours, certainly."

"Of course it wouldn't. But it would make the point that in the world of reality we can't be held responsible for the 'what ifs.' "

Livvy's nostrils flared. She said nothing.

Norman said, "Look! You remember the big New Year's celebration at Winnie's place year before last?"

"I certainly do. You spilled a keg of alcohol all over me."

"That's beside the point, and besides, it was only a cocktail shaker's worth. What I'm trying to say is that Winnie is just about your best friend and had been long before you married me."

"What of it?"

"Georgette was a good friend of hers too, wasn't she?"

"Yes."

"All right, then. You and Georgette would have gone to the party regardless of which one of you I had married. I would have had nothing to do with it. Let him show us the party as it would have been if I had married Georgette, and I'll bet you'd be there with either your fiancé or your husband."

Livvy hesitated. She felt honestly afraid of just that.

He said, "Are you afraid to take the chance?"

And that, of course, decided her. She turned on him furiously. "No, I'm not! And I hope I *am* married. There's no reason I should pine for you. What's more, I'd like to see what happens when you spill the shaker all over Georgette. She'll fill both your ears for you, and in public, too. I know *her*. Maybe you'll see a certain difference in the jigsaw pieces then." She faced forward and crossed her arms angrily and firmly across her chest.

Norman looked across at the little man, but there was no need to say anything. The glass slab was on his lap already. The sun slanted in from the west, and the white foam of hair that topped his head was edged with pink.

Norman said tensely, "Ready?"

Livvy nodded and let the noise of the train slide away again.

LIVVY STOOD, A little flushed with recent cold, in the doorway. She had just removed her coat, with its sprinkling of snow, and her bare arms were still rebelling at the touch of open air.

She answered the shouts that greeted her with "Happy New Years" of her own, raising her voice to make herself heard over the squealing of the radio. Georgette's shrill tones were almost the first thing she heard upon entering, and now she steered toward her. She hadn't seen Georgette, or Norman, in weeks.

Georgette lifted an eyebrow, a mannerism she had lately cultivated, and said, "Isn't anyone with you, Olivia?" Her eyes swept the immediate surroundings and then returned to Livvy.

Livvy said indifferently, "I think Dick will be around later. There was something or other he had to do first." She felt as indifferent as she sounded.

Georgette smiled tightly. "Well, Norman's here. That ought to keep you from being lonely, dear. At least, it's turned out that way before."

And as she said so, Norman sauntered in from the kitchen. He had a cocktail shaker in his hand, and the rattling of ice cubes castanetted his words. "Line up, you rioting revelers, and get a mixture that will really revel your riots— Why, Livvy!"

He walked toward her, grinning his welcome, "Where've you been keeping yourself? I haven't seen you in twenty years, seems like. What's the matter? Doesn't Dick want anyone else to see you?"

"Fill my glass, Norman," said Georgette sharply.

"Right away," he said, not looking at her. "Do you want one too, Livvy? I'll get you a glass." He turned, and everything happened at once.

Livvy cried, "Watch out!" She saw it coming, even had a vague feeling that all this had happened before, but it played itself out inexorably. His heel caught the edge of the carpet; he lurched, tried to right himself, and lost the cocktail shaker. It seemed to jump out of his hands, and a pint of ice-cold liquor drenched Livvy from shoulder to hem.

She stood there, gasping. The noises muted about her, and for a few intolerable moments she made futile brushing gestures at her gown, while Norman kept repeating, "Damnation!" in rising tones.

Georgette said coolly, "It's too bad, Livvy. Just one of those things. I imagine the dress can't be very expensive."

Livvy turned and ran. She was in the bedroom, which was at least empty and relatively quiet. By the light of the fringe-shaded lamp on the dresser, she poked among the coats on the bed, looking for her own.

Norman had come in behind her. "Look, Livvy, don't pay any attention to what she said. I'm really devilishly sorry. I'll pay—"

"That's all right. It wasn't your fault." She blinked rapidly and didn't look at him. "I'll just go home and change."

"Are you coming back?"

"I don't know. I don't think so."

"Look, Livvy . . ." His warm fingers were on her shoulders—

Livvy felt a queer tearing sensation deep inside her, as though she were ripping away from clinging cobwebs and—

— AND THE TRAIN noises were back.

Something *did* go wrong with the time when she was in there—in the slab. It was deep twilight now. The train lights were on. But it didn't matter. She seemed to be recovering from the wrench inside her.

Norman was rubbing his eyes with thumb and forefinger. "What happened?"

Livvy said, "It just ended. Suddenly."

Norman said uneasily, "You know, we'll be putting into New Haven soon." He looked at his watch and shook his head.

Livvy said wonderingly, "You spilled it on me."

"Well, so I did in real life."

"But in real life I was your wife. You ought to have spilled it on Georgette this time. Isn't that queer?" But she was thinking of Norman pursuing her; his hands on her shoulders. . . .

She looked up at him and said with warm satisfaction, "I wasn't married."

"No, you weren't. But was that Dick Reinhardt you were going around with?"

"Yes."

"You weren't planning to marry him, were you, Livvy?"

"Jealous, Norman?"

Norman looked confused. "Of that? Of a slab of glass? Of course not."

"I don't think I would have married him."

Norman said, "You know, I wish it hadn't ended when it did. There was something that was about to happen, I think." He stopped, then added slowly, "It was as though I would rather have done it to anybody else in the room."

"Even to Georgette."

"I wasn't giving two thoughts to Georgette. You don't believe me, I suppose."

"Maybe I do." She looked up at him. "I've been silly, Norman. Let's—let's live our real life. Let's not play with all the things that just might have been."

But he caught her hands. "No, Livvy. One last time. Let's see what we would have been doing right now, Livvy! This very minute! If I had married Georgette."

Livvy was a little frightened. "Let's not, Norman." She was thinking of his eyes, smiling hungrily at her as he held the shaker, while Georgette stood beside her, unregarded. She didn't *want* to know what happened afterward. She just wanted this life now, this *good* life.

New Haven came and went.

Norman said again, "I want to try, Livvy."

She said, "If you want to, Norman." She decided fiercely that it wouldn't matter. Nothing would matter. Her hands reached out and encircled his arm. She held it tightly, and while she held it she thought: "Nothing in the make-believe can take him from me."

Norman said to the little man, "Set 'em up again."

In the yellow light the process seemed to be slower. Gently the frosted slab cleared, like clouds being torn apart and dispersed by an unfelt wind.

Norman was saying, "There's something wrong. That's just the two of us, exactly as we are now."

He was right. Two little figures were sitting in a train on the seats which were farthest toward the front. The field was enlarging now—they were merging into it. Norman's voice was distant and fading.

"It's the same train," he was saying. "The window in back is cracked just as—"

LIVVY WAS BLINDINGLY happy. She said, "I wish we were in New York."

He said, "It will be less than an hour, darling." Then he said, "I'm going to kiss you." He made a movement, as though he were about to begin.

"Not here! Oh, Norman, people are looking."

Norman drew back. He said, "We should have taken a taxi."

"From Boston to New York?"

"Sure. The privacy would have been worth it."

She laughed. "You're funny when you try to act ardent."

"It isn't an act." His voice was suddenly a little somber. "It's not just an hour, you know. I feel as though I've been waiting five years."

"I do, too."

"Why couldn't I have met you first? It was such a waste."

"Poor Georgette," Livvy sighed.

Norman moved impatiently. "Don't be sorry for her, Livvy. We never really made a go of it. She was glad to get rid of me."

"I know that. That's why I say 'Poor Georgette.' I'm just sorry for her for not being able to appreciate what she had."

"Well, see to it that *you* do," he said. "See to it that you're immensely appreciative, infinitely appreciative—or more than that, see that you're at least half as appreciative as I am of what *I've* got."

"Or else you'll divorce me, too?"

"Over my dead body," said Norman.

Livvy said, "It's all so strange. I keep thinking; 'What if you hadn't spilt the cocktails on me that time at the party?' You wouldn't have followed me out; you wouldn't have told me; I wouldn't have known. It would have been so different . . . everything."

"Nonsense. It would have been just the same. It would have all happened another time."

"I wonder," said Livvy softly.

TRAIN NOISES MERGED into train noises. City lights flickered outside, and the atmosphere of New York was about them. The coach was astir with travelers dividing the baggage among themselves.

Livvy was an island in the turmoil until Norman shook her.

She looked at him and said, "The jigsaw pieces fit after all."

He said, "Yes."

She put a hand on his. "But it wasn't good, just the same. I was very wrong. I thought that because we had each other, we should have all the *possible* each others. But all the possibles are none of our business. The real is enough. Do you know what I mean?"

He nodded.

She said, "There are millions of other *what ifs*. I don't want to know what happened in any of them. I'll never say 'What if' again."

Norman said, "Relax, dear. Here's your coat." And he reached for the suitcases.

Livvy said with sudden sharpness, "Where's Mr. If?"

Norman turned slowly to the empty seat that faced them. Together they scanned the rest of the coach.

"Maybe," Norman said, "he went into the next coach."

"But why? Besides, he wouldn't leave his hat." And she bent to pick it up.

Norman said, "What hat?"

And Livvy stopped her fingers hovering over nothingness. She said, "It was here—I almost touched it." She straightened and said, "Oh, Norman, what if—"

Norman put a finger on her mouth. "Darling . . ."

She said, "I'm sorry. Here, let me help you with the suitcases."

The train dived into the tunnel beneath Park Avenue, and the noise of the wheels rose to a roar.

PREFACE TO
SALLY

FIRST APPEARANCE—*FANTASTIC,* May–June, 1953. Copyright 1953, by Ziff-Davis Publishing Company.

As long as I mentioned the parlor psychoanalyst in the introduction to "What If—," I may as well go on to those fellows who analyze stories in Freudian fashion.

Given a Freudian cast of mind and sufficient ingenuity, it is possible, I think, to translate any collection of words (rational, irrational, or nonsensical) into sexual symbolism, and then prate learnedly about the writer's unconscious.

I have said this before and I'll say it again. I don't know what is in my unconscious mind and I don't care. I don't even know for sure that I have one.

I am told that the contents of one's unconscious may so distort his personality that he can only straighten out by a close study of those hidden mental factors under the guidance of an analyst.

Maybe so, but the only thing about myself that I consider to be severe enough to warrant psychoanalytic treatment is my compulsion to write. Perhaps if I vacuumed my mentality and got rid of the compulsion, I could spend more time sleeping in the sun and playing golf, or whatever it is that people do who have nothing better to do.

But I don't want to, thank you. I know all about my compulsion and I like it and intend to keep it. Someone else can have my ticket for sleeping in the sun and playing golf.

So I hope no one ever has the impulse to psychoanalyze my stories and come to me with a complete explanation of my compulsions and hangups and neuroses and expect me to be tearfully grateful. I'm not in the market. Nor am I interested in the hidden meanings of my stories. If you find them, keep them.

Which brings me to "Sally." It is well known that the average American male loves his car with a pseudosexual passion, and who am I to be un-American?

Anyone reading "Sally" can sense that I feel strongly attracted to the heroine of the story and that this probably reflects something of my own life. Toward the end of the story, in fact, Sally does something which will allow the amateur Freudian a field day. (Oh, find it for yourself; it won't be hard.) The sexual symbolism is blatant and the parlor psychoanalyst can chuckle himself to death with what he will be sure exists in my unconscious mind.

Except that he will be quite wrong, because none of that was put in by my unconscious mind. It was all carefully and deliberately inserted by my conscious mind, because I wanted to.

SALLY

Sally was coming down the lake road, so I waved to her and called her by name. I always liked to see Sally. I liked all of them, you understand, but Sally's the prettiest one of the lot. There just isn't any question about it.

She moved a little faster when I waved to her. Nothing undignified. She was never that. She moved just enough faster to show that she was glad to see me, too.

I turned to the man standing beside me. "That's Sally," I said.

He smiled at me and nodded.

Mrs. Hester had brought him in. She said, "This is Mr. Gellhorn, Jake. You remember he sent you the letter asking for an appointment."

That was just talk, really. I have a million things to do around the Farm, and one thing I just can't waste my time on is mail. That's why I have Mrs. Hester around. She lives pretty close by, she's good at attending to foolishness without running to me about it, and most of all, she likes Sally and the rest. Some people don't.

"Glad to see you, Mr. Gellhorn," I said.

"Raymond J. Gellhorn," he said, and gave me his hand, which I shook and gave back.

He was a largish fellow, half a head taller than I and wider, too. He was about half my age, thirtyish. He had black hair, plastered down slick, with a part in the middle, and a thin mustache, very neatly trimmed. His jawbones got big under his ears and made him look as if he had a slight case of mumps. On video he'd be a natural to play the villain, so I assumed he was a nice fellow. It goes to show that video can't be wrong all the time.

"I'm Jacob Folkers," I said. "What can I do for you?"

He grinned. It was a big, wide, white-toothed grin. "You can tell me a little about your Farm here, if you don't mind."

I heard Sally coming up behind me and I put out my hand. She slid right into it and the feel of the hard, glossy enamel of her fender was warm in my palm.

"A nice automatobile," said Gellhorn.

That's one way of putting it. Sally was a 2045 convertible with a Hennis-Carleton positronic motor and an Armat chassis. She had the cleanest, finest lines I've ever seen on any model, bar none. For five years, she'd been my favorite, and I'd put everything into her I could dream up. In all that time, there'd never been a human being behind her wheel.

Not once.

"Sally," I said, patting her gently, "meet Mr. Gellhorn."

Sally's cylinder-purr keyed up a little. I listened carefully for any knocking. Lately, I'd been hearing motor-knock in almost all the cars and changing the gasoline hadn't done a bit of good. Sally was as smooth as her paint job this time, however.

"Do you have names for all your cars?" asked Gellhorn.

He sounded amused, and Mrs. Hester doesn't like people to sound as though they were making fun of the Farm. She said, sharply, "Certainly. The cars have real personalities, don't they, Jake? The sedans are all males and the convertibles are females."

Gellhorn was smiling again. "And do you keep them in separate garages, ma'am?"

Mrs. Hester glared at him.

Gellhorn said to me, "And now I wonder if I can talk to you alone, Mr. Folkers?"

"That depends," I said. "Are you a reporter?"

"No, sir. I'm a sales agent. Any talk we have is not for publication. I assure you I am interested in strict privacy."

"Let's walk down the road a bit. There's a bench we can use."

We started down. Mrs. Hester walked away. Sally nudged along after us.

I said, "You don't mind if Sally comes along, do you?"

"Not at all. She can't repeat what we say, can she?" He laughed at his own joke, reached over and rubbed Sally's grille.

Sally raced her motor and Gellhorn's hand drew away quickly.

"She's not used to strangers," I explained.

We sat down on the bench under the big oak tree where we could look across the small lake to the private speedway. It was the warm part of the day and the cars were out in force, at least thirty of them. Even at this distance I could see that Jeremiah was pulling his usual stunt of sneaking up behind some staid older model, then putting on a jerk of speed and yowling past with deliberately squealing brakes. Two weeks before he had crowded old Angus off the asphalt altogether, and I had turned off his motor for two days.

It didn't help though, I'm afraid, and it looks as though there's nothing to be done about it. Jeremiah is a sports model to begin with and that kind is awfully hot-headed.

"Well, Mr. Gellhorn," I said. "Could you tell me why you want the information?"

But he was just looking around. He said, "This *is* an amazing place, Mr. Folkers."

"I wish you'd call me Jake. Everyone does."

"All right, Jake. How many cars do you have here?"

"Fifty-one. We get one or two new ones every year. One year we got five. We haven't lost one yet. They're all in perfect running order. We even have a '15 model Mat-O-Mot in working order. One of the original automatics. It was the first car here."

Good old Matthew. He stayed in the garage most of the day now, but then he was the granddaddy of all positronic-motored cars. Those were the days when blind war veterans, paraplegics and heads of state were the only ones who drove automatics. But Samson Harridge was my boss and he was rich enough to be able to get one. I was his chauffeur at the time.

The thought makes me feel old. I can remember when there wasn't an automobile in the world with brains enough to find its own way home. I chauffeured dead lumps of machines that needed a man's hand at their controls every minute. Every year machines like that used to kill tens of thousands of people.

The automatics fixed that. A positronic brain can react much faster than a human one, of course, and it paid people to keep hands off the controls. You got in, punched your destination and let it go its own way.

We take it for granted now, but I remember when the first laws came out forcing the old machines off the highways and limiting travel to automatics. Lord, what a fuss. They called it everything from communism to fascism, but it emptied the highways and stopped the killing, and still more people get around more easily the new way.

Of course, the automatics were ten to a hundred times as expensive as the hand-driven ones, and there weren't many that could afford a private vehicle. The industry specialized in turning out omni-bus-automatics. You could always call a company and have one stop at your door in a matter of minutes and take you where you wanted to go. Usually, you had to drive with others who were going your way, but what's wrong with that?

Samson Harridge had a private car though, and I went to him the minute it arrived. The car wasn't Matthew to me then. I didn't know it was going to be the dean of the Farm some day. I only knew it was taking my job away and I hated it.

I said, "You won't be needing me anymore, Mr. Harridge?"

He said, "What are you dithering about, Jake? You don't think I'll trust myself to a contraption like that, do you? You stay right at the controls."

I said, "But it works by itself, Mr. Harridge. It scans the road, reacts properly to obstacles, humans, and other cars, and remembers routes to travel."

"So they say. So they say. Just the same, you're sitting right behind the wheel in case anything goes wrong."

Funny how you can get to like a car. In no time I was calling it Matthew and was spending all my time keeping it polished and humming. A positronic brain stays in condition best when it's got control of its chassis at all times, which means it's worth keeping the gas tank filled so that the motor can turn over slowly day and night. After a while, it got so I could tell by the sound of the motor how Matthew felt.

In his own way, Harridge grew fond of Matthew, too. He had no one else to like. He'd divorced or outlived three wives and outlived five children and three grandchildren. So when he died, maybe it wasn't surprising that he had his estate converted into a Farm for Retired Automobiles, with me in charge and Matthew the first member of a distinguished line.

It's turned out to be my life. I never got married. You can't get married and still tend to automatics the way you should.

The newspapers thought it was funny, but after a while they stopped joking about it. Some things you can't joke about. Maybe you've never been able to afford an automatic and maybe you never will, either, but take it from me, you get to love them. They're hard-working and affectionate. It takes a man with no heart to mistreat one or to see one mistreated.

It got so that after a man had an automatic for a while, he would make provisions for having it left to the Farm, if he didn't have an heir he could rely on to give it good care.

I explained that to Gellhorn.

He said, "Fifty-one cars! That represents a lot of money."

"Fifty thousand minimum per automatic, original investment," I said. "They're worth a lot more now. I've done things for them."

"It must take a lot of money to keep up the Farm."

"You're right there. The Farm's a non-profit organization, which gives us a break on taxes and, of course, new automatics that come in usually have trust funds attached. Still, costs are always going up. I have to keep the place landscaped; I keep laying down new asphalt and keeping the old in repair; there's gasoline, oil, repairs, and new gadgets. It adds up."

"And you've spent a long time at it."

"I sure have, Mr. Gellhorn. Thirty-three years."

"You don't seem to be getting much out of it yourself."

"I don't? You surprise me, Mr. Gellhorn. I've got Sally and fifty others. Look at her."

I was grinning. I couldn't help it. Sally was so clean, it almost hurt. Some insect must have died on her windshield or one speck of dust too many had landed, so she was going to work. A little tube protruded and spurted Tergosol over the glass. It spread quickly over the silicone surface film and squeegees snapped into place instantly, passing over the windshield and forcing the water into the little channel that led it, dripping, down to the ground. Not a speck of water got onto her glistening apple-green hood. Squeegee and detergent tube snapped back into place and disappeared.

Gellhorn said, "I never saw an automatic do that."

"I guess not," I said. "I fixed that up specially on our cars. They're clean. They're always scrubbing their glass. They like it. I've even got Sally fixed up with wax jets. She polishes herself every night till you can see your face in any part of her and shave by it. If I can scrape up the money, I'd be putting it on the rest of the girls. Convertibles are very vain."

"I can tell you how to scrape up the money, if that interests you."

"That always does. How?"

"Isn't it obvious, Jake? Any of your cars is worth fifty thousand minimum, you said. I'll bet most of them top six figures."

"So?"

"Ever think of selling a few?"

I shook my head. "You don't realize it, I guess, Mr. Gellhorn, but I can't sell any of these. They belong to the Farm, not to me."

"The money would go to the Farm."

"The incorporation papers of the Farm provide that the cars receive perpetual care. They can't be sold."

"What about the motors, then?"

"I don't understand you."

Gellhorn shifted position and his voice got confidential. "Look here, Jake, let me explain the situation. There's a big market for private automatics if they could only be made cheaply enough. Right?"

"That's no secret."

"And ninety-five percent of the cost is the motor. Right? Now, I know where we can get a supply of bodies. I also know where we can sell automatics at a good price—twenty or thirty thousand for the cheaper models, maybe fifty or sixty for the better ones. All I need are the motors. You see the solution?"

"I don't, Mr. Gellhorn." I did, but I wanted him to spell it out.

"It's right here. You've got fifty-one of them. You're an expert automatobile mechanic, Jake. You must be. You could unhook a motor and place it in another car so that no one would know the difference."

"It wouldn't be exactly ethical."

"You wouldn't be harming the cars. You'd be doing them a favor. Use your older cars. Use that old Mat-O-Mot."

"Well, now, wait a while, Mr. Gellhorn. The motors and bodies aren't two separate items. They're a single unit. Those motors are used to their own bodies. They wouldn't be happy in another car."

"All right, that's a point. That's a very good point, Jake. It would be like taking your mind and putting it in someone else's skull. Right? You don't think you would like that?"

"I don't think I would. No."

"But what if I took your mind and put it into the body of a young athlete. What about that, Jake? You're not a youngster anymore. If you had the chance, wouldn't you enjoy being twenty again? That's what I'm offering some of your positronic motors. They'll be put into new '57 bodies. The latest construction."

I laughed. "That doesn't make much sense, Mr. Gellhorn. Some of our cars may be old, but they're well-cared for. Nobody drives them. They're allowed their own way. They're *retired*, Mr. Gellhorn. I wouldn't want a twenty-year-old body if it meant I had to dig ditches for the rest of my new life and never have enough to eat. . . . What do you think, Sally?"

Sally's two doors opened and then shut with a cushioned slam.

"What that?" said Gellhorn.

"That's the way Sally laughs."

Gellhorn forced a smile. I guess he thought I was making a bad joke. He said, "Talk sense, Jake. Cars are *made* to be driven. They're probably not happy if you don't drive them."

I said, "Sally hasn't been driven in five years. She looks happy to me."

"I wonder."

He got up and walked toward Sally slowly. "Hi, Sally, how'd you like a drive?"

Sally's motor revved up. She backed away.

"Don't push her, Mr. Gellhorn," I said. "She's liable to be a little skittish."

Two sedans were about a hundred yards up the road. They had stopped. Maybe, in their own way, they were watching. I didn't bother about them. I had my eyes on Sally, and I kept them there.

Gellhorn said, "Steady now, Sally." He lunged out and seized the door handle. It didn't budge, of course.

He said, "It opened a minute ago."

I said, "Automatic lock. She's got a sense of privacy, Sally has."

He let go, then said, slowly and deliberately, "A car with a sense of privacy shouldn't go around with its top down."

He stepped back three or four paces, then quickly, so quickly I couldn't take a step to stop him, he ran forward and vaulted into the car. He caught Sally completely by surprise, because as he came down, he shut off the ignition before she could lock it in place.

For the first time in five years, Sally's motor was dead.

I think I yelled, but Gellhorn had the switch on "Manual" and locked that in place, too. He kicked the motor into action. Sally was alive again but she had no freedom of action.

He started up the road. The sedans were still there. They turned and drifted away, not very quickly. I suppose it was all a puzzle to them.

One was Giuseppe, from the Milan factories, and the other was Stephen. They were always together. They were both new at the Farm, but they'd been here long enough to know that our cars just didn't have drivers.

Gellhorn went straight on, and when the sedans finally got it through their heads that Sally wasn't going to slow down, that she *couldn't* slow down, it was too late for anything but desperate measures.

They broke for it, one to each side, and Sally raced between them like a streak. Steve crashed through the lakeside fence and rolled to a halt on the grass and mud not six inches from the water's edge. Giuseppe bumped along the land side of the road to a shaken halt.

I had Steve back on the highway and was trying to find out what harm, if any, the fence had done him, when Gellhorn came back.

Gellhorn opened Sally's door and stepped out. Leaning back, he shut off the ignition a second time.

"There," he said. "I think I did her a lot of good."

I held my temper. "Why did you dash through the sedans? There was no reason for that."

"I kept expecting them to turn out."

"They did. One went through a fence."

"I'm sorry, Jake," he said. "I thought they'd move more quickly. You know how it is. I've been in lots of buses, but I've only been in a private automatic two or three times in my life, and this is the first time I ever drove one. That just shows you, Jake. It got me, driving one, and

I'm pretty hard-boiled. I tell you, we don't have to go more than twenty percent below list price to reach a good market, and it would be ninety percent profit."

"Which we would split?"

"Fifty-fifty. And I take all the risks, remember."

"All right. I listened to you. Now you listen to me." I raised my voice because I was just too mad to be polite anymore. "When you turn off Sally's motor, you hurt her. How would you like to be kicked unconscious? That's what you do to Sally, when you turn her off."

"You're exaggerating, Jake. The automatobuses get turned off every night."

"Sure, that's why I want none of my boys or girls in your fancy '57 bodies, where I won't know what treatment they'll get. Buses need major repairs in their positronic circuits every couple of years. Old Matthew hasn't had his circuits touched in twenty years. What can you offer him compared with that?"

"Well, you're excited now. Suppose you think over my proposition when you've cooled down and get in touch with me."

"I've thought it over all I want to. If I ever see you again, I'll call the police."

His mouth got hard and ugly. He said, "Just a minute, old-timer."

I said, "Just a minute, you. This is private property and I'm ordering you off."

He shrugged. "Well, then, goodbye."

I said, "Mrs. Hester will see you off the property. Make that good-bye permanent."

BUT IT WASN'T permanent. I saw him again two days later. Two and a half days, rather, because it was about noon when I saw him first and a little after midnight when I saw him again.

I sat up in bed when he turned the light on, blinking blindly till I made out what was happening. Once I could see, it didn't take much explaining. In fact, it took none at all. He had a gun in his right fist, the nasty little needle barrel just visible between two fingers. I knew that all he had to do was to increase the pressure of his hand and I would be torn apart.

He said, "Put on your clothes, Jake."

I didn't move. I just watched him.

He said, "Look, Jake, I know the situation. I visited you two days ago, remember. You have no guards on this place, no electrified fences, no warning signals. Nothing."

I said, "I don't need any. Meanwhile there's nothing to stop you from leaving, Mr. Gellhorn. I would if I were you. This place can be very dangerous."

He laughed a little. "It is, for anyone on the wrong side of a fist gun."

"I see it," I said. "I know you've got one."

"Then get a move on. My men are waiting."

"No, sir, Mr. Gellhorn. Not unless you tell me what you want, and probably not then."

"I made you a proposition day before yesterday."

"The answer's still no."

"There's more to the proposition now. I've come here with some men and an automatobus. You have your chance to come with me and disconnect twenty-five of the positronic motors. I don't care which twenty-five you choose. We'll load them on the bus and take them away. Once they're disposed of, I'll see to it that you get your fair share of the money."

"I have your word on that, I suppose."

He didn't act as if he thought I was being sarcastic. He said, "You have."

I said, "No."

"If you insist on saying no, we'll go about it in our own way. I'll disconnect the motors myself, only I'll disconnect all fifty-one. Every one of them."

"It isn't easy to disconnect positronic motors, Mr. Gellhorn. Are you a robotics expert? Even if you are, you know, these motors have been modified by me."

"I know that, Jake. And to be truthful, I'm not an expert. I may ruin quite a few motors trying to get them out. That's why I'll have to work over all fifty-one if you don't cooperate. You see, I may only end up with twenty-five when I'm through. The first few I'll tackle will probably suffer the most. Till I get the hang of it, you see. And if I go it myself, I think I'll put Sally first in line."

I said, "I can't believe you're serious, Mr. Gellhorn."

He said, "I'm serious, Jake." He let it all dribble in. "If you want to help, you can keep Sally. Otherwise, she's liable to be hurt very badly. Sorry."

I said, "I'll come with you, but I'll give you one more warning. You'll be in trouble, Mr. Gellhorn."

He thought that was very funny. He was laughing very quietly as we went down the stairs together.

THERE WAS AN automatobus waiting outside the driveway to the garage apartments. The shadows of three men waited beside it, and their flash beams went on as we approached.

Gellhorn said in a low voice, "I've got the old fellow. Come on. Move the truck up the drive and let's get started."

One of the others leaned in and punched the proper instructions on the control panel. We moved up the driveway with the bus following submissively.

"It won't go inside the garage," I said. "The door won't take it. We don't have buses here. Only private cars."

"All right," said Gellhorn. "Pull it over onto the grass and keep it out of sight."

I could hear the thrumming of the cars when we were still ten yards from the garage.

Usually they quieted down if I entered the garage. This time they didn't. I think they knew that strangers were about, and once the faces of Gellhorn and the others were visible they got noisier. Each motor was a warm rumble, and each motor was knocking irregularly until the place rattled.

The lights went up automatically as we stepped inside. Gellhorn didn't seem bothered by the car noise, but the three men with him looked surprised and uncomfortable. They had the look of the hired thug about them, a look that was not compounded of physical features so much as of a certain wariness of eye and hang-dogness of face. I knew the type and I wasn't worried.

One of them said, "Damn it, they're burning gas."

"My cars always do," I replied stiffly.

"Not tonight," said Gellhorn. "Turn them off."

"It's not that easy, Mr. Gellhorn," I said.

"Get started!" he said.

I stood there. He had his fist gun pointed at me steadily. I said, "I told you, Mr. Gellhorn, that my cars have been well-treated while they've been at the Farm. They're used to being treated that way, and they resent anything else."

"You have one minute," he said. "Lecture me some other time."

"I'm trying to explain something. I'm trying to explain that my cars can understand what I say to them. A positronic motor will learn to do that with time and patience. My cars have learned. Sally understood your proposition two days ago. You'll remember she laughed when I asked her opinion. She also knows what you did to her and so do the two sedans you scattered. And the rest know what to do about trespassers in general."

"Look, you crazy old fool—"

"All I have to say is—" I raised my voice. "Get them!"

One of the men turned pasty and yelled, but his voice was drowned completely in the sound of fifty-one horns turned loose at once. They held their notes, and within the four walls of the garage the echoes rose to a wild, metallic call. Two cars rolled forward, not hurriedly, but with no possible mistake as to their target. Two cars fell in line behind the first two. All the cars were stirring in their separate stalls.

The thugs stared, then backed.

I shouted, "Don't get up against a wall."

Apparently, they had that instinctive thought themselves. They rushed madly for the door of the garage.

At the door one of Gellhorn's men turned, brought up a fist gun of his own. The needle pellet tore a thin, blue flash toward the first car. The car was Giuseppe.

A thin line of paint peeled up Giuseppe's hood, and the right half of his windshield crazed and splintered but did not break through.

The men were out the door, running, and two by two the cars crunched out after them into the night, their horns calling the charge.

I kept my hand on Gellhorn's elbow, but I don't think he could have moved in any case. His lips were trembling.

I said, "That's why I don't need electrified fences or guards. My property protects itself."

Gellhorn's eyes swiveled back and forth in fascination as, pair by pair, they whizzed by. He said, "They're killers!"

"Don't be silly. They won't kill your men."

"They're killers!"

"They'll just give your men a lesson. My cars have been specially trained for cross-country pursuit for just such an occasion; I think what your men will get will be worse than an outright quick kill. Have you ever been chased by an automatobile?"

Gellhorn didn't answer.

I went on. I didn't want him to miss a thing. "They'll be shadows going no faster than your men, chasing them here, blocking them there, blaring at them, dashing at them, missing with a screech of brake and a thunder of motor. They'll keep it up till your men drop, out of breath and half-dead, waiting for the wheels to crunch over their breaking bones. The cars won't do that. They'll turn away. You can bet, though, that your men will never return here in their lives. Not for all the money you or ten like you could give them. Listen—"

I tightened my hold on his elbow. He strained to hear.

I said, "Don't you hear car doors slamming?"

It was faint and distant, but unmistakable.

I said, "They're laughing. They're enjoying themselves."

His face crumpled with rage. He lifted his hand. He was still holding his fist gun.

I said, "I wouldn't. One automatocar is still with us."

I don't think he had noticed Sally till then. She had moved up so quietly. Though her right front fender nearly touched me, I couldn't hear her motor. She might have been holding her breath.

Gellhorn yelled.

I said, "She won't touch you, as long as I'm with you. But if you kill me. . . . You know, Sally doesn't like you."

Gellhorn turned the gun in Sally's direction.

"Her motor is shielded," I said, "and before you could ever squeeze the gun a second time she would be on top of you."

"All right, then," he yelled, and suddenly my arm was bent behind my back and twisted so I could hardly stand. He held me between Sally and himself, and his pressure didn't let up. "Back out with me and don't try to break loose, old-timer, or I'll tear your arm out of its socket."

I had to move. Sally nudged along with us, worried, uncertain what to do. I tried to say something to her and couldn't. I could only clench my teeth and moan.

Gellhorn's automatobus was still standing outside the garage. I was forced in. Gellhorn jumped in after me, locking the doors.

He said, "All right, now. We'll talk sense."

I was rubbing my arm, trying to get life back into it, and even as I did I was automatically and without any conscious effort studying the control board of the bus.

I said, "This is a rebuilt job."

"So?" he said caustically. "It's a sample of my work. I picked up a discarded chassis, found a brain I could use and spliced me a private bus. What of it?"

I tore at the repair panel, forcing it aside.

He said, "What the hell. Get away from that." The side of his palm came down numbingly on my left shoulder.

I struggled with him. "I don't want to do this bus any harm. What kind of a person do you think I am? I just want to take a look at some of the motor connections."

It didn't take much of a look. I was boiling when I turned to him. I said, "You're a hound and a bastard. You had no right installing this motor yourself. Why didn't you get a robotics man?"

He said, "Do I look crazy?"

"Even if it was a stolen motor, you had no right to treat it so. I wouldn't treat a man the way you treated that motor. Solder, tape, and pinch clamps! It's brutal!"

"It works, doesn't it?"

"Sure it works, but it must be hell for the bus. You could live with migraine headaches and acute arthritis, but it wouldn't be much of a life. This car is *suffering*."

"Shut up!" For a moment he glanced out the window at Sally, who had rolled up as close to the bus as she could. He made sure the doors and windows were locked.

He said, "We're getting out of here now, before the other cars come back. We'll stay away."

"How will that help you?"

"Your cars will run out of gas someday, won't they? You haven't got them fixed up so they can tank up on their own, have you? We'll come back and finish the job."

"They'll be looking for me," I said. "Mrs. Hester will call the police."

He was past reasoning with. He just punched the bus in gear. It lurched forward. Sally followed.

He giggled. "What can she do if you're here with me?"

Sally seemed to realize that, too. She picked up speed, passed us and was gone. Gellhorn opened the window next to him and spat through the opening.

The bus lumbered on over the dark road, its motor rattling unevenly. Gellhorn dimmed the periphery light until the phosphorescent green stripe down the middle of the highway, sparkling in the moonlight, was all that kept us out of the trees. There was virtually no traffic. Two cars passed ours, going the other way, and there was none at all on our side of the highway, either before or behind.

I heard the door-slamming first. Quick and sharp in the silence, first on the right and then on the left. Gellhorn's hands quivered as he punched savagely for increased speed. A beam of light shot out from among a scrub of trees, blinding us. Another beam plunged at us from behind the guard rails on the other side. At a crossover, four hundred yards ahead, there was sque-e-e-e-e as a car darted across our path.

"Sally went for the rest," I said. "I think you're surrounded."

"So what? What can they do?"

He hunched over the controls, peering through the windshield.

"And don't *you* try anything, old-timer," he muttered.

I couldn't. I was bone-weary; my left arm was on fire. The motor sounds gathered and grew closer. I could hear the motors hissing in odd patterns; suddenly it seemed to me that my cars were speaking to one another.

A medley of horns came from behind. I turned and Gellhorn looked quickly into the rearview mirror. A dozen cars were following in both lanes.

Gellhorn yelled and laughed madly.

I cried, "Stop! Stop the car!"

Because not a quarter of a mile ahead, plainly visible in the light beams of two sedans on the roadside was Sally, her trim body plunked square across the road. Two cars shot into the opposite lane to our left, keeping perfect time with us and preventing Gellhorn from turning out.

But he had no intention of turning out. He put his finger on the full-speed-ahead button and kept it there.

He said, "There'll be no bluffing here. This bus outweighs her five to one, old-timer, and we'll just push her off the road like a dead kitten."

I knew he could. The bus was on manual and his finger was on the button. I knew he would.

I lowered the window, and stuck my head out. "Sally," I screamed. "Get out of the way. *Sally!*"

It was drowned out in the agonized squeal of maltreated brake-bands. I felt myself thrown forward and heard Gellhorn's breath puff out of his body.

I said, "What happened?" It was a foolish question. We had stopped. That was what had happened. Sally and the bus were five feet apart. With five times her weight tearing down on her, she had not budged. The guts of her.

Gellhorn yanked at the Manual toggle switch. "It's got to," he kept muttering. "It's got to."

I said, "Not the way you hooked up the motor, expert. Any of the circuits could cross over."

He looked at me with a tearing anger and growled deep in his throat. His hair was matted over his forehead. He lifted his fist.

"That's all the advice out of you there'll ever be, old-timer."

And I knew the needle gun was about to fire.

I pressed back against the bus door, watching the fist come up, and when the door opened I went over backward and out, hitting the ground with a thud. I heard the door slam closed again.

I got to my knees and looked up in time to see Gellhorn struggle uselessly with the closing window, then aim his fist-gun quickly through the glass. He never fired. The bus got under way with a tremendous roar, and Gellhorn lurched backward.

Sally wasn't in the way any longer, and I watched the bus's rear lights flicker away down the highway.

I was exhausted. I sat down right there, right on the highway, and put my head down in my crossed arms, trying to catch my breath.

I heard a car stop gently at my side. When I looked up, it was Sally. Slowly—lovingly, you might say—her front door opened.

No one had driven Sally for five years—except Gellhorn, of course—and I know how valuable such freedom was to a car. I appreciated the gesture, but I said, "Thanks, Sally, but I'll take one of the newer cars."

I got up and turned away, but skillfully and neatly as a pirouette, she wheeled before me again. I couldn't hurt her feelings. I got in. Her front seat had the fine, fresh scent of an automatobile that kept itself spotlessly clean. I lay down across it, thankfully, and with even, silent, and rapid efficiency, my boys and girls brought me home.

MRS. HESTER BROUGHT me the copy of the radio transcript the next evening with great excitement.

"It's Mr. Gellhorn," she said. "The man who came to see you."

"What about him?"

I dreaded her answer.

"They found him dead," she said. "Imagine that. Just lying dead in a ditch."

"It might be a stranger altogether," I mumbled.

"Raymond J. Gellhorn," she said, sharply. "There can't be two, can there? The description fits, too. Lord, what a way to die? They found tire marks on his arms and body. Imagine! I'm glad it turned out to be a bus; otherwise they might have come poking around here."

"Did it happen near here?" I asked, anxiously.

"No . . . Near Cooksville. But, goodness, read about it yourself if you—What happened to Giuseppe?"

I welcomed the diversion. Giuseppe was waiting patiently for me to complete the repaint job. His windshield had been replaced.

After she left, I snatched up the transcript. There was no doubt about it. The doctor reported he had been running and was in a state of totally spent exhaustion. I wondered for how many miles the bus had played with him before the final lunge. The transcript had no notion of anything like that, of course.

They had located the bus and identified it by the tire tracks. The police had it and were trying to trace its ownership.

There was an editorial in the transcript about it. It had been the first traffic fatality in the state for that year and the paper warned strenuously against manual driving after night.

There was no mention of Gellhorn's three thugs and for that, at least, I was grateful. None of our cars had been seduced by the pleasure of the chase into killing.

That was all. I let the paper drop. Gellhorn had been a criminal. His treatment of the bus had been brutal. There was no question in my mind he deserved death. But still I felt a bit queasy over the manner of it.

A month has passed now and I can't get it out of my mind.

My cars talk to one another. I have no doubt about it anymore. It's as though they've gained confidence; as though they're not bothering to keep it secret anymore. Their engines rattle and knock continuously.

And they don't talk among themselves only. They talk to the cars and buses that come into the Farm on business. How long have they been doing that?

They must be understood, too. Gellhorn's bus understood them, for all it hadn't been on the grounds more than an hour. I can close my eyes and bring back that dash along the highway, with our cars flanking the bus on either side, clacking their motors at it till it understood, stopped, let me out, and ran off with Gellhorn.

Did my cars tell him to kill Gellhorn? Or was that his idea?

Can cars have such ideas? The motor designers say no. But they mean under ordinary conditions. Have they foreseen *everything*?

Cars get ill-used, you know.

Some of them enter the Farm and observe. They get told things. They find out that cars exist whose motors are never stopped, whom no one ever drives, whose every need is supplied.

Then maybe they go out and tell others. Maybe the word is spreading quickly. Maybe they're going to think that the Farm way should be the way all over the world. They don't understand. You couldn't expect them to understand about legacies and the whims of rich men.

There are millions of automatobiles on Earth, tens of millions. If the thought gets rooted in them that they're slaves; that they should do something about it . . . If they begin to think the way Gellhorn's bus did. . . .

Maybe it won't be till after my time. And then they'll have to keep a few of us to take care of them, won't they? They wouldn't kill us all.

And maybe they would. Maybe they wouldn't understand about how someone would have to care for them. Maybe they won't wait.

Every morning I wake up and think, Maybe today. . . .

I don't get as much pleasure out of my cars as I used to. Lately, I notice that I'm even beginning to avoid Sally.

PREFACE TO
FLIES

FIRST APPEARANCE—*THE MAGAZINE OF Fantasy and Science Fiction,* June 1953. Copyright 1953, by Fantasy House, Inc.

In late 1949, a new magazine appeared on the newsstands: *The Magazine of Fantasy.* By the second issue it had expanded its name to *The Magazine of Fantasy and Science Fiction,* and it is universally known by the initials *F & SF.*

I found *F & SF* daunting at first. It stressed style, it seemed to me, even more than idea, and I wasn't at all sure that I could manage style, or that I even knew what style might be. It was only a few months ago, indeed, that a reviewer, referring to me in her review of one of my books, said, "He is no stylist." I wrote at once to ask what a stylist was, but she never answered, so it looks as though I'll never find out.

As it happened, though, Anthony Boucher, the co-editor of the magazine, wrote me a letter after the appearance of "Hostess"—the first communication on record between us. In "Hostess," I had spoken of "the paler emotional surges of the late thirties," and Tony wrote in mild expostulation, having himself just turned forty at the time. (I had just turned thirty.) He told me that I had a delightful surprise ahead of me, and he was entirely right.

This initiated a pleasant correspondence and I lost some of my fear of *F & SF*. I thought I would try a story that stressed style but since I didn't (either then or now) know what style was, or how one went about getting it, I hadn't the faintest idea whether I had succeeded or not. I guess I did, though, for it was "Flies" I wrote and Mr. Boucher accepted and published it.

I had no way of telling it at the time, but this began what turned out to be the happiest of all my associations with science fiction magazines. I have no complaints about *Astounding, Galaxy*, or any of the rest, heaven knows, but *F & SF* has become something special to me, and it is only honest of me to say so.

By the way, if anyone thinks I am so arrogant that I can never accept any editorial correction, he is quite wrong. I don't *enjoy* editorial correction (no writer does) but I accept it quite often. (This, actually, is intended for my brother, who is a newspaper editor and who seems to think that all writers are fiendishly anti-editor out of sheer malevolent stupidity.)

Anyway, here is my example of how sweetly compliant I can be. When I first wrote "Flies," I named it "*King Lear*, IV, i, 36–37." Mr. Boucher wrote me, somewhat in horror, and asked if I insisted on the title, because nobody would look it up and it would be meaningless.

I thought it over and decided he was right and renamed the story "Flies." After you read the story, however, you're welcome to look it up. You'll find out what started the train of thought that ended in this particular story.

FLIES

"Flies!" said Kendell Casey, wearily. He swung his arm. The fly circled, returned and nestled on Casey's shirt-collar.

From somewhere there sounded the buzzing of a second fly.

Dr. John Polen covered the slight uneasiness of his chin by moving his cigarette quickly to his lips.

He said, "I didn't expect to meet you, Casey. Or you, Winthrop. Or ought I call you Reverend Winthrop?"

"Ought I call you Professor Polen?" said Winthrop, carefully striking the proper vein of rich-toned friendship.

They were trying to snuggle into the cast-off shell of twenty years back, each of them. Squirming and cramming and not fitting.

Damn, thought Polen fretfully, why do people attend college reunions?

Casey's hot blue eyes were still filled with the aimless anger of the college sophomore who has discovered intellect, frustration, and the tag-ends of cynical philosophy all at once.

Casey! Bitter man of the campus!

He hadn't outgrown that. Twenty years later and it was Casey, bitter ex-man of the campus! Polen could see that in the way his finger tips moved aimlessly and in the manner of his spare body.

As for Winthrop? Well, twenty years older, softer, rounder. Skin pinker, eyes milder. Yet no nearer the quiet certainty he would never find. It was all there in the quick smile he never entirely abandoned, as though he feared there would be nothing to take its place, that its absence would turn his face into a smooth and featureless flesh.

Polen was tired of reading the aimless flickering of a muscle's end; tired of usurping the place of his machines; tired of the too much they told him.

Could they read him as he read them? Could the small restlessness of his own eyes broadcast the fact that he was damp with the disgust that had bred mustily within him?

Damn, thought Polen, why didn't I stay away?

They stood there, all three, waiting for one another to say something, to flick something from across the gap and bring it, quivering, into the present.

Polen tried it. He said, "Are you still working in chemistry, Casey?"

"In my own way, yes," said Casey, gruffly. "I'm not the scientist you're considered to be. I do research on insecticides for E. J. Link at Chatham."

Winthrop said, "Are you really? You said you would work on insecticides. Remember, Polen? And with all that, the flies dare still be after you, Casey?"

Casey said, "Can't get rid of them. I'm the best proving ground in the labs. No compound we've made keeps them away when I'm around. Someone once said it was my odor. I attract them."

Polen remembered the someone who had said that.

Winthrop said, "Or else—"

Polen felt it coming. He tensed.

"Or else," said Winthrop, "it's the curse, you know." His smile intensified to show that he was joking, that he forgave past grudges.

Damn, thought Polen, they haven't even changed the words. And the past came back.

"FLIES," SAID CASEY, swinging his arm, and slapping. "Ever see such a thing? Why don't they light on you two?"

Johnny Polen laughed at him. He laughed often then. "It's something in your body odor, Casey. You could be a boon to science. Find out the nature of the odorous chemical, concentrate it, mix it with DDT, and you've got the best fly-killer in the world."

"A fine situation. What do I smell like? A lady fly in heat? It's a shame they have to pick on me when the whole damned world's a dung heap."

Winthrop frowned and said with a faint flavor of rhetoric, "Beauty is not the only thing, Casey, in the eye of the beholder."

Casey did not deign a direct response. He said to Polen, "You know what Winthrop told me yesterday? He said those damned flies were the curse of Beelzebub."

"I was joking," said Winthrop.

"Why Beelzebub?" asked Polen.

"It amounts to a pun," said Winthrop. "The ancient Hebrews used it as one of their many terms of derision for alien gods. It comes from *Ba'al*, meaning *lord* and *zevuv*, meaning *fly*. The lord of flies."

Casey said, "Come on, Winthrop, don't say you don't believe in Beelzebub."

"I believe in the existence of evil," said Winthrop, stiffly.

"I mean Beelzebub. Alive. Horns. Hooves. A sort of competition deity."

"Not at all." Winthrop grew stiffer. "Evil is a short-term affair. In the end it must lose—"

Polen changed the subject with a jar. He said, "I'll be doing graduate work for Venner, by the way. I talked with him day before yesterday, and he'll take me on."

"No! That's wonderful." Winthrop glowed and leaped to the subject-change instantly. He held out a hand with which to pump Polen's. He was always conscientiously eager to rejoice in another's good fortune. Casey often pointed that out.

Casey said, "Cybernetics Venner? Well, if you can stand him, I suppose he can stand you."

Winthrop went on. "What did he think of your idea? Did you tell him your idea?"

"What idea?" demanded Casey.

Polen had avoided telling Casey so far. But now Venner had considered it and had passed it with a cool, "Interesting!" How could Casey's dry laughter hurt it now?

Polen said, "It's nothing much. Essentially, it's just a notion that emotion is the common bond of life, rather than reason or intellect. It's practically a truism, I suppose. You can't tell what a baby thinks or even *if* it thinks, but it's perfectly obvious that it can be angry, frightened or contented even when a week old. See?

"Same with animals. You can tell in a second if a dog is happy or if a cat is afraid. The point is that their emotions are the same as those we would have under the same circumstances."

"So?" said Casey. "Where does it get you?"

"I don't know yet. Right now, all I can say is that emotions are universals. Now suppose we could properly analyze all the actions of men and certain familiar animals and equate them with the visible emotion. We might find a tight relationship. Emotion A might always involve Motion B. Then we could apply it to animals whose emotions we couldn't guess at by common sense alone. Like snakes, or lobsters."

"Or flies," said Casey, as he slapped viciously at another and flicked its remains off his wrist in furious triumph.

He went on. "Go ahead, Johnny. I'll contribute the flies and you study them. We'll establish a science of flychology and labor to make them happy by removing their neuroses. After all, we want the greatest good of the greatest number, don't we? And there are more flies than men."

"Oh, well," said Polen.

CASEY SAID, "SAY, Polen, did you ever follow up that weird idea of yours? I mean, we all know you're a shining cybernetic light, but I haven't been reading your papers. With so many ways of wasting time, something has to be neglected, you know."

"What idea?" asked Polen, woodenly.

"Come on. You know. Emotions of animals and all that sort of guff. Boy, those were the days. I used to know madmen. Now I only come across idiots."

Winthrop said, "That's right, Polen. I remember it very well. Your first year in graduate school you were working on dogs and rabbits. I believe you even tried some of Casey's flies."

Polen said, "It came to nothing in itself. It gave rise to certain new principles of computing, however, so it wasn't a total loss."

Why did they talk about it?

Emotions! What right had anyone to meddle with emotions? Words were invented to conceal emotions. It was the dreadfulness of raw emotion that had made language a basic necessity.

Polen knew. His machines had bypassed the screen of verbalization and dragged the unconscious into the sunlight. The boy and the girl, the son and the mother. For that matter, the cat and the mouse or the snake and the bird. The data rattled together in its universality and it had all poured into and through Polen until he could no longer bear the touch of life.

In the last few years he had so painstakingly schooled his thoughts in other directions. Now these two came, dabbling in his mind, stirring up its mud.

Casey batted abstractedly across the tip of his nose to dislodge a fly. "Too bad," he said. "I used to think you could get some fascinating things out of, say, rats. Well, maybe not fascinating, but then not as boring as the stuff you would get out of our somewhat-human beings. I used to think—"

Polen remembered what he used to think.

CASEY SAID, "DAMN this DDT. The flies feed on it, I think. You know, I'm going to do graduate work in chemistry and then get a job on insecticides. So help me. I'll personally get something that *will* kill the vermin."

They were in Casey's room, and it had a somewhat keroseney odor from the recently applied insecticide.

Polen shrugged and said, "A folded newspaper will always kill."

Casey detected a non-existent sneer and said instantly, "How would you summarize your first year's work, Polen? I mean aside from the true summary any scientist could state if he dared, by which I mean: 'Nothing.' "

"Nothing," said Polen. "There's your summary."

"Go on," said Casey. "You use more dogs than the physiologists do and I bet the dogs mind the physiological experiments less. I would."

"Oh, leave him alone," said Winthrop. "You sound like a piano with 87 keys eternally out of order. You're a bore!"

You couldn't say that to Casey.

He said, with sudden liveliness, looking carefully away from Winthrop, "I'll tell you what you'll probably find in animals, if you look closely enough. Religion."

"What the dickens!" said Winthrop, outraged. "That's a foolish remark."

Casey smiled. "Now, now, Winthrop. *Dickens* is just a euphemism for *devil* and you don't want to be swearing."

"Don't teach me morals. And don't be blasphemous."

"What's blasphemous about it? Why shouldn't a flea consider the dog as something to be worshipped? It's the source of warmth, food, and all that's good for a flea."

"I don't want to discuss it."

"Why not? Do you good. You could even say that to an ant, an anteater is a higher order of creation. He would be too big for them to comprehend, too mighty to dream of resisting. He would move among them like an unseen, inexplicable whirlwind, visiting them with destruction and death. But that wouldn't spoil things for the ants. They would reason that destruction was simply their just punishment for evil. And the anteater wouldn't even know he was a deity. Or care."

Winthrop had gone white. He said, "I know you're saying this only to annoy me and I am sorry to see you risking your soul for a moment's amusement. Let me tell you this," his voice trembled a little, "and let me say it very seriously. The flies that torment you are your punishment in this life. Beelzebub, like all the forces of evil, may think he does evil, but it's only the ultimate good after all. The curse of Beelzebub is on you for *your* good. Perhaps it will succeed in getting you to change your way of life before it's too late."

He ran from the room.

Casey watched him go. He said, laughing, "I told you Winthrop believed in Beelzebub. It's funny the respectable names you can give to superstition." His laughter died a little short of its natural end.

There were two flies in the room, buzzing through the vapors toward him.

Polen rose and left in heavy depression. One year had taught him little, but it was already too much, and his laughter was thinning. Only his machines could analyze the emotions of animals properly, but he was already guessing too deeply concerning the emotions of men.

He did not like to witness wild murder-yearnings where others could see only a few words of unimportant quarrel.

CASEY SAID, SUDDENLY, "Say, come to think of it, you did try some of my flies, the way Winthrop says. How about that?"

"Did I? After twenty years, I scarcely remember," murmured Polen.

Winthrop said, "You must. We were in your laboratory and you complained that Casey's flies followed him even there. He suggested you analyze them and you did. You recorded their motions and buzzings and wing-wiping for half an hour or more. You played with a dozen different flies."

Polen shrugged.

"Oh, well," said Casey. "It doesn't matter. It was good seeing you, old man." The hearty handshake, the thump on the shoulder, the broad grin—to Polen it all translated into sick disgust on Casey's part that Polen was a "success" after all.

Polen said, "Let me hear from you sometimes."

The words were dull thumps. They meant nothing. Casey knew that. Polen knew that. Everyone knew that. But words were meant to hide emotion and when they failed, humanity loyally maintained the pretense.

Winthrop's grasp of the hand was gentler. He said. "This brought back old times, Polen. If you're ever in Cincinnati, why don't you stop in at the meeting-house? You'll always be welcome."

To Polen, it all breathed of the man's relief at Polen's obvious depression. Science, too, it seemed, was not the answer, and Winthrop's basic and ineradicable insecurity felt pleased at the company.

"I will," said Polen. It was the usual polite way of saying, I won't.

He watched them thread separately to other groups.

Winthrop would never know. Polen was sure of that. He wondered if Casey knew. It would be the supreme joke if Casey did not.

He *had* run Casey's flies, of course, not that once alone, but many times. Always the same answer! Always the same unpublishable answer.

With a cold shiver he could not quite control, Polen was suddenly conscious of a single fly loose in the room, veering aimlessly for a moment, then beating strongly and reverently in the direction Casey had taken a moment before.

Could Casey *not* know? Could it be the essence of the primal punishment that he never learn he was Beelzebub?

Casey! Lord of the Flies!

NOBODY HERE BUT—

FIRST APPEARANCE—*STAR SCIENCE FICTION Stories,* 1953. Copyright 1953, by Ballantine Books, Inc.

I suppose that one of those stock phrases for which everyone is responsible at one time or another is: "Well, whatever does he see in *her*?" Or, "Well, whatever does she see in *him*?"

It's a ridiculous question because the sort of thing that he sees in her or she sees in him that isn't visible to the general population is probably you-know-very-well-what.

Just the same, I'm as prone to sneer as the next fellow and when I see a movie in which the girl falls in love with a fellow who has no visible advantages outside of being tall, lean, strong, fearless, and incredibly handsome, I am naturally disgusted. "Whatever does she see in *him*?" I ask.

Pressed for a reason for the sneer, I can point out that this tall, lean, strong, fearless, and incredibly handsome fellow almost invariably has the brain capacity of a gnat. He speaks in an occasional grunt and views the world with dim eyes backed by a lackluster brain. He is known to all and sundry, and particularly to the girl who is trying to mask her mad passion for him, as a "big lug," or, possibly, as a "big galoot."

These lugs or galoots are particularly impervious to even subhuman understanding of feminine psychology and the more they display this the more desperately they are loved.

I tell you I can't stand it. The fact that I know darned well that if I ever tried to compete for a girl with one of these tall, lean cretins, I would lose out, makes it worse. So I took my revenge; I decided never to write a big lug into one of my stories.

As far as I knew I never did. As of yesterday, I would have sworn to that, and backed the oath with any sum of money. Yet when I read over "Nobody Here But—" just now, prior to writing a fitting introduction, I realized with sinking heart and disbelieving mind that here was a story with a galoot.

Good Lord!

NOBODY HERE BUT—

You see, it wasn't our fault. We had no idea anything was wrong until I called Cliff Anderson and spoke to him when he wasn't there. What's more, I wouldn't have known he wasn't there, if it wasn't that he walked in while I was talking to him.

No, no, no, *no*—

I never seem to be able to tell this straight. I get too excited.—Look, I might as well begin at the beginning. I'm Bill Billings; my friend is Cliff Anderson. I'm an electrical engineer, he's a mathematician, and we're on the faculty of Midwestern Institute of Technology. Now you know who we are.

Ever since we got out of uniform, Cliff and I have been working on calculating machines. You know what they are. Norbert Wiener popularized them in his book, *Cybernetics*. If you've seen pictures of them, you know that they're great big things. They take up a whole wall and they're very complicated; also expensive.

But Cliff and I had ideas. You see, what makes a thinking machine so big and expensive is that it has to be full of relays and vacuum tubes just so that microscopic electric currents can be controlled and made to flicker on and off, here and there. Now the really important things are those little electric currents, so—

I once said to Cliff, "Why can't we control the currents without all the salad dressing?"

Cliff said, "Why not, indeed," and started working on the mathematics.

How we got where we did in two years is no matter. It's what we got after we finished that made the trouble. It turned out that we ended with something about this high and maybe so wide and just about this deep—

No, no. I forget that you can't see me. I'll give you the figures. It was about three feet high, six feet long, and two feet deep. Got that? It took two men to carry it but it could be carried and that was the point. And still, mind you, it could do anything the wall-size calculators could. Not as fast, maybe, but we were still working.

We had big ideas about that thing, the very biggest. We could put it on ships or airplanes. After a while, if we could make it small enough, an automobile could carry one.

We were especially interested in the automobile angle. Suppose you had a little thinking machine on the dashboard, hooked to the engine and battery and equipped with photo-electric eyes. It could choose an ideal course, avoid cars, stop at red lights, pick the optimum speed for the terrain. Everybody could sit in the back seat and automobile accidents would vanish.

All of it was fun. There was so much excitement to it, so many thrills every time we worked out another consolidation, that I could still cry when I think of the time I picked up the telephone to call our lab and tumbled everything into the discard.

I was at Mary Ann's house that evening— Or have I told you about Mary Ann yet? No. I guess I haven't.

Mary Ann was the girl who would have been my fiancee but for two ifs. One, if she were willing, and two, if I had the nerve to ask her. She has red hair and crams something like two tons of energy into about 110 pounds of body which fills out very nicely from the ground to five and a half feet up. I was dying to ask her, you understand, but each time I'd see her coming into sight, setting a match to my heart with every movement, I'd just break down.

It's not that I'm not good-looking. People tell me I'm adequate. I've got all my hair; I'm nearly six feet tall; I can even dance. It's just that

I've nothing to offer. I don't have to tell you what college teachers make. With inflation and taxes, it amounts to just about nothing. Of course, if we got the basic patents rolled up on our little thinking machine, things would be different. But I couldn't ask her to wait for that, either. Maybe, after it was all set—

Anyway, I just stood there, wishing, that evening, as she came into the living room. My arm was groping blindly for the phone.

Mary Ann said, "I'm all ready, Bill. Let's go."

I said, "Just a minute. I want to ring up Cliff."

She frowned a little, "Can't it wait?"

"I was supposed to call him two hours ago," I explained.

It only took two minutes. I rang the lab. Cliff was putting in an evening of work and so he answered. I asked something, then he said something, I asked some more and he explained. The details don't matter, but as I said, he's the mathematician of the combination. When I build the circuits and put things together in what look like impossible ways, he's the guy who shuffles the symbols and tells me whether they're really impossible. Then, just as I finished and hung up, there was a ring at the door.

For a minute, I thought Mary Ann had another caller and got sort of stiff-backed as I watched her go to the door. I was scribbling down some of what Cliff had just told me while I watched. But then she opened the door and it was only Cliff Anderson after all.

He said, "I thought I'd find you here— Hello, Mary Ann. Say, weren't you going to ring me at six? You're as reliable as a cardboard chair." Cliff is short and plump and always willing to start a fight, but I know him and pay no attention.

I said, "Things turned up and it slipped my mind. But I just called, so what's the difference?"

"Called? Me? When?"

I started to point to the telephone and gagged. Right then, the bottom fell out of things. Exactly five seconds before the doorbell had sounded I had been on the phone talking to Cliff in the lab, and the lab was six miles away from Mary Ann's house.

I said, "I—just spoke to you."

I wasn't getting across. Cliff just said, "To me?" again.

I was pointing to the phone with both hands now, "On the phone. I called the lab. On this phone here! Mary Ann heard me. Mary Ann, wasn't I just talking to—"

Mary Ann said, "I don't know whom you were talking to. —Well, shall we go?" That's Mary Ann. She's a stickler for honesty.

I sat down. I tried to be very quiet and clear. I said, "Cliff, I dialed the lab's phone number, you answered the phone, I asked you if you had the details worked out, you said, yes, and gave them to me. Here they are. I wrote them down. Is this correct or not?"

I handed him the paper on which I had written the equations.

Cliff looked at them. He said, "They're correct. But where could you have gotten them? You didn't work them out yourself, did you?"

"I just told you. You gave them to me over the phone."

Cliff shook his head, "Bill, I haven't been in the lab since seven fifteen. There's nobody there."

"I spoke to somebody, I tell you."

Mary Ann was fiddling with her gloves. "We're getting late," she said.

I waved my hands at her to wait a bit, and said to Cliff, "Look, are you sure—"

"There's nobody there, unless you want to count Junior." Junior was what we called our pint-sized mechanical brain.

We stood there, looking at one another. Mary Ann's toe was still hitting the floor like a time bomb waiting to explode.

Then Cliff laughed. He said, "I'm thinking of a cartoon I saw, somewhere. It shows a robot answering the phone and saying, 'Honest, boss, there's nobody here but us complicated thinking machines."

I didn't think that was funny. I said, "Let's go to the lab."

Mary Ann said, "Hey! We won't make the show."

I said, "Look, Mary Ann, this is very important. It's just going to take a minute. Come along with us and we'll go straight to the show from there."

She said, "The show starts—" And then she stopped talking, because I grabbed her wrist and we left.

That just shows how excited I was. Ordinarily, I wouldn't ever have dreamed of shoving her around. I mean, Mary Ann is quite the lady. It's just that I had so many things on my mind. I don't even really remember grabbing her wrist, come to think of it. It's just that the next thing I knew, I was in the auto and so was Cliff and so was she, and she was rubbing her wrist and muttering under her breath about big gorillas.

I said, "Did I hurt you, Mary Ann?"

She said, "No, of course not. I have my arm yanked out of its socket every day, just for fun." Then she kicked me in the shin.

She only does things like that because she has red hair. Actually, she has a very gentle nature, but she tries very hard to live up to the redhead mythology. I see right through that, of course, but I humor her, poor kid.

We were at the laboratory in twenty minutes.

THE INSTITUTE IS empty at night. It's emptier than a building would ordinarily be. You see, it's designed to have crowds of students rushing through the corridors and when they aren't there, it's unnaturally lonely. Or maybe it was just that I was afraid to see what might be sitting in our laboratory upstairs. Either way, footsteps were uncomfortably loud and the self-service elevator was downright dingy.

I said to Mary Ann, "This won't take long." But she just sniffed and looked beautiful.

She can't help looking beautiful.

Cliff had the key to the laboratory and I looked over his shoulder when he opened the door. There was nothing to see. Junior was there, sure, but he looked just as he had when I saw him last. The dials in front registered nothing and except for that, there was just a large box, with a cable running back into the wall socket.

Cliff and I walked up on either side of Junior. I think we were planning to grab it if it made a sudden move. But then we stopped because Junior just wasn't doing anything. Mary Ann was looking at it, too. In fact, she ran her middle finger along its top and then looked at the finger tip and twiddled it against her thumb to get rid of the dust.

I said, "Mary Ann, don't you go near it. Stay at the other end of the room."

She said, "It's just as dirty there."

She'd never been in our lab before, and of course she didn't realize that a laboratory wasn't the same thing as a baby's bedroom, if you know what I mean. The janitor comes in twice a day and all he does is empty the wastebaskets. About once a week, he comes in with a dirty mop, makes mud on the floor, and shoves it around a little.

Cliff said, "The telephone isn't where I left it."

I said, "How do you know?"

"Because I left it there." He pointed. "And now it's here."

If he were right, the telephone had moved closer to Junior. I swallowed and said, "Maybe you don't remember right." I tried to laugh without sounding very natural and said, "Where's the screwdriver?"

"What are you going to do?"

"Just take a look inside. For laughs."

Mary Ann said, "You'll get yourself all dirty." So I put on my lab coat. She's a very thoughtful girl, Mary Ann.

I got to work with a screwdriver. Of course, once Junior was really perfected, we were going to have models manufactured in welded, one-piece cases. We were even thinking of molded plastic in colors, for home use. In the lab model, though, we held it together with screws so that we could take it apart and put it together as often as we wanted to.

Only the screws weren't coming out. I grunted and yanked and said, "Some joker was putting his weight on these when he screwed these things in."

Cliff said, "You're the only one who ever touches the thing."

He was right, too, but that didn't make it any easier. I stood up and passed the back of my hand over my forehead. I held out the screwdriver to him, "Want to try?"

He did, and didn't get any further than I did. He said, "That's funny."

I said, "What's funny?"

He said, "I had a screw turning just now. It moved about an eighth of an inch and then the screwdriver slipped."

"What's funny about that?"

Cliff backed away and put down the screwdriver with two fingers. "What's funny is that I saw the screw move back an eighth of an inch and tighten up again."

Mary Ann was fidgeting again. She said, "Why don't your scientific minds think of a blowtorch, if you're so anxious." There was a blowtorch on one of the benches and she was pointing to it.

Well, ordinarily, I wouldn't think any more of using a blowtorch on Junior than on myself. But I was thinking something and Cliff was thinking something and we were both thinking the same thing. *Junior didn't want to be opened up.*

Cliff said, "What do you think, Bill?"

And I said, "I don't know, Cliff."

Mary Ann said, "Well, hurry up, lunkhead, we'll miss the show."

So I picked up the blowtorch and adjusted the gauge on the oxygen cylinder. It was going to be like stabbing a friend.

But Mary Ann stopped the proceedings by saying, "Well, how stupid can men be? These screws are loose. You must have been turning the screwdriver the wrong way."

Now there isn't much chance of turning a screwdriver the wrong way. Just the same, I don't like to contradict Mary Ann, so I just said, "Mary Ann, don't stay too close to Junior. Why don't you wait by the door."

But she just said, "Well, look!" And there was a screw in her hand and an empty hole in the front of Junior's case. She had removed it by hand.

Cliff said, "Holy Smoke!"

They were turning, all dozen screws. They were doing it by themselves, like little worms crawling out of their holes, turning round and round, then dropping out. I scrabbled them up and only one was left. It hung on for a while, the front panel sagging from it, till I reached out. Then the last screw dropped and the panel fell gently into my arms. I put it to one side.

Cliff said, "It did that on purpose. It heard us mention the blowtorch and gave up." His face is usually pink, but it was white then.

I was feeling a little queer myself. I said, "What's it trying to hide?"

"I don't know."

We bent before its open insides and for a while we just looked. I could hear Mary Ann's toe begin to tap the floor again. I looked at my wristwatch and I had to admit to myself we didn't have much time. In fact, we didn't have any time left.

And then I said, "It's got a diaphragm."

Cliff said, "Where?" and bent closer.

I pointed. "And a loud speaker."

"You didn't put them in?"

"Of course I didn't put them in. I ought to know what I put in. If I put it in, I'd remember."

"Then how did it get in?"

We were squatting and arguing. I said, "It made them itself, I suppose. Maybe it grows them. Look at that."

I pointed again. Inside the box at two different places, were coils of something that looked like thin garden hose, except that they were of metal. They spiraled tightly so that they lay flat. At the end of each coil, the metal divided into five or six thin filaments that were in little subspirals.

"You didn't put those in either?"

"No, I didn't put those in either."

"What are they?"

He knew what they were and I knew what they were. Something had to reach out to get materials for Junior to make parts for itself; something had to snake out for the telephone. I picked up the front panel and looked at it again. There were two circular bits of metal cut out and hinged so that they could swing forward and leave a hole for something to come through.

I poked a finger through one and held it up for Cliff to see, and said, "I didn't put this in either."

Mary Ann was looking over my shoulder now, and without warning she reached out. I was wiping my fingers with a paper towel to get off the dust and grease and didn't have time to stop her. I should have known Mary Ann, though; she's always so anxious to help.

Anyway, she reached in to touch one of the—well, we might as well say it—tentacles. I don't know if she actually touched them or not. Later on she claimed she hadn't. But anyway, what happened then was that she let out a little yell and suddenly sat down and began rubbing her arm.

"The same one," she whimpered. "First you, and then *that.*"

I helped her up. "It must have been a loose connection, Mary Ann. I'm sorry, but I told you—"

Cliff said, "Nuts! That was no loose connection. Junior's just protecting itself."

I had thought the same thing, myself. I had thought lots of things. Junior was a new kind of machine. Even the mathematics that controlled it were different from anything anybody had worked with before. Maybe it had something no machine previously had ever had. Maybe it felt a desire to stay alive and grow. Maybe it would have a desire to make more machines until there were millions of them all over the earth, fighting with human beings for control.

I opened my mouth and Cliff must have known what I was going to say, because he yelled, "No. No, don't say it!"

But I couldn't stop myself. It just came out and I said, "Well, look, let's disconnect Junior— What's the matter?"

Cliff said bitterly, "Because he's listening to what we say, you jackass. He heard about the blowtorch, didn't he? I was going to sneak up behind it, but now it will probably electrocute me if I try."

Mary Ann was still brushing at the back of her dress and saying how dirty the floor was, even though I kept telling her I had nothing to do with that. I mean, it's the janitor that makes the mud.

Anyway, she said, "Why don't you put on rubber gloves and yank the cord out?"

I could see Cliff was trying to think of reasons why that wouldn't work. He didn't think of any, so he put on the rubber gloves and walked towards Junior.

I yelled, "Watch out!"

It was a stupid thing to say. He *had* to watch out; he had no choice. One of the tentacles moved and there was no doubt what they were now. It whirled out and drew a line between Cliff and the power cable. It remained there, vibrating a little with its six finger-tendrils splayed out. Tubes inside Junior were beginning to glow. Cliff didn't try to go past that tentacle. He backed away and after a while, it spiraled inward again. He took off his rubber gloves.

"Bill," he said, "we're not going to get anywhere. That's a smarter gadget than we dreamed we could make. It was smart enough to use my voice as a model when it built its diaphragm. It may become smart enough to learn how to—" He looked over his shoulder, and whispered, "how to generate its own power and become self-contained."

"Bill, we've got to stop it, or someday someone will telephone the planet Earth and get the answer, 'Honest, boss, there's nobody here anywhere but us complicated thinking machines!' "

"Let's get in the police," I said, "We'll explain. A grenade, or something—"

Cliff shook his head, "We can't have anyone else find out. They'll build other Juniors and it looks like we don't have enough answers for that kind of a project after all."

"Then what do we do?"

"I don't know."

I felt a sharp blow on my chest. I looked down and it was Mary Ann, getting ready to spit fire. She said, "Look, lunkhead, if we've got a date, we've got one, and if we haven't, we haven't. Make up your mind."

I said, "Now, Mary Ann—"

She said, "Answer me. I never heard such a ridiculous thing. Here I get dressed to go to a play, and you take me to a dirty laboratory with a foolish machine and spend the rest of the evening twiddling dials."

"Mary Ann, I'm not—"

She wasn't listening; she was talking. I wish I could remember what she said after that. Or maybe I don't; maybe it's just as well I can't remember, since none of it was very complimentary. Every once in a while I would manage a "But, Mary Ann—" and each time it would get sucked under and swallowed up.

Actually, as I said, she's a very gentle creature and it's only when she gets excited that she's ever talkative or unreasonable. Of course, with red hair, she feels she ought to get excited rather often. That's my theory, anyway. She just feels she has to live up to her red hair.

Anyway, the next thing I *do* remember clearly is Mary Ann finishing with a stamp on my right foot and then turning to leave. I ran after her, trying once again, "But, Mary Ann—"

Then Cliff yelled at us. Generally, he doesn't pay any attention to us, but this time he was shouting, "Why don't you ask her to marry you, you lunkhead?"

Mary Ann stopped. She was in the doorway by then but she didn't turn around. I stopped too, and felt the words get thick and clogged up in my throat. I couldn't even manage a "But, Mary Ann—"

Cliff was yelling in the background. I heard him as though he were a mile away. He was shouting, "I got it! I got it!" over and over again.

Then Mary Ann turned and she looked so beautiful— Did I tell you that she's got green eyes with a touch of blue in them? Anyway she looked so beautiful that all the words in my throat jammed together very tightly and came out in that funny sound you make when you swallow.

She said, "Were you going to say something, Bill?"

Well, Cliff had put it in my head. My voice was hoarse and I said, "Will you marry me, Mary Ann?"

The minute I said it, I wished I hadn't, because I thought she would never speak to me again. Then two minutes after that I was glad I had, because she threw her arms around me and reached up to kiss me. It was a while before I was quite clear what was happening, and then I began to kiss back. This went on for quite a long time, until Cliff's banging on my shoulder managed to attract my attention.

I turned and said, snappishly, "What the devil do you want?" It was a little ungrateful. After all, he had started this.

He said, "Look!"

In his hand, he held the main lead that had connected Junior to the power supply.

I had forgotten about Junior, but now it came back. I said, "He's disconnected, then."

"Cold!"

"*How did you do it?*"

He said, "Junior was so busy watching you and Mary Ann fight that I managed to sneak up on it. Mary Ann put on one good show."

I didn't like that remark because Mary Ann is a very dignified and self-contained sort of girl and doesn't put on "shows." However, I had too much in hand to take issue with him.

I said to Mary Ann, "I don't have much to offer, Mary Ann; just a school teacher's salary. Now that we've dismantled Junior, there isn't even any chance of—"

Mary Ann said, "I don't care, Bill. I just gave up on you, you lunk-headed darling. I've tried practically everything—"

"You've been kicking my shins and stamping on my toes."

"I'd run out of everything else. I was desperate."

The logic wasn't quite clear, but I didn't answer because I remembered about the show. I looked at my watch and said, "Look, Mary Ann, if we hurry we can still make the second act."

She said, "Who wants to see the show?"

So I kissed her some more; and we never did get to see the show at all.

THERE'S ONLY ONE thing that bothers me now. Mary Ann and I are married, and we're perfectly happy. I just had a promotion; I'm an associate professor now. Cliff keeps working away at plans for building a controllable Junior and he's making progress.

None of that's it.

You see, I talked to Cliff the next evening, to tell him Mary Ann and I were going to marry and to thank him for giving me the idea. And after staring at me for a minute, he swore he hadn't said it; he hadn't shouted for me to propose marriage.

Of course, there was something else in the room with Cliff's voice.

I keep worrying Mary Ann will find out. She's the gentlest girl I know, but she *has* got red hair. She can't help trying to live up to that, or have I said that already?

Anyway, what will she say if she ever finds out that I didn't have the sense to propose till a *machine* told me to?

IT'S SUCH A BEAUTIFUL DAY

FIRST APPEARANCE—*STAR SCIENCE FICTION Stories* #3. Copyright 1954, by Ballantine Books, Inc.

We all have our lovable eccentricities and I have a few that are all my own.

For instance, I hate nice days. Show me a day in which the temperature is just 78, and a light breeze has the lush foliage of June, or the just turning leaves of September, rustling with a soft murmur; a day in which there is a drowsy softness over the landscape, and a sweet freshness to the air, and a general peacefulness over the world, and I'll show you one unhappy fellow—namely, me.

There's a reason for it, a good one. (You don't think I'm irrational, do you?) As I said in the preface to "Sally," I am a compulsive writer. That means that my idea of a pleasant time is to go up to my attic, sit at my electric typewriter (as I am doing right now), and bang away, watching the words take shape like magic before my eyes. To minimize distractions, I keep the window-shades down at all times and work exclusively by artificial light.

No one has any particular objection to this as long as we have the sleet of a typical New England late fall day darting through the air, or the blustering wind of a typical New England early spring day, or the leaden weight of Gulf air that splats out over New England in the summer, or the dancing flakes of that third foot of snow that blankets New England in the winter. Everyone says, "Boy, you're lucky *you* don't have to go out in that weather."

And I agree with them.

But then comes a beautiful day in May–June or September–October and everyone says to me, "What are you doing indoors on a day like this, you creep?" Sometimes out of sheer indignation they pick me up and throw me out the window so I can enjoy the nice day.

The niceness of being a writer, of course, is that you can take all your frustrations and annoyances and spread them out on paper. This prevents them from building up to dangerous levels and explains why writers in general are such lovable, normal people and are a joy to all who know them.

For instance, I wrote a novel in 1953 which pictured a world in which everyone lived in underground cities, comfortably enclosed away from the open air.

People would say, "How could you imagine such a nightmarish situation?"

And I would answer in astonishment, "What nightmarish situation?"

But with me everything becomes a challenge. Having made my pitch in favor of enclosure, I wondered if I could reverse the situation.

So I wrote "It's Such a Beautiful Day"—and did such a good job at convincing myself, that very often these days, sometimes twice in one week, when I feel I've put in a good day's work, I go out in the late afternoon and take a walk through the neighborhood.

But I don't know. That thing you people have up there in the sky. It's got quite a glare to it.

IT'S SUCH A BEAUTIFUL DAY

On April 12, 2117, the field-modulator brake-valve in the Door belonging to Mrs. Richard Hanshaw depolarized for reasons unknown. As a result, Mrs. Hanshaw's day was completely upset and her son, Richard, Jr., first developed his strange neurosis.

It was not the type of thing you would find listed as a neurosis in the usual textbooks and certainly young Richard behaved, in most respects, just as a well-brought-up twelve-year-old in prosperous circumstances ought to behave.

And yet from April 12 on, Richard Hanshaw, Jr., could only with regret ever persuade himself to go through a Door.

OF ALL THIS, on April 12, Mrs. Hanshaw had no premonition. She woke in the morning (an ordinary morning) as her mekkano slithered gently into her room, with a cup of coffee on a small tray.

Mrs. Hanshaw was planning a visit to New York in the afternoon and she had several things to do first that could not quite be trusted to a mekkano, so after one or two sips, she stepped out of bed.

The mekkano backed away, moving silently along the diamagnetic field that kept its oblong body half an inch above the floor, and moved back to the kitchen, where its simple computer was quite adequate to set the proper controls on the various kitchen appliances in order that an appropriate breakfast might be prepared.

Mrs. Hanshaw, having bestowed the usual sentimental glance upon the cubograph of her dead husband, passed through the stages of her morning ritual with a certain contentment. She could hear her son across the hall clattering through his, but she knew she need not interfere with him. The mekkano was well adjusted to see to it, as a matter of course, that he was showered, that he had on a change of clothing, and that he would eat a nourishing breakfast. The tergo-shower she had had installed the year before made the morning wash and dry so quick and pleasant that, really, she felt certain Dickie would wash even without supervision.

On a morning like this, when she was busy, it would certainly not be necessary for her to do more than deposit a casual peck on the boy's cheek before he left. She heard the soft chime the mekkano sounded to indicate approaching school time and she floated down the force-lift to the lower floor (her hairstyle for the day only sketchily designed, as yet) in order to perform that motherly duty.

She found Richard standing at the door, with his text-reels and pocket projector dangling by their strap and a frown on his face.

"Say, Mom," he said, looking up, "I dialed the school's co-ords but nothing happens."

She said, almost automatically, "Nonsense, Dickie. I never heard of such a thing."

"Well, you try."

Mrs. Hanshaw tried a number of times. Strange, the school Door was always set for general reception. She tried other co-ordinates. Her friends' Doors might not be set for reception, but there would be a signal at least, and then she could explain.

But nothing happened at all. The Door remained an inactive gray barrier despite all her manipulations. It was obvious that the Door was out of order—and only five months after its annual fall inspection by the company.

She was quite angry about it.

It *would* happen on a day when she had so much planned. She thought petulantly of the fact that a month earlier she had decided against installing a subsidiary Door on the grounds that it was an unnecessary expense. How was she to know that Doors were getting to be so *shoddy*?

She stepped to the visiphone while the anger still burned in her and said to Richard, "You just go down the road, Dickie, and use the Williamsons' Door."

Ironically, in view of later developments, Richard balked. "Aw, gee, Mom, I'll get dirty. Can't I stay home till the Door is fixed?"

And, as ironically, Mrs. Hanshaw insisted. With her finger on the combination board of the phone, she said, "You won't get dirty if you put flexies on your shoes, and don't forget to brush yourself well before you go into their house."

"But, golly—"

"No back talk, Dickie. You've got to be in school. Just let me see you walk out of here. And quickly, or you'll be late."

The mekkano, an advanced model and very responsive, was already standing before Richard with flexies in one appendage.

Richard pulled the transparent plastic shields over his shoes and moved down the hall with visible reluctance. "I don't even know how to work this thing, Mom."

"You just push that button," Mrs. Hanshaw called. "The red button. Where it says 'For Emergency Use.' And don't dawdle. Do you want the mekkano to go along with you?"

"Gosh, no," he called back, morosely, "what do you think I am? A baby? Gosh!" His muttering was cut off by a slam.

With flying fingers, Mrs. Hanshaw punched the appropriate combination on the phone board and thought of the things she intended saying to the company about this.

Joe Bloom, a reasonable young man, who had gone through technology school with added training in force-field mechanics, was at the Hanshaw residence in less than half an hour. He was really quite competent, though Mrs. Hanshaw regarded his youth with deep suspicion.

She opened the movable house-panel when he first signaled and her sight of him was as he stood there, brushing at himself vigorously to remove the dust of the open air. He took off his flexies and dropped them where he stood. Mrs. Hanshaw closed the house-panel against the flash of raw sunlight that had entered. She found herself irrationally hoping that the step-by-step trip from the public Door had been an un-pleasant one. Or perhaps that the public Door itself had been out of order and the youth had had to lug his tools even farther than the necessary two hundred yards. She wanted the Company, or its representative at least, to suffer a bit. It would teach them what broken Doors meant.

But he seemed cheerful and unperturbed as he said, "Good morning, ma'am. I came to see about your Door."

"I'm glad someone did," said Mrs. Hanshaw, ungraciously. "My day is quite ruined."

"Sorry, ma'am. What seems to be the trouble?"

"It just won't work. Nothing at all happens when you adjust co-ords," said Mrs. Hanshaw. "There was no warning at all. I had to send my son out to the neighbors through that—that thing."

She pointed to the entrance through which the repair man had come.

He smiled and spoke out of the conscious wisdom of his own specialized training in Doors. "That's a door, too, ma'am. You don't give that kind a capital letter when you write it. It's a hand-door, sort of. It used to be the only kind once."

"Well, at least it works. My boy's had to go out in the dirt and germs."

"It's not bad outside today, ma'am," he said, with the connoisseur-like air of one whose profession forced him into the open nearly every day. "Sometimes it *is* real unpleasant. But I guess you want I should fix this here Door, ma'am, so I'll get on with it."

He sat down on the floor, opened the large tool case he had brought in with him and in half a minute, by use of a point-demagnetizer, he had the control panel removed and a set of intricate vitals exposed.

He whistled to himself as he placed the fine electrodes of the field-analyzer on numerous points, studying the shifting needles on the dials. Mrs. Hanshaw watched him, arms folded.

Finally, he said, "Well, here's something," and with a deft twist, he disengaged the brake valve.

He tapped it with a fingernail and said, "This here brake valve is depolarized, ma'am. There's your whole trouble." He ran his finger along the little pigeonholes in his tool case and lifted out a duplicate of the object he had taken from the door mechanism. "These things just go all of a sudden. Can't predict it."

He put the control panel back and stood up. "It'll work now, ma'am."

He punched a reference combination, blanked it, then punched another. Each time, the dull gray of the Door gave way to a deep, velvety blackness. He said, "Will you sign here, ma'am? And put down your charge number, too, please? Thank you, ma'am."

He punched a new combination, that of his home factory, and with a polite touch of finger to forehead, he stepped through the Door. As his body entered the blackness, it cut off sharply. Less and less of him was visible and the tip of his tool case was the last thing that showed. A second after he had passed through completely, the Door turned back to dull gray.

Half an hour later, when Mrs. Hanshaw had finally completed her interrupted preparations and was fuming over the misfortune of the morning, the phone buzzed annoyingly and her real troubles began.

MISS ELIZABETH ROBBINS was distressed. Little Dick Hanshaw had always been a good pupil. She hated to report him like this. And yet, she told herself, his actions were certainly queer. And she would talk to his mother, not to the principal.

She slipped out to the phone during the morning study period, leaving a student in charge. She made her connection and found herself staring at Mrs. Hanshaw's handsome and somewhat formidable head.

Miss Robbins quailed, but it was too late to turn back. She said, diffidently, "Mrs. Hanshaw, I'm Miss Robbins." She ended on a rising note.

Mrs. Hanshaw looked blank, then said, "Richard's teacher?" That, too, ended on a rising note.

"That's right. I called you, Mrs. Hanshaw," Miss Robbins plunged right into it, "to tell you that Dick was quite late to school this morning."

"He *was*? But that couldn't be. I saw him leave."

Miss Robbins looked astonished. She said, "You mean you saw him use the Door?"

Mrs. Hanshaw said quickly, "Well, no. Our Door was temporarily out of order. I sent him to a neighbor and he used that Door."

"Are you sure?"

"Of course I'm sure. I wouldn't lie to you."

"No, no, Mrs. Hanshaw. I wasn't implying that at all. I meant are you sure he found the way to the neighbor? He might have got lost."

"Ridiculous. We have the proper maps, and I'm sure Richard knows the location of every house in District A-3." Then, with the quiet pride of one who knows what is her due, she added, "Not that he ever needs to know, of course. The co-ords are all that are necessary at any time."

Miss Robbins, who came from a family that had always had to economize rigidly on the use of its Doors (the price of power being what it was) and who had therefore run errands on foot until quite an advanced age, resented the pride. She said, quite clearly, "Well, I'm afraid, Mrs. Hanshaw, that Dick did not use the neighbor's Door. He was over an hour late to school and the condition of his flexies made it quite obvious that he tramped cross-country. They were *muddy*."

"*Muddy?*" Mrs. Hanshaw repeated the emphasis on the word. "What did he say? What was his excuse?"

Miss Robbins couldn't help but feel a little glad at the discomfiture of the other woman. She said, "He wouldn't talk about it. Frankly, Mrs. Hanshaw, he seems ill. That's why I called you. Perhaps you might want to have a doctor look at him."

"Is he running a temperature?" The mother's voice went shrill.

"Oh, no. I don't mean physically ill. It's just his attitude and the look in his eyes." She hesitated, then said with every attempt at delicacy, "I thought perhaps a routine checkup with a psychic probe——"

She didn't finish. Mrs. Hanshaw, in a chilled voice and with what was as close to a snort as her breeding would permit, said, "Are you implying that Richard is *neurotic*?"

"Oh, no, Mrs. Hanshaw, but——"

"It certainly sounded so. The idea! He has always been perfectly healthy. I'll take this up with him when he gets home. I'm sure there's a perfectly normal explanation which he'll give to *me*."

The connection broke abruptly, and Miss Robbins felt hurt and uncommonly foolish. After all she had only tried to help, to fulfill what she considered an obligation to her students.

She hurried back to the classroom with a glance at the metal face of the wall clock. The study period was drawing to an end. English Composition next.

But her mind wasn't completely on English Composition. Automatically, she called the students to have them read selections from their literary creations. And occasionally she punched one of those selections on tape and ran it through the small vocalizer to show the students how English *should* be read.

The vocalizer's mechanical voice, as always, dripped perfection, but, again as always, lacked character. Sometimes, she wondered if it was wise to try to train the students into a speech that was divorced from individuality and geared only to a mass-average accent and intonation.

Today, however, she had no thought for that. It was Richard Hanshaw she watched. He sat quietly in his seat, quite obviously indifferent to his surroundings. He was lost deep in himself and just not the same boy he had been. It was obvious to her that he had had some unusual experience that morning and, really, she was right to call his mother, although perhaps she ought not to have made the remark about the probe. Still it was quite the thing these days. All sorts of people get probed. There wasn't any disgrace attached to it. Or there shouldn't be, anyway.

She called on Richard, finally. She had to call twice, before he responded and rose to his feet.

The general subject assigned had been: "If you had your choice of traveling on some ancient vehicle, which would you choose, and why?" Miss Robbins tried to use the topic every semester. It was a good one because it carried a sense of history with it. It forced the youngster to think about the manner of living of people in past ages.

She listened while Richard Hanshaw read in a low voice.

"If I had my choice of ancient vehicles," he said, pronouncing the "h" in vehicles, "I would choose the stratoliner. It travels slow like all vehicles but it is clean. Because it travels in the stratosphere, it must be all enclosed so that you are not likely to catch disease. You can see the stars if it is night time almost as good as in a planetarium. If you look down you see the Earth like a map or maybe see clouds——" He went on for several hundred more words.

She said brightly when he had finished reading, "It's pronounced vee-ick-ulls, Richard. No 'h.' Accent on the first syllable. And you don't say 'travels slow' or 'see good.' What do you say, class?"

There was a small chorus of responses and she went on, "That's right. Now what is the difference between an adjective and an adverb? Who can tell me?"

And so it went. Lunch passed. Some pupils stayed to eat; some went home. Richard stayed. Miss Robbins noted that, as usually he didn't.

The afternoon passed, too, and then there was the final bell and the usual upsurging hum as twenty-five boys and girls rattled their belongings together and took their leisurely place in line.

Miss Robbins clapped her hands together. "Quickly, children. Come, Zelda, take your place."

"I dropped my tape-punch, Miss Robbins," shrilled the girl, defensively.

"Well, pick it up, pick it up. Now children, be brisk, be brisk."

She pushed the button that slid a section of the wall into a recess and revealed the gray blankness of a large Door. It was not the usual Door that the occasional student used in going home for lunch, but an advanced model that was one of the prides of this well-to-do private school.

In addition to its double width, it possessed a large and impressively gear-filled "automatic serial finder" which was capable of adjusting the door for a number of different co-ordinates at automatic intervals.

At the beginning of the semester, Miss Robbins always had to spend an afternoon with the mechanic, adjusting the device for the co-ordinates of the homes of the new class. But then, thank goodness, it rarely needed attention for the remainder of the term.

The class lined up alphabetically, first girls, then boys. The Door went velvety black and Hester Adams waved her hand and stepped through. "By-y-y——"

The 'bye' was cut off in the middle, as it almost always was.

The Door went gray, then black again, and Theresa Cantrocchi went through. Gray, black, Zelda Charlowicz. Gray, black, Patricia Coombs. Gray, black, Sara May Evans.

The line grew smaller as the Door swallowed them one by one, depositing each in her home. Of course, an occasional mother forgot to leave the house Door on special reception at the appropriate time and then the school Door remained gray. Automatically, after a minute-long wait, the Door went on to the next combination in line and the pupil in question had to wait till it was all over, after which a phone call to the forgetful parent would set things right. This was always bad for the pupils involved, especially the sensitive ones who took seriously the implication that they were little thought of at home. Miss Robbins always tried to impress this on visiting parents, but it happened at least once every semester just the same.

The girls were all through now. John Abramowitz stepped through and then Edwin Byrne——

Of course, another trouble, and a more frequent one was the boy or girl who got into line out of place. They *would* do it despite the teacher's sharpest watch, particularly at the beginning of the term when the proper order was less familiar to them.

When that happened, children would be popping into the wrong houses by the half-dozen and would have to be sent back. It always meant a mixup that took minutes to straighten out and parents were invariably irate.

Miss Robbins was suddenly aware that the line had stopped. She spoke sharply to the boy at the head of the line.

"Step through, Samuel. What are you waiting for?"

Samuel Jones raised a complacent countenance and said, "It's not my combination, Miss Robbins."

"Well, whose is it?" She looked impatiently down the line of five remaining boys. Who was out of place?

"It's Dick Hanshaw's, Miss Robbins."

"Where is he?"

Another boy answered, with the rather repulsive tone of self-righteousness all children automatically assume in reporting the deviations of their friends to elders in authority, "He went through the fire door, Miss Robbins."

"What?"

The schoolroom Door had passed on to another combination and Samuel Jones passed through. One by one, the rest followed.

Miss Robbins was alone in the classroom. She stepped to the fire door. It was a small affair, manually operated, and hidden behind a bend in the wall so that it would not break up the uniform structure of the room.

She opened it a crack. It was there as a means of escape from the building in case of fire, a device which was enforced by an anachronistic law that did not take into account the modern methods of automatic fire-fighting that all public buildings used. There was nothing outside, but the—outside. The sunlight was harsh and a dusty wind was blowing.

Miss Robbins closed the door. She was glad she had called Mrs.

Hanshaw. She had done her duty. More than ever, it was obvious that something was wrong with Richard. She suppressed the impulse to phone again.

MRS. HANSHAW DID not go to New York that day. She remained home in a mixture of anxiety and an irrational anger, the latter directed against the impudent Miss Robbins.

Some fifteen minutes before school's end, her anxiety drove her to the Door. Last year she had had it equipped with an automatic device which activated it to the school's co-ordinates at five of three and kept it so, barring manual adjustment, until Richard arrived.

Her eyes were fixed on the Door's dismal gray (why couldn't an inactive force-field be any other color, something more lively and cheerful?) and waited. Her hands felt cold as she squeezed them together.

The Door turned black at the precise second but nothing happened. The minutes passed and Richard was late. Then quite late. Then very late.

It was a quarter of four and she was distracted. Normally, she would have phoned the school, but she couldn't, she couldn't. Not after that teacher had deliberately cast doubts on Richard's mental well-being. How could she?

Mrs. Hanshaw moved about restlessly, lighting a cigarette with fumbling fingers, then smudging it out. Could it be something quite normal? Could Richard be staying after school for some reason? Surely he would have told her in advance. A gleam of light struck her; he knew she was planning to go to New York and might not be back till late in the evening——

No, he would surely have told her. Why fool herself?

Her pride was breaking. She would have to call the school, or even (she closed her eyes and teardrops squeezed through between the lashes) the police.

And when she opened her eyes, Richard stood before her, eyes on the ground and his whole bearing that of someone waiting for a blow to fall.

"Hello, Mom."

Mrs. Hanshaw's anxiety transmuted itself instantly (in a manner known only to mothers) into anger. "Where have you been, Richard?"

And then, before she could go further into the refrain concerning

careless, unthinking sons and broken-hearted mothers, she took note
of his appearance in greater detail, and gasped in utter horror.

She said, "You've been in the open."

Her son looked down at his dusty shoes (minus flexies), at the dirt
marks that streaked his lower arms and at the small, but definite tear in
his shirt. He said, "Gosh, Mom, I just thought I'd—" and he faded out.

She said, "Was there anything wrong with the school Door?"

"No, Mom."

"Do you realize I've been worried sick about you?" She waited
vainly for an answer. "Well, I'll talk to you afterward, young man.
First, you're taking a bath, and every stitch of your clothing is being
thrown out. Mekkano!"

But the mekkano had already reacted properly to the phrase "taking
a bath" and was off to the bathroom in its silent glide.

"You take your shoes off right here," said Mrs. Hanshaw, "then
march after mekkano."

Richard did as he was told with a resignation that placed him beyond futile protest.

Mrs. Hanshaw picked up the soiled shoes between thumb and forefinger and dropped them down the disposal chute which hummed in
faint dismay at the unexpected load. She dusted her hands carefully on
a tissue which she allowed to float down the chute after the shoes.

She did not join Richard at dinner but let him eat in the worse-
than-lack-of-company of the mekkano. This, she thought, would be an
active sign of her displeasure and would do more than any amount of
scolding or punishment to make him realize that he had done wrong.
Richard, she frequently told herself, was a sensitive boy.

But she went up to see him at bedtime.

She smiled at him and spoke softly. She thought that would be the
best way. After all, he had been punished already.

She said, "What happened today, Dickie-boy?" She had called him
that when he was a baby and just the sound of the name softened her
nearly to tears.

But he only looked away and his voice was stubborn and cold. "I
just don't like to go through those darn Doors, Mom."

"But why ever not?"

He shuffled his hands over the filmy sheet (fresh, clean, antiseptic and,
of course, disposable after each use) and said, "I just don't like them."

"But then how do you expect to go to school, Dickie?"

"I'll get up early," he mumbled.

"But there's nothing wrong with Doors."

"Don't like 'em." He never once looked up at her.

She said, despairingly, "Oh, well, you have a good sleep and tomorrow morning you'll feel much better."

She kissed him and left the room, automatically passing her hand through the photo-cell beam and in that manner dimming the room-lights.

But she had trouble sleeping herself that night. Why should Dickie dislike Doors so suddenly? They had never bothered him before. To be sure, the Door had broken down in the morning but that should make him appreciate them all the more.

Dickie was behaving so unreasonably.

Unreasonably? That reminded her of Miss Robbins and her diagnosis and Mrs. Hanshaw's soft jaw set in the darkness and privacy of her bedroom. Nonsense! The boy was upset and a night's sleep was all the therapy he needed.

But the next morning when she arose, her son was not in the house. The mekkano could not speak but it could answer questions with gestures of its appendages equivalent to a yes or no, and it did not take Mrs. Hanshaw more than half a minute to ascertain that the boy had arisen thirty minutes earlier than usual, skimped his shower, and darted out of the house.

But not by way of the Door.

Out the other way—through the door. Small "d."

MRS. HANSHAW'S VISIPHONE signaled genteelly at 3:10 P.M. that day. Mrs. Hanshaw guessed the caller and having activated the receiver, saw that she had guessed correctly. A quick glance in the mirror to see that she was properly calm after a day of abstracted concern and worry and then she keyed in her own transmission.

"Yes, Miss Robbins," she said coldly.

Richard's teacher was a bit breathless. She said, "Mrs. Hanshaw, Richard has deliberately left through the fire door although I told him to use the regular Door. I do not know where he went."

Mrs. Hanshaw said, carefully, "He left to come home."

Miss Robbins looked dismayed. "Do you approve of this?"

Pale-faced, Mrs. Hanshaw set about putting the teacher in her place. "I don't think it is up to you to criticize. If my son does not choose to use the Door, it is his affair and mine. I don't think there is any school ruling that would force him to use the Door, is there?" Her bearing quite plainly intimated that if there were she would see to it that it was changed.

Miss Robbins flushed and had time for one quick remark before contact was broken. She said, "I'd have him probed. I really would."

Mrs. Hanshaw remained standing before the quartzinium plate, staring blindly at its blank face. Her sense of family placed her for a few moments quite firmly on Richard's side. Why *did* he have to use the Door if he chose not to? And then she settled down to wait and pride battled the gnawing anxiety that something after all was wrong with Richard.

He came home with a look of defiance on his face, but his mother, with a strenuous effort at self-control, met him as though nothing were out of the ordinary.

For weeks, she followed that policy. It's nothing, she told herself. It's a vagary. He'll grow out of it.

It grew into an almost normal state of affairs. Then, too, every once in a while, perhaps three days in a row, she would come down to breakfast to find Richard waiting sullenly at the Door, then using it when school time came. She always refrained from commenting on the matter.

Always, when he did that, and especially when he followed it up by arriving home via the Door, her heart grew warm and she thought, "Well, it's over." But always with the passing of one day, two or three, he would return like an addict to his drug and drift silently out by the door—small "d"—before she woke.

And each time she thought despairingly of psychiatrists and probes, and each time the vision of Miss Robbins' low-bred satisfaction at (possibly) learning of it, stopped her, although she was scarcely aware that that was the true motive.

Meanwhile, she lived with it and made the best of it. The mekkano was instructed to wait at the door—small "d"—with a Tergo kit and a change of clothing. Richard washed and changed without resistance. His underthings, socks and flexies were disposable in any case, and Mrs.

Hanshaw bore uncomplainingly the expense of daily disposal of shirts. Trousers she finally allowed to go a week before disposal on condition of rigorous nightly cleansing.

One day she suggested that Richard accompany her on a trip to New York. It was more a vague desire to keep him in sight than part of any purposeful plan. He did not object. He was even happy. He stepped right through the Door, unconcerned. He didn't hesitate. He even lacked the look of resentment he wore on those mornings he used the Door to go to school.

Mrs. Hanshaw rejoiced. This could be a way of weaning him back into Door usage, and she racked her ingenuity for excuses to make trips with Richard. She even raised her power bill to quite unheard-of heights by suggesting, and going through with, a trip to Canton for the day in order to witness a Chinese festival.

That was on a Sunday, and the next morning Richard marched directly to the hole in the wall he always used. Mrs. Hanshaw, having wakened particularly early, witnessed that. For once, badgered past endurance, she called after him plaintively, "Why not the Door, Dickie?"

He said, briefly, "It's all right for Canton," and stepped out of the house.

So that plan ended in failure. And then, one day, Richard came home soaking wet. The mekkano hovered above him uncertainly and Mrs. Hanshaw, just returned from a four-hour visit with her sister in Iowa, cried, "Richard Hanshaw!"

He said, hang-dog fashion, "It started raining. All of a sudden, it started raining."

For a moment, the word didn't register with her. Her own school days and her studies of geography were twenty years in the past. And then she remembered and caught the vision of water pouring recklessly and endlessly down from the sky—a mad cascade of water with no tap to turn off, no button to push, no contact to break.

She said, "And you stayed out in it?"

He said, "Well, gee, Mom, I came home fast as I could. I didn't know it was going to rain."

Mrs. Hanshaw had nothing to say. She was appalled and the sensation filled her too full for words to find a place.

Two days later, Richard found himself with a running nose, and a dry, scratchy throat. Mrs. Hanshaw had to admit that the virus of disease had found a lodging in her house, as though it were a miserable hovel of the Iron Age.

It was over that that her stubbornness and pride broke and she admitted to herself that, after all, Richard had to have psychiatric help.

MRS. HANSHAW CHOSE a psychiatrist with care. Her first impulse was to find one at a distance. For a while, she considered stepping directly into the San Francisco Medical Center and choosing one at random.

And then it occurred to her that by doing that she would become merely an anonymous consultant. She would have no way of obtaining any greater consideration for herself than would be forthcoming to any public-Door user of the city slums. Now if she remained in her own community, her word would carry weight——

She consulted the district map. It was one of that excellent series prepared by Doors, Inc., and distributed free of charge to their clients. Mrs. Hanshaw couldn't quite suppress that little thrill of civic pride as she unfolded the map. It wasn't a fine-print directory of Door coordinates only. It was an actual map, with each house carefully located.

And why not? District A-3 was a name of moment in the world, a badge of aristocracy. It was the first community on the planet to have been established on a completely Doored basis. The first, the largest, the wealthiest, the best-known. It needed no factories, no stores. It didn't even need roads. Each house was a little secluded castle, the Door of which had entry anywhere the world over where other Doors existed.

Carefully, she followed down the keyed listing of the five thousand families of District A-3. She knew it included several psychiatrists. The learned professions were well represented in A-3.

Doctor Hamilton Sloane was the second name she arrived at and her finger lingered upon the map. His office was scarcely two miles from the Hanshaw residence. She liked his name. The fact that he lived in A-3 was evidence of worth. And he was a neighbor, practically a neighbor. He would understand that it was a matter of urgency—and confidential.

Firmly, she put in a call to his office to make an appointment.

DOCTOR HAMILTON SLOANE was a comparatively young man, not quite forty. He was of good family and he had indeed heard of Mrs. Hanshaw.

He listened to her quietly and then said, "And this all began with the Door breakdown."

"That's right, Doctor."

"Does he show any fear of the Doors?"

"Of course not. What an idea!" She was plainly startled.

"It's possible, Mrs. Hanshaw, it's possible. After all, when you stop to think of how a Door works it is rather a frightening thing, really. You step into a Door, and for an instant your atoms are converted into field-energies, transmitted to another part of space and reconverted into matter. For that instant you're not alive."

"I'm sure no one thinks of such things."

"But your son may. He witnessed the breakdown of the Door. He may be saying to himself, 'What if the Door breaks down just as I'm half-way through?'"

"But that's nonsense. He still uses the Door. He's even been to Canton with me; Canton, China. And as I told you, he uses it for school about once or twice a week."

"Freely? Cheerfully?"

"Well," said Mrs. Hanshaw, reluctantly, "he does seem a bit put out by it. But really, Doctor, there isn't much use talking about it, is there? If you would do a quick probe, see where the trouble was," and she finished on a bright note, "why, that would be all. I'm sure it's quite a minor thing."

Dr. Sloane sighed. He detested the word "probe" and there was scarcely any word he heard oftener.

"Mrs. Hanshaw," he said patiently, "there is no such thing as a quick probe. Now I know the mag-strips are full of it and it's a rage in some circles, but it's much overrated."

"Are you serious?"

"Quite. The probe is very complicated and the theory is that it traces mental circuits. You see, the cells of the brain are interconnected in a large variety of ways. Some of those interconnected paths are more used than others. They represent habits of thought, both conscious and unconscious. Theory has it that these paths in any given brain can be used to diagnose mental ills early and with certainty."

"Well, then?"

"But subjection to the probe is quite a fearful thing, especially to a child. It's a traumatic experience. It takes over an hour. And even then, the results must be sent to the Central Psychoanalytical Bureau for analysis, and that could take weeks. And on top of all that, Mrs. Hanshaw, there are many psychiatrists who think the theory of probe-analyses to be most uncertain."

Mrs. Hanshaw compressed her lips. "You mean nothing can be done."

Dr. Sloane smiled. "Not at all. There were psychiatrists for centuries before there were probes. I suggest that you let me talk to the boy."

"Talk to him? Is that all?"

"I'll come to you for background information when necessary, but the essential thing, I think, is to talk to the boy."

"Really, Dr. Sloane, I doubt if he'll discuss the matter with you. He won't talk to me about it and I'm his mother."

"That often happens," the psychiatrist assured her. "A child will sometimes talk more readily to a stranger. In any case, I cannot take the case otherwise."

Mrs. Hanshaw rose, not at all pleased. "When can you come, Doctor?"

"What about this coming Saturday? The boy won't be in school. Will you be busy?"

"We will be ready."

She made a dignified exit. Dr. Sloane accompanied her through the small reception room to his office Door and waited while she punched the co-ordinates of her house. He watched her pass through. She became a half-woman, a quarter-woman, an isolated elbow and foot, a nothing.

It *was* frightening.

Did a Door ever break down during passage, leaving half a body here and half there? He had never heard of such a case, but he imagined it could happen.

He returned to his desk and looked up the time of his next appointment. It was obvious to him that Mrs. Hanshaw was annoyed and disappointed at not having arranged for a psychic probe treatment.

Why, for God's sake? Why should a thing like the probe, an obvious piece of quackery in his own opinion, get such a hold on the general public? It must be part of this general trend toward machines. Anything man can do, machines can do better. Machines! More machines! Machines for anything and everything! O tempora! O mores!

Oh, hell!

His resentment of the probe was beginning to bother him. Was it a fear of technological unemployment, a basic insecurity on his part, a mechanophobia, if that was the word—

He made a mental note to discuss this with his own analyst.

DR. SLOANE HAD to feel his way. The boy wasn't a patient who had come to him, more or less anxious to talk, more or less anxious to be helped.

Under the circumstances it would have been best to keep his first meeting with Richard short and noncommittal. It would have been sufficient merely to establish himself as something less than a total stranger. The next time he would be someone Richard had seen before. The time after he would be an acquaintance, and after that a friend of the family.

Unfortunately, Mrs. Hanshaw was not likely to accept a long-drawn-out process. She would go searching for a probe and, of course, she would find it.

And harm the boy. He was certain of that.

It was for that reason he felt he must sacrifice a little of the proper caution and risk a small crisis.

An uncomfortable ten minutes had passed when he decided he must try. Mrs. Hanshaw was smiling in a rather rigid way, eyeing him narrowly, as though she expected verbal magic from him. Richard wriggled in his seat, unresponsive to Dr. Sloane's tentative comments, overcome with boredom and unable not to show it.

Dr. Sloane said, with casual suddenness, "Would you like to take a walk with me, Richard?"

The boy's eyes widened and he stopped wriggling. He looked directly at Dr. Sloane. "A walk, sir?"

"I mean, outside."

"Do you go—outside?"

"Sometimes. When I feel like it."

Richard was on his feet, holding down a squirming eagerness. "I didn't think anyone did."

"I do. And I like company."

The boy sat down, uncertainly. "Mom?———"

Mrs. Hanshaw had stiffened in her seat, her compressed lips radiating horror, but she managed to say, "Why certainly, Dickie. But watch yourself."

And she managed a quick and baleful glare at Dr. Sloane.

IN ONE RESPECT, Dr. Sloane had lied. He did *not* go outside "sometimes." He hadn't been in the open since early college days. True, he had been athletically inclined (still was to some extent) but in his time the indoor ultraviolet chambers, swimming pools and tennis courts had flourished. For those with the price, they were much more satisfactory than the outdoor equivalents, open to the elements as they were, could possibly be. There was no occasion to go outside.

So there was a crawling sensation about his skin when he felt wind touch it, and he put down his flexied shoes on bare grass with a gingerly movement.

"Hey, look at that." Richard was quite different now, laughing, his reserve broken down.

Dr. Sloane had time only to catch a flash of blue that ended in a tree. Leaves rustled and he lost it.

"What was it?"

"A bird," said Richard. "A blue kind of bird."

Dr. Sloane looked about him in amazement. The Hanshaw residence was on a rise of ground, and he could see for miles. The area was only lightly wooded and between clumps of trees, grass gleamed brightly in the sunlight.

Colors set in deeper green made red and yellow patterns. They were flowers. From the books he had viewed in the course of his lifetime and from the old video shows, he had learned enough so that all this had an eerie sort of familiarity.

And yet the grass was so trim, the flowers so patterned. Dimly, he realized he had been expecting something wilder. He said, "Who takes care of all this?"

Richard shrugged. "I dunno. Maybe the mekkanos do it."

"Mekkanos?"

"There's loads of them around. Sometimes they got a sort of atomic knife they hold near the ground. It cuts the grass. And they're always fooling around with the flowers and things. There's one of them over there."

It was a small object, half a mile away. Its metal skin cast back highlights as it moved slowly over the gleaming meadow, engaged in some sort of activity that Dr. Sloane could not identify.

Dr. Sloane was astonished. Here it was a perverse sort of estheticism, a kind of conspicuous consumption——

"What's that?" he asked suddenly.

Richard looked. He said, "That's a house. Belongs to the Froehlichs. Co-ordinates A-3, 23, 461. That little pointy building over there is the public Door."

Dr. Sloane was staring at the house. Was that what it looked like from the outside? Somehow he had imagined something much more cubic, and taller.

"Come along," shouted Richard, running ahead.

Dr. Sloane followed more sedately. "Do you know all the houses about here?"

"Just about."

"Where is A-23, 26, 475?" It was his own house, of course.

Richard looked about. "Let's see. Oh, sure, I know where it is—you see that water there?"

"Water?" Dr. Sloane made out a line of silver curving across the green.

"Sure. Real water. Just sort of running over rocks and things. It keeps running all the time. You can get across it if you step on the rocks. It's called a river."

More like a creek, thought Dr. Sloane. He had studied geography, of course, but what passed for the subject these days was really economic and cultural geography. Physical geography was almost an extinct science except among specialists. Still, he knew what rivers and creeks were, in a theoretical sort of way.

Richard was still talking. "Well, just past the river, over that hill with the big clump of trees and down the other side a way is A-23, 26, 475. It's a light green house with a white roof."

"It is?" Dr. Sloane was genuinely astonished. He hadn't known it was green.

Some small animal disturbed the grass in its anxiety to avoid the oncoming feet. Richard looked after it and shrugged. "You can't catch them. I tried."

A butterfly flitted past, a wavering bit of yellow. Dr. Sloane's eyes followed it.

There was a low hum that lay over the fields, interspersed with an occasional harsh, calling sound, a rattle, a twittering, a chatter that rose, then fell. As his ear accustomed itself to listening, Dr. Sloane heard a thousand sounds, and none were man-made.

A shadow fell upon the scene, advancing toward him, covering him. It was suddenly cooler and he looked upward, startled.

Richard said, "It's just a cloud. It'll go away in a minute—looka these flowers. They're the kind that smell."

They were several hundred yards from the Hanshaw residence. The cloud passed and the sun shone once more. Dr. Sloane looked back and was appalled at the distance they had covered. If they moved out of sight of the house and if Richard ran off, would he be able to find his way back?

He pushed the thought away impatiently and looked out toward the line of water (nearer now) and past it to where his own house must be. He thought wonderingly: Light green?

He said, "You must be quite an explorer."

Richard said, with a shy pride, "When I go to school and come back, I always try to use a different route and see new things."

"But you don't go outside every morning, do you? Sometimes you use the Doors, I imagine."

"Oh, sure."

"Why is that, Richard?" Somehow, Dr. Sloane felt there might be significance in that point.

But Richard quashed him. With his eyebrows up and a look of astonishment on his face, he said, "Well, gosh, some mornings it rains and I *have* to use the Door. I hate that, but what can you do? About two weeks ago, I got caught in the rain and I—" he looked about him automatically, and his voice sank to a whisper "—caught a cold, and wasn't Mom upset, though."

Dr. Sloane sighed. "Shall we go back now?"

There was a quick disappointment on Richard's face. "Aw, what for?"

"You remind me that your mother must be waiting for us."

"I guess so." The boy turned reluctantly.

They walked slowly back. Richard was saying, chattily, "I wrote a composition at school once about how if I could go on some ancient vehicle" (he pronounced it with exaggerated care) "I'd go in a strato-liner and look at stars and clouds and things. Oh, boy, I was sure nuts."

"You'd pick something else now?"

"You bet. I'd go in an aut'm'bile, real slow. Then I'd see everything there was."

MRS. HANSHAW SEEMED troubled, uncertain. "You don't think it's ab-normal, then, Doctor?"

"Unusual, perhaps, but not abnormal. He likes the outside."

"But how can he? It's so dirty, so unpleasant."

"That's a matter of individual taste. A hundred years ago our ances-tors were all outside most of the time. Even today, I dare say there are a million Africans who have never seen a Door."

"But Richard's always been taught to behave himself the way a de-cent person in District A-3 is supposed to behave," said Mrs. Hanshaw, fiercely. "Not like an African or—or an ancestor."

"That may be part of the trouble, Mrs. Hanshaw. He feels this urge to go outside and yet he feels it to be wrong. He's ashamed to talk about it to you or to his teacher. It forces him into sullen retreat and it could eventually be dangerous."

"Then how can we persuade him to stop?"

Dr. Sloane said, "Don't try. Channel the activity instead. The day your Door broke down, he was forced outside, found he liked it, and that set a pattern. He used the trip to school and back as an excuse to repeat that first exciting experience. Now suppose you agree to let him out of the house for two hours on Saturdays and Sundays. Suppose he gets it through his head that after all he can go outside without neces-sarily having to go anywhere in the process. Don't you think he'll be willing to use the Door to go to school and back thereafter? And don't you think that will stop the trouble he's now having with his teacher and probably with his fellow pupils?"

"But then will matters remain so? Must they? Won't he ever be nor-mal again?"

Dr. Sloane rose to his feet. "Mrs. Hanshaw, he's as normal as need be right now. Right now, he's tasting the joys of the forbidden. If you cooperate with him, show that you don't disapprove, it will lose some of its attraction right there. Then, as he grows older, he will become more aware of the expectations and demands of society. He will learn to conform. After all, there is a little of the rebel in all of us, but it generally dies down as we grow old and tired. Unless, that is, it is unreasonably suppressed and allowed to build up pressure. Don't do that. Richard will be all right."

He walked to the Door.

Mrs. Hanshaw said, "And you don't think a probe will be necessary, Doctor?"

He turned and said vehemently, "No, definitely not! There is nothing about the boy that requires it. Understand? Nothing."

His fingers hesitated an inch from the combination board and the expression on his face grew lowering.

"What's the matter, Dr. Sloane?" asked Mrs. Hanshaw.

But he didn't hear her because he was thinking of the Door and the psychic probe and all the rising, choking tide of machinery. There is a little of the rebel in all of us, he thought.

So he said in a soft voice, as his hand fell away from the board and his feet turned away from the Door, "You know, it's such a beautiful day that I think I'll walk."

PREFACE TO
STRIKEBREAKER

FIRST APPEARANCE—*THE ORIGINAL SCIENCE Fiction Stories,* January 1957, under the title "Male Strikebreaker." Copyright 1956, by Columbia Publications, Inc.

Surprises work both ways; I explained in my introduction to "Nightfall" that its success had been completely unexpected. Well, in the case of "Strikebreaker," I thought I had a blockbuster. It seemed to me to be fresh and original; I felt it contained a stirring sociological theme, with lots of meaning, and with considerable pathos. Yet, as nearly as I can make out, it dropped silently into the sea of audience reaction without as much as marking out a single circular ripple on its surface.

But I can be stubborn about such things. If I like a story, I like it, and I include it here to give the audience a second chance.

This is one of those stories where I can remember the exact occasion that put it into my mind. It involved one of my periodic trips to New York which have, more and more, become a kind of highlight to my life. They are the only occasions on which I can stop writing for as much as three or four days at a time without feeling either guilty or restless.

Naturally, anything that would tend to interfere with one of my trips would ruffle my otherwise imperturable *sang-froid*. Actually, I would throw a fit. It was bad enough when something enormous would get in my way—a hurricane or a blizzard, for instance. But a subway strike? And not of all the subway employees, but only a few key men, say thirty-five. They would stall the entire subway system and, with that, the entire city. And if the strike came to pass, I could scarcely venture into a stalled city.

"Where will this all end?" I apostrophized the heavens in my best tragical manner, one fist raised high and the other clenched in my hair. "A mere handful of men can paralyze an entire megalopolis. Where will it end?"

My gesture remained frozen as, in thought, I carried the situation to its logical extreme. I carefully unhooked the gesture, went upstairs, and wrote "Strikebreaker."

The happy ending is that the threatened strike did not come to pass, and I went to New York.

One more point about this story. It represents my personal record for stupid title changes. The editor of the magazine in which this story first appeared was Robert W. Lowndes, as sweet and as erudite a man as I have ever known. He had nothing to do with it. Some idiot in the higher echelons decided to call the story "Male Strikebreaker."

Why "Male"? What possible addition to the sense of the title can be made by that adjective? What illumination? What improvement? Heavens, I can understand (though not approve) a ridiculous title change which the publisher felt would imply something salacious and thus increase sales, but the modified title doesn't even do that.

Oh, well—I'll just change it back.

STRIKEBREAKER

Elvis Blei rubbed his plump hands and said, "Self-containment is the word." He smiled uneasily as he helped Steven Lamorak of Earth to a light. There was uneasiness all over his smooth face with its small wide-set eyes.

Lamorak puffed smoke appreciatively and crossed his lanky legs.

His hair was powdered with gray and he had a large and powerful jawbone. "Home grown?" he asked, staring critically at the cigarette. He tried to hide his own disturbance at the other's tension.

"Quite," said Blei.

"I wonder," said Lamorak, "that you have room on your small world for such luxuries."

(Lamorak thought of his first view of Elsevere from the spaceship visiplate. It was a jagged, airless planetoid, some hundred miles in diameter—just a dust-gray rough-hewn rock, glimmering dully in the light of its sun, 200,000,000 miles distant. It was the only object more than a mile in diameter that circled that sun, and now men had burrowed into that miniature world and constructed a society in it. And he himself, as a sociologist, had come to study the world and see how humanity had made itself fit into that queerly specialized niche.)

Blei's polite fixed smile expanded a hair. He said, "We are not a small world, Dr. Lamorak; you judge us by two-dimensional standards. The surface area of Elsevere is only three-quarters that of the State of New York, but that's irrelevant. Remember, we can occupy, if we wish, the entire interior of Elsevere. A sphere of 50 miles radius has a volume of well over half a million cubic miles. If all of Elsevere were occupied by levels 50 feet apart, the total surface area within the planetoid would be 56,000,000 square miles, and that is equal to the total land area of Earth. And none of these square miles, Doctor, would be unproductive."

Lamorak said, "Good Lord," and stared blankly for a moment. "Yes, of course you're right. Strange I never thought of it that way. But then, Elsevere is the only thoroughly exploited planetoid world in the Galaxy; the rest of us simply can't get away from thinking of two-dimensional surfaces, as you pointed out. Well, I'm more than ever glad that your Council has been so cooperative as to give me a free hand in this investigation of mine."

Blei nodded convulsively at that.

Lamorak frowned slightly and thought: He acts for all the world as though he wished I had not come. Something's wrong.

Blei said, "Of course, you understand that we are actually much smaller than we could be; only minor portions of Elsevere have as yet been hollowed out and occupied. Nor are we particularly anxious to expand, except very slowly. To a certain extent we are limited by the capacity of our pseudo-gravity engines and Solar energy converters."

"I understand. But tell me, Councillor Blei—as a matter of personal curiosity, and not because it is of prime importance to my project— could I view some of your farming and herding levels first? I am fascinated by the thought of fields of wheat and herds of cattle inside a planetoid."

"You'll find the cattle small by your standards, Doctor, and we don't have much wheat. We grow yeast to a much greater extent. But there will be some wheat to show you. Some cotton and tobacco, too. Even fruit trees."

"Wonderful. As you say, self-containment. You recirculate everything, I imagine."

Lamorak's sharp eyes did not miss the fact that this last remark twinged Blei. The Elseverian's eyes narrowed to slits that hid his expression.

He said, "We must recirculate, yes. Air, water, food, minerals—everything that is used up—must be restored to its original state; waste products are reconverted to raw materials. All that is needed is energy, and we have enough of that. We don't manage with one hundred per-cent efficiency, of course; there is a certain seepage. We import a small amount of water each year; and if our needs grow, we may have to import some coal and oxygen."

Lamorak said, "When can we start our tour, Councillor Blei?"

Blei's smile lost some of its negligible warmth. "As soon as we can, Doctor. There are some routine matters that must be arranged."

Lamorak nodded, and having finished his cigarette, stubbed it out.

Routine matters? There was none of this hesitancy during the pre-liminary correspondence. Elsevere had seemed proud that its unique planetoid existence had attracted the attention of the Galaxy.

He said, "I realize I would be a disturbing influence in a tightly knit society," and watched grimly as Blei leaped at the explanation and made it his own.

"Yes," said Blei, "we feel marked off from the rest of the Galaxy. We have our own customs. Each individual Elseverian fits into a comfortable niche. The appearance of a stranger without fixed caste is unsettling."

"The caste system does involve a certain inflexibility."

"Granted," said Blei quickly; "but there is also a certain self-assurance. We have firm rules of intermarriage and rigid inheritance of occupation. Each man, woman and child knows his place, accepts it, and is accepted in it; we have virtually no neurosis or mental illness."

"And are there no misfits?" asked Lamorak.

Blei shaped his mouth as though to say no, then clamped it suddenly shut, biting the word into silence; a frown deepened on his forehead. He said, at length, "I will arrange for the tour, Doctor. Meanwhile, I imagine you would welcome a chance to freshen up and to sleep."

They rose together and left the room, Blei politely motioning the Earthman to precede him out the door.

Lamorak felt oppressed by the vague feeling of crisis that had per-vaded his discussion with Blei.

The newspaper reinforced that feeling. He read it carefully before getting into bed, with what was at first merely a clinical interest. It was an eight-page tabloid of synthetic paper. One-quarter of its items consisted of "personals": births, marriages, deaths, record quotas, expanding habitable volume (not area! three dimensions!). The remainder included scholarly essays, educational material, and fiction. Of news, in the sense to which Lamorak was accustomed, there was virtually nothing.

One item only could be so considered and that was chilling in its incompleteness.

It said, under a small headline: *DEMANDS UNCHANGED: There has been no change in his attitude of yesterday. The Chief Councillor, after a second interview, announced that his demands remain completely unreasonable and cannot be met under any circumstances.*

Then, in parentheses, and in different type, there was the statement: *The editors of this paper agree that Elsevere cannot and will not jump to his whistle, come what may.*

Lamorak read it over three times. *His* attitude. *His* demands. *His* whistle.

Whose?

He slept uneasily, that night.

HE HAD NO time for newspapers in the days that followed; but spasmodically, the matter returned to his thoughts.

Blei, who remained his guide and companion for most of the tour, grew ever more withdrawn.

On the third day (quite artificially clock-set in an Earth-like twenty-four hour pattern), Blei stopped at one point, and said, "Now this level is devoted entirely to chemical industries. That section is not important—"

But he turned away a shade too rapidly, and Lamorak seized his arm. "What are the products of that section?"

"Fertilizers. Certain organics," said Blei stiffly.

Lamorak held him back, looking for what sight Blei might be evading. His gaze swept over the close-by horizons of lined rock and the buildings squeezed and layered between the levels.

Lamorak said, "Isn't that a private residence there?"

Blei did not look in the indicated direction.

Lamorak said, "I think that's the largest one I've seen yet. Why is it here on a factory level?" That alone made it noteworthy. He had already seen that the levels on Elsevere were divided rigidly among the residential, the agricultural and the industrial.

He looked back and called, "Councillor Blei!"

The councillor was walking away and Lamorak pursued him with hasty steps. "Is there something wrong, sir?"

Blei muttered, "I am rude, I know. I am sorry. There are matters that prey on my mind—" He kept up his rapid pace.

"Concerning *his* demands."

Blei came to a full halt. "What do *you* know about that?"

"No more than I've said. I read that much in the newspaper."

Blei muttered something to himself.

Lamorak said, "Ragusnik? What's that?"

Blei sighed heavily. "I suppose you ought to be told. It's humiliating, deeply embarrassing. The Council thought that matters would certainly be arranged shortly and that your visit need not be interfered with, that you need not know or be concerned. But it is almost a week now. I don't know what will happen and, appearances notwithstanding, it might be best for you to leave. No reason for an Outworlder to risk death."

The Earthman smiled incredulously. "Risk death? In this little world, so peaceful and busy. I can't believe it."

The Elseverian councillor said, "I can explain. I think it best I should." He turned his head away. "As I told you, everything on Elsevere must recirculate. You understand that."

"Yes."

"That includes—uh, human wastes."

"I assumed so," said Lamorak.

"Water is reclaimed from it by distillation and absorption. What remains is converted into fertilizer for yeast use; some of it is used as a source of fine organics and other by-products. These factories you see are devoted to this."

"Well?" Lamorak had experienced a certain difficulty in the drinking of water when he first landed on Elsevere, because he had been realistic enough to know what it must be reclaimed from; but he had conquered the feeling easily enough. Even on Earth, water was reclaimed by natural processes from all sorts of unpalatable substances.

Blei, with increasing difficulty, said, "Igor Ragusnik is the man who is in charge of the industrial processes immediately involving the wastes. The position has been in his family since Elsevere was first colonized. One of the original settlers was Mikhail Ragusnik and he—he—"

"Was in charge of waste reclamation."

"Yes. Now that residence you singled out is the Ragusnik residence; it is the best and most elaborate on the planetoid. Ragusnik gets many privileges the rest of us do not have; but, after all—" Passion entered the Councillor's voice with great suddenness, "we cannot *speak* to him."

"What?"

"He demands full social equality. He wants his children to mingle with ours, and our wives to visit— Oh!" It was a groan of utter disgust.

Lamorak thought of the newspaper item that could not even bring itself to mention Ragusnik's name in print, or to say anything specific about his demands. He said, "I take it he's an outcast because of his job."

"Naturally. Human wastes and—" words failed Blei. After a pause, he said more quietly, "As an Earthman, I suppose you don't understand."

"As a sociologist, I think I do." Lamorak thought of the Untouchables in ancient India, the ones who handled corpses. He thought of the position of swineherds in ancient Judea.

HE WENT ON, "I gather Elsevere will not give in to those demands."

"Never," said Blei, energetically. "Never."

"And so?"

"Ragusnik has threatened to cease operations."

"Go on strike, in other words."

"Yes."

"Would that be serious?"

"We have enough food and water to last quite a while; reclamation is not essential in that sense. But the wastes would accumulate; they would infect the planetoid. After generations of careful disease control, we have low natural resistance to germ diseases. Once an epidemic started—and one would—we would drop by the hundred."

"Is Ragusnik aware of this?"

"Yes, of course."

"Do you think he is likely to go through with his threat, then?"

"He is mad. He has already stopped working; there has been no waste reclamation since the day before you landed." Blei's bulbous nose sniffed at the air as though it already caught the whiff of excrement.

Lamorak sniffed mechanically at that, but smelled nothing.

Blei said, "So you see why it might be wise for you to leave. We are humiliated, of course, to have to suggest it."

But Lamorak said, "Wait; not just yet. Good Lord, this is a matter of great interest to me professionally. May I speak to Ragusnik?"

"On no account," said Blei, alarmed.

"But I would like to understand the situation. The sociological conditions here are unique and not to be duplicated elsewhere. In the name of science—"

"How do you mean, speak? Would image-reception do?"

"Yes."

"I will ask the Council," muttered Blei.

THEY SAT ABOUT Lamorak uneasily, their austere and dignified expressions badly marred with anxiety. Blei, seated in the midst of them, studiously avoided the Earthman's eyes.

The Chief Councillor, gray-haired, his face harshly wrinkled, his neck scrawny, said in a soft voice, "If in any way you can persuade him, sir, out of your own convictions, we will welcome that. In no case, however, are you to imply that we will, in any way, yield."

A gauzy curtain fell between the Council and Lamorak. He could make out the individual councillors still, but now he turned sharply toward the receiver before him. It glowed to life.

A head appeared in it, in natural color and with great realism. A strong dark head, with massive chin faintly stubbled, and thick, red lips set into a firm horizontal line.

The image said, suspiciously, "Who are you?"

Lamorak said, "My name is Steven Lamorak; I am an Earthman."

"An Outworlder?"

"That's right. I am visiting Elsevere. You are Ragusnik?"

"Igor Ragusnik, at your service," said the image, mockingly. "Except that there is no service and will be none until my family and I are treated like human beings."

Lamorak said, "Do you realize the danger that Elsevere is in? The possibility of epidemic disease?"

"In twenty-four hours, the situation can be made normal, if they allow me humanity. The situation is theirs to correct."

"You sound like an educated man, Ragusnik."

"So?"

"I am told you're denied of no material comforts. You are housed and clothed and fed better than anyone on Elsevere. Your children are the best educated."

"Granted. But all by servo-mechanism. And motherless girl-babies are sent us to care for until they grow to be our wives. And they die young for loneliness. Why?" There was sudden passion in his voice. "Why must we live in isolation as if we were all monsters, unfit for human beings to be near? Aren't we human beings like others, with the same needs and desires and feelings. Don't we perform an honorable and useful function—?"

THERE WAS A rustling of sighs from behind Lamorak. Ragusnik heard it, and raised his voice. "I see you of the Council behind there. Answer me: Isn't it an honorable and useful function? It is *your* waste made into food for *you*. Is the man who purifies corruption worse than the man who produces it?—Listen, Councillors, I will *not* give in. Let all of Elsevere die of disease—including myself and my son, if necessary—but I will not give in. My family will be better dead of disease, than living as now."

Lamorak interrupted. "You've led this life since birth, haven't you?"

"And if I have?"

"Surely you're used to it."

"Never. Resigned, perhaps. My father was resigned, and I was resigned for a while; but I have watched my son, my only son, with no other little boy to play with. My brother and I had each other, but my son will never have anyone, and I am no longer resigned. I am through with Elsevere and through with talking."

The receiver went dead.

The Chief Councillor's face had paled to an aged yellow. He and Blei were the only ones of the group left with Lamorak. The Chief Councillor said, "The man is deranged; I do not know how to force him."

He had a glass of wine at his side; as he lifted it to his lips, he spilled a few drops that stained his white trousers with purple splotches.

Lamorak said, "Are his demands so unreasonable? Why can't he be accepted into society?"

There was momentary rage in Blei's eyes. "A dealer in excrement." Then he shrugged. "You are from Earth."

Incongruously, Lamorak thought of another unacceptable, one of the numerous classic creations of the medieval cartoonist, Al Capp. The variously named "inside man at the skonk works."

He said, "Does Ragusnik really deal with excrement? I mean, is there physical contact? Surely, it is all handled by automatic machinery."

"Of course," said the Chief Councillor.

"Then exactly what is Ragusnik's function?"

"He manually adjusts the various controls that assure the proper functioning of the machinery. He shifts units to allow repairs to be made; he alters functional rates with the time of day; he varies end production with demand." He added sadly, "If we had the space to make the machinery ten times as complex, all this could be done automatically; but that would be such needless waste."

"But even so," insisted Lamorak, "all Ragusnik does he does simply by pressing buttons or closing contacts or things like that."

"Yes."

"Then his work is no different from any Elseverian's."

Blei said, stiffly, "You don't understand."

"And for that you will risk the death of your children?"

"We have no other choice," said Blei. There was enough agony in his voice to assure Lamorak that the situation was torture for him, but that he had no other choice indeed.

Lamorak shrugged in disgust. "Then break the strike. Force him."

"How?" said the Chief Councillor. "Who would touch him or go near him? And if we kill him by blasting from a distance, how will that help us?"

LAMORAK SAID, THOUGHTFULLY, "Would you know how to run his machinery?"

The Chief Councillor came to his feet. "I?" he howled.

"I don't mean *you*," cried Lamorak at once. "I used the pronoun in its indefinite sense. Could *someone* learn how to handle Ragusnik's machinery?"

Slowly, the passion drained out of the Chief Councillor. "It is in the handbooks, I am certain—though I assure you I have never concerned myself with it."

"Then couldn't someone learn the procedure and substitute for Ragusnik until the man gives in?"

Blei said, "Who would agree to do such a thing? Not I, under any circumstances."

Lamorak thought fleetingly of Earthly taboos that might be almost as strong. He thought of cannibalism, incest, a pious man cursing God. He said, "But you must have made provision for vacancy in the Ragusnik job. Suppose he died."

"Then his son would automatically succeed to his job, or his nearest other relative," said Blei.

"What if he had no adult relatives? What if all his family died at once?"

"That has never happened; it will never happen."

The Chief Councillor added, "If there were danger of it, we might, perhaps, place a baby or two with the Ragusniks and have it raised to the profession."

"Ah. And how would you choose that baby?"

"From among children of mothers who died in childbirth, as we choose the future Ragusnik bride."

"Then choose a substitute Ragusnik now, by lot," said Lamorak.

The Chief Councillor said, "*No! Impossible!* How can you suggest that? If we select a baby, that baby is brought up to the life; it knows no other. At this point, it would be necessary to choose an adult and subject him to Ragusnik-hood. No, Dr. Lamorak, we are neither monsters nor abandoned brutes."

No use, thought Lamorak helplessly. *No use, unless*—

He couldn't bring himself to face that *unless* just yet.

THAT NIGHT, LAMORAK slept scarcely at all. Ragusnik asked for only the basic elements of humanity. But opposing that were thirty thousand Elseverians who faced death.

The welfare of thirty thousand on one side; the just demands of one family on the other. Could one say that thirty thousand who would support such injustice deserved to die? Injustice by what standards? Earth's? Elsevere's? And who was Lamorak that he should judge?

And Ragusnik? He was willing to let thirty thousand die, including men and women who merely accepted a situation they had been taught to accept and could not change if they wished to. And children who had nothing at all to do with it.

Thirty thousand on one side; a single family on the other.

Lamorak made his decision in something that was almost despair; in the morning he called the Chief Councillor.

He said, "Sir, if you can find a substitute, Ragusnik will see that he has lost all chance to force a decision in his favor and will return to work."

"There can be no substitute," sighed the Chief Councillor; "I have explained that."

"No substitute among the Elseverians, but I am not an Elseverian; it doesn't matter to me. *I* will substitute."

THEY WERE EXCITED, much more excited than Lamorak himself. A dozen times they asked him if he was serious.

Lamorak had not shaved, and he felt sick, "Certainly, I'm serious. And any time Ragusnik acts like this, you can always import a substitute. No other world has the taboo and there will always be plenty of temporary substitutes available if you pay enough."

(He was betraying a brutally exploited man, and he knew it. But he told himself desperately: *Except for ostracism, he's very well treated. Very well.*)

They gave him the handbooks and he spent six hours, reading and re-reading. There was no use asking questions. None of the Elseverians knew anything about the job, except for what was in the handbook; and all seemed uncomfortable if the details were as much as mentioned.

"Maintain zero reading of galvanometer A-2 at all times during red signal of the Lunge-howler," read Lamorak. "Now what's a lunge-howler?"

"There will be a sign," muttered Blei, and the Elseverians looked at each other hang-dog and bent their heads to stare at their finger-ends.

THEY LEFT HIM long before he reached the small rooms that were the central headquarters of generations of working Ragusniks, serving their world. He had specific instructions concerning which turnings to take and what level to reach, but they hung back and let him proceed alone.

He went through the rooms painstakingly, identifying the instruments and controls, following the schematic diagrams in the handbook.

There's a Lunge-howler, he thought, with gloomy satisfaction. The sign did indeed say so. It had a semi-circular face bitten into holes that were obviously designed to glow in separate colors. Why a "howler" then?

He didn't know.

Somewhere, thought Lamorak, *somewhere wastes are accumulating, pushing against gears and exits, pipelines and stills, waiting to be handled in half a hundred ways. Now they just accumulate.*

Not without a tremor, he pulled the first switch as indicated by the handbook in its directions for "Initiation." A gentle murmur of life made itself felt through the floors and walls. He turned a knob and lights went on.

At each step, he consulted the handbook, though he knew it by heart; and with each step, the rooms brightened and the dial-indicators sprang into motion and a humming grew louder.

Somewhere deep in the factories, the accumulated wastes were being drawn into the proper channels.

A HIGH-PITCHED SIGNAL sounded and startled Lamorak out of his painful concentration. It was the communications signal and Lamorak fumbled his receiver into action.

Ragusnik's head showed, startled; then slowly, the incredulity and outright shock faded from his eyes. "*That's* how it is, then."

"I'm not an Elseverian, Ragusnik; I don't mind doing this."

"But what business is it of yours? Why do you interfere?"

"I'm on your side, Ragusnik, but I must do this."

"Why, if you're on my side? Do they treat people on your world as they treat me here?"

"Not any longer. But even if you are right, there are thirty thousand people on Elsevere to be considered."

"They would have given in; you've ruined my only chance."

"They would *not* have given in. And in a way, you've won; they know now that you're dissatisfied. Until now, they never dreamed a Ragusnik could be unhappy, that he could make trouble."

"What if they know? Now all they need do is hire an Outworlder anytime."

Lamorak shook his head violently. He had thought this through in these last bitter hours. "The fact that they know means that the Elseverians will begin to think about you; some will begin to wonder if it's right to treat a human so. And if Outworlders are hired, they'll spread the word that this goes on upon Elsevere and Galactic public opinion will be in your favor."

"And?"

"Things will improve. In your son's time, things will be much better."

"In my son's time," said Ragusnik, his cheeks sagging. "I might have had it now. Well, I lose. I'll go back to the job."

Lamorak felt an overwhelming relief. "If you'll come here now, sir, you may have your job and I'll consider it an honor to shake your hand."

Ragusnik's head snapped up and filled with a gloomy pride. "You call me 'sir' and offer to shake my hand. Go about your business, Earthman, and leave me to my work, for I would not shake yours."

LAMORAK RETURNED THE way he had come, relieved that the crisis was over, and profoundly depressed, too.

He stopped in surprise when he found a section of corridor cordoned off, so he could not pass. He looked about for alternate routes, then startled at a magnified voice above his head. "Dr. Lamorak do you hear me? This is Councillor Blei."

Lamorak looked up. The voice came over some sort of public address system, but he saw no sign of an outlet.

He called out, "Is anything wrong? Can you hear me?"

"I hear you."

Instinctively, Lamorak was shouting. "Is anything wrong? There seems to be a block here. Are there complications with Ragusnik?"

"Ragusnik has gone to work," came Blei's voice. "The crisis is over, and you must make ready to leave."

"Leave?"

"Leave Elsevere; a ship is being made ready for you now."

"But wait a bit." Lamorak was confused by this sudden leap of events. "I haven't completed my gathering of data."

Blei's voice said, "This cannot be helped. You will be directed to the ship and your belongings will be sent after you by servo-mechanisms. We trust—we trust—"

Something was becoming clear to Lamorak. "You trust *what?*"

"We trust you will make no attempt to see or speak directly to any Elseverian. And of course we hope you will avoid embarrassment by not attempting to return to Elsevere at any time in the future. A colleague of yours would be welcome if further data concerning us is needed."

"I understand," said Lamorak, tonelessly. Obviously, he had himself become a Ragusnik. He had handled the controls that in turn had handled the wastes; he was ostracized. He was a corpse-handler, a swineherd, an inside man at the skonk works.

He said, "Good-bye."

Blei's voice said, "Before we direct you, Dr. Lamorak—. On behalf of the Council of Elsevere, I thank you for your help in this crisis."

"You're welcome," said Lamorak, bitterly.

INSERT KNOB A
IN HOLE B

FIRST APPEARANCE—*THE MAGAZINE OF Fantasy and Science Fiction,* December 1957. © 1957, by Fantasy House, Inc.

In some ways, this story has the strangest background of any I ever wrote. It is also the shortest story I ever wrote—only 350 words. The two go together.

It came about this way. On August 21, 1957, I took part in a panel discussion on means of communicating science on WGBH, Boston's educational TV station. With me were John Hansen, a technical writer of directions for using machinery, and David O. Woodbury, the well-known science writer.

We all bemoaned the inadequacy of most science writing and technical writing and there was some comment on my own prolificity. With my usual modesty, I attributed my success entirely to an incredible fluency of ideas and a delightful facility in writing. I stated incautiously that I could write a story anywhere, any time, under any conditions within reason. I was instantly challenged to write one right then and there with the television cameras on me.

I accepted the challenge and began to write, taking for my theme the subject of discussion. The other two did not try to make life easier for me, either. They deliberately kept interrupting in order to drag me into their discussion and interrupt my line of thought, and I was just vain enough to try to answer sensibly while I continued scribbling.

Before the half-hour program was over I had finished and read the story (which is why it is so short, by the way) and it was the one you see here as "Insert Knob A in Hole B." In his own introduction to the story, when it appeared in *F & SF*, Mr. Boucher said he was printing it just as it was (I had sent him the handwritten script, after typing a copy for myself) "even to the retention of its one grammatical error." I have kept that error here, too. It's yours for the finding.

I cheated, though. (Would I lie to you?) The three of us were talking before the program started and somehow I got the idea they might ask me to write a story on the program. So, just in case they did, I spent a few minutes before its start blocking out something.

Consequently, when they asked me, I had it roughly in mind. All I had to do was work out the details, write it down, and then read it. After all, I had twenty minutes.

INSERT KNOB A
IN HOLE B

Dave Woodbury and John Hansen, grotesque in their spacesuits, supervised anxiously as the large crate swung slowly out and away from the freight-ship and into the airlock. With nearly a year of their hitch on Space Station A5 behind them, they were understandably weary of filtration units that clanked, hydroponic tubs that leaked, air generators that hummed constantly and stopped occasionally.

"Nothing works," Woodbury would say mournfully, "because everything is hand-assembled by ourselves."

"Following directions," Hansen would add, "composed by an idiot."

There were undoubtedly grounds for complaint there. The most expensive thing about a spaceship was the room allowed for freight so all equipment had to be sent across space disassembled and nested. All equipment had to be assembled at the Station itself with clumsy hands, inadequate tools and with blurred and ambiguous direction sheets for guidance.

Painstakingly Woodbury had written complaints to which Hansen had added appropriate adjectives, and formal requests for relief of the situation had made its way back to Earth.

And Earth had responded. A special robot had been designed, with a positronic brain crammed with the knowledge of how to assemble properly any disassembled machine in existence.

That robot was in the crate being unloaded now and Woodbury was trembling as the airlock closed behind it.

"First," he said, "it overhauls the Food-Assembler and adjusts the steak-attachment knob so we can get it rare instead of burnt."

They entered the station and attacked the crate with dainty touches of the demoleculizer rods in order to make sure that not a precious metal atom of their special assembly-robot was damaged.

The crate fell open!

And there within it were five hundred separate pieces—and one blurred and ambiguous direction sheet for assemblage.

PREFACE TO
THE UP-TO-DATE
SORCERER

FIRST APPEARANCE—*THE MAGAZINE OF Fantasy and Science Fiction*, July 1958. © 1958, by Mercury Press, Inc.

I have frequently (rather to my own uneasy surprise) been accused of writing humorously. Oh, I try, I try, but only very cautiously, and for a long time I thought nobody noticed.

You see, there is no margin for error in humor. You can try to write suspense and not quite hit the mark, and have a story that is only moderately suspenseful. In analogous manner, you can have a story be only moderately romantic, moderately exciting, moderately eerie, even moderately science-fictiony.

But what happens when you miss the mark in humor? Is the result moderately humorous? Of course not! The not-quite-humorous remark, the not-quite-witty rejoinder, the not-quite-farcical episode are, respectively, dreary, stupid, and ridiculous.

Well, with a target that is all bull's-eye and no larger than a bull's-eye at that, am I going to blaze away carelessly? Certainly not! I'm fantastically courageous, but I'm not stupid.

So I have tried being funny only occasionally, and usually only gently and unobtrusively (as in "Nobody Here But—"). On the few occasions in which I tried to write a purely funny story, I wasn't completely satisfied.

Mostly, therefore, I kept my stories grave and sober (as you can tell).

Yet, I never quite gave up, either. One day, at the prodding of Mr. Boucher, I tried my hand at a Gilbert and Sullivan parody and finally (in my own eyes, at any rate) I clicked without reservation. I read the story over and laughed heartily.

That was it. I had found my métier in humor. All I had to do was to assume a very slightly exaggerated pseudo-Victorian style and I found I had no trouble at all in being funny.

Did I enter a full-fledged career as science fiction humorist at once? Not at all. I kept the humor at the previous level and remained, for the most part, grave and sober. That's still what I do best.

However, in the middle 1960s, I took to writing a series of articles for *TV Guide* which are nothing but this kind of humor, and I love them. (I am sometimes taken to task, by the way, for saying, in my artless way, that I like my own material, but why shouldn't I? Is it conceivable that I would spend seventy hours a week on writing and related reading if I *didn't* like what I wrote? Come on!)

By the way, a final word about "The Up-to-Date Sorcerer"—It is not essential to read Gilbert and Sullivan's *The Sorcerer* first, but it would make my story funnier if you did (I think), and I would like to give it every break.

THE UP-TO-DATE SORCERER

It always puzzled me that Nicholas Nitely, although a Justice of the Peace, was a bachelor. The atmosphere of his profession, so to speak, seemed so conducive to matrimony that surely he could scarcely avoid the gentle bond of wedlock.

When I said as much over a gin and tonic at the Club recently, he said, "Ah, but I had a narrow escape some time ago," and he sighed.

"Oh, really?"

"A fair young girl, sweet, intelligent, pure yet desperately ardent, and withal most alluring to the physical senses for even such an old fogy as myself."

I said, "How did you come to let her go?"

"I had no choice." He smiled gently at me and his smooth, ruddy complexion, his smooth gray hair, his smooth blue eyes, all combined to give him an expression of near-saintliness. He said, "You see, it was really the fault of her fiancé——"

"Ah, she was engaged to someone else."

"—and of Professor Wellington Johns, who was, although an endocrinologist, by way of being an up-to-date sorcerer. In fact, it was just that———" He sighed, sipped at his drink, and turned on me the bland and cheerful face of one who is about to change the subject.

I said firmly, "Now, then, Nitely, old man, you cannot leave it so. I want to know about your beautiful girl—the flesh that got away."

He winced at the pun (one, I must admit, of my more abominable efforts) and settled down by ordering his glass refilled. "You understand," he said, "I learned some of the details later on."

PROFESSOR WELLINGTON JOHNS had a large and prominent nose, two sincere eyes and a distinct talent for making clothes appear too large for him. He said, "My dear children, love is a matter of chemistry."

His dear children, who were really students of his, and not his children at all, were named Alexander Dexter and Alice Sanger. They looked perfectly full of chemicals as they sat there holding hands. Together, their age amounted to perhaps 45, evenly split between them, and Alexander said, fairly inevitably, "*Vive la chémie!*"

Professor Johns smiled reprovingly. "Or rather endocrinology. Hormones, after all, affect our emotions and it is not surprising that one should, specifically, stimulate that feeling we call love."

"But that's so unromantic," murmured Alice. "I'm sure I don't need any." She looked up at Alexander with a yearning glance.

"My dear," said the professor, "your blood stream was crawling with it at that moment you, as the saying is, fell in love. Its secretion had been stimulated by"—for a moment he considered his words carefully, being a highly moral man—"by some environmental factor involving your young man, and once the hormonal action had taken place, inertia carried you on. I could duplicate the effect easily."

"Why, Professor," said Alice, with gentle affection. "It would be delightful to have you try," and she squeezed Alexander's hand shyly.

"I do not mean," said the professor, coughing to hide his embarrassment, "that I would personally attempt to reproduce—or, rather, to duplicate—the conditions that created the natural secretion of the hormone. I mean, instead, that I could inject the hormone itself by hypodermic or even by oral ingestion, since it is a steroid hormone. I have, you see," and here he removed his glasses and polished them proudly, "isolated and purified the hormone."

Alexander sat erect. "Professor! And you have said nothing?"

"I must know more about it first."

"Do you mean to say," said Alice, her lovely brown eyes shimmering with delight, "that you can make people feel the wonderful delight and heaven-surpassing tenderness of true love by means of a . . . a pill?"

The professor said, "I can indeed duplicate the emotion to which you refer in those rather cloying terms."

"Then why don't you?"

Alexander raised a protesting hand. "Now, darling, your ardor leads you astray. Our own happiness and forthcoming nuptials make you forget certain facts of life. If a married person were, by mistake, to accept this hormone——"

Professor Johns said, with a trace of hauteur, "Let me explain right now that my hormone, or my amatogenic principle, as I call it——" (for he, in common with many practical scientists, enjoyed a proper scorn for the rarefied niceties of classical philology).

"Call it a love-philtre, Professor," said Alice, with a melting sigh.

"My amatogenic cortical principle," said Professor Johns, sternly, "has no affect on married individuals. The hormone cannot work if inhibited by other factors, and being married is certainly a factor that inhibits love."

"Why, so I have heard," said Alexander, gravely, "but I intend to disprove that callous belief in the case of my own Alice."

"Alexander," said Alice. "My love."

The professor said, "I mean that marriage inhibits extramarital love."

Alexander said, "Why, it has come to my ears that sometimes it does not."

Alice said, shocked, "Alexander!"

"Only in rare instances, my dear, among those who have not gone to college."

The professor said, "Marriage may not inhibit a certain paltry sexual attraction, or tendencies toward minor trifling, but true love, as Miss Sanger expressed the emotion, is something which cannot blossom when the memory of a stern wife and various unattractive children hobbles the subconscious."

"Do you mean to say," said Alexander, "that if you were to feed your love-philtre—beg pardon, your amatogenic principle—to a number of people indiscriminately, only the *un*married individuals would be affected?"

"That is right, I have experimented on certain animals which, though not going through the conscious marriage rite, do form monogamous attachments. Those with the attachments already formed are not affected."

"Then, Professor, I have a perfectly splendid idea. Tomorrow night is the night of the Senior Dance here at college. There will be at least fifty couples present, mostly unmarried. Put your philtre in the punch."

"What? Are you mad?"

But Alice had caught fire. "Why, it's a heavenly idea, Professor. To think that all my friends will feel as I feel! Professor, you would be an angel from heaven.—But oh, Alexander, do you suppose the feelings might be a trifle uncontrolled? Some of our college chums are a little wild and if, in the heat of discovery of love, they should, well, kiss——"

Professor Johns said, indignantly, "My dear Miss Sanger. You must not allow your imagination to become overheated. My hormone induces only those feelings which lead to marriage and not to the expression of anything that might be considered indecorous."

"I'm sorry," murmured Alice, in confusion. "I should remember, Professor, that you are the most highly moral man I know—excepting always dear Alexander—and that no scientific discovery of yours could possibly lead to immorality."

She looked so woebegone that the professor forgave her at once.

"Then you'll do it, Professor?" urged Alexander. "After all, assuming there will be a sudden urge for mass marriage afterward, I can take care of that by having Nicholas Nitely, an old and valued friend of the family, present on some pretext. He is a Justice of the Peace and can easily arrange for such things as licenses and so on."

"I could scarcely agree," said the professor, obviously weakening, "to perform an experiment without the consent of those experimented upon. It would be unethical."

"But you would be bringing only joy to them. You would be contributing to the moral atmosphere of the college. For surely, in the absence of overwhelming pressure toward marriage, it sometimes happens even in college that the pressure of continuous propinquity breeds a certain danger of—of——"

"Yes, there is that," said the professor. "Well, I shall try a dilute solution. After all, the results may advance scientific knowledge tremendously and, as you say, it will also advance morality."

Alexander said, "And, of course, Alice and I will drink the punch, too."

Alice said, "Oh, Alexander, surely such love as ours needs no artificial aid."

"But it would not be artificial, my soul's own. According to the professor, your love began as a result of just such a hormonal effect, induced, I admit, by more customary methods."

Alice blushed rosily. "But then, my only love, why the need for the repetition?"

"To place us beyond all vicissitudes of Fate, my cherished one."

"Surely, my adored, you don't doubt my love."

"No, my heart's charmer, but——"

"*But?* Is it that you do not trust me, Alexander?"

"Of course I trust you, Alice, but——"

"*But?* Again but!" Alice rose, furious. "If you cannot trust me, sir, perhaps I had better leave——" And she did leave indeed, while the two men stared after her, stunned.

Professor Johns said, "I am afraid my hormone has, quite indirectly, been the occasion of spoiling a marriage rather than of causing one."

Alexander swallowed miserably, but his pride upheld him. "She will come back," he said, hollowly. "A love such as ours is not so easily broken."

THE SENIOR DANCE was, of course, the event of the year. The young men shone and the young ladies glittered. The music lilted and the dancing feet touched the ground only at intervals. Joy was unrestrained.

Or, rather, it was unrestrained in most cases. Alexander Dexter stood in one corner, eyes hard, expression icily bleak. Straight and handsome he might be, but no young woman approached him. He was known to belong to Alice Sanger, and under such circumstances, no college girl would dream of poaching. Yet where was Alice?

She had not come with Alexander and Alexander's pride prevented him from searching for her. From under grim eyelids, he could only watch the circulating couples cautiously.

Professor Johns, in formal clothes that did not fit although made to measure, approached him. He said, "I will add my hormone to the punch shortly before the midnight toast. Is Mr. Nitely still here?"

"I saw him a moment ago. In his capacity as chaperon he was busily engaged in making certain that the proper distance between dancing couples was maintained. Four fingers, I believe, at the point of closest approach. Mr. Nitely was most diligently making the necessary measurements."

"Very good. Oh, I had neglected to ask: Is the punch alcoholic? Alcohol would affect the workings of the amatogenic principle adversely."

Alexander, despite his sore heart, found spirit to deny the unintended slur upon his class. "Alcoholic, Professor? This punch is made along those principles firmly adhered to by all young college students. It contains only the purest of fruit juices, refined sugar, and a certain quantity of lemon peel—enough to stimulate but not inebriate."

"Good," said the professor. "Now I have added to the hormone a sedative designed to put our experimental subjects to sleep for a short time while the hormone works. Once they awaken, the first individual each sees—that is, of course, of the opposite sex—will inspire that individual with a pure and noble ardor that can end only in marriage."

Then, since it was nearly midnight, he made his way through the happy couples, all dancing at four-fingers' distance, to the punch bowl.

Alexander, depressed nearly to tears, stepped out to the balcony. In doing so, he just missed Alice, who entered the ballroom from the balcony by another door.

"Midnight," called out a happy voice. "Toast! Toast! Toast to the life ahead of us."

They crowded about the punch bowl; the little glasses were passed round.

"To the life ahead of us," they cried out and, with all the enthusiasm of young college students, downed the fiery mixture of pure fruit juices, sugar, and lemon peel, with—of course—the professor's sedated amatogenic principle.

As the fumes rose to their brains, they slowly crumpled to the floor.

Alice stood there alone, still holding her drink, eyes wet with unshed tears. "Oh, Alexander, Alexander, though you doubt, yet are you my only love. You wish me to drink and I shall drink." Then she, too, sank gracefully downward.

NICHOLAS NITELY HAD gone in search of Alexander, for whom his warm heart was concerned. He had seen him arrive without Alice and he could only assume that a lovers' quarrel had taken place. Nor did he feel any dismay at leaving the party to its own devices. These were not wild youngsters, but college boys and girls of good family and gentle upbringing. They could be trusted to the full to observe the four-finger limit, as he well knew.

He found Alexander on the balcony, staring moodily out at a star-riddled sky.

"Alexander, my boy." He put his hand on the young man's shoulder. "This is not like you. To give way so to depression. Chut, my young friend, chut."

Alexander's head bowed at the sound of the good old man's voice. "It is unmanly, I know, but I yearn for Alice. I have been cruel to her and I am justly treated now. And yet, Mr. Nitely, if you could but know——" He placed his clenched fist on his chest, next his heart. He could say no more.

Nitely said, sorrowfully, "Do you think because I am unmarried that I am unacquainted with the softer emotions? Be undeceived. Time was when I, too, knew love and heartbreak. But do not do as I did once and allow pride to prevent your reunion. Seek her out, my boy, seek her out and apologize. Do not allow yourself to become a solitary old bachelor such as I myself.—But, tush, I am puling."

Alexander's back had straightened. "I will be guided by you, Mr. Nitely. I will seek her out."

"Then go on in. For shortly before I came out, I believe I saw her there."

Alexander's heart leaped. "Perhaps she searches for me even now. I will go—— But, no. Go you first, Mr. Nitely, while I stay behind to recover myself. I would not have her see me a prey to womanish tears."

"Of course, my boy."

NITELY STOPPED AT the door into the ballroom in astonishment. Had a universal catastrophe struck all low? Fifty couples were lying on the floor, some heaped together most indecorously.

But before he could make up his mind to see if the nearest were dead, to sound the fire alarm, to call the police, to anything, they were rousing and struggling to their feet.

Only one still remained. A lonely girl in white, one arm outstretched gracefully beneath her fair head. It was Alice Sanger and Nitely hastened to her, oblivious to the rising clamor about him.

He sank to his knees. "Miss Sanger. My dear Miss Sanger. Are you hurt?"

She opened her beautiful eyes slowly, and said, "Mr. Nitely! I never realized you were such a vision of loveliness."

"I?" Nitely started back with horror, but she had now risen to her feet and there was light in her eyes such as Nitely had not seen in a maiden's eyes for thirty years—and then only weakly.

She said, "Mr. Nitely, surely you will not leave me?"

"No, no," said Nitely, confused. "If you need me, I shall stay."

"I need you. I need you with all my heart and soul. I need you as a thirsty flower needs the morning dew. I need you as Thisbe of old needed Pyramus."

Nitely, still backing away, looked about hastily, to see if anyone could be hearing this unusual declaration, but no one seemed to be paying any attention. As nearly as he could make out, the air was filled with other declarations of similar sort, some being even more forceful and direct.

His back was up against a wall, and Alice approached him so closely as to break the four-finger rule to smithereens. She broke, in fact, the no-finger rule, and at the resulting mutual pressure, a certain indefinable something seemed to thud away within Nitely.

"Miss Sanger. Please."

"Miss Sanger? Am I Miss Sanger to you?" exclaimed Alice, passionately. "Mr. Nitely! Nicholas! Make me your Alice, your own. Marry me. Marry me!"

All around there was the cry of "Marry me. Marry me!" and young men and women crowded around Nitely, for they knew well that he was a Justice of the Peace. They cried out, "Marry us, Mr. Nitely. Marry us!"

He could only cry in return, "I must get you all licenses."

They parted to let him leave on that errand of mercy. Only Alice followed him.

NITELY MET ALEXANDER at the door of the balcony and turned him back toward the open and fresh air. Professor Johns came at that moment to join them all.

Nitely said, "Alexander. Professor Johns. The most extraordinary thing has occurred—"

"Yes," said the professor, his mild face beaming with joy. "The experiment has been a success. The principle is far more effective on the human being, in fact, than on any of my experimental animals." Noting Nitely's confusion, he explained what had occurred in brief sentences.

Nitely listened and muttered, "Strange, strange. There is a certain elusive familiarity about this." He pressed his forehead with the knuckles of both hands, but it did not help.

Alexander approached Alice gently, yearning to clasp her to his strong bosom, yet knowing that no gently nurtured girl could consent to such an expression of emotion from one who had not yet been forgiven.

He said, "Alice, my lost love, if in your heart you could find—"

But she shrank from him, avoiding his arms though they were outstretched only in supplication. She said, "Alexander, I drank the punch. It was your wish."

"You needn't have. I was wrong, wrong."

"But I did, and oh, Alexander, I can never be yours."

"Never be mine? But what does this mean?"

And Alice, seizing Nitely's arm, clutched it avidly. "My soul is intertwined indissolubly with that of Mr. Nitely, of Nicholas, I mean. My passion for him—that is, my passion for marriage with him—cannot be withstood. It racks my being."

"You are false?" cried Alexander, unbelieving.

"You are cruel to say 'false,' " said Alice, sobbing. "I cannot help it."

"No, indeed," said Professor Johns, who had been listening to this in the greatest consternation, after having made his explanation to Nitely. "She could scarcely help it. It is simply an endocrinological manifestation."

"Indeed that is so," said Nitely, who was struggling with endocrinological manifestations of his own. "There, there, my—my dear." He patted Alice's head in a most fatherly way and when she held her enticing face up toward his, swooningly, he considered whether it might not be a fatherly thing—nay, even a neighborly thing—to press those lips with his own, in pure fashion.

But Alexander, out of his heart's despair, cried, "You are false, false—false as Cressid," and rushed from the room.

And Nitely would have gone after him, but that Alice had seized him about the neck and bestowed upon his slowly melting lips a kiss that was not daughterly in the least.

It was not even neighborly.

THEY ARRIVED AT Nitely's small bachelor cottage with its chaste sign of
JUSTICE OF THE PEACE in Old English letters, its air of melancholy peace,
its neat serenity, its small stove on which the small kettle was quickly
placed by Nitely's left hand (his right arm being firmly in the clutch of
Alice, who, with a shrewdness beyond her years, chose that as one sure
method of rendering impossible a sudden bolt through the door on his
part).

Nitely's study could be seen through the open door of the dining
room, its walls lined with gentle books of scholarship and joy.

Again Nitely's hand (his left hand) went to his brow. "My dear," he
said to Alice, "it is amazing the way—if you would release your hold
the merest trifle, my child, so that circulation might be restored—the
way in which I persist in imagining that all this has taken place before."

"Surely never before, my dear Nicholas," said Alice, bending her
fair head upon his shoulder, and smiling at him with a shy tenderness
that made her beauty as bewitching as moonlight upon still waters,
"could there have been so wonderful a modern-day magician as our
wise Professor Johns, so up-to-date a sorcerer."

"So up-to-date a——" Nitely had started so violently as to lift the
fair Alice a full inch from the floor. "Why, surely that must be it. Dickens take me, if that's not it." (For on rare occasions, and under the stress
of overpowering emotions, Nitely used strong language.)

"Nicholas. What is it? You frighten me, my cherubic one."

But Nitely walked rapidly into his study, and she was forced to run
with him. His face was white, his lips firm, as he reached for a volume
from the shelves and reverently blew the dust from it.

"Ah," he said with contrition, "how I have neglected the innocent
joys of my younger days. My child, in view of this continuing incapac-
ity of my right arm, would you be so kind as to turn the pages until I
tell you to stop?"

Together they managed, in such a tableau of preconnubial bliss as is
rarely seen, he holding the book with his left hand, she turning the
pages slowly with her right.

"I am right!" Nitely said with sudden force. "Professor Johns, my
dear fellow, do come here. This is the most amazing coincidence—a

frightening example of the mysterious unfelt power that must sport with us on occasion for some hidden purpose."

Professor Johns, who had prepared his own tea and was sipping it patiently, as befitted a discreet gentleman of intellectual habit in the presence of two ardent lovers who had suddenly retired to the next room, called out, "Surely you do not wish my presence?"

"But I do, sir. I would fain consult one of your scientific attainments."

"But you are in a position——"

Alice screamed, faintly, "Professor!"

"A thousand pardons, my dear," said Professor Johns, entering. "My cobwebby old mind is filled with ridiculous fancies. It is long since I——" and he pulled mightily at his tea (which he had made strong) and was himself again at once.

"Professor," said Nitely. "This dear child referred to you as an up-to-date sorcerer and that turned my mind instantly to Gilbert and Sullivan's *The Sorcerer*."

"What," asked Professor Johns, mildly, "are Gilbert and Sullivan?"

Nitely cast a devout glance upward, as though with the intention of gauging the direction of the inevitable thunderbolt and dodging. He said in a hoarse whisper, "Sir William Schwenck Gilbert and Sir Arthur Sullivan wrote, respectively, the words and music of the greatest musical comedies the world has ever seen. One of these is entitled *The Sorcerer*. In it, too, a philtre was used: a highly moral one which did not affect married people, but which did manage to deflect the young heroine away from her handsome young lover and into the arms of an elderly man."

"And," asked Professor Johns, "were matters allowed to remain so?"

"Well, no.—Really, my dear, the movements of your fingers in the region of the nape of my neck, while giving rise to undeniably pleasurable sensations, *do* rather distract me.—There is a reunion of the young lovers, Professor."

"Ah," said Professor Johns. "Then in view of the close resemblance of the fictional plot to real life, perhaps the solution in the play will help point the way to the reunion of Alice and Alexander. At least, I presume you do not wish to go through life with one arm permanently useless."

Alice said, "I have no wish to be reunited. I want only my own Nicholas."

"There is something," said Nitely, "to be said for that refreshing point of view, but tush—youth must be served. There *is* a solution in the play, Professor Johns, and it is for that reason that I most particularly wanted to talk to you." He smiled with a gentle benevolence. "In the play, the effects of the potion were completely neutralized by the actions of the gentleman who administered the potion in the first place: the gentleman, in other words, analogous to yourself."

"And those actions were?"

"Suicide! Simply that! In some manner unexplained by the authors, the effect of this suicide was to break the sp——"

But by now Professor Johns had recovered his equilibrium and said in the most sepulchrally forceful tone that could be imagined, "My dear sir, may I state instantly that, despite my affection for the young persons involved in this sad dilemma, I cannot under any circumstances consent to self-immolation. Such a procedure might be extremely efficacious in connection with love potions of ordinary vintage, but my amatogenic principle, I assure you, would be completely unaffected by my death."

Nitely sighed. "I feared that. As a matter of fact, between ourselves, it was a very poor ending for the play, perhaps the poorest in the canon," and he looked up briefly in mute apology to the spirit of William S. Gilbert. "It was pulled out of a hat. It had not been properly foreshadowed earlier in the play. It punished an individual who did not deserve the punishment. In short, it was, alas, completely unworthy of Gilbert's powerful genius."

Professor Johns said, "Perhaps it was not Gilbert. Perhaps some bungler had interfered and botched the job."

"There is no record of that."

But Professor Johns, his scientific mind keenly aroused by an unsolved puzzle, said at once, "We can test this. Let us study the mind of this—this Gilbert. He wrote other plays, did he?"

"Fourteen, in collaboration with Sullivan."

"Were there endings that resolved analogous situations in ways which were more appropriate?"

Nitely nodded. "One, certainly. There was *Ruddigore*."

"Who was he?"

"Ruddigore is a place. The main character is revealed as the true bad baronet of Ruddigore and is, of course, under a curse."

"To be sure," muttered Professor Johns, who realized that such an eventuality frequently befell bad baronets and was even inclined to think it served them right.

Nitely said, "The curse compelled him to commit one crime or more each day. Were one day to pass without a crime, he would inevitably die in agonizing torture."

"How horrible," murmured the sofe-hearted Alice.

"Naturally," said Nitely, "no one can think up a crime each day, so our hero was forced to use his ingenuity to circumvent the curse."

"How?"

"He reasoned thus: If he deliberately refused to commit a crime, he was courting death by his own act. In other words, he was attempting suicide, and attempting suicide is, of course, a crime—and so he fulfills the conditions of the curse."

"I see. I see," said Professor Johns. "Gilbert obviously believes in solving matters by carrying them forward to their logical conclusions." He closed his eyes, and his noble brow clearly bulged with the numerous intense thought waves it contained.

He opened them. "Nitely, old chap, when was *The Sorcerer* first produced?"

"In eighteen hundred and seventy-seven."

"Then that is it, my dear fellow. In eighteen seventy-seven, we were faced with the Victorian age. The institution of marriage was not to be made sport of on the stage. It could not be made a comic matter for the sake of the plot. Marriage was holy, spiritual, a sacrament———"

"Enough," said Nitely, "of this apostrophe. What is in your mind?"

"Marriage. Marry the girl, Nitely. Have all your couples marry, and that at once. I'm sure that was Gilbert's original intention."

"But that," said Nitely, who was strangely attracted by the notion, "is precisely what we are trying to avoid."

"I am not," said Alice, stoutly (though she was not stout, but, on the contrary, enchantingly lithe and slender).

Professor Johns said, "Don't you see? Once each couple is married, the amatogenic principle—which does not affect married people—loses its power over them. Those who would have been in love without the aid of the principle remain in love; those who would not are no longer in love—and consequently apply for an annulment."

"Good heavens," said Nitely. "How admirably simple. Of course!

Gilbert must have intended that until a shocked producer or theater manager—a bungler, as you say—forced the change."

"AND DID IT work?" I asked. "After all, you said quite distinctly that the professor had said its effect on married couples was only to inhibit extra-marital re——"

"It worked," said Nitely, ignoring my comment. A tear trembled on his eyelid, but whether it was induced by memories or by the fact that he was on his fourth gin and tonic, I could not tell.

"It worked," he said. "Alice and I were married, and our marriage was almost instantly annulled by mutual consent on the grounds of the use of undue pressure. And yet, because of the incessant chaperoning to which we were subjected, the incidence of undue pressure between ourselves was, unfortunately, virtually nil." He sighed again. "At any rate, Alice and Alexander were married soon after and she is now, I understand, as a result of various concomitant events, expecting a child."

He withdrew his eyes from the deep recesses of what was left of his drink and gasped with sudden alarm. "Dear me! She again."

I looked up, startled. A vision in pastel blue was in the doorway. Imagine, if you will, a charming face made for kissing; a lovely body made for loving.

She called, "Nicholas! Wait!"

"Is that Alice?" I asked.

"No, no. This is someone else entirely: a completely different story.—But I must not remain here."

He rose and, with an agility remarkable in one so advanced in years and weight, made his way through a window. The feminine vision of desirability, with an agility only slightly less remarkable, followed.

I shook my head in pity and sympathy. Obviously, the poor man was continually plagued by these wondrous things of beauty who, for one reason or another, were enamored of him. At the thought of this horrible fate, I downed my own drink at a gulp and considered the odd fact that no such difficulties had ever troubled me.

And at that thought, strange to tell, I ordered another drink savagely, and a scatological exclamation rose, unbidden, to my lips.

PREFACE TO
UNTO THE
FOURTH GENERATION

FIRST APPEARANCE—*THE MAGAZINE OF Fantasy and Science Fiction*, April 1959. © 1959, by Mercury Press, Inc.

Not long after the appearance of "The Up-to-Date Sorcerer," Mr. Boucher retired as editor of *F & SF*, and was succeeded in the post by Robert P. Mills.

Mr. Mills proceeded to do me the largest single favor of my writing life since Mr. Campbell had started the discussion that had led to "Nightfall." Mr. Mills asked me to write a monthly column on science for *F & SF* and I complied at once. Since the November 1958 issue, in which my first column appeared, I have kept right on going, month after month, and, as I write this, I am about to celebrate my tenth anniversary as monthly columnist for the magazine.

Of all the writing I do, fiction, non-fiction, adult, or juvenile, the *F & SF* articles are by far the most fun, and in them, during Mr. Mills' tenure I never referred to him as other than the "Kindly Editor."

Anyway, over lunch one day, Mr. Mills said he had seen the name Lefkowitz on several different and unrelated occasions that day, which struck him as a curious coincidence. Could I make a story out of it? In my usual offhand manner, I said, "Sure!" and gave it a little thought.

The result was a story that served as a tribute to Mr. Boucher, too. He was, you see, a devout Catholic. (I must say "was," for he died in April 1968 to the heartfelt grief of all who knew him. He was so kind a man that he was loved by the very authors he rejected, even while he was rejecting them, and there simply isn't any harsher test of true love than that.) And because Mr. Boucher was a sincere Catholic, there was very often a faintly Catholic air about *F & SF* under his leadership; always a pleasant and liberal one, though, for that was the kind of man he was.

So I thought that as my tribute to Mr. Boucher's editorship, I would try my hand at that kind of flavor myself. I couldn't handle it Catholic-fashion, of course, for I am not Catholic. I did it the only way I could manage, and wrote a Jewish story—the only Jewish story it ever occurred to me to write, I think.

And I made Mr. Mills' remark about Lefkowitz become "Unto the Fourth Generation."

UNTO THE
FOURTH GENERATION

At ten of noon, Sam Marten hitched his way out of the taxicab, trying as usual to open the door with one hand, hold his briefcase in another and reach for his wallet with a third. Having only two hands, he found it a difficult job and, again as usual, he thudded his knee against the cab-door and found himself still groping uselessly for his wallet when his feet touched pavement.

The traffic of Madison Avenue inched past. A red truck slowed its crawl reluctantly, then moved on with a rasp as the light changed. White script on its side informed an unresponsive world that its owner-ship was that of *F. Lewkowitz and Sons, Wholesale Clothiers*.

Levkowich, thought Marten with brief inconsequence, and finally fished out his wallet. He cast an eye on the meter as he clamped his briefcase under his arm. Dollar sixty-five, make that twenty cents more as a tip, two singles gone would leave him only one for emergencies, better break a fiver.

"Okay," he said, "take out one-eighty-five, bud."

"Thanks," said the cabbie with mechanical insincerity and made the change.

Marten crammed three singles into his wallet, put it away, lifted his briefcase and breasted the human currents on the sidewalk to reach the glass doors of the building.

Levkovich? he thought sharply, and stopped. A passerby glanced off his elbow.

"Sorry," muttered Marten, and made for the door again.

Levkovich? That wasn't what the sign on the truck had said. The name had read Lewkowitz, Loo-koh-itz. Why did he *think* Levkovich? Even with his college German in the near past changing the w's to v's, where did he get the "-ich" from?

Levkovich? He shrugged the whole matter away roughly. Give it a chance and it would haunt him like a Hit Parade tinkle.

Concentrate on business. He was here for a luncheon appointment with this man, Naylor. He was here to turn a contract into an account and begin, at twenty-three, the smooth business rise which, as he planned it, would marry him to Elizabeth in two years and make him a paterfamilias in the suburbs in ten.

He entered the lobby with grim firmness and headed for the banks of elevators, his eye catching at the white-lettered directory as he passed.

It was a silly habit of his to want to catch suite numbers as he passed, without slowing, or (heaven forbid) coming to a full halt. With no break in his progress, he told himself, he could maintain the impression of belonging, of knowing his way around, and that was important to a man whose job involved dealing with other human beings.

Kulin-etts was what he wanted, and the word amused him. A firm specializing in the production of minor kitchen gadgets, striving manfully for a name that was significant, feminine, and coy, all at once—

His eyes snagged at the M's and moved upward as he walked. Mandel, Lusk, Lippert Publishing Company (two full floors), Lafkowitz, Kulin-etts. There it was—1024. Tenth floor. OK.

And then, after all, he came to a dead halt, turned in reluctant fascination, returned to the directory, and stared at it as though he were an out-of-towner.

Lafkowitz?

What kind of spelling was that?

It was clear enough. Lafkowitz, Henry J., 701. With an A. That was no good. That was useless.

Useless? Why useless? He gave his head one violent shake as though to clear it of mist. Damn it, what did he care how it was spelled? He turned away, frowning and angry, and hastened to an elevator door, which closed just before he reached it, leaving him flustered.

Another door opened and he stepped in briskly. He tucked his briefcase under his arm and tried to look bright alive—junior executive in its finest sense. He had to make an impression on Alex Naylor, with whom so far he had communicated only by telephone. If he was going to brood about Lewkowitzes and Lafkowitzes—

The elevator slid noiselessly to a halt at seven. A youth in shirt-sleeves stepped off, balancing what looked like a desk-drawer in which were three containers of coffee and three sandwiches.

Then, just as the doors began closing, frosted glass with black letter-ing loomed before Marten's eyes. It read: 701—HENRY J. LEFKOWITZ—IMPORTER and was pinched off by the inexorable coming together of the elevator doors.

Marten leaned forward in excitement. It was his impulse to say: Take me back down to 7.

But there were others in the car. And after all, he had no reason.

Yet there was a tingle of excitement within him. The Directory *had* been wrong. It wasn't A, it was E. Some fool of a non-spelling menial with a packet of small letters to go on the board and only one hind foot to do it with.

Lefkowitz. Still not right, though.

Again, he shook his head. Twice. Not right for what?

The elevator stopped at ten and Marten got off.

Alex Naylor of Kulin-etts turned out to be a bluff, middle-aged man with a shock of white hair, a ruddy complexion, and a broad smile. His palms were dry and rough, and he shook hands with a con-siderable pressure, putting his left hand on Marten's shoulder in an ear-nest display of friendliness.

He said, "Be with you in two minutes. How about eating right here in the building? Excellent restaurant, and they've got a boy who makes a good martini. That sound all right?"

"Fine. Fine." Marten pumped up enthusiasm from a somehow-clogged reservoir.

It was nearer ten minutes than two, and Marten waited with the usual uneasiness of a man in a strange office. He stared at the upholstery on the chairs and at the little cubby-hole within which a young and bored switchboard operator sat. He gazed at the pictures on the wall and even made a half-hearted attempt to glance through a trade journal on the table next to him.

What he did not do was think of Lev—

He did *not* think of it.

THE RESTAURANT WAS good, or it would have been good if Marten had been perfectly at ease. Fortunately, he was freed of the necessity of carrying the burden of the conversation. Naylor talked rapidly and loudly, glanced over the menu with a practiced eye, recommended the Eggs Benedict, and commented on the weather and the miserable traffic situation.

On occasion, Marten tried to snap out of it, to lose that edge of fuzzed absence of mind. But each time the restlessness would return. Something was wrong. The name was wrong. It stood in the way of what he had to do.

With main force, he tried to break through the madness. In sudden verbal clatter, he led the conversation into the subject of wiring. It was reckless of him. There was no proper foundation; the transition was too abrupt.

But the lunch had been a good one; the dessert was on its way; and Naylor responded nicely.

He admitted dissatisfaction with existing arrangements. Yes, he had been looking into Marten's firm and, actually, it seemed to him that, yes, there was a chance, a good chance, he thought, that—

A hand came down on Naylor's shoulder as a man passed behind his chair. "How's the boy, Alex?"

Naylor looked up, grin ready-made and flashing. "Hey, Lefk, how's business?"

"Can't complain. See you at the—" He faded into the distance.

Marten wasn't listening. He felt his knees trembling, as he half-rose. "Who was that man?" he asked, intensely. It sounded more peremptory than he intended.

"Who? Lefk? Jerry Lefkovitz. You know him?" Naylor stared with cool surprise at his lunch companion.

"No. How do you spell his name?"

"L-E-F-K-O-V-I-T-Z, I think. Why?"

"With a V?"

"An F. . . . Oh, there's a V in it, too." Most of the good nature had left Naylor's face.

Marten drove on. "There's a Lefkowitz in the building. With a W. You know, Lef-COW-itz."

"Oh?"

"Room 701. This is not the same one?"

"Jerry doesn't work in this building. He's got a place across the street. I don't know this other one. This is a big building, you know. I don't keep tabs, on everyone in it. What is all this, anyway?"

Marten shook his head and sat back. He didn't know what all this was, anyway. Or at least, if he did, it was nothing he dared explain. Could he say: I'm being haunted by all manner of Lefkowitzes today.

He said, "We were talking about wiring."

Naylor said, "Yes. Well, as I said, I've been considering your company. I've got to talk it over with the production boys, you understand. I'll let you know."

"Sure," said Marten, infinitely depressed. Naylor wouldn't let him know. The whole thing was shot.

And yet, through and beyond his depression, there was still that restlessness.

The hell with Naylor. All Marten wanted was to break this up and get on with it. (*Get on with what?* But the question was only a whisper. Whatever did the questioning inside him was ebbing away, dying down . . .)

The lunch frayed to an ending. If they had greeted each other like long-separated friends at last reunited, they parted like strangers.

Marten felt only relief.

He left with pulses thudding, threading through the tables, out of the haunted building, onto the haunted street.

Haunted? Madison Avenue at 1:20 P.M. in an early fall afternoon with the sun shining brightly and ten thousand men and women behiving its long straight stretch.

But Marten felt the haunting. He tucked his briefcase under his arm and headed desperately northward. A last sigh of the normal within him warned him he had a three o'clock appointment on 36th Street. Never mind. He headed uptown. Northward.

AT 54TH STREET, he crossed Madison and walked west, came abruptly to a halt and looked upward.

There was a sign on the window, three stories up. He could make it out clearly: A. S. LEFKOWICH, CERTIFIED ACCOUNTANT.

It had an F and an OW, but it was the first "-ich" ending he had seen. The first one. He was getting closer. He turned north again on Fifth Avenue, hurrying through the unreal streets of an unreal city, panting with the chase of something, while the crowds about him began to fade.

A sign in a ground floor window, M. R. LEFKOWICZ, M.D.

A small gold-leaf semi-circle of letters in a candy-store window: JACOB LEVKOW.

(Half a name, he thought savagely. Why is he disturbing me with half a name?)

The streets were empty now except for the varying clan of Lefkowitz, Levkowitz, Lefkowicz to stand out in the vacuum.

He was dimly aware of the park ahead, standing out in painted motionless green. He turned west. A piece of newspaper fluttered at the corner of his eyes, the only movement in a dead world. He veered, stooped, and picked it up, without slackening his pace.

It was in Yiddish, a torn half-page.

He couldn't read it. He couldn't make out the blurred Hebrew letters, and could not have read it if they were clear. But one word was clear. It stood out in dark letters in the center of the page, each letter clear in its every serif. And it said Lefkovitsch, he knew, and as he said it to himself, he placed its accent on the second syllable: Lef-KUH-vich.

He let the paper flutter away and entered the empty park.

The trees were still and the leaves hung in odd, suspended attitudes. The sunlight was a dead weight upon him and gave no warmth.

He was running, but his feet kicked up no dust and a tuft of grass on which he placed his weight did not bend.

AND THERE ON a bench was an old man; the only man in the desolate park. He wore a dark felt cap, with a visor shading his eyes. From underneath it, tufts of gray hair protruded. His grizzled beard reached the uppermost button of his rough jacket. His old trousers were patched, and a strip of burlap was wrapped about each worn and shapeless shoe.

Marten stopped. It was difficult to breathe. He could only say one word and he used it to ask his question: "Levkovich?"

He stood there, while the old man rose slowly to his feet; brown old eyes peering close.

"Marten," he sighed. "Samuel Marten. You have come." The words sounded with an effect of double exposure, for under the English, Marten heard the faint sigh of a foreign tongue. Under the "Samuel" was the unheard shadow of a "Schmu-el."

The old man's rough, veined hands reached out, then withdrew as though he were afraid to touch. "I have been looking but there are so many people in this wilderness of a city-that-is-to-come. So many Martins and Martines and Mortons and Mertons. I stopped at last when I found greenery, but for a moment only—I would not commit the sin of losing faith. And then you came."

"It is I," said Marten, and knew it was. "And you are Phinehas Levkovich. Why are we here?"

"I am Phinehas ben Jehudah, assigned the name Levkovich by the ukase of the Tsar that ordered family names for all. And we are here," the old man said, softly, "because I prayed. When I was already old, Leah, my only daughter, the child of my old age, left for America with her husband, left the knouts of the old for the hope of the new. And my sons died, and Sarah, the wife of my bosom, was long dead and I was alone. And the time came when I, too, must die. But I had not seen Leah since her leaving for the far country and word had come but rarely. My soul yearned that I might see sons born unto her; sons of my seed; sons in whom my soul might yet live and not die."

His voice was steady and the soundless shadow of sound beneath his words was the stately roll of an ancient language.

"And I was answered and two hours were given me that I might see the first son of my line to be born in a new land and in a new time. My daughter's daughter's daughter's son, have I found you, then, amidst the splendor of this city?"

"But why the search? Why not have brought us together at once?"

"Because there is pleasure in the hope of the seeking, my son," said the old man, radiantly, "and in the delight of the finding. I was given two hours in which I might seek, two hours in which I might find . . . and behold, thou art here, and I have found that which I had not looked to see in life." His voice was old, caressing. "Is it well with thee, my son?"

"It is well, my father, now that I have found thee," said Marten, and dropped to his knees. "Give me thy blessing, my father, that it may be well with me all the days of my life, and with the maid whom I am to take to wife and the little ones yet to be born of my seed and thine."

He felt the old hand resting lightly on his head and there was only the soundless whisper.

Marten rose. The old man's eyes gazed into his yearningly. Were they losing focus?

"I go to my fathers now in peace, my son," said the old man, and Marten was alone in the empty park.

There was an instant of renewing motion, of the Sun taking up its interrupted task, of the wind reviving, and even with that first instant of sensation, all slipped back—

At ten of noon, Sam Marten hitched his way out of the taxicab, and found himself groping uselessly for his wallet while traffic inched on.

A red truck slowed, then moved on. A white script on its side announced: *F. Lewkowitz and Sons, Wholesale Clothiers.*

Marten didn't see it. Yet somehow he knew that all would be well with him. Somehow, as never before, he knew. . . .

WHAT IS THIS THING CALLED LOVE?

FIRST APPEARANCE—*AMAZING STORIES,* March 1961, under the title "Playboy and the Slime God." Copyright © 1961, by Ziff-Davis Publishing Company.

This one is complicated. It goes back to 1938–39 when, for some half a dozen issues or so, a magazine I won't name tried to make a go of what I can only call "spicy science fiction stories." Considering the sexual freedom allowed the writers of today, those old spicy s.f. stories read like "The Bobbsey Twins in Outer Space" now, but they were sizzlers to the magazine's few readers then.

The stories dealt very heavily with the hot passion of alien monsters for Earth-women. Clothes were always getting ripped off and breasts were described in a variety of elliptical phrases. (Yes, I know that's a pun.) The magazine died a deserved death, not so much for its sex and sadism, as for the deadly sameness of its stories and the abysmal quality of its "writing."

The curtain falls, and rises again in 1960. The magazine *Playboy* decided to have a little fun with science fiction. They published an article entitled "Girls for the Slime God" in which they pretended (good-naturedly) that all science fiction was sex and sadism. They could find very little real stuff to satirize, however, for until 1960 there was no branch of literature anywhere (except perhaps for the children's stories in Sunday school bulletins) as puritanical as science fiction. Since 1960, to be sure, sexual libertarianism has penetrated even science fiction.

Playboy therefore had to illustrate its article with the funny-sexy covers of fictitious magazines and had to draw all its quotations from only one source—that 1938–39 magazine I mentioned above.

Cele Goldsmith, the editor of *Amazing Stories*, read the article and called me at once. She suggested I write a story entitled "Playboy and the Slime God" satirizing the satire. I was strongly tempted to do so for several reasons:

1) Miss Goldsmith had to be seen to be believed. She was the only science fiction editor I've ever seen who looked like a show girl, and I happen to be aesthetically affected (or something) by show-girl types.

2) I take science fiction seriously and I was annoyed that that 1938–39 magazine should have given *Playboy* a handle for satire. I wanted to satire back at them.

3) I quickly thought up exactly what I wanted to say.

So I wrote "Playboy and the Slime God" using some of the same quotes that *Playboy* had used and trying to show what an encounter between sex-interested aliens and an Earth-woman might *really* be like. (I might say that Miss Goldsmith wrote the final three paragraphs of the story. I had a quite pretentious ending and Miss Goldsmith's was much better. So I let it stand, not only in the magazine, but here.)

The title was a problem, though. It's disgusting. When the late (alas!) Groff Conklin, who was one of the most indefatigable anthologizers in the business, was considering the story for one of his collections, he asked rather piteously if I had an alternate title. "You bet!" I said. "How about 'What Is This Thing Called Love?' "

Mr. Conklin was delighted and so was I, and that is the title that he used, and the one that I am now using.

WHAT IS THIS
THING CALLED LOVE?

"But these are two species," said Captain Garm, peering closely at the creatures that had been brought up from the planet below. His optic organs adjusted focus to maximum sharpness, bulging outwards as they did so. The color patch above them gleamed in quick flashes.

Botax felt warmly comfortable to be following color-changes once again, after months in a spy cell on the planet, trying to make sense out of the modulated sound waves emitted by the natives. Communication by flash was almost like being home in the far-off Perseus arm of the Galaxy. "Not two species," he said, "but two forms of one species."

"Nonsense, they look quite different. Vaguely Perse-like, thank the Entity, and not as disgusting in appearance as so many out-forms are. Reasonable shape, recognizable limbs. But no color-patch. Can they speak?"

"Yes, Captain Garm," Botax indulged in a discreetly disapproving prismatic interlude. "The details are in my report. These creatures form sound waves by way of throat and mouth, something like complicated coughing. I have learned to do it myself." He was quietly proud. "It is very difficult."

"It must be stomach-turning. Well, that accounts for their flat, unex-tensible eyes. Not to speak by color makes eyes largely useless. Mean-while, how can you insist these are a single species? The one on the left is smaller and has longer tendrils, or whatever it is, and seems differently proportioned. It bulges where this other does not. Are they alive?"

"Alive but not at the moment conscious, Captain. They have been psycho-treated to repress fright in order that they might be studied easily."

"But are they worth study? We are behind our schedule and have at least five worlds of greater moment than this one to check and explore. Maintaining a Time-stasis unit is expensive and I would like to return them and go on—"

But Botax's moist spindly body was fairly vibrating with anxiety. His tubular tongue flicked out and curved up and over his flat nose, while his eyes sucked inward. His splayed three-fingered hand made a gesture of negation as his speech went almost entirely into the deep red.

"Entity save us, Captain, for no world is of greater moment to us than this one. We may be facing a supreme crisis. These creatures could be the most dangerous life-forms in the Galaxy, Captain, just *because* there are two forms."

"I don't follow you."

"Captain, it has been my job to study this planet, and it has been most difficult, for it is unique. It is so unique that I can scarcely compre-hend its facets. For instance, almost all life on the planet consists of species in two forms. There are no words to describe it, no concepts even. I can only speak of them as first form and second form. If I may use their sounds, the little one is called 'female,' and the big one, here, 'male,' so the creatures themselves are aware of the difference."

Garm winced, "What a disgusting means of communication."

"And, Captain, in order to bring forth young, the two forms must cooperate."

The Captain, who had bent forward to examine the specimens closely with an expression compounded of interest and revulsion, straightened at once. "Cooperate? What nonsense is this? There is no more fundamental attribute of life than that each living creature bring forth its young in innermost communication with itself. What else makes life worth living?"

"The one form does bring forth life but the other form must coop-erate."

"How?"

"That has been difficult to determine. It is something very private and in my search through the available forms of literature I could find no exact and explicit description. But I have been able to make reasonable deductions."

Garm shook his head. "Ridiculous. Budding is the holiest, most private function in the world. On tens of thousands of worlds it is the same. As the great photo-bard, Levuline, said, 'In budding-time, in budding time, in sweet, delightful budding time; when—' "

"Captain, you don't understand. This cooperation between forms brings about somehow (and I am not certain exactly how) a mixture and recombination of genes. It is a device by which in every generation, new combinations of characteristics are brought into existence. Variations are multiplied; mutated genes hastened into expression almost at once where under the usual budding system, millennia might pass first."

"Are you trying to tell me that the genes from one individual can be combined with those of another? Do you know how completely ridiculous that is in the light of all the principles of cellular physiology?"

"It must be so," said Botax nervously under the other's pop-eyed glare. "Evolution *is* hastened. This planet is a riot of species. There are supposed to be a million and a quarter different species of creatures."

"A dozen and a quarter more likely. Don't accept too completely what you read in the native literature."

"I've seen dozens of radically different species myself in just a small area. I tell you, Captain, give these creatures a short space of time and they will mutate into intellects powerful enough to overtake us and rule the Galaxy."

"Prove that this cooperation you speak of exists, Investigator, and I shall consider your contentions. If you cannot, I shall dismiss all your fancies as ridiculous and we will move on."

"I can prove it." Botax's color-flashes turned intensely yellow-green. "The creatures of this world are unique in another way. They foresee advances they have not yet made, probably as a consequence of their belief in rapid change which, after all, they constantly witness. They therefore indulge in a type of literature involving the space-travel they have never developed. I have translated their term for the literature as 'science-fiction.' Now I have dealt in my readings almost exclusively with science-fiction, for there I thought, in their dreams and fancies, they would expose themselves and their danger to us. And it was from that science-fiction that I deduced the method of their inter-form cooperation."

"How did you do that?"

"There is a periodical on this world which sometimes publishes science-fiction which is, however, devoted almost entirely to the various aspects of the cooperation. It does not speak entirely freely, which is annoying, but persists in merely hinting. Its name as nearly as I can put it into flashes is 'Recreationlad.' The creature in charge, I deduce, is interested in nothing but inter-form cooperation and searches for it everywhere with a systematic and scientific intensity that has roused my awe. He has found instances of cooperation described in science-fiction and I let material in his periodical guide me. From the stories he instanced I have learned how to bring it about.

"And Captain, I beg of you, when the cooperation is accomplished and the young are brought forth before your eyes, give orders not to leave an atom of this world in existence."

"Well," said Captain Garm, wearily, "bring them into full consciousness and do what you must do quickly."

MARGE SKIDMORE WAS suddenly completely aware of her surroundings. She remembered very clearly the elevated station at the beginning of twilight. It had been almost empty, one man standing near her, another at the other end of the platform. The approaching train had just made itself known as a faint rumble in the distance.

There had then come the flash, a sense of turning inside out, the half-seen vision of a spindly creature, dripping mucus, a rushing upward, and now—

"Oh, God," she said, shuddering. "It's still here. And there's another one, too."

She felt a sick revulsion, but no fear. She was almost proud of herself for feeling no fear. The man next to her, standing quietly as she herself was, but still wearing a battered fedora, was the one that had been near her on the platform.

"They got you, too?" she asked. "Who else?"

Charlie Grimwold, feeling flabby and paunchy, tried to lift his hand to remove his hat and smooth the thin hair that broke up but did not entirely cover the skin of his scalp and found that it moved only with difficulty against a rubbery but hardening resistance. He let his hand drop and looked morosely at the thin-faced woman facing him. She was in her middle thirties, he decided, and her hair was nice and her dress fit well, but at the moment, he just wanted to be somewhere else and it did him no good at all that he had company, even female company.

He said, "I don't know, lady. I was just standing on the station platform."

"Me, too."

"And then I see a flash. Didn't hear nothing. Now here I am. Must be little men from Mars or Venus or one of them places."

Marge nodded vigorously, "That's what I figure. A flying saucer? You scared?"

"No. That's funny, you know. I think maybe I'm going nuts or I *would* be scared."

"Funny thing. I ain't scared, either. Oh, God, here comes one of them now. If he touches me, I'm going to scream. Look at those wiggly hands. And that wrinkled skin, all slimy; makes me nauseous."

Botax approached gingerly and said, in a voice at once rasping and screechy, this being the closest he could come to imitating the native timbre, "Creatures! We will not hurt you. But we must ask you if you would do us the favor of cooperating."

"Hey, it talks!" said Charlie. "What do you mean, cooperate."

"Both of you. With each other," said Botax.

"Oh?" He looked at Marge. "You know what he means, lady?"

"Ain't got no idea whatsoever," she answered loftily.

Botax said, "What I mean—" and he used the short term he had once heard employed as a synonym for the process.

Marge turned red and said, "What!" in the loudest scream she could manage. Both Botax and Captain Garm put their hands over their midregions to cover the auditory patches that trembled painfully with the decibels.

Marge went on rapidly, and nearly incoherently. "Of all things. I'm a married woman, you. If my Ed was here, you'd hear from *him*. And you, wise guy," she twisted toward Charlie against rubbery resistance, "whoever you are, if you think—"

"Lady, lady," said Charlie in uncomfortable desperation. "It ain't my idea. I mean, far be it from me, you know, to turn down some lady, you know; but me, I'm married, too. I got three kids. Listen—"

CAPTAIN GARM SAID, "What's happening, Investigator Botax? These cacophonous sounds are awful."

"Well," Botax flashed a short purple patch of embarrassment. "This forms a complicated ritual. They are supposed to be reluctant at first. It heightens the subsequent result. After that initial stage, the skins must be removed."

"They have to be *skinned?*"

"Not really skinned. Those are artificial skins that can be removed painlessly, and must be. Particularly in the smaller form."

"All right, then. Tell it to remove the skins. Really, Botax, I don't find this pleasant."

"I don't think I had better tell the smaller form to remove the skins. I think we had better follow the ritual closely. I have here sections of those space-travel tales which the man from the 'Recreationlad' periodical spoke highly of. In those tales the skins are removed forcibly. Here is a description of an accident, for instance 'which played havoc with the girl's dress, ripping it nearly off her slim body. For a second, he felt the warm firmness of her half-bared bosom against his cheek—' It goes on that way. You see, the ripping, the forcible removal, acts as a stimulus."

"Bosom?" said the Captain. "I don't recognize the flash."

"I invented that to cover the meaning. It refers to the bulges on the upper dorsal region of the smaller form."

"I see. Well, tell the larger one to rip the skins off the smaller one. What a dismal thing this is."

Botax turned to Charlie. "Sir," he said, "rip the girl's dress nearly off her slim body, will you? I will release you for the purpose."

Marge's eyes widened and she twisted toward Charlie in instant outrage. "Don't you dare do that, you. Don't you *dast* touch me, you sex maniac."

"Me?" said Charlie plaintively. "It ain't my idea. You think I go around ripping dresses? Listen," he turned to Botax, "I got a wife and three kids. She finds out I go around ripping dresses, I get clobbered. You know what my wife does when I just look at some dame? *Listen*—"

"Is he still reluctant?" said the Captain, impatiently.

"Apparently," said Botax. "The strange surroundings, you know, may be extending that stage of the cooperation. Since I know this is unpleasant for you, I will perform this stage of the ritual myself. It is frequently written in the space-travel tales that an outer-world species performs the task. For instance, here," and he riffled through his notes finding the one he wanted, "they describe a very awful such species. The creatures on the planet have foolish notions, you understand. It never occurs to them to imagine handsome individuals such as ourselves, with a fine mucous cover."

"Go on! Go on! Don't take all day," said the Captain.

"Yes, Captain. It says here that the extraterrestrial 'came forward to where the girl stood. Shrieking hysterically, she was cradled in the monster's embrace. Talons ripped blindly at her body, tearing the kirtle away in rags.' You see, the native creature is shrieking with stimulation as her skins are removed."

"Then go ahead, Botax, remove it. But please, allow no shrieking. I'm trembling all over with the sound waves."

Botax said politely to Marge, "If you don't mind—"

One spatulate finger made as though to hook on to the neck of the dress.

Marge wiggled desperately. "Don't touch. Don't touch! You'll get slime on it. Listen, this dress cost $24.95 at Ohrbach's. Stay away, you monster. Look at those eyes on him." She was panting in her desperate efforts to dodge the groping, extraterrestrial hand. "A slimy, bug-eyed monster, that's what he is. Listen, I'll take it off myself. Just don't touch it with slime, for God's sake."

She fumbled at the zipper, and said in a hot aside to Charlie, "Don't you dast look."

Charlie closed his eyes and shrugged in resignation.

She stepped out of the dress. "All right? You satisfied?"

Captain Garm's fingers twitched with unhappiness. "Is that the bosom? Why does the other creature keep its head turned away?"

"Reluctance. Reluctance," said Botax. "Besides, the bosom is still covered. Other skins must be removed. When bared, the bosom is a very strong stimulus. It is constantly described as ivory globes, or white spheres, or otherwise after that fashion. I have here drawings, visual picturizations, that come from the outer covers of the space-travel magazines. If you will inspect them, you will see that upon every one of them, a creature is present with a bosom more or less exposed."

The Captain looked thoughtfully from the illustrations to Marge and back. "What is ivory?"

"That is another made-up flash of my own. It represents the tusky material of one of the large sub-intelligent creatures on the planet."

"Ah," and Captain Garm went into a pastel green of satisfaction. "That explains it. This small creature is one of a warrior sect and those are tusks with which to smash the enemy."

"No, no. They are quite soft, I understand." Botax's small brown hand flicked outward in the general direction of the objects under discussion and Marge screamed and shrank away.

"Then what other purpose do they have?"

"I think," said Botax with considerable hesitation, "that they are used to feed the young."

"The young eat them?" asked the Captain with every evidence of deep distress.

"Not exactly. The objects produce a fluid which the young consume."

"Consume a fluid from a living body? Yech-h-h." The Captain covered his head with all three of his arms, calling the central supernumerary into use for the purpose, slipping it out of its sheath so rapidly as almost to knock Botax over.

"A three-armed, slimy, bug-eyed monster," said Marge.

"Yeah," said Charlie.

"All right you, just watch those eyes. Keep them to yourself."

"Listen, lady. I'm trying not to look."

Botax approached again. "Madam, would you remove the rest?"

Marge drew herself up as well as she could against the pinioning field. "Never!"

"I'll remove it, if you wish."

"Don't touch! For God's sake, don't touch. Look at the slime on him, will you? All right, I'll take it off." She was muttering under her breath and looking hotly in Charlie's direction as she did so.

"NOTHING IS HAPPENING," said the Captain, in deep dissatisfaction, "and this seems an imperfect specimen."

Botax felt the slur on his own efficiency. "I brought you two perfect specimens. What's wrong with the creature?"

"The bosom does not consist of globes or spheres. I know what globes or spheres are and in these pictures you have shown me, they are so depicted. Those are large globes. On this creature, though, what we have are nothing but small flaps of dry tissue. And they're discolored, too, partly."

"Nonsense," said Botax. "You must allow room for natural variation. I will put it to the creature herself."

He turned to Marge, "Madam, is your bosom imperfect?"

Marge's eyes opened wide and she struggled vainly for moments without doing anything more than gasp loudly. *"Really!"* she finally managed. "Maybe I'm no Gina Lollobrigida or Anita Ekberg, but I'm perfectly all right, thank you. Oh boy, if my Ed were only here." She turned to Charlie. "Listen, you, you tell this bug-eyed slimy thing here, there ain't nothing wrong with my development."

"Lady," said Charlie, softly. "I ain't looking, remember?"

"Oh, sure, you ain't looking. You been peeking enough, so you might as well just open your crummy eyes and stick up for a lady, if you're the least bit of a gentleman, which you probably ain't."

"Well," said Charlie, looking sideways at Marge, who seized the opportunity to inhale and throw her shoulders back, "I don't like to get mixed up in a kind of delicate matter like this, but you're all right—I guess."

"You *guess*? You blind or something? I was once runner-up for Miss Brooklyn, in case you don't happen to know, and where I missed out was on waist-line, *not* on—"

Charlie said, "All right, all right. They're fine. Honest." He nodded vigorously in Botax's direction. "They're okay. I ain't that much of an expert, you understand, but they're okay by me."

Marge relaxed.

Botax felt relieved. He turned to Garm. "The bigger form expresses interest, Captain. The stimulus is working. Now for the final step."

"And what is that?"

"There is no flash for it, Captain. Essentially, it consists of placing the speaking-and-eating apparatus of one against the equivalent apparatus of the other. I have made up a flash for the process, thus: kiss."

"Will nausea never cease?" groaned the Captain.

"It is the climax. In all the tales, after the skins are removed by force, they clasp each other with limbs and indulge madly in burning kisses, to translate as nearly as possible the phrase most frequently used. Here is one example, just one, taken at random: 'He held the girl, his mouth avid on her lips.' "

"Maybe one creature was devouring the other," said the Captain.

"Not at all," said Botax impatiently. "Those were burning kisses."

"How do you mean, burning? Combustion takes place?"

"I don't think literally so. I imagine it is a way of expressing the fact that the temperature goes up. The higher the temperature, I suppose, the more successful the production of young. Now that the big form is properly stimulated, he need only place his mouth against hers to produce young. The young will not be produced without that step. It is the cooperation I have been speaking of."

"That's all? Just this—" The Captain's hands made motions of coming together, but he could not bear to put the thought into flash form.

"That's all," said Botax. "In none of the tales; not even in 'Recreationlad,' have I found a description of any further physical activity in connection with young-bearing. Sometimes after the kissing, they write a line of symbols like little stars, but I suppose that merely means more kissing; one kiss for each star, when they wish to produce a multitude of young."

"Just one, please, right now."

"Certainly, Captain."

BOTAX SAID WITH grave distinctness, "Sir, would you kiss the lady?"

Charlie said, "Listen, I can't move."

"I will free you, of course."

"The lady might not like it."

Marge glowered. "You bet your damn boots, I won't like it. You just stay away."

"I would like to, lady, but what do they do if I don't? Look, I don't want to get them mad. We can just—you know—make like a little peck."

She hesitated, seeing the justice of the caution. "All right. No funny stuff, though. I ain't in the habit of standing around like this in front of every Tom, Dick and Harry, you know."

"I know that, lady. It was none of my doing. You got to admit that."

Marge muttered angrily, "Regular slimy monsters. Must think they're some kind of gods or something, the way they order people around. Slime gods is what they are!"

Charlie approached her. "If it's okay now, lady." He made a vague motion as though to tip his hat. Then he put his hands awkwardly on her bare shoulders and leaned over in a gingerly pucker.

Marge's head stiffened so that lines appeared in her neck. Their lips met.

Captain Garm flashed fretfully. "I sense no rise in temperature." His heat-detecting tendril had risen to full extension at the top of his head and remained quivering there.

"I don't either," said Botax, rather at a loss, "but we're doing it just as the space travel stories tell us to. I think his limbs should be more extended—Ah, like that. See, it's working."

Almost absently, Charlie's arm had slid around Marge's soft, nude torso. For a moment, Marge seemed to yield against him and then she suddenly writhed hard against the pinioning field that still held her with fair firmness.

"Let go." The words were muffled against the pressure of Charlie's lips. She bit suddenly, and Charlie leaped away with a wild cry, holding his lower lip, then looking at his fingers for blood.

"What's the idea, lady?" he demanded plaintively.

She said, "We agreed just a peck, is all. What were you starting there? You some kind of playboy or something? What am I surrounded with here? Playboy and the slime gods?"

CAPTAIN GARM FLASHED rapid alternations of blue and yellow. "Is it done? How long do we wait now?"

"It seems to me it must happen at once. Throughout all the universe, when you have to bud, you bud, you know. There's no waiting."

"Yes? After thinking of the foul habits you have been describing, I don't think I'll ever bud again. Please get this over with."

"Just a moment, Captain."

But the moments passed and the Captain's flashes turned slowly to a brooding orange, while Botax's nearly dimmed out altogether.

Botax finally asked hesitantly, "Pardon me, madam, but when will you bud?"

"When will I *what*?"

"Bear young?"

"I've got a kid."

"I mean bear young now."

"I should say not. I ain't ready for another kid yet."

"What? What?" demanded the Captain. "What's she saying?"

"It seems," said Botax, "she does not intend to have young at the moment."

The Captain's color patch blazed brightly. "Do you know what I think, Investigator? I think you have a sick, perverted mind. Nothing's happening to these creatures. There is no cooperation between them, and no young to be borne. I think they're two different species and that you're playing some kind of foolish game with me."

"But, Captain—" said Botax.

"Don't but Captain me," said Garm. "I've had enough. You've upset me, turned my stomach, nauseated me, disgusted me with the whole notion of budding and wasted my time. You're just looking for headlines and personal glory and I'll see to it that you don't get them. Get rid of these creatures now. Give that one its skins back and put them back where you found them. I ought to take the expense of maintaining Time-stasis all this time out of your salary."

"But, Captain—"

"Back, I say. Put them back in the same place and at the same instant of time. I want this planet untouched, and I'll see to it that it stays untouched." He cast one more furious glance at Botax. "One species, two forms, bosoms, kisses, cooperation, BAH— You are a fool, Investigator, a dolt as well and, most of all, a sick, sick, sick creature."

There was no arguing. Botax, limbs trembling, set about returning the creatures.

THEY STOOD THERE at the elevated station, looking around wildly. It was twilight over them, and the approaching train was just making itself known as a faint rumble in the distance.

Marge said, hesitantly, "Mister, did it really happen?"

Charlie nodded. "I remember it."

Marge said, "We can't tell anybody."

"Sure not. They'd say we was nuts. Know what I mean?"

"Uh-huh. Well," she edged away.

Charlie said, "Listen. I'm sorry you was embarrassed. It was none of my doing."

"That's all right. I know." Marge's eyes considered the wooden platform at her feet. The sound of the train was louder.

"I mean, you know, lady, you wasn't really bad. In fact, you looked good, but I was kind of embarrassed to say that."

Suddenly, she smiled. "It's all right."

"You want maybe to have a cup of coffee with me just to relax you? My wife, she's not really expecting me for a while."

"Oh? Well, Ed's out of town for the weekend so I got only an empty apartment to go home to. My little boy is visiting at my mother's." She explained.

"Come on, then. We been kind of introduced."

"I'll say." She laughed.

The train pulled in, but they turned away, walking down the narrow stairway to the street.

They had a couple of cocktails actually, and then Charlie couldn't let her go home in the dark alone, so he saw her to her door. Marge was bound to invite him in for a few moments, naturally.

MEANWHILE, BACK IN the spaceship, the crushed Botax was making a final effort to prove his case. While Garm prepared the ship for departure Botax hastily set up the tight-beam visiscreen for a last look at his specimens. He focused in on Charlie and Marge in her apartment. His tendril stiffened and he began flashing in a coruscating rainbow of colors.

"Captain Garm! Captain! Look what they're doing now!"

But at that very instant the ship winked out of Time-stasis.

PREFACE TO

THE MACHINE THAT WON THE WAR

FIRST APPEARANCE—*THE MAGAZINE OF Fantasy and Science Fiction*, October 1961. © 1961, by Mercury Press, Inc.

Toward the end of the 1950s some rather unexpected changes took place in my life. My writing career had been constantly expanding. I had been driven on by my own compulsion and by editorial cooperation to undertake more and more tasks in greater and greater variety and by 1958 I found that I could no longer do the writing I wanted to do and maintain a full academic schedule.

The Medical School and I came to an amicable understanding, therefore. I kept my title (Associate Professor of Biochemistry, if you're curious) and continued to do odd jobs, like giving several lectures a year, sitting on committees, and so on. In the main, however, I became a full-time writer and relieved them of the trouble of paying me a salary.

For a while, it seemed to me that with virtually no academic duties and an infinite amount of time each and every day, I could finally do all the writing I had to do with plenty of time left over for fun and games.

It didn't work out. One of Parkinson's laws is: "Work expands to fill the time available." It did in my case. In no time at all, I found I was typing as assiduously full-time as I had previously been typing half-time and I quickly discovered the Asimov corollary to Parkinson's law: "In ten hours a day you have time to fall twice as far behind your commitments as in five hours a day."

The worst of it was that just about the time I was arranging to make myself a full-time writer, the Soviet Union sent up Sputnik I and the United States went into a kind of tizzy, and so did I.

I was overcome by the ardent desire to write popular science for an America that might be in great danger through its neglect of science, and a number of publishers got an equally ardent desire to publish popular science for the same reason. As a result of combining the two ardencies I found myself plunging into a shoreless sea in which I am still immersed.

The trouble is—it's all non-fiction. In the last ten years, I've done a couple of novels, some collections, a dozen or so stories, but that's *nothing*.

From the aggrieved letters I get, one would think I was doing this on purpose. I'm *not*. I try desperately not to lose touch with science fiction altogether. It's my life in a way that nothing else can quite be. There's my monthly article in *F & SF*, of course, but that's not quite the same thing.

And so it happens that each short individual piece of fiction I manage to get the typewriter to put out for me is dearer to me in the nowadays of my dimness, than in the old times when I did two dozen or more long ones a year.

"The Machine That Won the War" is one of those that serves as my periodic proof to the world of fandom that I am, too, alive.

THE MACHINE THAT WON THE WAR

The celebration had a long way to go and even in the silent depths of Multivac's underground chambers, it hung in the air.

If nothing else, there was the mere fact of isolation and silence. For the first time in a decade, technicians were not scurrying about the vitals of the giant computer, the soft lights did not wink out their erratic patterns, the flow of information in and out had halted.

It would not be halted long, of course, for the needs of peace would be pressing. Yet now, for a day, perhaps for a week, even Multivac might celebrate the great time, and rest.

Lamar Swift took off the military cap he was wearing and looked down the long and empty main corridor of the enormous computer. He sat down rather wearily in one of the technician's swing-stools, and his uniform, in which he had never been comfortable, took on a heavy and wrinkled appearance.

He said, "I'll miss it all after a grisly fashion. It's hard to remember when we weren't at war with Deneb, and it seems against nature now to be at peace and to look at the stars without anxiety."

The two men with the Executive Director of the Solar Federation were both younger than Swift. Neither was as gray. Neither looked quite as tired.

John Henderson, thin-lipped and finding it hard to control the relief he felt in the midst of triumph, said, "They're destroyed! They're destroyed! It's what I keep saying to myself over and over and I still can't believe it. We all talked so much, over so many years, about the menace hanging over Earth and all its worlds, over every human being, and all the time it was true, every word of it. And now we're alive and it's the Denebians who are shattered and destroyed. They'll be no menace now, ever again."

"Thanks to Multivac," said Swift, with a quiet glance at the imperturbable Jablonsky, who through all the war had been Chief Interpreter of science's oracle. "Right, Max?"

Jablonsky shrugged. Automatically, he reached for a cigarette and decided against it. He alone, of all the thousands who had lived in the tunnels within Multivac, had been allowed to smoke, but toward the end he had made definite efforts to avoid making use of the privilege.

He said, "Well, that's what *they* say." His broad thumb moved in the direction of his right shoulder, aiming upward.

"Jealous, Max?"

"Because they're shouting for Multivac? Because Multivac is the big hero of mankind in this war?" Jablonsky's craggy face took on an air of suitable contempt. "What's that to me? Let Multivac be the machine that won the war, if it pleases them."

Henderson looked at the other two out of the corners of his eyes. In this short interlude that the three had instinctively sought out in the one peaceful corner of a metropolis gone mad; in this entr'acte between the dangers of war and the difficulties of peace; when, for one moment, they might all find surcease; he was conscious only of his weight of guilt.

Suddenly, it was as though that weight were too great to be borne longer. It had to be thrown off, along with the war; now!

Henderson said, "Multivac had nothing to do with victory. It's just a machine."

"A big one," said Swift.

"Then just a big machine. No better than the data fed it." For a moment, he stopped, suddenly unnerved at what he was saying.

Jablonsky looked at him, his thick fingers once again fumbling for a cigarette and once again drawing back. "You should know. You supplied the data. Or is it just that you're taking the credit?"

"*No*," said Henderson, angrily. "There is no credit. What do you know of the data Multivac had to use; predigested from a hundred subsidiary computers here on Earth, on the Moon, on Mars, even on Titan. With Titan always delayed and always that feeling that its figures would introduce an unexpected bias."

"It would drive anyone mad," said Swift, with gentle sympathy.

Henderson shook his head. "It wasn't just that. I admit that eight years ago when I replaced Lepont as Chief Programmer, I was nervous. But there was an exhilaration about things in those days. The war was still long-range; an adventure without real danger. We hadn't reached the point where manned vessels had had to take over and where interstellar warps could swallow up a planet clean, if aimed correctly. But then, when the real difficulties began—"

Angrily—he could finally permit anger—he said, "You know nothing about it."

"Well," said Swift. "Tell us. The war is over. We've won."

"Yes." Henderson nodded his head. He had to remember that. Earth had won so all had been for the best. "Well, the data became meaningless."

"Meaningless? You mean that literally?" said Jablonsky.

"Literally. What would you expect? The trouble with you two was that you weren't out in the thick of it. You never left Multivac, Max, and you, Mr. Director, never left the Mansion except on state visits where you saw exactly what they wanted you to see."

"I was not as unaware of that," said Swift, "as you may have thought."

"Do you know," said Henderson, "to what extent data concerning our production capacity, our resource potential, our trained manpower—everything of importance to the war effort, in fact—had become unreliable and untrustworthy during the last half of the war? Group leaders, both civilian and military, were intent on projecting their own improved image, so to speak, so they obscured the bad and magnified the good. Whatever the machines might do, the men who programmed them and interpreted the results had their own skins to think of and competitors to stab. There was no way of stopping that. I tried, and failed."

"Of course," said Swift, in quiet consolation. "I can see that you would."

This time Jablonsky decided to light his cigarette. "Yet I presume you provided Multivac with data in your programming. You said nothing to us about unreliability."

"How could I tell you? And if I did, how could you afford to believe me?" demanded Henderson, savagely. "Our entire war effort was geared to Multivac. It was the one great weapon on our side, for the Denebians had nothing like it. What else kept up morale in the face of doom but the assurance that Multivac would always predict and circumvent any Denebian move, and would always direct and prevent the circumvention of our moves? Great Space, after our Spy-warp was blasted out of hyperspace we lacked any reliable Denebian data to feed Multivac and we didn't dare make *that* public."

"True enough," said Swift.

"Well, then," said Henderson, "if I told you the data was unreliable, what could you have done but replace me and refuse to believe me? I couldn't allow that."

"What did you do?" said Jablonsky.

"Since the war is won, I'll tell you what I did. I corrected the data."

"How?" asked Swift.

"Intuition, I presume. I juggled them till they looked right. At first, I hardly dared. I changed a bit here and there to correct what were obvious impossibilities. When the sky didn't collapse about us, I got braver. Toward the end, I scarcely cared. I just wrote out the necessary data as it was needed. I even had the Multivac Annex prepare data for me according to a private programming pattern I had devised for the purpose."

"Random figures?" said Jablonsky.

"Not at all. I introduced a number of necessary biases."

Jablonsky smiled, quite unexpectedly, his dark eyes sparkling behind the crinkling of the lower lids. "Three times a report was brought me about unauthorized uses of the Annex, and I let it go each time. If it had mattered, I would have followed it up and spotted you, John, and found out what you were doing. But, of course, nothing about Multivac mattered in those days, so you got away with it."

"What do you mean, nothing mattered?" asked Henderson, suspiciously.

"Nothing did. I suppose if I had told you this at the time, it would have spared you your agony, but then if you had told me what you were doing, it would have spared me mine. What made you think Multivac was in working order, whatever the data you supplied it?"

"Not in working order?" said Swift.

"Not really. Not reliably. After all, where were my technicians in the last years of the war? I'll tell you, they were feeding computers on a thousand different space devices. They were gone! I had to make do with kids I couldn't trust and veterans who were out-of-date. Besides, do you think I could trust the solid-state components coming out of Cryogenics in the last years? Cryogenics wasn't any better placed as far as personnel was concerned than I was. To me, it didn't matter whether the data being supplied Multivac were reliable or not. The *results* weren't reliable. That much I knew."

"What did you do?" asked Henderson.

"I did what you did, John. I introduced the bugger factor. I adjusted matters in accordance with intuition—and that's how the machine won the war."

Swift leaned back in the chair and stretched his legs out before him. "Such revelations. It turns out then that the material handed me to guide me in my decision-making capacity was a man-made interpretation of man-made data. Isn't that right?"

"It looks so," said Jablonsky.

"Then I perceive I was correct in not placing too much reliance upon it," said Swift.

"You didn't?" Jablonsky, despite what he had just said, managed to look professionally insulted.

"I'm afraid I didn't. Multivac might seem to say, Strike here, not there; do this, not that; wait, don't act. But I could never be certain that what Multivac seemed to say, it really did say; or what it really said, it really meant. I could never be certain."

"But the final report was always plain enough, sir," said Jablonsky.

"To those who did not have to make the decision, perhaps. Not to me. The horror of the responsibility of such decisions was unbearable and not even Multivac was sufficient to remove the weight. But the point is I was justified in doubting and there is tremendous relief in that."

Caught up in the conspiracy of mutual confession, Jablonsky put titles aside, "What was it you did then, Lamar? After all, you did make decisions. How?"

"Well, it's time to be getting back perhaps but—I'll tell you first. Why not? I did make use of a computer, Max, but an older one than Multivac, much older."

He groped in his own pocket for cigarettes, and brought out a package along with a scattering of small change; old-fashioned coins dating to the first years before the metal shortage had brought into being a credit system tied to a computer-complex.

Swift smiled rather sheepishly. "I still need these to make money seem substantial to me. An old man finds it hard to abandon the habits of youth." He put a cigarette between his lips and dropped the coins one by one back into his pocket.

He held the last coin between his fingers, staring absently at it. "Multivac is not the first computer, friends, nor the best-known, nor the one that can most efficiently lift the load of decision from the shoulders of the executive. A machine *did* win the war, John; at least a very simple computing device did; one that I used every time I had a particularly hard decision to make."

With a faint smile of reminiscence, he flipped the coin he held. It glinted in the air as it spun and came down in Swift's outstretched palm. His hand closed over it and brought it down on the back of his left hand. His right hand remained in place, hiding the coin.

"Heads or tails, gentlemen?" said Swift.

PREFACE TO
MY SON,
THE PHYSICIST

FIRST APPEARANCE—*SCIENTIFIC AMERICAN*, February 1962. © 1962, Hoffman Electronics Corporation.

One of the side effects of the growing respectability of science fiction was that it began to appear in markets where, a few short years earlier, the Sanitation Department would have been called in to remove any such manuscripts that had inadvertently found their way into the editorial office.

I'll never forget the shock that rumbled through the entire world of science fiction fandom when, after World War II, our own Robert A. Heinlein broke the "slicks" barrier by having an undiluted science fiction story of his published in *The Saturday Evening Post*.

Nowadays, it is routine to find science fiction writers and their science fiction in such wide-circulation markets as *Playboy*. Indeed, the competition of the mass markets is such that the small specialty science fiction magazines find it hard to hold on to the more experienced writers and they do not benefit, as they ought, from the field's new-won respectability. It is unjust!

But the strangest market for science fiction, in my opinion, was the advertising columns of that excellent (and, for me, indispensable) periodical, *Scientific American*. It seems that a company called Hoffman Electronics Corporation got the idea of running a series of advertisements that would include a two-page (minus one column) illustrated science fiction story—real science fiction stories by the acknowledged masters. The final column would then be used to promote their product in a dignified manner. There was no direct tie-in between story and advertising and the writer was to have carte blanche, except that it would be nice to have the story involve communications in one form or another (since communications technology was what Hoffman was selling).

The challenge was interesting and artistic integrity was preserved, so when I was asked to do a story for the program, I accepted and wrote "My Son, the Physicist." As you see, it deals with communications but is in no way a "commercial" for such things. Hoffman accepted the story without changing a word or a comma and it ran not only in the ad columns of *Scientific American* but in *Fortune* as well.

It was an experience, you may be sure, because it is not likely that my by-line would ever have appeared in either magazine otherwise. Not under a piece of science fiction, anyway.

I am a little uneasy, though, as to how well the idea worked out. There were only six such advertisements altogether, as far as I know, and then they stopped. Well, maybe they just had difficulty getting appropriate stories. I don't know.

MY SON,
THE PHYSICIST

Her hair was light apple-green in color, very subdued, very old-fashioned. You could see she had a delicate hand with the dye, the way they did thirty years ago, before the streaks and stipples came into fashion.

She had a sweet smile on her face, too, and a calm look that made something serene out of elderliness.

And, by comparison, it made something shrieking out of the confusion that enfolded her in the huge government building.

A girl passed her at a half-run, stopped and turned toward her with a blank stare of astonishment. "How did you get in?"

The woman smiled. "I'm looking for my son, the physicist."

"Your son, the—"

"He's a communications engineer, really. Senior Physicist Gerard Cremona."

"Dr. Cremona. Well, he's— Where's your pass?"

"Here it is. I'm his mother."

"Well, Mrs. Cremona, I don't know. I've got to— His office is down there. You just ask someone." She passed on, running.

Mrs. Cremona shook her head slowly. Something had happened, she supposed. She hoped Gerard was all right.

She heard voices much farther down the corridor and smiled happily. She could tell Gerard's.

She walked into the room and said, "Hello, Gerard."

Gerard was a big man, with a lot of hair still and the gray just beginning to show because he didn't use dye. He said he was too busy. She was very proud of him and the way he looked.

Right now, he was talking volubly to a man in army uniform. She couldn't tell the rank, but she knew Gerard could handle him.

Gerard looked up and said, "What do you— Mother! What are you doing here?"

"I was coming to visit you today."

"Is today Thursday? Oh Lord, I forgot. Sit down, Mother, I can't talk now. Any seat. Any seat. Look, General."

General Reiner looked over his shoulder and one hand slapped against the other in the region of the small of his back. "Your mother?"

"Yes."

"Should she be here?"

"Right now, no, but I'll vouch for her. She can't even read a thermometer so nothing of this will mean anything to her. Now look, General. They're on Pluto. You see? They are. The radio signals can't be of natural origin so they must originate from human beings, from our men. You'll have to accept that. Of all the expeditions we've sent out beyond the planetoid belt, one turns out to have made it. And they've reached Pluto."

"Yes, I understand what you're saying, but isn't it impossible just the same? The men who are on Pluto now were launched four years ago with equipment that could not have kept them alive more than a year. That is my understanding. They were aimed at Ganymede and seem to have gone eight times the proper distance."

"Exactly. And we've got to know how and why. They may—just— have—had—help."

"What kind? How?"

Cremona clenched his jaws for a moment as though praying inwardly. "General," he said, "I'm putting myself out on a limb but it is just barely possible non-humans are involved. Extra-terrestrials. We've got to find out. We don't know how long contact can be maintained."

"You mean" (the General's grave face twitched into an almost-smile) "they may have escaped from custody and they may be recaptured again at any time."

"Maybe. Maybe. The whole future of the human race may depend on our knowing exactly what we're up against. Knowing it *now*."

"All right. What is it you want?"

"We're going to need Army's Multivac computer at once. Rip out every problem it's working on and start programing our general semantic problem. Every communications engineer you have must be pulled off anything he's on and placed into coordination with our own."

"But why? I fail to see the connection."

A gentle voice interrupted. "General, would you like a piece of fruit? I brought some oranges?"

Cremona said, "Mother! Please! Later! General, the point is a simple one. At the present moment Pluto is just under four billion miles away. It takes six hours for radio waves, traveling at the speed of light, to reach from here to there. If we say something, we must wait twelve hours for an answer. If they say something and we miss it and say 'what' and they repeat—bang, goes a day."

"There's no way to speed it up?" said the General.

"Of course not. It's the fundamental law of communications. No information can be transmitted at more than the speed of light. It will take months to carry on the same conversation with Pluto that would take hours between the two of us right now."

"Yes, I see that. And you really think extraterrestrials are involved?"

"I do. To be honest, not everyone here agrees with me. Still, we're straining every nerve, every fiber, to devise some method of concentrating communication. We must get in as many bits per second as possible and pray we get what we need before we lose contact. And there's where I need Multivac and your men. There must be some communications strategy we can use that will reduce the number of signals we need send out. Even an increase of ten percent in efficiency can mean perhaps a week of time saved."

The gentle voice interrupted again. "Good grief, Gerard, are you trying to get some talking done?"

"Mother! Please!"

"But you're going about it the wrong way. Really."

"Mother." There was a hysterical edge to Cremona's voice.

"Well, all right, but if you're going to say something and then wait twelve hours for an answer, you're silly. You shouldn't."

The General snorted. "Dr. Cremona, shall we consult—"

"Just one moment, General," said Cremona. "What are you getting at, Mother?"

"While you're waiting for an answer," said Mrs. Cremona, earnestly, "just keep on transmitting and tell them to do the same. You talk all the time and they talk all the time. You have someone listening all the time and they do, too. If either one of you says anything that needs an answer, you can slip one in at your end, but chances are, you'll get all you need without asking."

Both men stared at her.

Cremona whispered, "Of course. Continuous conversation. Just twelve hours out of phase, that's all. God, we've got to get going."

He strode out of the room, virtually dragging the General with him, then strode back in.

"Mother," he said, "if you'll excuse me, this will take a few hours, I think. I'll send in some girls to talk to you. Or take a nap, if you'd rather."

"I'll be all right, Gerard," said Mrs. Cremona.

"Only, how did you think of this, Mother? What made you suggest this?"

"But, Gerard, all women know it. Any two women—on the videophone, or on the stratowire, or just face to face—know that the whole secret to spreading the news is, no matter what, to Just Keep Talking."

Cremona tried to smile. Then, his lower lip trembling, he turned and left.

Mrs. Cremona looked fondly after him. Such a fine man, her son, the physicist. Big as he was and important as he was, he still knew that a boy should always listen to his mother.

PREFACE TO
EYES DO MORE THAN SEE

FIRST APPEARANCE—*THE MAGAZINE OF Fantasy and Science Fiction*, April 1965. © 1965, by Mercury Press, Inc.

I have a rule which I state loudly on every possible occasion. The rule is, that I never write anything unless I am asked to do so. That sounds awfully haughty and austere, but it's a fake. As a matter of fact, I take it for granted that the various science fiction magazines and certain of my book publishers have standing requests for material, so I write for them freely. It's just the scattering of others that have to ask.

In 1964, I was finally asked by *Playboy* to write a story for them. They sent me a dim photograph of a clay head, without ears, and with the other features labeled in block letters, and asked me to write a story based on that photo. Two other writers were also asked to write a story based on that same photo and all three stories were to be published together.

It was an interesting challenge and I was tempted. I wrote "Eyes Do More Than See."

In case I have given the impression in the previous introductions in this volume that my writing career has been one long succession of triumphs ever since "Nightfall"; that with me, to write is to sell; that I wouldn't recognize a rejection slip if some fellow writer showed me one—rest easy, it is not so.

"Eyes Do More Than See" was rejected with muscular vigor. The manuscript came flying through my window all the way from Chicago, bounced off the wall and lay there quivering. (At least that's how it seemed.) The other two stories were accepted by *Playboy*, and a third story, by someone hastily called in to backstop me, was also accepted.

Fortunately, I am a professional of enviable imperturbability and these things do not bother me. I doubt whether anyone could have guessed that I was disturbed except for the short screaming fit of rage I indulged myself with.

I checked with *Playboy* and made sure the story was mine to do with as I please, despite the fact it was based on their photo. It was!

My next step was to send the story to *F & SF*, explaining to them (as is my wont in such cases) that it was a reject and giving them the exact circumstances. They took it, anyway.

Fortunately, *F & SF* works reasonably quickly and *Playboy* works abominably slowly. Consequently "Eyes Do More Than See" appeared in *F & SF* a year and a half before the story-triad appeared in *Playboy*. I spent an appreciable length of time hoping *Playboy* would get indignant letters complaining that the situations in the triad had been stolen from an Asimov story. I was even tempted to write such a letter myself under a false name (but I didn't).

I contented myself, instead, with the thought that by the time *Playboy* had published its triad, my little story had not only been published elsewhere but had been reprinted twice and was slated to appear in still a third anthology. (And this collection represents a fourth, and how do you like that, Mr. Hefner?)

EYES DO MORE
THAN SEE

After hundreds of billions of years, he suddenly thought of himself as Ames. Not the wavelength combination which, through all the universe was now the equivalent of Ames—but the sound itself. A faint memory came back of the sound waves he no longer heard and no longer could hear.

The new project was sharpening his memory for so many more of the old, old, eons-old things. He flattened the energy vortex that made up the total of his individuality and its lines of force stretched beyond the stars.

Brock's answering signal came.

Surely, Ames thought, he could tell Brock. Surely he could tell somebody.

Brock's shifting energy pattern communed, "Aren't you coming, Ames?"

"Of course."

"Will you take part in the contest?"

"Yes!" Ames's lines of force pulsed erratically. "Most certainly. I have thought of a whole new art-form. Something really unusual."

"What a waste of effort! How can you think a new variation can be thought of after two hundred billion years. There can be nothing new."

For a moment Brock shifted out of phase and out of communion, so that Ames had to hurry to adjust his lines of force. He caught the drift of other-thoughts as he did so, the view of the powdered galaxies against the velvet of nothingness, and the lines of force pulsing in end-less multitudes of energy-life, lying between the galaxies.

Ames said, "Please absorb my thoughts, Brock. Don't close out. I've thought of manipulating Matter. Imagine! A symphony of Matter. Why bother with Energy. Of course, there's nothing new in Energy; how can there be? Doesn't that show we must deal with Matter?"

"Matter!"

Ames interpreted Brock's energy-vibrations as those of disgust.

He said, "Why not? We were once Matter ourselves back—back—Oh, a trillion years ago anyway! Why not build up objects in a Matter medium, or abstract forms or—listen, Brock—why not build up an imitation of ourselves in Matter, ourselves as we used to be?"

Brock said, "I don't remember how that was. No one does."

"I do," said Ames with energy, "I've been thinking of nothing else and I am beginning to remember. Brock, let me show you. Tell me if I'm right. Tell me."

"No. This is silly. It's—repulsive."

"Let me try, Brock. We've been friends; we've pulsed energy to-gether from the beginning—from the moment we became what we are. Brock, please!"

"Then, quickly."

Ames had not felt such a tremor along his own lines of force in—well, in how long? If he tried it now for Brock and it worked, he could dare manipulate Matter before the assembled Energy-beings who had so drearily waited over the eons for something new.

The Matter was thin out there between the galaxies, but Ames gath-ered it, scraping it together over the cubic light-years, choosing the atoms, achieving a clayey consistency and forcing matter into an ovoid form that spread out below.

"Don't you remember, Brock?" he asked softly. "Wasn't it some-thing like this?"

Brock's vortex trembled in phase. "Don't make me remember. I don't remember."

"That was the head. They called it the head. I remember it so clearly, I want to say it. I mean with sound." He waited, then said, "Look, do you remember that?"

On the upper front of the ovoid appeared HEAD.

"What is that?" asked Brock.

"That's the word for head. The symbols that meant the word in sound. Tell me you remember, Brock!"

"There was something," said Brock hesitantly, "something in the middle." A vertical bulge formed.

Ames said, "Yes! Nose, that's it!" And NOSE appeared upon it. "And those are eyes on either side," LEFT EYE—RIGHT EYE.

Ames regarded what he had formed, his lines of force pulsing slowly. Was he sure he liked this?

"Mouth," he said, in small quiverings, "and chin and Adam's apple, and the collarbones. How the words come back to me." They appeared on the form.

Brock said, "I haven't thought of them for hundreds of billions of years. Why have you reminded me? Why?"

Ames was momentarily lost in his thoughts, "Something else. Organs to hear with; something for the sound waves. Ears! Where do they go? I don't remember where to put them!"

Brock cried out, "Leave it alone! Ears and all else! Don't remember!"

Ames said, uncertainly, "What is wrong with remembering?"

"Because the outside wasn't rough and cold like that but smooth and warm. Because the eyes were tender and alive and the lips of the mouth trembled and were soft on mine." Brock's lines of force beat and wavered, beat and wavered.

Ames said, "I'm sorry! I'm sorry!"

"You're reminding me that once I was a woman and knew love; that eyes do more than see and I have none to do it for me."

With violence, she added matter to the rough-hewn head and said, "Then let *them* do it" and turned and fled.

And Ames saw and remembered, too, that once he had been a man. The force of his vortex split the head in two and he fled back across the galaxies on the energy-track of Brock—back to the endless doom of life.

And the eyes of the shattered head of Matter still glistened with the moisture that Brock had placed there to represent tears. The head of Matter did that which the energy-beings could do no longer and it wept for all humanity, and for the fragile beauty of the bodies they had once given up, a trillion years ago.

PREFACE TO
SEGREGATIONIST

FIRST APPEARANCE—*ABBOTTEMPO,* Book 4, 1967. Copyright 1968, by Isaac Asimov.

In the spring of 1967, I received an interesting request.

It seems there is a periodical called *Abbottempo,* supported by Abbott Laboratories, a respected pharmaceutical firm. It is a slickpaper, impressively designed job, with excellent articles on various medical and near-medical subjects. It is printed in the Netherlands and is distributed free of charge to physicians in Great Britain and on the Continent. It is not distributed in the United States.

The editor of *Abbottempo* wrote to ask me to write a 2000-word science fiction story on a subject of medical interest that physicians would find at once interesting, amusing, and thought-provoking.

I was just as swamped with work at that moment as I am at all other moments, so I sighed and put a piece of letter paper in the typewriter, intending to write out a polite refusal.

Unfortunately, or fortunately, it takes time to pick up letter paper and a yellow second sheet, put a piece of carbon paper between, and roll the sandwich into the typewriter. It takes additional time to center the paper properly, type the date, address, and salutation.

What with all that time, I happened to think up a story I couldn't resist, so when I actually got past the "Dear Sir," I found myself typing a polite acceptance.

I wrote "Segregationist" in April 1967, on a theme that was completely and entirely science-fictional. It appeared in December 1967, just in time to be slightly behind the headlines in *some* respects.

The nicest result of the publication of the story, by the way, was that *Abbottempo* published it in each of their eight editions. They sent me a boxed collection of the set in 1) English, 2) French, 3) Spanish, 4) German, 5) Italian, 6) Japanese, 7) Greek, and 8) Turkish. I had never before had anything I had written translated into either Greek or Turkish, and the set remains one of the more interesting oddities of my personal library of Asimoviana.

SEGREGATIONIST

The surgeon looked up without expression. "Is he ready?"

"Ready is a relative term," said the med-eng. "*We*'re ready. He's restless."

"They always are. . . . Well, it's a serious operation."

"Serious or not, he should be thankful. He's been chosen for it over an enormous number of possibles and frankly, I don't think . . ."

"Don't say it," said the surgeon. "The decision is not ours to make."

"We accept it. But do we have to agree?"

"Yes," said the surgeon, crisply. "We agree. Completely and whole-heartedly. The operation is entirely too intricate to approach with mental reservations. This man has proven his worth in a number of ways and his profile is suitable for the Board of Mortality."

"All right," said the med-eng, unmollified.

The surgeon said, "I'll see him right in here, I think. It is small enough and personal enough to be comforting."

"It won't help. He's nervous, and he's made up his mind."

"Has he indeed?"

"Yes. He wants metal; they always do."

The surgeon's face did not change expression. He stared at his hands. "Sometimes one can talk them out of it."

"Why bother?" said the med-eng, indifferently. "If he wants metal, let it be metal."

"You don't care?"

"Why should I?" The med-eng said it almost brutally. "Either way it's a medical engineering problem and I'm a medical engineer. Either way, I can handle it. Why should I go beyond that?"

The surgeon said stolidly, "To me, it is a matter of the fitness of things."

"Fitness! You can't use that as an argument. What does the patient care about the fitness of things?"

"I care."

"You care in a minority. The trend is against you. You have no chance."

"I have to try." The surgeon waved the med-eng into silence with a quick wave of his hand—no impatience to it, merely quickness. He had already informed the nurse and he had already been signaled concerning her approach. He pressed a small button and the double-door pulled swiftly apart. The patient moved inward in his motorchair, the nurse stepping briskly along beside him.

"You may go, nurse," said the surgeon, "but wait outside. I will be calling you." He nodded to the med-eng, who left with the nurse, and the door closed behind them.

The man in the chair looked over his shoulder and watched them go. His neck was scrawny and there were fine wrinkles about his eyes. He was freshly shaven and the fingers of his hands, as they gripped the arms of the chair tightly, showed manicured nails. He was a high-priority patient and he was being taken care of. . . . But there was a look of settled peevishness on his face.

He said, "Will we be starting today?"

The surgeon nodded. "This afternoon, Senator."

"I understand it will take weeks."

"Not for the operation itself, Senator. But there are a number of subsidiary points to be taken care of. There are some circulatory renovations that must be carried through, and hormonal adjustments. These are tricky things."

"Are they dangerous?" Then, as though feeling the need for establishing a friendly relationship, but patently against his will, he added, ". . . doctor?"

The surgeon paid no attention to the nuances of expression. He said, flatly, "Everything is dangerous. We take our time in order that it be less dangerous. It is the time required, the skill of many individuals united, the equipment, that makes such operations available to so few . . ."

"I know that," said the patient, restlessly. "I refuse to feel guilty about that. Or are you implying improper pressure?"

"Not at all, Senator. The decisions of the Board have never been questioned. I mention the difficulty and intricacy of the operation merely to explain my desire to have it conducted in the best fashion possible."

"Well, do so, then. That is my desire, also."

"Then I must ask you to make a decision. It is possible to supply you with either of two types of cyber-hearts, metal or . . ."

"Plastic!" said the patient, irritably. "Isn't that the alternative you were going to offer, doctor? Cheap plastic. I don't want that. I've made my choice. I want the metal."

"But . . ."

"See here. I've been told the choice rests with me. Isn't that so?"

The surgeon nodded. "Where two alternate procedures are of equal value from a medical standpoint, the choice rests with the patient. In actual practice, the choice rests with the patient even when the alternate procedures are *not* of equal value, as in this case."

The patient's eyes narrowed. "Are you trying to tell me the plastic heart is superior?"

"It depends on the patient. In my opinion, in your individual case, it is. And we prefer not to use the term, plastic. It is a fibrous cyber-heart."

"It's plastic as far as I am concerned."

"Senator," said the surgeon, infinitely patient, "the material is not plastic in the ordinary sense of the word. It is a polymeric material true, but one that is far more complex than ordinary plastic. It is a complex protein-like fibre designed to imitate, as closely as possible, the natural structure of the human heart you now have within your chest."

"Exactly, and the human heart I now have within my chest is worn out although I am not yet sixty years old. I don't want another one like it, thank you. I want something better."

"We all want something better for you, Senator. The fibrous cyber-heart will be better. It has a potential life of centuries. It is absolutely non-allergenic . . ."

"Isn't that so for the metallic heart, too?"

"Yes, it is," said the surgeon. "The metallic cyber is of titanium alloy that . . ."

"And it doesn't wear out? And it is stronger than plastic? Or fibre or whatever you want to call it?"

"The metal is physically stronger, yes, but mechanical strength is not a point at issue. Its mechanical strength does you no particular good since the heart is well protected. Anything capable of reaching the heart will kill you for other reasons even if the heart stands up under manhandling."

The patient shrugged. "If I ever break a rib, I'll have that replaced by titanium, also. Replacing bones is easy. Anyone can have that done anytime. I'll be as metallic as I want to be, doctor."

"That is your right, if you so choose. However, it is only fair to tell you that although no metallic cyber-heart has ever broken down mechanically, a number have broken down electronically."

"What does that mean?"

"It means that every cyber-heart contains a pacemaker as part of its structure. In the case of the metallic variety, this is an electronic device that keeps the cyber in rhythm. It means an entire battery of miniaturized equipment must be included to alter the heart's rhythm to suit an individual's emotional and physical state. Occasionally something goes wrong there and people have died before that wrong could be corrected."

"I never heard of such a thing."

"I assure you it happens."

"Are you telling me it happens often?"

"Not at all. It happens very rarely."

"Well, then, I'll take my chance. What about the plastic heart? Doesn't that contain a pacemaker?"

"Of course it does, Senator. But the chemical structure of a fibrous cyber-heart is quite close to that of human tissue. It can respond to the ionic and hormonal controls of the body itself. The total complex that need be inserted is far simpler than in the case of the metal cyber."

"But doesn't the plastic heart ever pop out of hormonal control?"

"None has ever yet done so."

"Because you haven't been working with them long enough. Isn't that so?"

The surgeon hesitated. "It is true that the fibrous cybers have not been used nearly as long as the metallic."

"There you are. What is it anyway, doctor? Are you afraid I'm making myself into a robot . . . into a Metallo, as they call them since citizenship went through?"

"There is nothing wrong with a Metallo as a Metallo. As you say, they are citizens. But you're *not* a Metallo. You're a human being. Why not stay a human being?"

"Because I want the best and that's a metallic heart. You see to that."

The surgeon nodded. "Very well. You will be asked to sign the necessary permissions and you will then be fitted with a metal heart."

"And you'll be the surgeon in charge? They tell me you're the best."

"I will do what I can to make the changeover an easy one."

The door opened and the chair moved the patient out to the waiting nurse.

THE MED-ENG CAME in, looking over his shoulder at the receding patient until the doors had closed again.

He turned to the surgeon. "Well, I can't tell what happened just by looking at you. What was his decision?"

The surgeon bent over his desk, punching out the final items for his records. "What you predicted. He insists on the metallic cyber-heart."

"After all, they are better."

"Not significantly. They've been around longer; no more than that. It's this mania that's been plaguing humanity ever since Metallos have become citizens. Men have this odd desire to make Metallos out of themselves. They yearn for the physical strength and endurance one associates with them."

"It isn't one-sided, doc. You don't work with Metallos but I do; so I know. The last two who came in for repairs have asked for fibrous elements."

"Did they get them?"

"In one case, it was just a matter of supplying tendons; it didn't make much difference there, metal or fibre. The other wanted a blood system or its equivalent. I told him I couldn't; not without a complete rebuilding of the structure of his body in fibrous material. . . . I suppose it will come to that some day. Metallos that aren't really Metallos at all, but a kind of flesh and blood."

"You don't mind that thought?"

"Why not? And metallized human beings, too. We have two varieties of intelligence on Earth now and why bother with two. Let them approach each other and eventually we won't be able to tell the difference. Why should we want to? We'd have the best of both worlds; the advantages of man combined with those of robot."

"You'd get a hybrid," said the surgeon, with something that approached fierceness. "You'd get something that is not both, but neither. Isn't it logical to suppose an individual would be too proud of his structure and identity to want to dilute it with something alien? Would he *want* mongrelization?"

"That's segregationist talk."

"Then let it be that." The surgeon said with calm emphasis, "I believe in being what one is. I wouldn't change a bit of my own structure for any reason. If some of it absolutely required replacement, I would have that replacement as close to the original in nature as could possibly be managed. I am *myself*; well pleased to be myself; and would not be anything else."

He had finished now and had to prepare for the operation. He placed his strong hands into the heating oven and let them reach the dull red-hot glow that would sterilize them completely. For all his impassioned words, his voice had never risen, and on his burnished metal face there was (as always) no sign of expression.

BE SURE NOT TO MISS

ANY OF THESE UNFORGETTABLE BOOKS

BY

ISAAC ASIMOV

THE FOUNDATION SERIES

Foundation

For twelve thousand years the Galactic Empire has ruled supreme. Now it is dying. Only Hari Seldon, creator of the revolutionary science of psychohistory, can see into the future—a dark age of ignorance, barbarism, and warfare that will last thirty thousand years. To preserve knowledge and save humanity, Seldon gathers the best minds in the Empire—both scientists and scholars—and brings them to a bleak planet at the edge of the galaxy to serve as a beacon of hope for future generations. He calls this sanctuary the Foundation.

But soon the fledgling Foundation finds itself at the mercy of corrupt warlords rising in the wake of the receding Empire. And mankind's last best hope is faced with an agonizing choice: submit to the barbarians and live as slaves—or take a stand for freedom and risk total destruction.

Foundation and Empire

Led by its founding father, the psychohistorian Hari Seldon, the Foundation survived the greed and barbarism of its neighboring warrior-planets utilizing science and technology. Now cleverness and courage may not be enough. For the Empire—the mightiest force in the Galaxy—is even more dangerous in its death throes. Even worse, a mysterious entity called the Mule has appeared with powers beyond anything humanly conceivable. Who—or what—is the Mule? And how is humanity to defend itself against this invulnerable avatar of annihilation?

Filled with nail-biting suspense, nonstop action, and cutting-edge speculation, *Foundation and Empire* is the story of humanity's perpetual struggle against the darkness that forever threatens to overwhelm the light—and of how the courage of even a determined few can make all the difference in the universe.

Second Foundation

The Foundation lies in ruins—destroyed by a mutant mind bent on humanity's annihilation. But it's rumored that there's a Second Foundation hidden somewhere at the end of the Galaxy, established as insurance to preserve the knowledge of mankind. Now a desperate race has begun between the survivors of the First Foundation and an alien entity to find this last flicker of humanity's shining past—and future hope. Yet the key to it all might be a fourteen-year-old girl burdened with a terrible secret. Is she the Foundation's savior—or its deadliest enemy?

Unforgettable, thought-provoking, and riveting, *Second Foundation* is a stunning novel of adventure and ideas writ huge across the Galaxy—a powerful tale of humankind's struggle to preserve the fragile light of wisdom against the threat of its own dark barbarism.

Foundation's Edge

At last, the costly and bitter war between the two Foundations has come
to an end. The scientists of the First Foundation have proved victorious;
and now they return to Hari Seldon's long-established plan to build a
new Empire on the ruins of the old. But rumors persist that the Second
Foundation is not destroyed after all—and that its still-defiant survivors
are preparing their revenge. Now two exiled citizens of the Foundation—
a renegade Councilman and a doddering historian—set out in search of
the mythical planet Earth . . . and proof that the Second Foundation still
exists.

Meanwhile someone—or something—outside of both Foundations
seems to be orchestrating events to suit its own ominous purpose. Soon
representatives of both the First and Second Foundations will find themselves racing toward a mysterious world called Gaia and a final, shocking
destiny at the very end of the universe!

Foundation and Earth

Golan Trevize, former Councilman of the First Foundation, has chosen
the future, and it is Gaia. A superorganism, Gaia is a holistic planet with
a common consciousness so intensely united that every dewdrop, every
pebble, every being, can speak for all—and feel for all. It is a realm in
which privacy is not only undesirable, it is incomprehensible.

But is it the right choice for the destiny of mankind? While Trevize
feels it is, that is not enough. He must know.

Trevize believes the answer lies at the site of humanity's roots: fabled
Earth . . . if it still exists. For no one is sure where the planet of Gaia's
first settlers is to be found in the immense wilderness of the Galaxy. Nor
can anyone explain why no record of Earth has been preserved, no mention of it made anywhere in Gaia's vast world-memory. It is an enigma
Trevize is determined to resolve, and a quest he is determined to undertake, at any cost.

Prelude to Foundation

It is the year 12,020 G. E. and Emperor Cleon I sits uneasily on the Imperial throne of Trantor. Here in the great multidomed capital of the Galactic Empire, forty billion people have created a civilization of unimaginable technological and cultural complexity. Yet Cleon knows there are those who would see him fall—those whom he would destroy if only he could read the future.

Hari Seldon has come to Trantor to deliver his paper on psychohistory, his remarkable theory of prediction. Little does the young Outworld mathematician know that he has already sealed his fate and the fate of humanity. For Hari possesses the prophetic power that makes him the most wanted man in the Empire . . . the man who holds the key to the future—an apocalyptic power to be known forever after as the Foundation.

Forward the Foundation

As Hari Seldon struggles to perfect his revolutionary theory of psychohistory and ensure a place for humanity among the stars, the great Galactic Empire totters on the brink of apocalyptic collapse. Caught in the maelstrom are Seldon and all he holds dear, pawns in the struggle for dominance. Whoever can control Seldon will control psychohistory—and with it the future of the Galaxy.

Among those seeking to turn psychohistory into the greatest weapon known to man are a populist political demagogue, the weak-willed Emperor Cleon I, and a ruthless militaristic general. In his last act of service to humankind, Hari Seldon must somehow save his life's work from their grasp as he searches for its true heirs—a search that begins with his own granddaughter and the dream of a new Foundation.

THE GALACTIC EMPIRE SERIES

The Stars, Like Dust

The Stars, Like Dust is the first book in the Galactic Empire series, the spectacular precursor to the classic Foundation series. His name was Biron Farrill and he was a student at the University of Earth. A native of one of the helpless Nebular Kingdoms, he saw his home world conquered and controlled by the planet Tyrann—a ruthless, barbaric Empire that was building a dynasty of cruelty and domination among the stars.

Farrill's own father had been executed for trying to resist the Tyrann dictatorship and now someone was trying to kill Biron. But why?

His only hope for survival lay in fleeing Earth and joining the rebellion that was rumored to be forming somewhere in the Kingdoms. But once he cast his lot with the freedom fighters, he would find himself guarding against treachery on every side and facing the most difficult choice of all: to betray either the woman he loved or the revolution that was the last hope for the future.

The Currents of Space

Trantor had extended its rule over half the Galaxy, but the other half defied its authority, defending their corrupt fiefdoms with violence and repression. On the planet Florina, the natives labored as slaves for their arrogant masters on nearby Sark. But now both worlds were hurtling toward a cataclysmic doom, and only one man knew the truth—a slave unaware of the secret knowledge locked inside his own brain.

Rik had once been a prominent scientist until a psychic probe erased all memories of his past. Now he was a humble laborer in the kyrt mills of Florina. Then the memories began to return, bringing with them the terrible truth about the future—a truth that his masters on Sark would kill to keep secret . . . even at the cost of their own survival.

Pebble in the Sky

After years of bitter struggle, Trantor at last completed its work—its Galactic Empire ruled all 200 million planets of the Galaxy . . . all but one. On a backward planet called Earth were those who nurtured bitter dreams of a mythical, half-remembered past when the planet was humanity's only home. The other worlds despised it or merely patronized it—until a man from the past miraculously stepped through a time fault that spanned a millennium, living proof of Earth's most preposterous claims.

Joseph Schwartz was a happily retired Chicago tailor circa 1949. Trapped in an incredible future he could barely comprehend, the unlikely time traveler would soon become a pawn in a desperate conspiracy to bring down the Empire in a twist of agony and death—a mad plan to restore Earth's tarnished glory by ending human life on every other world.

THE ROBOT SERIES

I, Robot

I, Robot, the first and most widely read book in Asimov's Robot series, forever changed the world's perception of artificial intelligence. Here are stories of robots gone mad, of mind-reading robots, and robots with a sense of humor. Of robot politicians, and robots who secretly run the world—all told with the dramatic blend of science fact and science fiction that has become Asimov's trademark.

THE THREE LAWS OF ROBOTICS:

1) A robot may not injure a human being or, through inaction, allow a human being to come to harm.

2) A robot must obey orders given to it by human beings except where such orders would conflict with the First Law.

3) A robot must protect its own existence as long as such protection does not conflict with the First or Second Law.

With these three, simple directives, Isaac Asimov formulated the laws governing robots' behavior. In *I, Robot*, Asimov chronicles the development of the robot from its primitive origins in the present to its ultimate perfection in the not-so-distant future—a future in which humanity itself may be rendered obsolete.

The Caves of Steel

A millennium into the future two advances have altered the course of human history: the colonization of the Galaxy and the creation of the positronic brain. Isaac Asimov's Robot novels chronicle the unlikely partnership between a New York City detective and a humanoid robot who must learn to work together.

Like most people left behind on an overpopulated Earth, New York City police detective Elijah Baley had little love for either the arrogant Spacers or their robotic companions. But when a prominent Spacer is murdered under mysterious circumstances, Baley is ordered to the Outer Worlds to help track down the killer.

The relationship between Lije and his Spacer superiors, who distrusted all Earthmen, was strained from the start. Then he learned that they had assigned him a partner: R. Daneel Olivaw. Worst of all was that the "R" stood for *robot*—and his positronic partner was made in the image and likeness of the murder victim!

The Naked Sun

On the beautiful Outer World planet of Solaria, a handful of human colonists lead a hermitlike existence, their every need attended to by their faithful robot servants. To this strange and provocative planet comes Detective Elijah Baley, sent from the streets of New York with his positronic partner, the robot R. Daneel Olivaw, to solve an incredible murder that has rocked Solaria to its foundations.

The victim had been so reclusive that he appeared to his associates only through holographic projection. Yet someone had gotten close enough to bludgeon him to death while his robots looked on. Now Baley and Olivaw are faced with two clear impossibilities: Either the Solarian was killed by one of his robots—unthinkable under the Laws of Robotics—or he was killed by the woman who loved him so much that she never came into his presence!

The Robots of Dawn

Detective Elijah Baley is called to the Spacer world Aurora to solve a bizarre case of roboticide. The prime suspect is a gifted roboticist who had the means, the motive, and the opportunity to commit the crime. There's only one catch: Baley and his positronic partner, R. Daneel Olivaw, must prove the man innocent. For in a case of political intrigue and love between woman and robot gone tragically wrong, there's more at stake than simple justice. This time Baley's career, his life, and Earth's right to pioneer the Galaxy hang in the delicate balance.

THE STAND-ALONES

The End of Eternity

The End of Eternity is a spellbinding novel set in the universe of Isaac Asimov's classic Galactic Empire series and Foundation series. The Eternals, the ruling class of the Future, had the power of life and death not only over every human being but over the very centuries into which they were born. Past, Present, and Future could be created or destroyed at will.

You had to be special to become an Eternal. Andrew Harlan was special. Until he committed the one unforgivable sin—falling in love.

Eternals weren't supposed to have feelings. But Andrew Harlan could not deny the sensations that were struggling within him. He knew he could not keep this secret forever. And so he began to plan his escape, a plan that changed his own past . . . and threatened Eternity itself.

Fantastic Voyage

Four men and one woman are reduced to a microscopic fraction of their original size. Boarding a miniaturized atomic sub, they are injected into a dying man's carotid artery. Passing through the heart and entering the inner ear, where even the slightest sound would destroy them, they battle relentlessly into the cranium. Their objective: to reach a blood clot and destroy it with the piercing rays of a laser. At stake: the fate of the entire world.

The Gods Themselves

In the twenty-second century, Earth obtains limitless free energy from a source that science little understands: an exchange between Earth and a parallel universe, using a process devised by the aliens. But even free energy has a price. The transference process will eventually lead to the destruction of Earth's Sun—and of Earth itself.

Only a few know the terrifying truth—an outcast Earth scientist, a rebellious alien inhabitant of a dying planet, and a lunar-born human intuitionist who senses the immanent annihilation of the Sun. They know the truth—but who will listen? They have foreseen the cost of abundant energy—but who will believe? These few beings, human and alien, hold the key to Earth's survival—if they can get anyone to pay attention.

Nemesis

In the twenty-third century, pioneers have escaped the crowded Earth for life in self-sustaining orbital colonies. One of the colonies, Rotor, has broken away from the solar system to create its own renegade utopia around an unknown red star two light-years from Earth: a star named Nemesis.

Now a fifteen-year-old Rotorian girl has learned of the dire threat that Nemesis poses to Earth's people—but she is prevented from warning them. Soon she will realize that Nemesis endangers Rotor as well. And soon it will be up to her alone to save both Earth and Rotor as—drawn inexorably by Nemesis, the death star—they hurtle toward certain disaster.

ABOUT THE AUTHOR

ISAAC ASIMOV began his Foundation series at the age of twenty-one, not realizing that it would one day be considered a cornerstone of science fiction. During his legendary career, Asimov penned over 470 books on subjects ranging from science to Shakespeare to history, though he was most loved for his award-winning science fiction sagas, which include the Robot, Galactic Empire, and Foundation series. Named a Grand Master of Science Fiction by the Science Fiction Writers of America, Asimov entertained and educated readers of all ages for close to five decades. He died, at the age of seventy-two, in April 1992.

ABOUT THE TYPE

This book was set in Bembo, a typeface based on an old-style Roman face that was used for Cardinal) Pietro Bembo's tract *De Aetna* in 1495. Bembo was cut by Francesco Griffo (1450–1518) in the early sixteenth century for Italian Renaissance printer and publisher Aldus Manutius (1449–1515). The Lanston Monotype Company of Philadelphia brought the well-proportioned letterforms of Bembo to the United States in the 1930s.